There were certain things a woman noticed about a man. The way his shoulders curved, how his hands moved when he spoke, the style of his dress, the length of his hair. But these details, which had not escaped her attention, were made small by the way he *moved*. Gabriella watched, fascinated by the play of his muscles. Darius moved with an efficient grace of strength tempered by a harmony of perfect coordination. He stopped so close to her she could smell the salty tang of his sweat on her tongue.

"Was there some reason you didn't tell me?" In the stillness of the room, his voice cut through the silence.

"You never asked." Her chin lifted in automatic challenge. "You *assumed*."

As Gabriella reached past him to pick up her towel from the side bench, Darius moved again. He said nothing but pushed her back against the wall, locking her into place with his arms. Her head came up and before she could voice her protest, his lips came down hard on hers, bruising her with his mouth. She had nowhere to run, no place to hide from her body's response. He took without asking, and she offered him entrance, not because there was *no choice*, but it was *her choice* and she could deny him nothing, deny herself nothing. She placed her hands on the V of his uniform and settled on the smooth hardness of his chest where she could feel the rapid beating of his heart.

Angela Weaver

Blind Obsession

BET Publications, LLC
http://www.bet.com
http://www.arabesquebooks.com

ARABESQUE BOOKS are published by

BET Publications, LLC
c/o BET Books
One BET Plaza
1900 W Place NE
Washington, DC 20018-1211

All Kensington Titles, Imprints, and Distributed Lines are available at special quantity discounts for bulk purchases for sales promotions, premiums, fund-raising, and educational or institutional use. Special book excerpts for customized printings can also be created to fit specific needs. For details, write or phone the office of the Kensington special sales manager: Kensington Publishing Corp., 850 Third Avenue, New York, NY 10022, attn: Special Sales Department, Phone: 1-800-221-2647.

First Printing: June 2005

10 9 8 7 6 5 4 3 2 1

Printed in the United States of America

I would like to dedicate this book to my aunt, Bettye Wilcox, because she is always a source of support and encouragement. Also, when I'm down, she knocks me on the head to get me up again.

When you are joyous, look deep into your heart, and you shall find it is only that which has given you sorrow that is giving you joy.

When you are sorrowful, look again in your heart, and you shall see that in truth you are weeping for that which has been your delight.

—*The Prophet*

Chapter One

Family was the only thing that mattered in a man's life, and Darius Yassoud had been given three. The family he'd been born into, the one that had raised him, and the one that kept him from getting killed as he served his country. Today marked his first full day on leave, but half of him already wanted to hitch a ride on an Army transport back to Fort Bragg.

After putting on his jacket, he checked the G-shock watch on his wrist, locked the door to his empty apartment, and pocketed the keys.

Darius loved his uncle's family, but there were times when he loved the camaraderie of his Delta Special Forces team more. Even now, he missed his first months in the field when he'd spent days in the jungle doing reconnaissance. Despite Detroit's cold weather, he remembered well the call of the birds, the stench of rotting vegetation, and the constant wetness of the oppressive humidity on his skin.

As an expert communications specialist, he could speak many languages, program satellites, manipulate electronic devices, and go behind enemy lines at a moment's notice. For the past ten years, he'd been in and out of war torn countries while at the same time advancing to the rank of Sergeant Colonel. In combat, as the line between life and death thinned, he responded faster, pushed harder, becoming all the more lethal. He'd never left a man behind or failed a mission.

And yet, he had woken that morning contemplating whether he could leave active duty for Army Intelligence training. Darius keyed the car's ignition and pulled out of the parking space. His heart warmed as he thought of his uncle. Rashad had orchestrated a large family celebration the night before he went to West Point Academy. Even his own parents had journeyed from his father's newest posting in Turkey. Lowering the volume on the radio, he headed toward the highway.

Twenty minutes later, he entered Bloomfield. After their financial situation changed for the better, his uncle had moved the family into the affluent Michigan suburb. The large colonial residences differed greatly from the two-story duplex his aunt and uncle had called home when Darius first arrived in America.

He slowed the rental car as he drew near his destination. The neighborhood had changed little since he'd last seen it. It had the same large brick houses, manicured lawns, and pristine streets with elegant lamps lining the sidewalks. Darius pulled up to the front of the iron gates, rolled down his window, then pressed the intercom button while looking into the small videocamera lens.

Seconds later, the gates drew back and he drove up the circular driveway to park the car near the front entrance.

Reaching into the backseat, he grabbed two shopping bags full of gifts he'd gathered during a short visit to Nairobi. Darius got out of the car and strode up the pathway to the stained glass double doors. He pulled out a second set of keys and unlocked the door. With his hand still gripped on the knob, he eased the door open, quietly stepped inside, and paused in surprise at the lack of noise.

The two-story open foyer, usually filled with music, stood silent, meaning that his Aunt Inas wasn't home. Closing the door behind him, Darius shut his eyes as his lungs filled with the scent of jasmine. No matter where he traveled, the memorable smell always reminded him of family. He placed the gifts in the entranceway closet and shrugged off his coat.

"I'm in the kitchen." The older Yassoud's deep, authoritative voice came from the back of the dwelling.

Darius's booted feet slipped soundlessly over the thick carpet; he bypassed the formal living room and entered into the arched hallway, which led into the kitchen.

Leaning in the doorway, he watched his Uncle Rashad dig in the back of the cabinet and crow happily as he pulled out the Oreo cookies. "One bag left." He held it up as though discovering a priceless treasure.

"She knows about your hidden stash, *Amm*," Darius chuckled as he addressed his father's younger twin using the Arabic word for uncle.

"That wife of mine knows everything. I dare not wish, much less think about food anymore," Rashad Yassoud grumbled, but placed the bag on the counter. "Your aunt's newest diet will drive me insane. I am the head of an international multi-billion dollar enterprise, but I must hide cookies in my own house.

"Bah, enough of this," Rashad said briskly, then held out his arms. "Welcome home."

"It's good to be here." Slipping back into the affectionate manner of his childhood, Darius stepped forward and kissed his uncle on the cheek. His coal-colored hair had lightened with gray, and his walk had slowed, but Rashad's eyes continued to be sharp as ever.

"You're early," Rashad pointed out.

"I brought presents and thought it would be best to hide them so I don't get mobbed."

Uncle Rashad nodded his head before turning back toward the cabinets. "You were always the smart one. Last summer when Bashr returned from Fez, he didn't make it past the entryway before those grandchildren of mine bombarded him with pleas."

"Speaking of my cousin, how is he?"

His uncle looked up at the ceiling while raising his arms. "*Insha'allah*, soon to join the rest of Allah's blessed."

"Ahh, he's dying," Darius joked, while struggling not to chuckle at his uncle's weary expression of the Islamic prayer of God willing.

"No," Rashad shook his head. "He's getting married."

"When's the wedding?" Darius leaned back against the kitchen island. He had spent the best days of his life in this kitchen watching his aunt and cousins shout over pots and pans while he and Bashr sat at the breakfast table enjoying the chaos.

"In autumn. Plenty of time to make wedding preparations and to finish building their new house. Let us talk further over coffee." Rashad patted Darius on the back. "If you tell me pleasing news, I might share my cookies with you."

Darius pulled two small cups out of the cabinets. "Where is everyone?"

"Your aunt had to run to town to get your favorite dessert and pick up my grandchildren from their Arabic lessons."

Darius watched as Rashad poured a measured amount of water into the espresso machine. Less than a minute later, the strong bitter smell of Turkish coffee filled the air. After they'd settled into the plush chairs in the study, he waited until his uncle had consumed his third Oreo before speaking.

"How's business?"

Rashad took a sip of coffee and waved a hand. "Very good. So good, in fact, I'm thinking of retiring."

Darius looked at the other man intently. The import/export enterprise his uncle had built from the ground up had been less of a business and more of a child to him.

"Retire?" He leaned forward gripping the cup's porcelain handle.

Rashad waved his cup. "Inas worries about my health. All of my children nag me to spend more time at home. I will make the announcement at the board meeting next month."

Darius remained unconvinced. "Is that all?"

His uncle shifted uncomfortably and picked up another Oreo. "Why would you think there is something else?"

Darius's lips hitched upward while his gaze shifted downward toward the black and white Oreo cookie clutched between his uncle's fingers. "That's your fifth cookie. You only eat those when you're worried."

Rashad's eyebrows rose and chagrin filled his dark eyes. "It is mortifying to know I am that transparent."

"Only to family. Now, would you like to tell me about it?"

The other man leaned back and sighed. "It is not business that worries me. I have an opportunity to repay an old debt and now I find that I must decline."

The coffee on the tray sat forgotten as he examined his uncle. His mind shifted from concerns over Rashad's impending retirement to the new unknown issue of a debt. Darius linked his uncle's agitation to the problem of repayment. There was no doubt Rashad would pay, but at what price? "Now you've got me worried. What's got you in such a state?"

"Sebastian van Ryne."

Darius didn't straighten from his relaxed pose. Sebastian van Ryne had been the first major investor in his uncle's business. The Dutch shipping CEO had made it clear that Yassoud Enterprises cargo would be delivered on schedule. At a time when it was customary to overcharge and delay shipment, van Ryne had made good on his promises. The shipping magnate had acted with honor and integrity when his uncle had asked for dedicated cargo space on the New York to Turkey shipping run.

"What does he want?" Darius asked.

"Someone he can trust."

He froze and his eyes locked with his uncle's. "Tell me everything."

"He needs someone to be protected for a few weeks."

"Let me guess. He wants Bashr's help?" Darius's brow creased then smoothed at the mention of his younger cousin.

Why wouldn't van Ryne want a professional bodyguard? As if reading his mind, his uncle answered.

"We've talked throughout the years. Sebastian knew that your cousin was a police officer before leaving to work for the family business."

"Did Bashr agree to this?" he asked.

"Of course . . ."

"But—" Darius interjected.

"My wife did not." Rashad looked crestfallen. "The person in question is not only Sebastian's unmarried daughter, but it would also require him to go to New York City."

"I see," Darius chuckled, imagining the fierce scolding his aunt had unleashed upon the house. The younger member of the family had an unearned reputation with women. Bashr's Lawrence of Arabia good looks stirred more passion than sense where women were concerned.

"Now that she has finally succeeded in finding him a wife, Inas will hardly let Bashr go for short business trips. The sun will rise in the West and set in the East before she'll agree to this endeavor."

Darius watched as his uncle picked up another cookie; he couldn't keep the grin off his face.

"Don't be too smug, nephew." Rashad wagged a finger. "Mark my words, Inas will be after you next."

Darius shook his head. "I've many years before I reach the point where I'm ready to settle down."

"Exactly what all my children have said, and now I have five grandchildren and will have more if Bashr's future mother-in-law has her way," he said smiling proudly. "I'm sure you'll change your mind after she's finished with you."

Knowing his aunt, Darius had no doubts that she would begin parading marriageable daughters in front of him within the week. As the image of long family dinners with young women floated to the front of his mind, Darius mimicked his uncle in shifting uneasily in his chair. "It's been too long since I have seen Nadia."

In one shot, he could kill three birds with one stone: avoid his aunt's machinations, reconnect with Nadia, his cousin, and repay his uncle's debt.

Rashad deliberately rubbed his chin. "Ah, she and Mahmood have opened an Egyptian restaurant in Philadelphia. They sent me a newspaper review. It says her couscous is the best in the city."

Darius leaned forward and picked up the coffee carafe. "I'm not surprised; she learned from a master chef."

"Yes." His uncle sat back and smiled. "Yes, you're right. Having family stop in for a visit would be nice."

"New York isn't far from Philly," Darius commented, pouring both his Uncle and himself another cup of coffee. "With your permission, Uncle, I'll take Bashr's place."

"You have my deepest gratitude, Darius."

"There's nothing to thank me for, Uncle. You have raised me as your son. I would give thanks as to a father."

Before he could question his uncle further on the matter of why van Ryne's daughter needed protection, the quiet of the house gave way to the clamor of tiny feet running down the hall. He stood but didn't make it three feet before the doors burst open. "Uncle Darius!" the toddlers shouted in unison.

"Uncle Darius, remember me? I'm all big now," Suna giggled.

Darius looked down at the tops of their heads as his nieces and nephews poured into the room. Locking their hands together, they made a ring and began to circle round and round him, giving their greetings in an old Arabic nursery rhyme.

Bending down, he reached out and plucked his oldest niece from the circle. Leila had been but a small thing when he'd last held her in his arms. Tweaking her chubby cheeks, he hugged her close, inhaling the scent of baby powder.

"Uncle Darius, did you bring me a present?"

"Of course," he laughed, starting a chorus of demands and tugging of his pants. "I have gifts for all of you."

Darius looked up in time to see the relief and affection in

his aunt's expression. Her dark eyes disappeared behind soft gold cheeks as a smile enveloped her face. Now that his aunt had returned, the house would fill with the smell of bread, spices, lamb, fish, and vegetables.

He sighed contentedly. It was good to be home.

Chapter
Two

I will never escape him. . . .

Gabriella Josette Marie suppressed a shiver caused by the sudden drop in temperature as she disembarked from the transcontinental airplane at John F. Kennedy airport. Even after spending close to seventeen hours in the air or waiting in airport lounges, she still imagined him close at her heels.

Her eyes closed briefly as she waited for the people ahead to move up the jet way. She walked with a stiffness gained from sitting in one position during the flight and the fatigue brought about from the stress of always looking over her shoulder. She'd slept in many small, unfamiliar beds and stayed in different hotel rooms and hostels.

Before her engagement, she'd spent the majority of nights at her fiancé's designer loft, yet Gabriella still clung to the comforting memory of her one bedroom pied-à-terre, perfectly situated within walking distance of Berlin's Orchestra Academy. It was the only time in her adult life when she'd felt true happiness.

Pushing the memory aside, Gabriella followed the signs directing United States passport holders toward the proper immigration officials. After taking out travel documents and a passport from her handbag, she looked around at the happy groups of high school children and older adults as their raised voices intruded upon her deep thoughts.

It was a scene she'd witnessed time after time while traveling throughout Europe. At every train station, people waited for loved ones or parents greeted an excited child coming home on holiday. At one point in her life, she had craved that warm sense of family above everything; now she felt neither envy nor joy.

The line inched forward.

A knot had begun to tighten in her stomach the moment she'd landed. Gabriella swallowed hard in an attempt to keep down the few bites of food she'd managed to eat on the plane.

As time and distance from him increased, so did her ability to fool herself into believing that her journey would be little more than a travel adventure. She had seen more treasures and toured Europe's most prized architectural and historical buildings, but nothing could rid her of the sense of dread.

Vasilei.

Gabriella shivered as his name conjured up the feelings and memories she'd spent the past three months trying to lose. Before she had given them away, her mother's string of amber rosary beads had hung around her neck, and the feel of them warm against her skin would calm her. Now, she willed herself not to touch the exquisite diamond sapphire engagement ring that hung from a platinum chain underneath her black knit sweater.

On the eve of their engagement party, she'd gifted three of her most prized possessions to Vasilei: her trust, her heart, and her mother's rosary. He, in turn, had given her a ring bearing the insignia of his family crest, a mark of ownership.

Vasilei Lexer. Gabriella had put countries between them. Yet, no amount of distance could erase the fact that he was the only man she'd ever loved and trusted. If there had been some way to go back in time, she would never have looked in the window. They would have been married and she would have been wife to a stranger; sister-in-law to a ruthless killer.

She adjusted her grip on her bag and lowered her face in

order to avoid looking directly into one of the many surveillance cameras. It took her less than twenty minutes to pass
through immigration, but customs might not be so easy.

Following an airport official's instruction to move forward
into a newly formed queue, Gabriella bit the inside of her
cheek as her pulse jumped. *So close.*

Her gaze moved downward to focus on the front page of
her passport. While studying the picture, she wondered how
he'd gotten a copy of the yearbook photo taken at the beginning of her senior year at the Sorbonne in Paris.

Hers was a European face, angled and sharp-featured, with
only her mother's Afro-Caribbean blood to warm it. Professionally straightened raven hair lay perfectly arranged over
her shoulders. The photograph was one of the few things on
the passport that was not a lie.

She took another step forward, but her mind continued to
dwell in the past. When her mother died and they flew her
body back to Saint Martin, Gabriella had thought that she
would remain with her Aunt Colette. For days after the funeral, she'd wandered in the small wooded areas on the island
looking for her mother's favorite flowers.

Shaking her head, she came to a stop next to the small cu-
bicle. "Passport and customs form, please."

Gabriella placed her bag on the counter and noticed a
slight trembling in her hand as she handed the documents to
the agent.

While she waited for him to page through the document
and stamp it, an image of her mother flashed across her mind.
She too had boarded a plane to the Promised Land. Ten minutes later, she stood in front of another nameless official.

"You have nothing to declare?" the customs official asked.

"No, I didn't have time to do any shopping." She met the
man's direct stare. His gaze moved from the passport to linger
on her face.

He blinked. "Welcome back to the States, Ms. Cravell.
Please exit through the doors to your right."

"Thank you." Retrieving her passport, she returned the customs agent's warm smile with a practiced one of her own.

She'd changed her mind at least a half-dozen times as to whether or not to seek Sebastian's help. In the end, she'd had little choice.

In spite of all her doubts, everything had worked as he had assured her it would. This would be the first time the man had managed to keep his word. It had to be the grandest irony in her life that it happened to be Sebastian van Ryne who arranged her return to America.

Carefully placing her passport back in her handbag, Gabriella bent to pick up her carry-on and slowly walked through the doorway. For a moment, she didn't know whom she feared more: the man who had gotten her out of Europe or the ex-fiancé who chased her still.

Welcome to New York City.

She joined the crowd of people streaming out of the terminal heading toward the baggage claim area. Gabriella had come full circle, back to the place where everything had changed.

In the past, she had never run from a fight or hidden from the make-believe ghosts in her closet. Now, however, fear like a maestro's baton dictated her every move. The horrible memory of that fateful day still woke her late in the night with a cold sweat upon her brow. She couldn't forget seeing the shimmer of the blade in his hand and the chilling glitter of his blue eyes. Yet, in her nightmares, only her ex-fiancé's face was shown; Vasilei's perfect face contorted as the blood pooled on the flat surface of the boathouse floor.

As she struggled with the knowledge that her beloved ex-fiancé was, in truth, his father's son, she prayed the land of the brave could hide her from Vasilei's pursuit.

Following the flow of passengers through the airport corridor, she took her place beside the crowded luggage conveyor belt. Last summer, she'd left the Italian villa with nothing more than her duffle bag and the clothes she'd worn on her back. This winter, with her new identity, only two suitcases contained all of her worldly possessions.

After ten minutes, she loaded her bags onto the luggage trolley and set off in the direction of the taxi stands. People moved around her like phantoms, and in that place of arrivals and departures, she just wanted to disappear.

"Gabriella, wait."

Her breath quickened at the distinctive voice. Pretending not to recognize her name, she would have kept walking toward the exit doors if a hand hadn't come down on her shoulder. She'd begun to move away, when she caught sight of a police officer patrolling the terminal.

"Gabriella," he called again.

She took a step back and drew in a deep breath, fighting to calm the rush of adrenaline. Seconds later, when she faced the owner of the Dutch-accented voice, Gabriella had schooled her features into a perfect mask of indifference.

"Sebastian." She nodded coolly as though they were merely business acquaintances, but the quicksilver hurt in his pale blue eyes didn't go unnoticed.

He looked exactly like he had in her memory, except that the patrician face had begun to show marks of passing time. Sebastian's silver blond hair was clipped short, and his thin straight nose and high cheekbones seemed harsh under the florescent light. His custom-tailored Italian suit and expensive wristwatch set him apart from the crowd. The corners of her mouth compressed with bitterness at the sight of the Rolex. His son had given it to him as a birthday present.

"My car is this way." He moved to take the bag from her hand, but she held it firmly.

Taking another step back, Gabriella replied in a firm but polite tone. "Thank you for your help, but I no longer require your assistance."

"Rella." He said her name the French way. It rolled off his tongue and reminded her of the time as a little girl she'd rush downstairs to greet him. "We need to talk."

Travelers continued to flow around them as they stood near the exit. Each time the automatic doors opened, an icy wind cut swiftly through the space between them. Dry. Everything was dry, her throat, her skin, the vast ocean of love a daughter should have for her father. "Later. You and I can talk tomorrow or the day after."

Gabriella felt the beginning of a headache behind her eyes. It was most likely caused by the fact that she hadn't slept more than a couple of hours since she'd departed Norway.

Barely managing to keep both her wits and her nerves together, she stood facing the man she hadn't seen in years. She wanted to send the message that her asking for his help wouldn't bridge the silence between them.

Sebastian turned from her. "Darius, could you please take her baggage out to the car?"

Gabriella turned toward the person who'd come to stand beside her unnoticed. Her eyes studied the man dressed all in black. Having lived and traveled throughout Western Europe, she'd seen men of all different hues and sizes—plain, handsome, and gorgeous. But the tall and broad-shouldered stranger who reached over and took the duffle bag from her cramped fingers also took her breath away and held it tight in his grasp.

The aristocratic bearing coupled with his aquiline nose, broad cheeks, and skin that glowed like well-burnished copper would not have looked out of place on an ancient sculpture. He was perfect except for a tiny half-moon scar stretched underneath his right cheekbone.

Between one blink and another, he raised his eyes in time to catch her staring. A slow flush heated Gabriella's cheeks. His expression, however, remained impassive as he looked from her face and then directed his penetrating gaze to Sebastian.

Shaking off her embarrassment of having been caught gawking like a schoolgirl, Gabriella turned back toward her father and hissed under her breath. "This is neither the time nor the place, Sebastian."

"Darius, I believe we need a moment alone." Her father was a tall man, and he had given his height to her as well as his stubbornness. He took the tone of a man born to control the actions of others.

Darius replied impatiently. "Take your moment someplace else, van Ryne. If you stay here any longer, there are enough cameras in here to guarantee future identification."

"You're right, of course. We can talk in the car." Sebastian touched her arm before she could step away. She caught Darius's eyes, then followed their movements toward the arm Sebastian had grasped.

"I'm not going anywhere with you until you tell me whether or not you were you able to get me an apartment in the Bronx."

"The neighborhood you chose is not safe, Gabriella," Sebastian said with the impatience of one who was used to having his opinion matter.

Gabriella let out a sharp laugh. Vasilei wouldn't rest until she was back in his bed, while his older brother, Anton . . . She suppressed a shudder as the thought of him filled her with dread; she wasn't a psychologist, but her survival instincts could be far more conclusive: he would kill her at the first chance. "There's no safe place for me now."

Again, her father reached out to place a hand on her arm; then he pulled back before she could reproach him. "Did you get the apartment?" she repeated.

"No, he didn't," Darius interrupted. He bent to pick up her luggage and then straightened. "I did."

This time when Sebastian's daughter looked toward him, Darius deliberately let his gaze pause on her face. Gabriella Josette Marie had changed. The picture of her that Sebastian had given him showed a girl with long straight hair. The woman who stood before him had a head full of heavy, shoulder-length curls and clear, honey-brown skin. A sharply inclined jaw un-

derwrote a soft mouth. She had the kind of face that etched itself in a man's memory, he decided. Unforgettable was a liabil-
ity in his duty to keep her hidden. Picking up her bag, he aimed
a hard look toward van Ryne. "Bring the girl and let's get out of
here before the car's towed."

"What is this about?" Gabriella demanded, uncaring of the
attention her outburst brought. "Who is this man and why is
he here?"

Her father clamped her arm more firmly. "Just come with
me to the car and I can explain."

"*Non, arrête.*" Gabriella lapsed into French as she attempted to pull away. "I don't need you."

"If you want to remain hidden from your ex-fiancé, you
will do as you are told, Gabriella." Somehow, the sharpness
of his tone penetrated the anger heating her blood. "Now is
not the time for childish tantrums."

"Let go of my arm, Sebastian." She enunciated each word
slowly. When he did so, Gabriella fought the urge to rub the
place of his touch.

Her fingers bit into the leather of her purse. "I asked for
your help to get me into the country so that I could hide from
Vasilei. That's all."

"Yes," Sebastian nodded, then took a step closer. "You
asked for my help and I gave it willingly, for you are my
daughter. But there are strings attached; either you come with
me or I will make sure Vasilei Lexer is reunited with the missing fiancée whom he is so desperate to find."

"You wouldn't," she hissed, then went still, so still her heart
stopped for a moment. He'd previously betrayed her once in
the name of fatherhood when he sent her away to boarding
school. But would he give her up to Vasilei? She hadn't told
her father of the murders, but she'd given good reasons for
her flight.

"It's your choice, Gabriella. I have done many things, but I
have never lied to you."

She met his gaze and a shudder wracked her chest. Her father was the man her mother had loved more than life, more than her own daughter. And just to prove his power over her life, he would threaten her when she'd come to him for help.

"I hate you." Her words came out scratchy and lacked the conviction needed to make them into the truth.

Sebastian nodded slowly and a part of her filled with a dark glee at the fleeting hurt she saw in his eyes. "Hate me all you want, but I will keep you safe."

Gabriella rubbed the back of her neck. She considered asking why he pretended to care but swallowed the question. It didn't matter. Shrugging her shoulders, she started toward the door.

She didn't turn to look as Sebastian fell into step alongside her as they exited through the automatic doors. The bitter cold air stung her lungs but she welcomed it as she pulled her long coat closer to her body, then tucked her hands into the pockets.

They walked only a few feet to a black Mercedes with diplomatic license plates parked at the corner. Once the car got underway, Gabriella turned her face toward the windows and watched the stream of traffic as they sped along the highway.

Sebastian asked, "Was your flight comfortable?"

Conscious of the ears listening to their conversation, Gabriella forced herself to be civil. "Of course."

"Good, good. Did you eat on the plane?"

"Very little, I wasn't hungry."

After making the decision to contact Sebastian, her appetite had disappeared and she felt numb to everything. It was as though a screen had risen around her emotions, cutting off the tide of long buried sentiments her father's presence had stirred up.

"Would you like to have dinner first, Gabriella?"

"No, I want to be alone," she replied, careful to keep her voice even. Not wanting to engage in more polite chatter, Gabriella yawned before snuggling deeper into the leather seat and turned her eyes back toward the window. So many questions tumbled in the back of her mind.

"Not to worry. I leave for Amsterdam tomorrow. I have personal and business matters to attend to."

Gabriella's lips curled with scorn, yet she did not turn her face from the window. "Give my regards to Jensen, *Father*." She mockingly used the title for the first time in over a decade.

"Rella," he softly chided. "Things are not as you imagine them to be. I will return soon and we will make things right between us."

She rubbed a hand across her brow. If she allowed herself to feel, her heart would shatter into pieces. Jensen van Ryne. She had a brother. No, a half-brother, whom she'd never met. An older brother she'd only seen in pictures. "Leave or stay; I don't care."

"You may not trust me, and I have given you just cause, but I promise that I will make it all up to you." His Dutch accent roughened with emotion.

Gabriella wanted to place her hands over her ears at the words she'd dreamed of him saying but instead kept her silence.

He continued. "You are my flesh, my blood, and the only woman I have ever loved except your mother. I won't let anything happen to you."

She curved her body closer to the door and stared at the passing scenery. Even as she fought against the tide of weariness and jet lag, the sound of the radio coupled with the rhythmic movement of the car drew her into an exhausted sleep.

Darius kept his eyes on the road, even as the temptation to turn and check on the woman in the backseat niggled at the back of his mind. His sharp eyes took in the passing taxis and cars as he drove along the Fifty-ninth Street Bridge into Manhattan.

As he made his way to the west side of the city, skyscrapers gave way to the trees of Central Park and then to limestone structures, shops, and lights. Turning from the passing scenery, he glanced into the rearview mirror in time to watch the Dutch businessman reach over and trail his fingertips across the sleeping woman's cheek.

The sight of the man's pale fingers on her burnt sienna skin tightened something in his gut. His cool gaze locked with the older man's blue eyes as the car slowed to a full stop in front of the high-rise building.

"Could you carry her inside? I need to make a phone call."

Darius nodded and exited the car. They'd parked in front of a high-rise apartment building. A doorman and valet stood at attention inside the lobby.

He opened the back door and unfastened the young woman's seat belt. When he lifted her out of the backseat, she hung limply in his arms. Pulling her closer, he inhaled the light floral scent that clung to her clothing. As the woman's silky hair fell over his arm, he looked down into her uncovered face.

If it had not been from the way the winter air made her breath visible, he would have sworn she was no longer breathing. The shadows under her eyes and her unresponsive body spoke of a deep fatigue. He adjusted his hold and carried her inside. Yet, he found himself wanting her to wake up so that he could gain another glimpse of their golden color.

As though she'd heard his thoughts, she stirred in his arms and her eyes opened slowly. "What? No—" she mumbled and pushed against his chest. Strengthening his hold on her squirming body, he entered into one of the building's multiple entrances. "Go back to sleep, little one. All is well," he spoke quietly.

He smiled at her as though reassuring a frightened child, then began to cross through the lavish lobby toward the elevator bank. The elevator doors had just opened when she lost her struggle against exhaustion. Darius watched her eyes flutter closed and he exhaled slowly. As the elevator swept them to the upper floors, he examined Gabriella's long thick eyelashes and could vividly recall the color of her eyes as they flashed with anger less than an hour ago. Although he knew his only purpose was to protect not admire her, Darius remained hypnotized by the delicate beauty of her face.

When the elevator doors opened to an empty hallway, he quickly located the apartment. Using a couple of tricks he'd learned while carrying passed out teammates from a local bar, he managed to unlock the door to the apartment while still carrying Gabriella in his arms. Without turning on the lights, Darius made his way through the spacious entryway, down the rug-carpeted hallway, and into one of the apartment's three bedrooms. He laid her upon the bed, then adjusted the lamplight on the bedside table.

Sebastian's daughter didn't stir as he removed her coat and shoes. Yet, when he started to move away, she shifted on the bed. "Wait." Her voice was as soothing as the lull of the Nile River.

As though commanded, Darius stilled at the foot of the bed.

"Who are you?" she questioned. Her voice was so soft it pulled him. For the second time that night, Darius put aside his thoughts of duty and stared at Gabriella. Careful to keep his eyes locked with hers, he moved to the side of the bed and bent his knees to bring his face within mere inches of hers.

She barely resembled the university ID photo van Ryne had given him, he thought. The black and white photo had missed her lion-colored amber eyes, the hollows of her dusky cheeks, the rich brown of her hair, the thick fan of her eyelashes.

His eyes followed the curve of her neck and focused on the measured pulse underneath flawless brown skin. When he took a breath, the haunting scent of vanilla and sandalwood swamped his senses. Her scent. His mind catalogued the new information and forever linked it with her, while his body tightened in response, forcing him to clamp down on his libido.

He gentled his voice and gave in to the urge to touch her.

Darius raised his hand and brushed the tendrils of her hair from her face. Underneath the surface of her sleep-filled eyes, he glimpsed the emotion that prevented her from rest. Sebastian's daughter was afraid. "I am the man who will keep you safe. Now go back to sleep."

She sighed and closed her eyes as requested. Darius pulled the duvet over her shoulder, then dimmed the light on the bedside table. He waited until he was sure that she had fallen asleep before he slipped out of the room and eased the door closed behind him, careful not to make any noise.

As he made his way back through the hallway to the front of the apartment, he turned on the lights, flooding the pre-war living area with the light of crystal chandeliers. The place was miles away from the sterility of the military barracks. It was apparent van Ryne had spared no expense in his bid to make his daughter's hiding place comfortable. His feet scarcely made a sound on the gleaming walnut flooring. With Manhattan real estate being what it was, he imagined the yearly rent alone to be more than eight times his pay.

He walked silently through the living room and stopped in front of French doors leading to a small terrace overlooking Central Park. He didn't move as the front door unlocked and Sebastian's heavy footfalls echoed in the entryway; instead, his eyes narrowed on the man's image in the windowpane.

"Gabriella?" van Ryne questioned.

"She's asleep." Darius turned. "We need to talk."

"Apologies, but I have to see my daughter first."

Ten minutes later, Sebastian returned and immediately headed over to the in-wall bar area to pour himself a drink from a glass decanter.

"Are you prepared to tell me what this is all about?" Up until that moment, he'd kept his questions limited to a need-to-know basis. Mainly, what he needed to do, when, how and where. But one look into the woman's eyes, coupled with the tension between father and daughter, had him questioning if he were playing the role of bodyguard or jailer.

Sebastian rubbed his brow. "As I told your uncle, I need you to protect her."

"Somehow I get the feeling she won't be happy about that." Darius waved his hand as the other man offered him a glass. He didn't strictly follow the ways of his faith, but in the commandment against imbibing alcohol he remained devout.

"You're right." Sebastian sat down on one of the numerous chairs. "But that's beside the point because I want her safe."

"From whom?" Darius took a step away from the glass doors and stood next to the Italian settee. The fingers of his left hand curled over the white-gold finish of the wood. His right hand was at his side. Darius had a habit of keeping his primary firing hand unencumbered and available to reach back and grab his weapon at the slightest hint of trouble.

"Does it matter?"

"For me to do my job properly, I need to know what I could be up against."

Sebastian continued to stare at the glass in his hand. "Vasilei Lexer."

Darius shook his head. "Sorry, the name doesn't ring a bell."

"He's rich, powerful, and ruthless. I don't want him anywhere near her." Sebastian finished his drink and poured another. Darius caught the way his hand trembled on the glass.

He looked pointedly toward the bedroom wing. "Why does he want her?"

"Why does any man want a woman as beautiful as my daughter?" Sebastian replied rhetorically.

Darius's eyes narrowed. It was a question, not an answer. "Do you trust me?"

"What do you mean?"

He took a step forward, consciously allowing his sidearm to show. "Do you trust me to protect her?"

"I trust Rashad and he says that you are the best."

"Then tell me why you need your daughter under 24/7 protection," he ordered simply.

Darius watched the man set aside the full glass of scotch before he stood, opened the lid of the Steinway grand piano, and ran his finger over the keys. Van Ryne's normally smooth brow furrowed with the intensity of his mood.

"She called me from a pay phone in Geneva, pretending to be my mistress. Of course, you can understand I was shocked because we haven't directly communicated in over three years. Gabriella asked that I get her out of Europe and hide her from Lexer."

"Why would she want to hide?"

"I assume it is because she broke off the engagement."

"There has to be more," Darius pressed. Marriages and engagements stirred deep emotions, but this was different. His daughter's actions portrayed a woman who had run for her life, not from a jilted fiancé. "What did she say to you?"

"To be blunt, Darius, I didn't ask because I didn't care. My daughter has asked for nothing since her mother died. All I know is that she is troubled and she has come back to me. She needs to be protected, and I have an opportunity to make things right."

"How can you be sure this won't be the first place he'll look for her? It makes sense that she would ask her father for help."

Sebastian shrugged. "Gabriella has never told anyone that I'm her father. Even if Lexer discovers my identity and suspects that I'm hiding her, the apartment cannot be traced back to me. The false passport will gain me more than enough time to settle my affairs back home and for us to start a new life in Canada."

"You seem certain that he'll continue to look for her. Why?"

Sebastian shook his head. "I may not have kept in close contact with my daughter since her mother's death, but I have kept watch over her from the moment she was born. I know about Vasilei Lexer because he *is* very much like me.

I loved her mother more than anything else in my life, and I could never have given her up."

Darius's gaze narrowed on the gold wedding band on van Ryne's finger. "Gabriella's mother was your mistress?"

"Yes." Sebastian nodded his head and in that instant, the Dutchman looked far older than his years.

Having traversed the globe, Darius was not surprised that a man as wealthy as van Ryne had discrete affairs. However modern the times had become, some European elites kept to their old ways of marriage alliances. In his mind's eye, he saw again the clear flushed skin drawn tight over Sebastian's high cheekbones.

Sebastian pointed to the coffee table. "Here are the keys to both the apartment and the vehicle. You'll find everything arranged to your specifications. I also took the liberty of allowing you access to a large amount of funds, both cash and credit."

Darius raised an eyebrow. "In order to protect her, I need to be close."

"You have your pick of the other two bedrooms."

"And I need her cooperation."

The other man inclined his head and shared a ghost of a smile. "If you're as good as your uncle says you are, then you'll be able to keep her in line."

"How long until you return?" Darius asked.

Sebastian paused before glancing toward the door. "Two or three weeks. My personal number has been programmed into the mobile phones I've provided."

Darius nodded. Three weeks. He would keep her hidden, then he would leave New York, stop in Philadelphia, then head back to Fort Bragg.

Sebastian moved toward the front door. "I will call you sometime tomorrow to check on Gabriella."

And tonight, Darius thought, I'll find out more about Vasilei Lexer.

Chapter Three

"There is no right and wrong in this life, my son. There is only yours: your power, your will, your soul, and your money."

His father's words haunted him that morning. Fear of failure instilled by years of living up to Dmitry Lexer's expectations had imprinted upon him an instinctual need to succeed.

Vasilei looked down at the signet ring on his right hand. In Germany and most Eastern European countries, the Lexer family name was synonymous with wealth and success. Yet, he had failed. He had failed to keep Gabriella from the truth, failed to keep her from running, and failed to keep the underside of his business from touching his personal life.

You must seize the moment and destroy those who seek to take from you. And when you strike, be forceful and relentless, decide upon your path and inflict all of your punishments at once," his father whispered once more.

Dmitry Lexer had all of his political rivals crushed or executed. The great man had helped rule a nation with the absolute power only granted to a few within the Communist regime. All his life Vasilei followed his father's tenets, yet with this betrayal, he'd chosen a less expedient repayment of his loss.

Last night, he'd watched another man die. And, for the first time, the consequence of taking a life weighed heavily on him. Looking up from the glass of vodka in his hand, Vasilei stared out over the glistening water as the morning light poured though the tinted windows of the boathouse. In another hour, the marina would fill with well-wishers and business acquaintances ready to board his yacht and celebrate his thirty-eighth birthday.

He'd forgotten his mother had arranged the little distraction. His waking thoughts dwelled on the emptiness and silence brought by Gabriella's disappearance. It had been from this villa in the south of Italy that she had vanished. He would not soon forget waking in bed without the woman he had chosen to sleep by his side. *Gabriella.*

"I am most sorry, Vasilei."

"It wasn't your fault, Karl." He continued to look out the window, careful to take small breaths.

Although the boathouse was clean of last night's deed, the rank stench of fear and blood continued to linger in his memories. It was superbly ironic that to the international business community he appeared to be the opposite of his father. Others saw him as exceptionally merciful, trustworthy, upright, and in possession of keen business acumen. Gabriella had only served to add to the illusion. She was perfect in every way, her manners impeccable, as was her beauty; she was a prize for any man, and he had won her when many had failed.

"Sir, we continue to look for your fiancée. My agents report that she has disappeared from Denmark."

"How did they lose her this time?" A smile played on the corners of his lips. Vasilei placed the glass on the windowsill and reached into his pocket. His fingers curled over the rosary beads, the only object of Gabriella's he still possessed.

He listened as Karl, Anton's second in command, cleared his throat. "She went into a church. The men waited outside but she never came out."

"What you meant to say is that she did not come out of the front door."

"Yes, of course," Karl paused. "There hasn't been any activity in her bank accounts and her flute performances have ceased.

"Based on the information we retrieved from Ms. Marie's secondary school admission file, I've dispatched two men on the ground in Saint Martin."

"I promise to have more information for you soon." A deeper voice entered into the conversation.

Vasilei faced his older brother, Anton, the one person on earth whom he trusted with his life. "Have you learned anything further about Gabriella's father?" he repeated.

"We have located a copy of the birth certificate. I have someone in America making inquiries."

"Good." Vasilei nodded dismissively and fell silent until the other men left the boathouse to give him time alone with his brother.

He didn't know why he felt like talking, but he did. "She was magnificent when I first saw her, Anton. I'd never seen a woman ride with the skill of a man. Then to hear her play the flute . . ." his voice trailed off.

His brother's winter blue eyes flashed as he leaned against the wall opposite Vasilei. "She led you on a merry chase, Vas."

"It seems that we are doomed to repeat this cycle, she and I."

"You don't have to chase her this time." Anton took a step forward. "Just let her go."

"Of all the things I could do, that is one which I cannot—" His fingers clenched and Vasilei tossed back the contents of his glass. The vodka's burn only served to heighten his emotional state. "Will not do."

Every part of him rejected the notion of letting anything go. From the moment he'd stood on the second floor balcony of his business associate's French chateau and looked over the grounds to see Gabriella, he'd been obsessed with her.

At first, his interest was just a passing curiosity, but the image of Gabriella had etched itself into his mind and he wanted her. She was an amazing horsewoman, the way she calmed the high-strung gelding and laughed. In that moment, she seemed to be the Goddess Athena reborn.

That weekend, he'd watched her unknowingly collect admirers. She placed the young bucks in her pocket and kept them as friends. A few discreet inquiries and he knew her name. Within two days, he knew her university scores, her favorite music, the color of her bedroom walls, and the scent of her perfume.

Vasilei had it all. Money, power, connections, everything but passion and love, everything but one special woman in his bed.

He spent the weeks following their initial meeting wooing her with flowers, jewelry, and expensive chocolates, yet she still wouldn't agree to have dinner with him. He'd hidden in the upper rows of the university music hall during her afternoon practices, listening to the mesmerizing sound of her flute.

"In the end, she could betray you," Anton argued.

He waved his hand and turned from the window. "No, she won't; she loves me."

"You mean she's blinded you." The other man raked his fingers through his silver peppered hair. "She saw me kill the Russian agents, Vas. We can't afford to have her running loose."

"She's running scared," Vasilei corrected. "If Gabriella had turned to the authorities, we wouldn't be standing here."

"Still."

Vasilei grinned. "Brother, you worry too much."

"How so?"

"All my life you have kept me from harm. Is it so hard to believe that Gabriella wishes to protect me as well?" Vasilei pondered aloud.

"No, it's not." Anton straightened and his light eyes narrowed. "I won't let anything happen to you ever, Vas. Do you doubt that?"

"Not at all," Vasilei sighed. "I want everything to be as it was before."

"I have never failed you," said Anton with steel in his voice. "I swore on Father's grave that I would take care of you. Rest easy, I'll find her."

Vasilei's green eyes darkened as his fingers squeezed the beads in his hand. They would bring Gabriella home; then he would punish her for leaving him. Returning the rosary to his pocket, he turned back toward the window and back to the days of their early acquaintance.

Gabriella hadn't yielded to romance, so he'd met her on the riding fields outside of Paris, and he'd wooed her with horse races and trips to the zoo before capturing her heart. He'd been her first and he'd be her last. Vasilei had taken her on the deck of his yacht and Gabriella had been magnificent, a pagan priestess under the stars. He grew aroused remembering the way he'd deflowered her, brought her to ecstasy. His hands tangled in her hair, the way she'd wanted him.

He shook his head and smiled as he left the boathouse. All of Europe whispered about his fiancée's disappearance. The tabloids were rife with speculation that family disapproval and Vasilei's supposed infidelity had driven her away. None of them could have been further from the truth.

She had fled because of the man who had lain mewling at his feet the night before. A man who'd failed to do his job and keep her from witnessing the killings.

Vasilei thought that Markus's crooked nose and flat inwardly curved mouth had lent him a permanent look of disdain, even as his blood spilled out over the floor. That night, during Anton's usual excellence at prolonged killing, the thought of Gabriella had stirred him even as he'd witnessed the torture. She was his mate, the one who would bare him magnificent sons, and he would hunt her down and bring her back to where she belonged.

* * *

Awareness came quickly to Gabriella as she woke to find sunlight streaming through the open-curtained windows. Closing her eyes and wrapping her arms around the pillow, she snuggled deeper into the lavender striped comforter. She wanted to stay there forever, but thirst stirred and stronger than the grumbling in her stomach, was the pounding in her head.

Rolling over, she got out of bed and sighed at her rumpled clothing. Taking a minute to orient herself, she exited the bedroom only to pause as she stepped into the hallway. On her journey from her bedroom to the kitchen, she ran her hands over the antique wood furniture and breathed in the lingering scent of fresh paint, while sounds of car horns stole in through closed windows.

As with many Manhattan pre-war apartments, the rooms were large with high ceilings that spread from a central gallery that separated the bedrooms and study from the living room, dining room, and kitchen. She remembered all of the architectural details, yet nothing was familiar to her.

After searching through the kitchen cabinets, she stood next to the sink and drank glass after glass of water. She ate an apple, then made her way to the bathroom adjoining her bedroom and stopped in the doorway. A large marble sink stood by itself next to a walnut vanity tower. The glass-framed shower stall stood separated from the bath. Gabriella crossed the marble floor to run her fingers over the edge of the white claw-footed bathtub whose deeply polished inside spoke of long soaks with low lights and burning candles.

For a lingering moment, Gabriella eyed the long, deep porcelain tub, then turned on the spigot. The gushing of water reminded her of her childhood love of water. Foregoing the temptation of taking a soak, she turned off the water and moved toward what she hoped was a closet. She pulled back the doors to see lotions, oils, soaps, gels, shampoos, conditioners, perfumes, scrubs, and towels lining the closet shelves.

Gabriella began to hum as she took off her two-day-old

clothing, then stepped into the stand-alone shower and shut the glass door. Later, once she'd finished showering and put on a thick cotton robe, she returned to the bedroom and stood by the window.

The sun peeked from behind a cloud and its rays turned Central Park's reservoir into gold. She touched her fingers to the glass and the chill spread quickly up her arm. As cold as it was outside, she loved this time of year and the deceptive way the sun glowed bright but the wind blew cold.

Vasilei had marveled at her love of the Alpine winters, while her heritage pointed to a predisposition for Caribbean beaches. She sighed and moved from the window; the wonder of the morning disappeared when the image of her ex-fiancé floated before her eyes.

Even now, far from his presence, she was afraid. Not of his finding her, for Sebastian had covered her tracks well, but that the time alone had not been enough. Gabriella feared he might still control her body. It terrified her to think that she could still be tethered to him, the man she'd thought she loved, the same man who stood by as Anton had committed murder.

The thought of Vasilei's brother sent a chill down her spine. He was a killer in every sense of the word. And Anton had seen her outside the boathouse window the night she watched him torture the two men to death. She shivered with dread. If not for Vasilei's presence, she would have been dead by his hand.

Running her fingers through her still damp hair, Gabriella looked down at the parchment dressing table and inhaled sharply at the sight of the antique furniture piece. Sebastian had given it to her mother as a Christmas present. Cautiously, she reached out and picked up a picture of her mother holding a baby in her arms. She put it down and touched everything—the lacquer jewelry box, perfume bottles, the makeup case, and perfume bottles she'd played with as a child. She cradled the wooden hairbrush to her chest and heard the opening strains

of a lullaby her mother had sung to her. Every night before bedtime, Gabriella had sat in the very same cushioned chair while
her mother gently untangled her hair, brushed, and plaited it
into a single braid.

"*Maman*," she whispered, then wiped a tear from her
cheek. Gabriella dropped the brush on the table, then hur-
riedly turned and walked into the closet. Needing a distraction from her memories, she passed her hands over the myriad
of hangers filled with clothing.

It seemed that Sebastian had spared no expense on her
wardrobe. Leafing through the garments, she ascertained that
he had even gone as far as to have included both a winter and
spring collection. Expensive leather shoes and handbags
stood in the back corner; designer shirts, skirts, dresses, and
pants hung on wooden hangers. Yet, he had deliberately
missed an essential. Sebastian hadn't left her with a single
pair of blue jeans. Unconsciously, a rueful smile curled her
lips. He'd not forgotten that her mother had heartily disliked
them.

Still, she had to search through the lower drawers until
she found what she was looking for. After ridding the garments of their price tags, she put on the jogging pants, sweatshirt, socks, athletic shoes, and a jacket.

Now that her headache had dissipated, she needed to clear
her mind. The only sure way to do that was with fresh air and
open sky. She spared a glance at the duffle bag on top of the
armoire. So much of her life had been lost or given away. She
barely had anything left and she wouldn't let it go, so she
picked up the bag and placed it into the back of the closet.

Taking a moment to search, she found the key to the apartment, a cell phone, and an envelope containing a mixed assortment of cash on a side table next to the door. Gabriella
stopped counting after identifying fifty, one hundred-dollar
bills. She tucked a single bill and a key into her pocket, then
put on a pair of suede gloves. Stepping out into the quiet,

carpet-lined hallway, she closed the door and pressed the button for the elevator.

"Going somewhere?"

She stiffened and turned her head to glance at the man leaning against the wall. Nothing could have kept her from recalling his presence in the airport the night before or observing that he retained his dangerously handsome looks. He was dressed in monochrome black from the tips of his shoes to the sunglasses perched behind the slight crook of his nose. Aware that she was staring, Gabriella turned and pressed the elevator call button again.

"It's cold outside," he continued.

Gabriella adjusted her gloves and stared straight ahead at the shiny silver doors.

"I take it we're going jogging?"

"Leave me alone, please," she finally bit out, stepping into the elevator car. Before the doors could close, the man had stepped in beside her.

"We were not properly introduced last night. My name's Darius."

Her memory wasn't that short. She still remembered with great clarity not only his name, but also the comfort of his strong arms as he'd carried her to bed last night. Looking away, she ignored his outstretched hand. Why couldn't he just leave her the hell alone? She wasn't a violent woman, but for a few moments she let clandestine thoughts of pushing him into an empty elevator shaft frolic in her imagination.

"That's not nice, Gabriella." The devilishly strong voice taunted.

"How much is he paying you?" she asked tightly.

"Why? Do you have a better offer?"

The arrogant way he regarded her from over the rim of his sunglasses infuriated Gabriella, even as the melodic pitch of his voice intrigued her. Barely managing to keep her tone even, she replied, "I'll double it."

The money her mother had set aside, along with the prize

money she'd won from flute competitions, would be more than enough, if she could touch it. It hadn't taken her long to realize that Vasilei had somehow gained access to her bank accounts and used them to track her. But, she could still sell her engagement ring.

In her travels, she'd rediscovered her fondness for being alone and going wherever she wanted without having Vasilei's men following her. The novelty of having Markus as a bodyguard wore off quickly. Vasilei insisted that she have someone with her at all times, that his family fortune and the Lexer name would make her vulnerable to enemies whose grudges stemmed from his father's role in the exiled Communist regime.

At the thought of her ex-bodyguard, Gabriella averted her attention to zipping up her jacket. The silent man who had been her constant shadow must have paid a high price for her disappearance. Yet, where Markus had been slightly menacing, this man had had such an air of resolution and self-confidence that he projected an almost visible aura of controlled, intelligent, and disciplined power.

"That's a nice offer," Darius replied. His brow crinkled.

A hopeful smile curved her lips upward. "You'll take it?"

Darius stepped out of the elevator first. Standing slightly back, Gabriella noticed his head rotate as he looked over the entire lobby area. "No," he replied without looking in her direction.

He caught her heated glare and smiled again as she sailed through the apartment building's doorway and, without saying a word, broke into a jog after crossing the busy Upper West Side street.

"Great weather," he commented, drawing alongside her. They turned a corner and entered the park.

Gabriella didn't respond verbally to his comment, but instead increased her speed in an attempt to pull away. What had been a promising morning was in the process of being ruined.

Blood pumped into her ears and her breath came hard in

the cold air. It had taken Sebastian less then twenty-four hours to intrude upon every facet of her life, and it galled her. Worse yet, she'd brought it upon herself by asking her father for help.

She put herself on autopilot and headed north through the park toward the reservoir. In the cause of love, her father had exiled her to boarding school. In the name of affection, Vasilei had deceived her.

Her heart caught at the thought of his confessions of the torture and death that he had seen as a child. She had wept for him and loved him all the more that he had been able to leave behind his father's brutal legacy and make his way to become a model business leader and humanitarian. Even her ex-fiancé's mother believed him to be the most wonderful of sons.

But Vasilei had managed to fool them all.

Over a half an hour later, she came to a stop and bent over, trying to catch her breath. Looking down, she could see the vestiges of the February frost that had left a blanket of white over the park grounds.

"That was nice." A deep voice came from over her shoulder.

Between pulling in deep gulps of the crisp air, Gabriella managed to get out, "What do you want?"

"Just to do my job."

"And that is?"

"Protecting you," Darius answered.

"From whom?" She finished stretching, then crossed her arms and raised her chin in a defiant manner. Golden eyes locked with obsidian. Leaned and muscled, his breath came evenly as hers clouded the air like smoke from a chimney. The evidence of his physical stamina increased her annoyance instead of garnering her respect. She'd halfway hoped he'd collapse at her feet.

"You tell me."

"I'm in no danger, Mr—" she pretended to have forgotten his name.

"Darius Said Yassoud. Call me Darius."

"Mr. Yassoud." Gabriella offered a cold smile.

"Darius," he corrected, taking a step forward and keeping his arms open and at his side. The dark eyes glinted and a lazy grin curled his lips. "Why not be on a first name basis? We'll be seeing quite a bit of one another over the next few weeks." He removed his sunglasses.

"Darius," she said smoothly. If she couldn't get rid of him by being rude, she would try tact. "Sebastian has always been a bit extreme in his work, but I don't need a babysitter."

"That's good, because I don't chase after spoiled rich girls."

Gabriella's blood, which was already flowing from the exercise, began to pound at the implication. She glared at him as he rubbed his gloved hands together and then raised a thick eyebrow. She couldn't discern if the twinkle in those sinfully dark chocolate eyes of his came from amusement or irritation.

"Triple," she blurted out, suddenly aware of Darius in a way that she shouldn't have been. Gabriella shivered and it had nothing to do with the sharp wind blowing off the water. Not only did the spark of attraction dance on her skin, but also the flare of hunger on her tongue had nothing to do with lack of food in her stomach. Gabriella lowered her gaze quickly as she caught herself staring at the beauty of his face in the winter sunlight. She was mesmerized by the ripples of midnight black hair and prominent cheekbones that left soft hollows around his eyes.

"Triple what?"

"I'll pay you triple your fee, if you leave and say nothing to Sebastian."

"Sorry." Darius shook his head, unable to remain entirely unmoved by the plea he saw in the golden glint of her eyes. "I gave him my word."

The woman clenched her hands into fists and struck out against the air. "I should never have called him."

Darius had noticed her slight French accent the moment

she'd spoken to him in the hallway that morning, but now as her temper flared, the Gallic intonation colored her voice.

"That may or may not be the case, but I'm here to look after you. Now that we've gotten the unpleasantness out of the way, why don't you join me for a cup of coffee back at the apartment?" His confident smile was a testament to his complete disregard of her feelings.

Her mouth compressed into a thin line. "Go to hell." Arrogant, that's what he was, and she would have none of it. Turning her back to him, she started toward the exit to Central Park.

Darius shook his head and chuckled before starting after her. Her curse was a joke because he'd be going *back* to hell. The places in the Middle East his Special Forces team had been sent were worse than any purgatory her pretty head could come up with.

At one time, all he'd ever wanted was the thrill of victory that came with the successful completion of the mission. Now, only a few days into his leave of absence, Darius wondered about the future direction of his life. It hadn't taken him long to figure out that he was at a crossroads. His choices had come down to two: stay in the clandestine fighting of Delta Force or take on the new role of intelligence instructor.

Darius increased his pace in order to keep Gabriella within his line of sight. She jogged, oblivious to the turned heads of men out walking with their dogs and lean cyclists who slowed at her approach. He couldn't blame them. He might have been assigned as her bodyguard, but he didn't keep a close eye on her just for protection. No, his gaze remained fixed because he couldn't tear his eyes away. With long legs extending from a curvy bottom, dainty ears, and hair that caught the light and uncovered veins of red, Gabriella was beautiful.

The rash of weddings by his current and former Delta team members increased his restlessness and distraction. He'd grown up in a family that had stressed the importance of faith; Darius believed the will of Allah was the mover of all actions and the originator of all events. And for that alone, he bore no doubts that he'd been chosen to watch over this woman.

Twenty minutes later, Gabriella picked up the eatery's menu from the side counter and glanced at the breakfast selections. It was a toss-up as to whether or not she would have stayed, but desire of human contact had her sitting in a booth near the back kitchen.

As she waited for the busboy to clear a table, the waitresses with their white blouses and black short skirts greeted and chatted with most of the diners. The small restaurant with its diverse clientele seemed filled with the heavy scent of freshly brewed coffee, pancakes, and bacon. It had been months since Gabriella had freely enjoyed eating in public places with the company of others.

Once she'd taken a seat in a booth and the waitress filled her cup with steaming hot coffee, she turned her attention back to the menu in her hand. So many choices and not enough room, she mused. The hint of a smile played on the corners of her mouth as she remembered her mother's scolding that her eyes were always bigger than her stomach.

"You don't like me, do you?"

Startled, Gabriella looked up in time to see Darius slide into the other side of the booth. For a minute, she just studied the man and the way he flashed a broad smile as she put down her menu. Just as she opened her mouth to tell him he was the rudest and most obnoxious man she'd ever met, one of her favorite songs came on the restaurant's audio system. The sound of the young British pop singer brought back memories of small French cafés and underground dance clubs.

Letting out a not so polite sigh, Gabriella gave him a sideways glance instead of a cold shoulder. "I don't know you enough to dislike you, but what I do know is that I don't like being followed."

She watched as Darius turned toward the waitress and thanked her for the extra menu and cup of coffee.

"And I don't like having to chase you." He picked up his cup and leaned back.

Gabriella added cream and sugar to her coffee. After taking a sip, she put down her cup and turned her attention back to her menu. Although butterflies stirred in her stomach, she wouldn't let him ruin her breakfast.

"Good morning. Are you folks ready to order or should I come back?" The waitress had come to stand beside their table.

"Yes, we're ready," Darius answered. "I'll have the fruit, toast, and a Spanish omelet."

Gabriella glared at him before looking up at the waitress. The middle-aged woman practically drooled over Darius, she resentfully observed. While she felt a little less than respectable in her jogging clothes, Darius, with his black pants and long-sleeved mock turtleneck, could have recently departed a symphony performance. She cleared her throat and closed her menu. "I would like the blueberry pancakes, scrambled eggs, and hash browns with onions and cheese."

"Coming right up."

"That's a rather large order," Darius commented as soon as the waitress left the vicinity.

"Are you my nutritionist as well as my guard?" Gabriella asked sarcastically. She'd had enough of being regulated in boarding school. For five years, she'd been told when to wake up, what to eat, how to dress, when to shower, and when to sleep.

"Not in this lifetime." Darius caught her eye and one brow quirked as his lips twitched in a smile. "That's something I wouldn't dare do. My older sister has a sweet tooth and my younger cousin has quite a fondness for figs. I would never get in the way of a woman and her meal."

Unconsciously, she found herself smiling along with him. It went against all her training to be rude, and it did her no good to take out her anger on him. Sebastian was the reason he sat across from her. Gabriella's smile dimmed at the prospect of facing her father again.

"Look, Gabriella, I wouldn't presume that you and I become friends, but I'd like for you to at least feel comfortable around me."

"Why?"

"Because it would make things a whole lot easier."

No, it wouldn't, she thought, feeling a flash of guilt. Markus had said the same thing after she'd argued with Vasilei about the need for a bodyguard. As a musician, she liked to have time alone and Markus's required presence, however unobtrusive, had bothered her.

After taking a long drink of her rapidly cooling beverage, Gabriella placed her hands on the table. She didn't say a word for a moment, and then she looked up into Darius's eyes. "Did Sebastian promise to give you a promotion?"

Darius sighed and leaned forward. "I don't work for Sebastian."

"Are you a professional bodyguard then?"

"On occasion I've had to protect people," he responded vaguely.

"What exactly did you do before this?" she persisted.

"Afraid I can't do my job?"

"Maybe."

"I'm in the military, Gabriella." He leaned back and stretched his arms out over the back of his booth seat. "I had a lot of time due to me and decided to take an extended leave."

"And you decided to do a little moonlighting on the side?" Her tone was mocking, but Darius saw the flash of wariness in her eyes.

The waitress chose that moment to deliver their order. The food-filled plates took up most of the space on the small rectangular table.

After taking a bite of his omelet, Darius scanned the

restaurant for the third time before returning his gaze to Gabriella. He didn't know why, but she had gotten under his skin. Maybe the mention of his sister influenced his emotions. Somehow, the woman was very different from the spoiled princess he imagined her to be earlier that morning. Sitting in the diner without makeup and her hair drawn back into a ponytail made her look more like a little girl than an accomplished concert flutist.

He'd spent half the night ensconced in the study utilizing the electronic means at his disposal to gather information on Lexer. The man's present situation didn't interest him so much as his past. Vasilei Lexer was the younger son of one of Eastern Europe's most brutal Communist dictators. His fortune, social position, and business dealings had been built from ill-gotten gains of a collapsed regime. He was a multimillionaire and a generous benefactor to the arts and International relief organizations.

Darius had dug around various governmental and international databases and found zero. The only clue as to why Gabriella broke off her engagement with Lexer was a rumor of an affair. No matter where he looked, it seemed Vasilei Lexer was the perfect corporate leader, a scion of wealth and privilege. But the image was too clean. He had studied a photograph of Gabriella and Lexer after a performance at the Berlin Philharmonic and something hard twisted in his stomach. The man's smile and possessive looks continued to bother him.

"No, Gabriella, I'm not here because of money. I'm doing this as a favor to my uncle."

"Your uncle?"

He watched as her forkful of syrup-laden pancake paused halfway to her lips. "He and van Ryne are business partners."

"Business partners," she repeated doubtfully, putting down her knife.

Darius observed Gabriella holding the knife in her right hand and the fork in her left hand to cut the pancakes and then change her fork from the left to the right hand to eat. While the woman ate with an American style, her accent was quite French, yet her father was Dutch. For a second, his brow wrinkled at the inherent contradictions.

"Sebastian van Ryne helped my uncle when he was just starting out in the export/import business."

"Oh, so you're doing this as a favor?" she asked. The response held genuine surprise.

"I'm doing this for family," he corrected.

Both of them continued to eat their breakfast. For the next twenty minutes, the sounds of other diners' voices filled the silence.

Darius realized that Gabriella had stopped eating her food and was instead shifting her scrambled eggs around the plate. Then she placed her fork down and looked up at him.

"Did I say something that bothered you?" he asked.

She wiped her mouth with the paper napkin. "What did Sebastian tell you about me?"

Darius shrugged and said, "Not much." But what he wanted to say was, *not enough*. Mystery clung to her like a second skin and he read biographies, not mysteries. The lack of answers surrounding her recent past intrigued him.

"Did he tell you why he wanted you to watch me?" she asked.

"He wants to make sure you're protected." Darius regarded her with a steady gaze.

"From who?"

"Vasilei Lexer."

Gabriella averted her eyes from his gaze, then gestured toward a passing waitress and got refills of their coffee. She placed her hand over the steaming mug and enjoyed the moist warmth.

"Van Ryne thinks that the man's a threat to you in some way," Darius asserted.

Denial sprang quickly to her lips but it disappeared in the next breath. She'd watched Vasilei stand by as his older brother tortured two men to death. The old Gabriella would have thought him incapable of such an act. She hadn't known the man she was to marry. The new Gabriella, who'd spent months running from her own shadow, knew better.

"Vasilei would never hurt me," she lied. She hadn't thought him capable of murder either. But would he harm her? She couldn't answer that question, but she wouldn't give Darius the satisfaction of being right.

"If that were the case, you wouldn't be hiding from him."

"What do you mean?"

Her eyes were the most unusual shade of amber, Darius thought. When she looked at him, he felt as though they were pulling him in, dragging him down like quicksand. "Lisa Cravell," he said simply.

"You supplied Sebastian with the fake passport?" Gabriella questioned. The job, the breakfast, the easygoing conversation had lulled her into dropping her guard. It was only years of self-training that allowed her to look at him with nothing more than a mild surprise.

"Yes, I did. But now that I think about it, it seems quite odd that you'd need a new identity and a bodyguard just to stay away from a man who isn't supposed to pose a threat."

She sat back while her mind searched for something to say. What she'd said was true. Vasilei might not wish her harm, but Anton would see her dead. She'd seen it in his eyes.

"I . . ." she began but was saved from continuing when his cell phone beeped discreetly.

Gabriella pretended interest in the comings and goings of the waitresses and busboys as Darius carried on his conversation. It took her a moment to recognize that Darius was speaking in Arabic.

He quickly ended the call. "You were saying?"

She shrugged one shoulder and slid over to exit the cushioned seat. "I just needed some time away from Vasilei, his family, and the paparazzi. Sebastian volunteered to help me resettle in New York. I had no idea he'd go to such lengths."

"Maybe he just wants to protect you."

"Well, I didn't ask for your opinion, thank you," she snapped, putting on her jacket and gloves.

He had the absolute gall to grin at her. "Excuse me, Princess. Guess I touched a nerve."

Unasked for, Darius tossed money onto the table and took her arm. She allowed him to lead her as far as the door, but once they were outside, Gabriella tried to pull away. Darius held tight.

He turned her around with one hand and raised her chin with the other. Looking directly into his eyes brought her heart to a stand-still while her breath rushed out of her chest. Whether in anger or desire, she couldn't tell.

"Princess, if you run, I'll run. Jog and I'll pace you like a drill sergeant. From now on, wherever you go, I go. Do you understand?"

She looked into his dark eyes and her lips tightened even as her stomach clenched. The steel she'd heard in his voice brooked no challenge.

"Release my arm," she ordered from behind clenched teeth. "I won't be going anywhere except to the shower, and you're not welcome there."

Darius slowly let go of her arm. Gabriella cast him a dirty look and put her hands in her pockets. When he fell into step beside her, she took a deep breath of diesel-scented air. She'd asked Sebastian for help and he'd taken over her life in the name of fatherhood. Not again, she silently vowed as she crossed the street in front of a row of shops. Somehow, some way, she would be free of all men . . . including her father, Sebastian.

Chapter Four

"This better be good, Sebastian." The high-powered attorney set his leather briefcase on the oval table, then came to a stop behind the executive chair.

Sebastian van Ryne continued to watch the slow-moving clouds from the window of his fifty-seventh floor executive office. "What diversion did I take you away from this time, Howard?"

"Best damn golf game of my life," the man replied.

"Sincerest apologies, but this business takes precedence." Sebastian turned from the window and regarded the heavyset New York attorney whom he also considered a close friend. His hair had once been brown, but age, stress, and long work hours had turned it silver. Yet, something about Howard's bluntness reminded him of the black and white cowboy movies he'd enjoyed in his youth. The attorney's tanned face and deep scowl only served to deepen this impression.

He took a seat and gathered his scattered thoughts. It had been difficult for him to concentrate today. Memories of his old life in New York had haunted him from the time he'd woken up this morning. Not only had his daughter returned to him, but her mother as well. Josette's ghost lay beside him in his dreams and walked beside him in the waking hours.

Born to an elite Dutch family, Sebastian had never known a material want. His family came from a long line of political leaders. He had been educated at the finest institutions and garnered the right connections and privileges of his class. He excelled in academics, thus meeting his father's expectations.

What he did not get from his cold and aloof parents was either affection or love. So when a marriage of old blood and new money was arranged between two proud families, he accepted because the match would make his parents proud and better the van Ryne name. His father-in-law had been the CEO of one of the Netherlands' largest shipping companies, which held significant interests in telecommunications, manufacturing, and chemicals.

"Gabriella's come back to America," Sebastian said softly before sitting down.

Howard sat up straight in his chair and adjusted his wire-framed glasses. "The girl's here? What does she want? It can't be money, because I've seen the bank statements from the trust fund you established at her birth. She's got millions."

"She didn't come back to see me." Sebastian waved his hand dismissively. "And she would not have contacted me if she hadn't been desperate."

"Desperate?"

"She's broken off with her fiancé."

Howard shifted in his chair. "I read about that when I was in France last month. If I recall correctly, she was supposed to marry the scion of the Lexer family. But three months before the wedding, she just disappeared; rumor surfaced that she caught him having an affair with a German actress. What does this have to do with her being desperate?"

"Apparently Lexer has yet to accept her refusal."

"So she's hiding from him here in New York?"

"Correct," Sebastian nodded. But in the back of his mind, he knew it was more than that. He had seen something that cut his heart. Far more disturbing than the cold anger he'd seen in his daughter's eyes was the panic he'd heard in her voice at the thought of Vasilei finding her. It was after her phone call that he'd contacted Rashad. He didn't just want a bodyguard; he wanted someone who wouldn't hesitate to employ lethal force should Lexer find Gabriella.

Howard's booming voice broke into his thoughts. "I hate to tell you, but there's really nothing I can do."

"I realize that, my friend. I need you for other matters. You're the only person I can trust to help me do the right thing."

"Whoa." Howard waved his thick hands. "Hold your horses. What are we talking about here?"

Sebastian watched as the attorney stood up and went over to the bar to pour a drink.

"I want to change my will. Gabriella should be named my legal heir and have my name."

"Sebastian." Howard almost succeeded in spilling the bourbon. "This isn't like you to make such rash decisions. Are you being blackmailed?"

"No." Sebastian smiled for the first time in days.

Howard took a deep drink. "Give me the bottom line. What does she want?"

"Nothing. You know that Gabriella has barely accepted anything I've given her. The graduation and birthday gifts she returned unopened. No, she blames me for her mother's death."

"Josette's illness wasn't your fault."

Sebastian shook his head. "I should have seen her pain, should have been there for both of them. I accept part of Gabriella's blame because it's the truth. But I will rectify my past mistakes and you, Howard, are going to help me."

"To tell the truth, I'm having a tough time with this." Howard took a seat and placed the empty glass firmly on the table.

"I've been responsible all my life, putting family and a misplaced sense of honor above all else, even my own blood, Howard." As he spoke, his accent thickened with emotion.

The attorney sat forward and took off his glasses before rubbing his brow. "You had an affair and more than fulfilled your duty by financially providing for the child and her mother."

Sebastian sat back and his eyes drifted toward the ceiling. He'd held the unspoken memory of his first meeting with Josette close to his heart for too long. Now, as he looked toward the future and felt hope for the first time, he wanted someone else to understand the bond that had formed between them. "I never told you that I met Gabriella's mother on the very night of my honeymoon."

"I knew that you didn't marry your wife out of affection, but . . ." Howard faltered.

Sebastian continued as though he had not heard the shock in his friend's voice. "I have never felt as cold and lonely as the first night in my own marriage bed. The price of being a van Ryne—family was everything. The wedding was more a merger of blood. I didn't love Catherine, didn't want to."

He stood and began to pace, propelled by the emotional memories. "She despised me because I had her father's attention and admiration. So on the night of our honeymoon, with my wife passed out in her separate suite, I walked alone on the beach."

Howard frowned. "This is where you met Josette?"

Sebastian stopped his pacing and sat back down. "Somehow the moonlight and the lush cocoon of the Caribbean had tricked me into believing in fairytales."

His breath had caught in his throat that night; it was as if he saw a mermaid swim from the water. *Josette.*

"I hid behind a tree when I saw her come walking out of the ocean, and I listened to her sing. I never wanted anything but to watch her. To know her name. Every night the scene repeated itself until the last night of my stay when she didn't walk down the beach away from me. Her bare feet came to my hiding place and I clutched the coconut tree as Josette read me like a book. All my sins, hope, guilt, and loneliness lay in her midnight eyes; I couldn't stop myself from kissing her."

He drew in a deep breath and opened his eyes. Sebastian couldn't keep from falling in love, couldn't keep her from wrapping around his soul and laying down her warm presence in his heart, even though their union could never last.

Josette's family had come to Curaçao from St. Martin. The townspeople had remarked that even as a little girl she possessed a woman's mind and a healer's heart. It amazed him that the lovely cadences of her voice could lull small animals from their hiding places and birds from the sky. Sebastian had seen it with his very own eyes. He would wake up as the sun came up just to see the transformation of the light as it touched her skin.

She was not simple, but clear in thought, action, life, and deed. Her sole motivation was to help people; and to fulfill that goal, she became a nurse. Josette was the best medicine any person could ask for. The woman Sebastian wished he'd had the courage to marry brought the aura of life and possibilities into the hospital room, and her eyes gave bedridden patients new hope and dreams.

"I went back to the island every chance I could get. And who wouldn't in my place? I welcomed the chance to leave that empty monstrosity of a mansion and the marble statue I had to call my wife. I would have given anything to just stay in our bungalow by the water."

The distance had killed him. Nothing could convince Josette to move closer. While in Europe, Sebastian worked like a madman and at night, after two-hour dinners, he sat at his desk with her letters while his wife went out to meet her friends and lovers. Maybe his father-in-law suspected or knew of his involvement with another woman.

Sebastian could never be sure of the man who treated him more as a son than a son-in-law. The man had a French marriage, his affairs were discreet, and he had kept the same woman for his mistress even after his wife's death. His own father-in-law had encouraged his frequent business trips to visit the oil refineries off the coast of the Antilles.

"Are you sure about this?" Howard's question broke his concentration.

"Absolutely," he nodded. Sebastian was more than ready to begin a new life out from of under his family's yoke. "One more thing, Howard." He turned from the window and sat back down.

"What's that?"

"Contact someone at the law firm in Amsterdam. I want a divorce."

"Your wife will fight this."

"No, she will not," he contradicted.

"What about your son?"

Sebastian drew in a deep breath before announcing the one secret only known by one other person. "She won't fight because of Jensen. You see, my friend, I've never slept with my wife."

As soon as Howard closed the large doors behind him, Sebastian relaxed in his chair and went back to his memories.

It had been two days after the anniversary of his third year of marriage when he read Josette's letter. She would come to New York; he would at long last become a real father. They named her Gabriella and she was beautiful. It was the happiest day of his life and the first and only time they ever fought. Josette wouldn't let him give the baby his name.

Because of his father-in-law's failing health and the potential scandal, Sebastian had agreed to keep his wife's secret. However, he'd told Catherine that as soon her child was born, he would relocate to New York without her. It was there that he was reunited with Josette. They were happy and in love for eight years until his father-in-law sickened and left the family business in Sebastian's hands, so he had to move back to Europe—without Josette. Yet, he'd continued his bicontinental affair for five years.

On a **trip to** Amsterdam for the holidays, his wife wanted to welc**ome he**r husband into her bed, but it was too late; Sebastian had received word that Josette was in the hospital. His grief had been so great that he had not been able to emotionally provide for his daughter. His fingers curled into the leather armrests of the executive chair.

A month after Josette's death, he journeyed to the Caribbean island to see his daughter, but she wouldn't speak to him. She'd gone so far as to refuse to see to him. Nothing had hurt deeper than when Gabriella had run away as Sebastian had tried to hug her. The relatives wanted to keep the child, but Sebastian thought it was a mistake; her grieved anger had been more than they could bear. They had let her run wild.

Acting upon the advice of his lawyer and his own inability to get past the grief caused by Gabriella's resemblance to her mother, Sebastian made a few phone calls and within two days had Gabriella sent to an elite girl's boarding school in Switzerland.

Grief at Josette's loss turned him from his own child. A twisted sense of love and self-protection kept him away from his daughter. His wife's increasing dependence upon him, coupled with his father-in-law's business demands, provided an escape. Becoming completely self-absorbed, he had focused on business and politics.

Sebastian unclenched his fingers and picked up a picture of Josette and Gabriella. Time was not on his side where Gabriella was concerned. He had not been there to love, guide, and protect her. Now he would rectify past mistakes and have his daughter back. He would keep her safe; nothing and no one would come between them again.

Darius stood outside of the mahogany bedroom door and hesitated again before knocking. Gabriella hadn't left her bedroom or stirred since their return from breakfast. Ensconced in the study, he'd made phone calls and answered a summons from van Ryne. When he'd asked the Dutchman if he wanted to speak with his daughter, the silence over the call told him more than he needed to know.

After hanging up the mobile phone, Darius returned to the computer and recommenced reading a file on Gabriella's ex-fiancé.

By evening, after hitting yet another wall in his background check, his gut and his head were in agreement. The information gaps were too jarring to put off as mere coincidence. Putting that thought aside, he raised his hand and knocked on the door.

"Come in."

He entered Gabriella's bedroom and stood to the side. Training made him automatically scan the area, but instinct led his eyes to her. Willpower alone kept him from taking another step forward. She was standing next to the window. The soft glow of the city lights shimmered along her wavy hair and made her eyes almost cat-like in their luminescence. His gaze slipped over her slender shoulders, the firm curve of her breasts, the long line of her stomach, down to the half-hidden toes. Sometime after returning, she'd exchanged her jogging outfit for a pair of wool slacks and a long cream-colored blouse. During various hours of the day, he'd stood outside her door listening, yet not once did he hear her stirring about.

"I came to see if you were ready for dinner."

The curtain swayed back into place and she turned from the window. As she did so, those golden eyes, which had never been far from his thoughts all day, rested inquiringly on his face.

"I seem to have slept the day away." She moved in closer to the center of the room. "We'll be dining out, of course."

"No, we won't." At the immediate look of disappointment, Darius allowed his lips to curl into an easy grin. "We'll be eating in the dining room."

"You cooked?"

"Better." He rubbed his hands together. "I ordered. Your father may have set you up in a nice place, but he left the refrigerator empty. I plan to go out tomorrow and stock up on supplies."

"Don't call him that." Her feet whispered over the hard-wood flooring as she took a step toward him.

He raised a brow at the angry retort. "It's the truth."

"It's a biological fact, but it doesn't mean he's worthy of the title." She paused and seemed to collect herself. "Please, Darius, I would prefer you not refer to him in that manner."

He nodded slowly, not bothering to keep the curiosity from his gaze. "Van Ryne called to check on you earlier."

"And what did you tell him?"

"That you were settling in nicely."

"I'm not too sure of that," she replied. "No offense, but I still neither want nor need a bodyguard."

"None taken." He caught a glimpse of a smile on her face and he wanted the frequency of the expression to stay. "How about you and I set aside our differences and eat before the food gets cold?"

"Pizza?" She came to stand beside him and he moved to the side so that they both entered the hallway and walked together into the kitchen.

Darius opened a brown bag and drew forth one of its plastic covered containers. "Same country but different menu." He grinned. "I took the liberty of ordering Italian."

"Looks like you ordered a lot," Gabriella commented. Her back was to him as she washed her hands in the double-sided sink, then dried them on a hand towel.

"You were sleeping and I don't know your food preferences yet. There are enough dishes in there to please anyone from a vegetarian to a carnivore."

Gabriella paused from reaching into the well-stocked, face-level cabinets. "That was very considerate of you."

"I aim to please."

They worked in silence. While Darius transferred the delicious smelling entrees into various serving dishes, she set the table. Yet, no matter what, his eyes came back to her. He watched her slender form as she bent over the round mahogany table and gathered silverware with ringless fingers.

She set the table with such military-like precision that he wanted to know how she could be so changeable. From a spoiled rich daughter one moment to a gracious hostess the next.

"Would you like beef, chicken, seafood, or risotto?"

"It's hard to choose. Everything smells and looks so lovely, I could eat it all," she replied.

He examined the thinness of her wrists and imagined that if he removed her blouse he could count her ribs from ten feet away. "How about I put everything on the table? There's more than enough for you to sample to your heart's content."

"Only if you join me."

"Gabriella," he grinned wickedly, "you'll never have to invite *me* to share a meal."

Darius placed the last dish on the table and stepped back to stand behind Gabriella's chair. As she brushed by him to take her seat in the slatback armchair, he caught the scent of her perfume. Darius took a step back as blood rushed to his groin. "How about I put on some music?"

"Sounds good."

"Any requests?" he tossed back over his shoulder.

"I think I'll leave that in your capable hands."

Darius grinned at the teasing tone in her voice. It took him less than three minutes to select a familiar CD from the wide selection and place it in the disc carousel. He lowered the volume and strolled back to the dining room.

The softness of her eyes and relaxed position of her shoulders confirmed that he'd made an excellent choice.

"Who, or better yet, what is this?" Gabriella forewent the urge to close her eyes and lose herself in the strong, enigmatic beats and poignant strings.

"It's a CD compilation series called *Café del Mar*. I first heard about it when one of my teammates picked it up in London. It's very relaxing and helps me wind down after a mission. You like it?"

"Can't you tell?" she laughed. "If it weren't for my growling stomach and table manners, I'd be standing in front of the stereo scanning through the songs and reading over the album notes to find out the name of the composer."

"Patience is a virtue," Darius commented as he picked up the cotton napkin and placed it in his lap.

"That you seem to have a lot of."

"I try." He gestured toward the table with its flowers and candles. "You've made the table beautiful."

"Thank you."

"Do you do this kind of thing often?"

She took a sip of water. "Are you asking if I've ever been a waitress?"

"Not exactly."

She smiled. "Actually, I worked as a waitress at an Italian bistro in Geneva, but I learned from my mother first and then from summer etiquette classes."

"How schools have changed since I made it out the door." Darius took a spoonful of minestrone soup.

"I went to boarding school in Switzerland. Many of the students are from various old families and new wealth."

"How are you adjusting to the time change?"

"Not as well as I expected." She tucked a stray strand of hair behind her ear. "I've been moving around a lot so I thought it'd be easier."

Under the light of the metal chandelier, with her head tilted to the side and her eyes downcast, Gabriella appeared much younger than the age he knew her to be.

"How long have you been moving around?" he asked even though he knew the answer. Darius reached out to place a piece of garlic bread on a small side plate. Too skinny by far, she needed to eat more, and he'd see to it that she finished her meal.

"Long enough to appreciate the prospect of sleeping in the same bed for more than one night," she stated ruefully.

He chuckled. "I know exactly how you feel."

Comprehension dawned and her eyes widened. "You must do this often then."

Darius put down his glass and waved a hand toward Gabriella. "Have dinner with a beautiful woman?" He paused. "Unfortunately, I don't."

He stared, fascinated by the sight of the blush brought about by his compliment.

"I meant you must protect people often."

"As I mentioned this morning, only on special occasions."

"Do you like it?" Her voice was low and intense.

Placing his silverware on the table, Darius forgot the beef stroganoff and narrowed his gaze at the woman across from him, willing her to look up. His gut said something important would be disclosed and he wanted to make certain he was well aware of all of it.

"That depends on two things: who I'm protecting and what I'm protecting them from. Why do you ask?"

"I never had dinner with Markus." Her fingers toyed with her fork.

"Who's Markus?"

"He was my bodyguard." She caught his look of surprise, then dropped her gaze back to the table.

"Bodyguard?" His voice rose with unfeigned skepticism. "I find that a little hard to swallow given you've had such a hard time accepting me."

This time she held his gaze. Her eyes, sparkling with anger, were hypnotic, and for Darius, the need to keep looking into them was akin to breathing.

"Like now. I had very little choice in the matter since I can't leave this apartment without you following me. I didn't run from Vasilei just to lock myself in the same situation."

"The man you were going to marry had you followed?" He made note of the extra information while watching her fingers tense on the fork. Her lips parted to reply but nothing came out. She shook her head, then seemed to remember herself and went back to toying with the food on her plate.

"For my *protection*," she explained. "Vasilei is from a very wealthy family. My being unescorted worried him."

"If that was the case, then how did you manage to get away?"

Gabriella looked away from his piercing eyes. "I lied," she said softly and left out the fact that she'd also stolen a car. Guilt clutched her heart. She'd lied to get away from Markus and she was sure that lie, along with the others she'd been forced to tell while on the run, would damn her soul.

"What made you lie? Why did you run away?"

"I don't want to talk about this. Can we just eat?"

"Avoiding the past won't make the problem go away," he countered.

"As far as I can see, there isn't a problem. Vasilei will forget about me, you'll go back to the military, and we can both chalk this up as a bad memory."

"Is that how you will think of our time? As a bad memory?"

Her gaze softened along with her tone. "No, I misspoke." She reached out, touched the back of his hand, then pulled back. The contact, no matter how brief, carried up her fingertips and sent heat coursing through her limbs. His hands must be so warm, she thought, and hot on the trail of the observation came the fantasy of those hands on her skin.

"Darius," Gabriella took a deep breath and arranged her face into a hopeful expression. "We have this delicious meal, good music, and a fresh bottle of vintage wine. Why don't we start over?"

"I can do that." He gestured toward the as yet untouched serving plate of linguini with shrimp and scallops. "I thought you liked Italian."

"I do."

"You're not eating."

"I'm savoring," she retorted after taking another bite. While she appreciated the meal, something else occurred to her. It was the simple feeling that she liked his company and his voice. She wondered if he were even aware of the rhythmic lilt and deepness of his tone. Gabriella swallowed and placed her fork down on the plate as Darius interrupted her musings.

"So that means you'll want to savor another dish, of course?"

"Maybe in a little while." Gabriella reached for her wine glass. Only after she'd indulged in a sip of the red wine did she notice that hers was the only wine glass on the table. "You don't drink alcohol?"

He finished taking a drink of water. "That's correct."

"Because of religion?"

"That's one reason. My father is Egyptian and my mother African-American, but that's not why I don't indulge. I simply don't like the taste."

"I understand. I never touched alcohol of any sort until Paris. The French have a penchant for wine. It flows like water and it's impossible to decline your host."

"*When in Rome, do as the Romans do.* Or so they say. If all countries heeded that advice, Egypt would still rule the Middle East."

"Are you from there?"

"I was born in Cairo."

Gabriella paused from taking a bite of chicken. She had suspected he had Turkish or Arabic in his background. She'd met many sons of wealthy oil families. Yet, she'd abandoned the notion of his being born in the Middle East because of the smoothness of his voice and the perfect American accent. Now she peered closer at Darius, taking in the yellow brown tone of his skin and his jet-black hair.

She shifted her legs underneath her and then leaned forward. "I couldn't tell from your accent."

"My parents work for the United Nations and have a tendency to move around a lot. They allowed me to choose to remain in Egypt or to join my uncle's family in America. I chose the latter."

"How could you leave Egypt? I've heard it's a wonderful place."

"It was once a beautiful city." Darius grimaced. "But that was thousands of years ago. Now, it's the poster child for

Westernization gone badly. Smog, pollution, decaying infra-
structure, traffic congestion, and overpopulation."

Gabriella's eyes widened and her lips twitched before
laughter spilled out of her mouth. "You make the city sound
like it's the worst place on earth, but I've heard so many great
things about it."

Darius sat forward and looked into her curious gold eyes.
Al-Qahiri, the Triumphant, in Arabic. To many people, Cairo
was the Mother of the World. Darius only remembered the
beauty of summers spent at the family's home in Alexandria.
Yet, he didn't want to spoil her impression. "Don't get me
wrong. I love the country, but I'm not blind to its faults.
There's a magic to living in the shadow of the Pyramids; the
wonder of having the Kings and Queens of Ancient Egypt
looking over your shoulder. My older sister never tired of visits to the Sphinx."

"It sounds lovely," Gabriella commented, not just entranced
by the thought of the city's historical wonders, but also by his
casual reference to his sister. There was no way she couldn't
see that Darius Yassoud loved his family. His tone hummed
with the softness of memories and connections. Although
pretending to concentrate on her meal, Gabriella stared at him
from underneath her thick lashes. His eyes crinkling into a
smile and that strong mouth curving upward in a grin set her
pulse racing.

"And you? The City of Lights didn't agree with you as a
child?"

"Paris," she sighed, and then shook her head to pull her
thoughts together. "I was a woman before I walked through the
Latin Quarter and bought a baguette to eat while sitting alongside the Seine. No, I spent my childhood here in New York."

"But, you have a beautiful French accent."

"I have a European accent," she corrected. "My friends at
the academy and later at the university were an eclectic mixture of Italian, French, German, and Swiss and their accents
rubbed off on me."

"Do you speak French?"

Unmindful of table manners, she leaned forward, placing her elbows on the table and resting her hands together. She could speak French, German, and a little Dutch. Wanting to show off, she told him just that but not in English. She chose the language of diplomacy and spoke French. "*Mais oui. Je peux parler Francaise, Allamand, et un peux de Néerlandais.*"

The corners of Darius's generous mouth lifted and he instantly replied in the same tongue. "*Tu peux parles Anglais tres bien aussi.*"

Her lips curved upward. "Thank you for the flattering remark, but since I was born in New York, I should be able to speak English well."

"So where did you study in France?"

"The Sorbonne."

Darius's brows rose as one. "That's a very well known French university. What was your major?"

"Music and literature. Mostly music. And you?"

"West Point."

"I'm sorry," she shook her head slightly, "but I'm not familiar with many American universities."

"It's a military academy where you begin to learn how to be a good officer."

"Are you still an officer?"

"I've gotten a few promotions since then."

"Do your parents approve of your profession?" Gabriella questioned after finishing off her second glass of wine. She crossed her legs and laid her hands open on the table, while thick lashes hooded her eyes.

"My father had his reservations, but my mother . . ." Darius smiled thinking of the way she'd scolded Siad Yassoud. The tall, broad-shouldered director of United Nations Relief Agencies and wielder of untold power had cringed before a woman half his weight and stature. "She had figured out at a young age that life is what you decide it is. She walked away from her upper middle-class African-American parents to save the world. While a member of the Peace Corps, my father fell in love with her and decided he had to keep her alive so that she could help others."

"Your mother sounds like a phenomenal woman. I'd love to meet her."

Darius chuckled silently at the prospect, imagining how his mother would gracefully maneuver Gabriella away for a private chat. "She and my father come back to New York at least twice a year for U.N. conferences. Maybe then?"

"No," she shook her head slowly. "I don't think I'll be in New York much longer."

"Where will you go?"

Gabriella shrugged a shoulder then placed her napkin on the table. "I don't know. I've lived without a schedule for the past three months. No place to be, no worries of being late. I'll live as the explorers who mapped this wonderful country did."

"You'd live your life as a modern Lewis and Clark?" Darius asked, referring to the famous explorers who first ventured into the Midwestern American wilderness.

"Exactly," she smiled. "I'll travel until I get tired; then I'll rest and travel some more."

"Travel or run?" he queried softly, even though he knew the truth in the way she flinched and averted her eyes. In the military, one was trained in the ways of war second to the ways of man. Besides, being able to speak four languages fluently, Darius continued to be a very apt student in the reading of body language. He could see the slight flush of the alcohol in her cheeks, the relaxed posture in her chair. But no matter the friendly rapport, which was seemingly growing between them, she continued to be wary of him.

"Travel," she replied after a moment had passed.

He sipped his sparkling water, looked into her eyes, and allowed her to change the topic. In all his adult life, he couldn't recall a time when he'd had a more pleasant dinner with such good company.

Who is Gabriella Josette Marie? He would ask himself that question over a hundred times.

He had accessed her university scores, academic and professional references. He'd skimmed online reviews of the orchestra's performances and her list of concert appearances, as well as looking at her credit card statements and copy of her original passport. But none of the information reached beneath Gabriella Marie's exotic looks, the sensual mouth, the graceful carriage, and unspoken passion.

On the stage of knowledge, she took center. He found her well-informed on world events, very liberal, always gracious, and intriguing. Like a child, she snuck sips of wine, and as she absentmindedly spoke, he placed small portions of food on her plate. Over coffee and dessert, she challenged him to a duel of words in philosophy, debating the effects of capitalism and the free market economy on unindustrialized nations.

After the plates were cleared and the leftovers stored in containers in the refrigerator, she'd helped him put the dishes in the dishwasher. That night, long after he'd completed his ritual of checking the TV monitors, the doors, and windows, Darius sat on the side of his bed and placed his sidearm on the nightstand. He thought of Gabriella and three words echoed in his head: protector, protect her. He would keep her safe from Vasilei Lexer, the perfect man on paper who remained an anathema to the woman in his care.

Chapter
Five

Gabriella stepped out of the shower and wrapped a towel around her hair before putting on a thick bathrobe. She had awoken filled with more energy than she'd had in weeks. But thoughts of going for a brisk morning jog were brushed aside as she pulled back the curtains and looked out the window to see the weather had taken a turn for the worse. The sound of light snowflakes hitting the window made her shiver while she watched the dreary sight of the slow-moving cars on the street below.

She had hoped to get out today, for she disliked being in such close proximity with Darius, a man who reminded her of all the feelings and emotions she'd labored to banish. Gabriella frowned as she pulled on a pair of slacks and an off-white cashmere sweater. Padding across the soft bedroom rug, she took the pillows off her bed. The routine of making a bed took on new meaning since she'd not done it in a long time. While her hands began to methodically pull back the sheets, her mind was on other things, more specifically on another person.

No man had touched her intimately before Vasilei and she'd thought no man ever would. Yet, no matter how much she wanted to deny the shadow of Darius in her mind, Gabriella couldn't ignore her body's traitorous response, like

the way her pulse sped when he was close, the way her skin
tingled, or the way tendrils of longing ran down her spine.

The only other time she'd felt such emotions was when she
played the flute. Gabriella paused as she tucked in the cotton
sheet. It had been in the shower that the urge to play had returned. The haunting sound of the flute called to her. She'd
enjoyed playing in small cafés to the smell of coffee and mint,
soft candlelight, and appreciative audiences. Yet, she'd had to
give it up after figuring out Vasilei's private investigators had
used her appearances to track her.

She finished making the bed and walked across the floor
to the bathroom. Unwrapping the towel from her hair, her fingers combed through the tangles, then let her thick tresses fall
to her shoulders to dry. Gabriella shook her head as she
placed the comb down on the marble sink. In retrospect, she
should have seen the signs of her ex-fiancé's ruthlessness;
should have paid attention to the convenient opening for a
solo flutist with the Orchestra Academy in Berlin. The same
city played host to the global headquarters of Lexer GmBH
Corporation.

Gabriella looked away from the mirror. From the first moment he'd held her in his arms, Vasilei had done everything in
his power to keep her. Even the nights her fingers moved
deftly over the keys and her flute commanded sleep to subdue
Vasilei's nightmares, had only served to bind her closer. No
one had needed her until him.

Undaunted by the prospect of reopening closed wounds,
she padded over to the bedroom closet and opened the door.
Inside on a wooden shelf lay her duffle bag. She pulled the
bag from the shelf, carried it into the other room, and carefully placed it on the bed before peeling back the zipper.
Slowly, she lifted out an old leather case the length of her
forearm.

Her fingers paused on the worn metal locks before flipping them back and opening the lid. The flute inside
gleamed silver in the light. There sat the only gift from Se-

bastian she'd ever kept. Nestled within the velvet burgundy lining, it shown in the incandescent lighting. Within seconds, she assembled the flute and moved to sit cross-legged in the center of the bed.

A soft smile curved her lips. Madame Elizabeth would scold her for having such bad posture. Gabriella had once played solo during a royal festival and the thrill of it had taken her breath away as the sound of her playing filled the music chamber. Not even winning the First Prize for a concerto performance could match the fact she'd brought tears to the eyes of the audience.

When she'd played at the Concertgebouw in Amsterdam, the image of her mother had danced and smiled lovingly as Gabriella stood next to her father's piano. She remembered the way the afternoon sunlight had filled what had once been a green room in the townhouse until her mother converted it into a sunroom when her father had purchased the piano.

Sebastian had loved the piano and she loved it through him. Some of her happiest memories centered on a gossamer black Steinway piano. Her eyes drifted closed to hold back the gathering wetness. God in Heaven, she silently prayed. How she missed her mother.

As anguish threatened to pull her down into the covers of the bed for a long hard cry, Gabriella picked up the instrument. Listening to the haunting memory of music as it echoed in her inner ear, she closed her eyes, lifted the silver flute to her lips, and blew.

Darius let the computer monitor default to the screen saver, rubbed his eyes, then pushed back from the desk and looked out the window to the street below. After exhausting all the military sources available to him as both a member of the Special Forces and a highly trained computer specialist, he'd called in a favor. He had a gut feeling that Vasilei Lexer was dirty, and the red flag on an Intelligence file had only deepened his suspicions. After making arrangements for a temporary replacement, he planned to go to Washington D.C. to gather more information.

He made it a practice to be cautious and good at his profession. He was as good at defense as he was at offense. The thought of why he was on defense brought him to the hallway and had his eyes focused speculatively down the corridor leading to the bedrooms.

An image of Gabriella's smile flashed into his mind. She was a curious mixture of fire and ice rolled into one. Darius clenched his teeth and swore under his breath. Less than seventy-two hours on the job and his objectivity was already shot. He'd protected ambassadors, presidents, dignitaries, and prime ministers; and the one constant in his line of work was that he must keep the relationship completely businesslike and at arm's length. If an operative became emotionally involved with a principal, he started making compromises that could eventually harm the very person he was supposed to protect. Never before had he wanted to be friends with the person he'd been protecting. Yet, what he wanted from the woman in his keeping was far less the simplicity of friendship and more the tangled knots that came as a consequence of an intense sexual relationship.

I'll do my job and then leave, Darius vowed. But in the meantime, he had some digging to do and if 'X' marked the spot, then he'd start his search with the woman down the hallway. Upon hearing the sound of music, however, all the questions he wanted to ask slipped from his mind like sand through open fingers.

Trying the door and finding it locked, he knocked; but apparently, she couldn't hear above the music. Darius pulled his keys out of his pocket and unlocked the door. The sight of her sitting in the middle of the bed stopped him cold. This wasn't the ladylike Gabriella Marie with whom he'd dined last night or the girl who'd jogged as though running with demons at her heels.

Hair as dark as raven wings curled about her shoulders, as her upturned face gave him an unobstructed view of the loveliest sight he'd seen in years. Her lush lips were pursed, and as she blew into the flute held suspended in her hands, the delicate skin over her cheeks tightened, leaving her face even more perfect.

His gaze drifted lower to her arched neck and paused to watch the slowly beating pulse in her throat before following the silver chain until it disappeared underneath her sweater. Her oval fingernails moved fluidly over the keys. The rise and fall of her chest and the remembered softness of the touch of her fingertips shuddered through him. In that moment, everything that was Gabriella seeped into his body, mesmerizing him.

Darius fixed his eyes on her face, willing her to open her lids even as the music stopped and a tear crept down her cheek.

"I met a lady in the meads,

Full beautiful, a fairy's child,

Her hair was long, her foot was light,

And her eyes were wild.

I set her on my pacing steed,

And nothing else saw all day long;

For sideways would she lean, and sing

A fairy's song . . . " Darius's voice trailed off, but the words still lingered in the silence.

Gabriella opened her eyes, let out a startled gasp, and almost lost her grip on the flute.

"John Keats," she murmured, feeling heat rise to her cheeks in response to the darkness of his eyes and the words of the poem she'd memorized at the Swiss Academy.

"La Belle Dame Sans Merci," Darius continued.

Nervously brushing her hands over her trousers, she busied herself with taking apart the flute. Afterward, she proceeded to clean and put it back into the case. "So you're a warrior, a poet, and a spy, huh?"

Darius shrugged. "I knocked on the door, but I guess you didn't hear me."

"Why am I not surprised that you have a key to my bedroom?" she tossed over her shoulder.

Darius grinned and held up the key chain. "The perks of being a bodyguard."

Gabriella took a step away from the bed and stretched, suddenly aware of how sore her arms were. The pain felt good. It reminded her of the first weeks of her training in Paris and the hours of grueling practice that had taken her from good to great. Although she loved playing, there could be no denying that a part of her wanted to show her father just how much she didn't need him to succeed. Her goal was to become a world famous concert flutist and that required a mastery that only came with intense studies alongside the world's elite. "How long were you standing there?"

"Not long enough." He watched her brows rise in surprise and barely managed to check the urge to grab her and pull her toward him. His indrawn breath brought the welcome scent of vanilla and sandalwood.

During his time in Saudi Arabia, Darius had spent time traveling through the region. Once on a stop in Medina, an oasis in the eastern slopes, they had camped beside the natives. Sometimes at night as the winds blew through the valley, the whirls would blend with the drumming of the Bedouin tribes. He'd thought it was the most perfect sound in the world, until today.

To say the sound of her playing was haunting would not have done justice to the music. Yet, the sight of Gabriella's smooth relaxed face as she swayed was reminiscent of the bedtime stories of *houri* his grandmother had told him as a boy. The dark-eyed and stunningly lovely spirits could steal a man's wits.

Darius took a step back, deliberately distancing himself from Gabriella. "What were you playing?"

"It was nothing," she shrugged. "Bits and pieces of different compositions I've studied in the past. I needed some practice."

He might have believed it if he hadn't seen the tear trail down her cheek or the lingering sadness in her eyes. And that image made him want to protect her—more than anything else in his life. The mix of vulnerability and innocence called to that part of him, the intrinsic part of him, that was the bridge between Darius the man and Darius the soldier.

"I'm no expert, but you're good," he stated casually.

"Thank you." She flashed a humble smile and looked away. Gabriella took two steps toward the hallway and stopped. "Would you like some tea?"

"Please."

They walked together to the kitchen. He'd grown up in a semi-traditional Egyptian home. His aunt and cousins ruled the kitchen, while the men in the family paid proper homage to their cooking. Even before he'd come to America, his own father had lectured him sternly about the importance of respect and courtesy. It was a lesson he'd taken to heart.

With all his dealings with women, he'd never failed to act with honesty and responsibility. Yet, the code of honor he adhered to was warring with him at that moment because he was drawn to Gabriella, a woman he didn't know—a woman whose relationship with two powerful men didn't need to be complicated further by a third.

Minutes later, after Gabriella had boiled the water and prepared the tea, he sat opposite her on the couch. "How long have you played the flute?" he inquired after taking a sip of Earl Grey.

"Since I was five years old."

"You're very dedicated."

"Of course." She peered at him over the rim of her cup. "They took music rather seriously at the academy and I played with the university orchestra, which is quite prestigious."

"Is that where you met Vasilei Lexer?" he inquired, letting

his curiosity get the better of him. "I read somewhere that he's a great patron of the arts."

Gabriella carefully placed her teacup and saucer on the table before returning her hands to her lap. "No, we met one weekend at a French country estate."

Darius watched as the reserve he'd encountered when they first met returned. The cool look of the lady could cut like a knife. "It would be difficult to play professionally without attracting his attention."

She raised an eyebrow before inclining her head. "You're right. I can't play publicly without attracting his notice, so I guess it's good that I've decided to do something different."

"You would give up something you enjoy so much?"

"How do you know I enjoy it?" She shrugged a single shoulder. "Maybe I hate it."

"And maybe elephants can really flap their ears and take to the skies." He shook his head as the corners of his mouth pulled back into a slow grin. "It's in your eyes, little one. They glow when you think of music. Are you so proud that you'd rather spend your life hiding than face a man who wronged you?"

"I'm going to travel, remember?" she replied lightly instead of giving into the temptation to defend herself. Music had once been her master, her passion, her career. Now it would be her private solace.

"Why do you fear him? Did he hurt you?" Darius's eyes narrowed into dark slits and focused on her face. For the third time since she'd met him, Gabriella called up every shred of training to keep from giving into the temptation to look away.

She shook her head. "Not in the way you imagine."

"Then tell me what happened." He leaned in closer. "What did Vasilei Lexer do or say to make you leave?"

Gabriella drew a shaky breath as the memory of that night, of the sound of the desperate whimpers, tried to tear through her wall of denial. She stood her ground and fought the urge to rise from the sofa and retreat to her bedroom. "I don't want to talk about it."

"Really don't like to talk about him, do you?"

"Most people don't like to talk about their exes, Darius," she replied, carefully modulating her voice to sound as flippant as she could. "I'm not so unusual in that aspect. Would you discuss your ex-wife or girlfriend with a stranger?"

The sight of his lips crinkling upward into a smile wiped away her thoughts of Vasilei and sent her blood racing.

"No, I wouldn't, but then again I don't have an ex-anything. And Gabriella?"

"Yes?" She replied reflexively, looking at his obsidian eyes and finding herself caught as he held her gaze, unable to look away, powerless to move from his presence even to save herself. When he moved forward and touched the back of her hand lightly with his fingertips, heat spread from the contact, and her breath came sharply through slightly parted lips.

"We've never been—nor will we ever be—strangers to one another."

The next time Darius knocked loudly on Gabriella's door. So she was bored, he mused. Well, he'd just have to give her something to do. After having to refuse her request to join the karate sessions taught in the building's fitness room and only allowing her to leave the apartment to go jogging in the park, even he had to admit the forced inactivity made him caged. But more than that, he was tired of catching mere glimpses of her during the day and wanted more than polite dinner conversation.

"What?"

Not bothering to hide the grin on his face, Darius took in Gabriella's disheveled state before looking over her shoulder to the unmade bed. "Have a nice nap?"

"Until you woke me, yes. Is this a social call or just general harassment?" Her gold eyes narrowed as she plopped back on the bed.

"Put this on." He dropped the white martial arts uniform in her open hands. The ease with which he'd purchased the garment reminded him of the convenience of New York City. Anything could be bought, anything delivered, for a price. A man long used to the basics of human comfort, the ease of his adjustment into the way of life amongst those of the wealthy made him keenly aware of the barrenness of his own military existence in the Detroit apartment he saw once or twice a year.

"The tai chi class ended hours ago, Darius."

He shrugged and on impulse reached out and pulled a lock of her hair gently. The gesture brought a smile to both their lips. "Today is your lucky day."

"You?" Gabriella's eyebrows rose upward.

"None better," he confidently replied.

"Were you an instructor as well as a bodyguard in the military?" she questioned.

"I was called on to do some training." He halfway chuckled at the understatement. If training equated to making a bunch of newly inducted Green Berets drop their pants, give up a day's worth of rations, and leave them tied to trees in the sweltering heat of the Louisiana panhandle, then yes. If that exercise could have been defined as an example of teaching, then he'd done an excellent job.

Looking back, Darius realized he hadn't had the time for formal training. The downside of being uniquely trained, in addition to having possession of knowledge and language of a region high on the U.S. Special Forces potential terrorist list, had kept their team in heavy demand. He'd spent over ninety percent of the past five years either deployed to an operation in the Middle East or on a transport plane to a new assignment.

"Did you give them a hard time?"

"They deserved it." Mistakes like theirs would have gotten

them killed if it had been a real covert operation instead of a training Joint Task Force exercise.

She picked up the clothing and stood up. "You really want to do this?"

He shrugged. "You might as well learn something about self-defense while we wait for Sebastian to return."

Her eyes flared, and he wondered if it was because of his verbal jab or the mention of her father's name. "I'm sure you're eager to be gone."

"Be ready in ten minutes." He didn't ask, didn't explain. Darius anticipated she'd be dressed and ready. Like recognized like, and Gabriella Marie was a fighter. He would just have to remind her of that fact.

Slipping off her sneakers, Gabriella glanced around the floor of the fitness room. Shined to perfection, the light wood gleamed under the fluorescent lighting. She leaned back and rested her body weight on the heels of her feet as the coolness of the floor underneath her socks crept up her skin.

"Want to give me a hand over here?"

Gabriella turned and caught sight of Darius in the long mirror that ran across the front of the windowless room. Busy dragging one of the half dozen stacked mats toward the center of the room, she was grateful he hadn't noticed her lingering glance at his form. The white *Gi* he wore left little to the imagination when it fell on his broad shoulders and narrowed over what she knew to be a firm stomach.

"Thank you for thinking of my safety," Gabriella said softly while helping Darius move another mat into position. She kept her eyes lowered so that he wouldn't glimpse the mischievous gleam she wouldn't be able to hide.

"Not a problem. Every woman needs to know how to protect herself."

For over an hour Gabriella followed Darius's instructions, shouts, and orders. She kept her nerve as he touched her arms, pushed her shoulders, and held her close. She gained new and intimate knowledge of how rock hard his thighs were, and the warmth of his breath on her bare shoulder sent chills down her body.

Yet, he didn't instruct through technique or have her memorize skills. No, he taught her what to do and not to do; how not to become a victim of panic.

Fight dirty and hit hard. Gabriella remembered Darius's instructions as she took a drink from her water bottle.

"Whenever you're ready, we can put those lessons into practice."

Gabriella screwed on the bottle cap. "Are you sure you shouldn't be wearing padding of some kind? I'd hate to hurt you."

"I'm not delicate, Princess. And I don't plan to pull any punches with you, so worry more about yourself than me."

Gabriella's chin went up at his reproachful answer. "Your goal has been for me to learn how to survive an attack, right?"

"Bull's eye, and that means no holding back."

She narrowed her eyes and took her place in the center of the mat, then tossed over her shoulder, "Don't worry. I won't."

"Remember, the key is not to pull away."

"Why?" she asked, already knowing the answer. She wanted to catch him off guard and to do that she would act exactly as he expected: inexperienced.

He shook his head and adjusted his hold. "Because it's what your attacker expects."

Gabriella nodded, then allowed a smile to curl her lips upward. "And I'm not to do as expected, right? The goal is to catch my attacker off guard and get away."

"Exactly. This isn't the time to play hero. Just scream and run like hell."

She chuckled and met his eyes. "I think I'll leave the hero business to the professionals—like you."

"Coming from you, I'll take that as high praise." The sight of his wide grin wiped away thoughts of self-defense and set her pulse to quicken. The last thing she'd expected when she'd dressed in the martial uniform and followed Darius downstairs to the aerobic room was to fall prey to attraction.

"Maybe I'm just trying to butter you up so you'll go easy on me," she quipped.

"Not a chance. We're not done yet and I don't intend to play around. Now let's get back to work. Remember you should stab the heel of your foot into my ankle and simultaneously jab me in the ribs with your elbow."

Sobering quickly at the reprimand, Gabriella flexed her fingers and rolled her shoulders. *He wanted to do real life?* She returned to the mat, deliberately turned her back toward Darius, and stood still. She didn't have to wait long. The only indication of his movement was the whisper of his feet against the rubber mat. She waited for the slight wind against her neck signaling his charge, then bent her body and slipped out of the way. He came for her with arms open to grab her and instead he met with air as her leg swung and connected solidly with his ankles. In one single move, she sent him into a headlong rush toward the opposite wall.

Gabriella backed away, marveling at the speed of his recovery.

"Nice move," he commented as he adjusted the belt of his *Gi.* "But that's not what I taught you."

"Beginner's luck." She flexed her wrists. "You did say I should do the unexpected. Shall we have a go at it again?"

This time she did as he expected, only better. Seconds after Darius locked his arms over her stomach, she slammed her heel into his foot, then raised the other to strike his shin after her elbow connected with his stomach. When his arms loosened, she broke free and sprinted a short distance away.

"That was a very good combination of movements."

"Thank you." She took a deep breath as her heart thudded in her chest. The hum of approval in his voice didn't match the perplexed look that marred his handsome face.

"But when the time comes for you to defend yourself, you

won't hesitate with fear, Gabriella. And you'll have to react with the proper amount of force."

"How do you know I wasn't?" She put a hand on her hip and leaned to the side.

"I know," he stated matter-of-factly before turning. "Now let's do this one last time."

Gabriella averted her eyes, but instead of focusing on the aerobic equipment in the corner of the room, they rested on the mirror image of Darius's muscled back. Her eyes lingered on the wide slope of his shoulders before moving to admire his firm backside. She thought of the feel of his arms, the heat of his chest, his scent. The temptation of attraction had momentarily taken over her common sense.

"Again?" She returned to her position on the exercise mat.

"This time don't hesitate," Darius ordered as he began to circle her slowly.

Gabriella turned with him, her eyes following every movement, watching and waiting while he looked for an opening but couldn't find it. This time he moved less like an opponent and more like a predator stalking his prey.

"Very good." He nodded his approval. "Always keep your eyes on your attacker." Darius narrowed his gaze and shifted slightly. If Gabriella hadn't been focused, she would have missed the sign. Still, she wasn't fully prepared for the swiftness of his advance.

Darius moved with the speed and agility of a cat. In comparison, she stumbled backward with feigned fear, and as his hand locked on her arms, she grabbed hold of his shoulders and let herself fall, adding enough momentum to his attack to propel him forward and catapult him over her head as her feet pushed him away. Gabriella rolled and was back on her feet in a defensive posture in seconds.

In anticipation of his fall, Darius lifted his hands over his head and, instead of hitting the mat, used his palms as a springboard and somersaulted to his feet. When he turned around it was to see Gabriella crouched in a defensive stance.

"Where the hell did you learn how to do that?"

"I started martial training in secondary school," she answered, silently amused by the shocked expressed on his face. The discipline of martial arts had appealed to her. If anything, it allowed her to be alone because she wasn't a team player. Only when she played flute did she enjoy being with others.

Darius's eyes narrowed as his hands remained out by his side. "What belt are you?"

"Black." Gabriella watched as he stood from his crouch. Only a healthy sense of self-preservation kept the corners of her lips at a one hundred and eighty degree angle instead of inching upward. This man didn't like surprises and being mocked wouldn't make him feel any better.

"What else?"

She blinked slowly before answering. "Girls are more than sugar and spice."

His brows almost touched. "So nuns are teaching martial arts now?"

"There were no nuns at my academy; only world class instructors in every subject. My music instructor felt it best if we pursued other disciplined activities in addition to our practice." She met his stare with confidence and swallowed.

There were certain things a woman noticed about a man. The way his shoulders curved, how his hands moved when he spoke, the style of his dress, the length of his hair. But these details, which had not escaped her attention, were made small by the way he *moved*. Gabriella watched, fascinated by the play of his muscles. Darius moved with an efficient grace of strength tempered by a harmony of perfect coordination. He stopped so close to her she could smell the salty tang of his sweat on her tongue.

"Was there some reason you didn't tell me?" In the stillness of the room, his voice cut through the silence.

"You never asked." Her chin lifted in automatic challenge. "You *assumed*."

As Gabriella reached past him to pick up her towel from

the side bench, Darius moved again. He said nothing but pushed her back against the wall, locking her into place with his arms. Her head came up and before she could voice her protest, his lips came down hard on hers, bruising her with his mouth. She had nowhere to run, no place to hide from her body's response. He took without asking, and she offered him entrance, not because there was *no choice*, but it was *her choice* and she could deny him nothing, deny herself nothing. She placed her hands on the V of his uniform and settled on the smooth hardness of his chest where she could feel the rapid beating of his heart.

Her body melted into his and their lips softened, even as his hands slid up her shoulders and his fingers found their new home at the nape of her neck, entangling in the soft curls of her hair. His tongue traced the outside of her lips, before entering to explore deep into her mouth. Gabriella closed her eyes to savor the taste of desire as her breasts began to swell against the wall of his chest. A shudder ran the length of her body as she kissed him back.

A surge of anticipation broke over her as his hands went from holding on to her shoulders to caressing the curve of her throat. She swallowed back a low moan when one of his fingers trailed down the V of her uniform. Skillful fingers stroked the firm rise of her breast, and the pad of his thumb ran rough over the sensitive nipple. Unlike the statue in Shakespeare's *Winters Tale*, desire not forgiveness brought her back to life, but the ache of remembrance hit her full in the chest. She'd only ever been with one man.

Dimly, Gabriella heard a low moan and realized it was from her throat and crept into her passion-slowed brain. The sound, coupled with her harsh breathing, broke through the haze clouding her mind. His tongue stroked her lip a last time as he slowly drew away, making her tremble, and heating the blood already throbbing in her veins. Gabriella's lashes rose and her gaze locked and stared into dark eyes glittering like chunks of black ice.

They stood in one another's arms, so close she had but to tilt her face to kiss him again. The sweetness of his breath warmed her cheek and a sense of recklessness flickered through her awareness while a delicious ache started at the apex of her thighs. If she hooked her leg around his, they would both go down hard and fast.

"Never drop your guard, little one," he whispered against her mouth, and moved away to continue folding the mats. For several moments, Gabriella remained immobile along the wall, afraid her knees might give out. Gathering her calm, she drew a ragged breath to bring air into her starving lungs. Her lips continued to tingle warmly from his kiss and she brought her hands to her cheeks hoping to cool them. Vasilei had taught her passion was dangerously addictive and something to be feared. Passion made sane people go to extreme lengths; it brought them a hairsbreadth away from obsession. A shiver snaked down her spine. Darius's words had been a warning. She only hoped they'd not come too late.

Chapter
Six

The next morning after breakfast, Darius pretended not to notice Gabriella's expectant look. He had yet to answer the question she'd asked as they'd run around the reservoir at sunrise. Giving her a sidelong glance, he kept silent as he rinsed the dishes, the glasses, the silverware, and then placed everything into the dishwasher.

"I need to go out," she announced.

Several moments passed before Darius repsonded. "Where?"

"To a rather large shopping establishment," she answered evasively.

Darius moved away from the sink and stopped a foot away from her, suppressing a shudder. Of all the things he'd been thinking she'd ask, that wouldn't have been on the list. Hell, he'd rather take apart his gun piece by piece and clean it with spit and a Q-tip than follow her around some high-end boutique. Still recuperating from a bullet wound, he'd had to work security detail for the President's wife while she was on a jewelry-shopping spree during a diplomatic visit to Bahrain. The half-day ordeal was worse than taking a bullet in the shoulder.

"You mean your *father* forgot something, or did you not include it on your list?" he asked, sarcasm lacing his tone. He still hadn't forgiven himself for kissing her yesterday. Only the thought of the kiss brought it all back, the feel of her tongue, and the softness of her fingertips on his skin. His stare dropped to her lips, then flicked upward to her eyes in time to catch a hint of remembrance in her gaze before her eyes cooled.

"If I'm not mistaken, *Sebastian* assigned you as my bodyguard, not my keeper." She shrugged. "If you don't want to come, then I'll go alone."

His lips compressed into a thin line. Darius placed his hand on the swinging door, then paused to look back in time to see Gabriella push her hair behind her shoulders. "Be ready in thirty minutes and try to come up with some measure of a disguise."

Less than an hour later, Darius looked down at the number on the paper and then back at the parking space. Sure enough they matched. He pressed the button on the remote control and was rewarded with a series of chirps from the Land Rover. It was only after inhaling the new car scent that Darius allowed a smile of satisfaction to creep onto his face.

Sebastian had done, or maybe overdone, exactly what he'd asked. He knew that if he ran the license plate, it would list the owner of the vehicle as an old woman in Buffalo. A fictitious woman. If he was going to be in a situation where he needed to do any surveillance, he preferred to be in a high suspension vehicle. The Land Rover didn't come close to the military vehicles he was used to, but it would give him the durability and the sight lines he needed to do his job.

He turned to Gabriella as she stood next to the tailgate and could have cursed all over again. It seemed she'd obeyed his instructions a little too well. With a black bucket hat and her hair braided, baggy sweatpants peeking out under a long fur-trimmed red coat, she looked like some rich college kid given a shopping spree at a thrift store or a celebrity hiding from the media.

"Let me guess." Darius walked over to the passenger side and opened the door. "You're auditioning for a music video?"

She narrowed her gaze, then moved past him. Ignoring his hand, Gabriella climbed into the SUV. Darius grinned as he shut the door and went around to the driver's side. This would be quick and quiet. No problem at all.

"God has forsaken me," Darius muttered under his breath as he followed Gabriella down another street filled with busy commuters streaming toward Penn Station. Keeping one eye on his impatient companion, the other on the shifting crowds, he kept well aware of his surroundings. The fleeting warmth of the winter sun had disappeared behind the tall buildings, leaving a lengthening trail of mauve and coral shadows across a clear sky.

As the traffic signal changed, he took the lead in crossing the street, making a path for her to follow through the on-coming tide of people. Gabriella's brief shopping expedition had turned one second into an hour, and a short wait into an eternity.

Once while gathering intelligence, he'd had to stay buried in a desert dugout for weeks at a time. But this was true torture. It was the fifth store in two hours and by far the largest. She hadn't even taken time for a proper lunch. At the reminder, his stomach rebelled against the greasy pizza he'd watched her consume with apparent relish.

"Macy's." He said the name of the store like a curse. In Egypt, men were exonerated from the chore of going to the market. Even after moving to Detroit, he and Bashr had been left at home because his female cousins couldn't stand their constant complaints.

As soon as he cleared the wooden circular door, Darius's chest tightened. It wasn't the shock of the temperature change. No, it was the loud music, the crowd of shoppers, and the hazard of sales people, jewelry counters, and cosmetics. The overpowering scent of perfume hit him in the face.

"Isn't this great?" Her childlike voice brought him back to the moment.

Darius followed behind a rapidly moving Gabriella, scanning the area as they went, noting high ceilings and a half-balconied second floor. Looking away to send a fierce stare to a rapidly approaching woman wielding multiple perfume bottles, he replied, "No, it's not."

Securing the red wool scarf she'd purchased from a street vendor near Penn Station around her neck, Gabriella turned a dazzling smile on him. "I didn't mean this part."

Undaunted by Darius's scowl, she linked her arm with his muscular one and led him toward the escalators. Nothing, not even her escort's cantankerous mood, was going to get her down. Gabriella loved the look and feel of Macy's with its endless racks of clothes and shoes, jewelry and linens, after holiday sales, and end of season rushes of bargain hunting shoppers. It had been her mother's favorite department store. They would come early on Saturday morning and afterward have lunch at a small bistro down the street.

After they transferred to another upward bound escalator, Gabriella broke the silence. "It has nine floors but we're only going to the third." She paused and scrutinized him from the collar of his black leather jacket, to the grey turtleneck sweater, to the cuffs of his black trousers. He wore no extra adornment except for a digital watch. "That is, unless you've decided to brighten up your wardrobe?"

"I like what I have just fine." He shrugged off her barb, then commented, "You seem to know this place very well."

Darius had noticed that the woman by his side walked straight down the rack-laden aisle as though she'd designed the place. He was trained to survey, trained to fight, and thus he kept a close eye on her. Yet, he found that he wanted to watch her, when she was aware of him and when she was not.

He shook his head and deliberately looked to the right and left of the floor. He knew the location of every exit and tracked the movements of sales personnel and mothers with baby strollers. He was careful to keep Gabriella to the left side of his body, so that his right would always be free to go for the gun nestled securely in the curve of his back.

He tried to concentrate on his job and do something, anything, to keep his mind off one woman—Gabriella Marie—who seemed to have taken over his thoughts the way the scent of her perfume tempted him to forget his duty.

Heaven knew, he wanted her. Not with the sweetness of a passion alluded to in many of the American fairytales. It would be more of the old stories of the Bedouins, desert tribesmen who stole brides from their parents' tents. He wanted her in all the ways and manners a man and a woman could love. This would not be casual sex necessitated partially by the reality of his life in the Special Forces, but something intimate and binding. There would not be just one time between them.

Again, she gave him a wide smile and he was aware that the sparkle in her eyes lit her face with an angelic glow. "I should be pretty familiar with this place since I spent many Saturdays riding up and down these escalators."

Darius's ears perked up on the word *days*. He couldn't imagine a more nonproductive use of time. They had been in and out of four stores; he'd waited beside three dressing rooms for the meager contents within the bag in Gabriella's hand. A hat and gloves. Damned if he could stomach any more of this. Darius moved to stand in front of Gabriella. "What exactly are you looking for here?"

She tilted her head and then stared past him. Darius turned to follow her gaze and froze. Faced with the bounty of more clothing in a magnitude of colors, sizes, shapes, and fabrics, his pulse quickened, triggering the fight-or-flee instinct that had in times past saved his life.

Darius shook his head. Devil take this shopping business. "No."

"Don't worry, I know what I want. We won't be here long."

When she moved to walk away, his hand snaked out and grabbed her hand firmly. "Enough."

The laughter drained out of her eyes as she tried to pull away from his grip. She looked down at his hand and by the time they returned to his face the golden glow had turned to a chilly glitter as her face reddened. "Remove your hand."

Instead he pulled her closer. "This is the second time that you've ordered me to let you go, Gabriella. Do you remember what I said the first time?"

She averted her gaze from his, then sighed. "If I say please with candy sprinkles on top, will you let me go?"

"Not until you promise me that we'll depart this house of horrors soon."

"Horrors?" she repeated. "It's a department store."

"No." Darius waved his hand. "It's a maze designed to trick unsuspecting men into waiting hours for their women to return."

Gabriella relaxed and placed her fingers on his shoulder. "You poor man." The laconic sharpness of her tongue could have drawn blood from the thickest armor. "I hadn't thought this would be so much of a strain on you."

Laughter rumbled in Darius's chest as he glanced down at the mock sympathy in her eyes. The woman was getting to him in the worst way. When he should have been dragging her out of the store, all he could think about was the bow of her lips, tasting the sweetness of her mouth, swallowing her sighs, and touching her skin.

"Thirty minutes," Gabriella promised with a smile.

"Ten."

"Twenty-five and I'll buy you dinner." Her eyebrows wiggled.

"Bribery?"

She shrugged before readjusting her grip on the bag in her hand. "Whatever works."

Darius worked hard to keep the corner of his mouth from inching upward. "Twenty minutes and we're out of here."

Thirty minutes and the purchase of three pairs of blue jeans later, Darius pressed a button on the car remote. Opening the passenger-side door, he took the shopping bags from Gabriella's hands before helping her into the Land Rover. Seconds later, after putting the bags away in the cargo space, he climbed into the driver's side and keyed the ignition. As soon as the engine started, he touched a few buttons and the temperature in the car warmed to a comfortable level.

"Do you like Moroccan food?"

Startled, Gabriella turned to look at Darius as he quickly pulled away from the curb and merged with the heavy traffic.

"I don't know. That's one international cuisine I haven't tasted."

"Would you like to try it?"

"Yes, I would. I take it that you know of a good place?"

Darius smiled in the darkness of the car. "Of course."

Gabriella leaned back in the leather seat. Looking out the windshield, she watched New York City roll slowly by. The town cars and yellow cabs whizzed by, speeding toward unknown destinations. She couldn't remember a time when she'd felt so relaxed and safe. For a few hours, she'd temporarily set aside her worries of Vasilei and anger at her father. She knew her problems wouldn't go away by ignoring them, yet she gave in to the temptation to push them to the back of her mind and enjoy the evening.

Turning her head, she studied Darius in the semi-light confines of the car, noting his profile and the confident way his hands gripped the leather-encased steering wheel. She had the feeling that there was little that could upset the man. Gabriella's curiosity about her bodyguard rose. Who was the man Sebastian had charged with her protection?

Darius glanced at the quiet woman at his side. "Sleepy?"

She shook her head. "Not at all. Shopping gives me energy."

Darius raised an eyebrow before bringing the car to a halt in front of a stoplight. "I hope it's also given you an appetite."

"That too," she laughed. "And yourself?"

"Always ready for a meal. Especially after skipping lunch."

Gabriella's smile disappeared and she nibbled the inside of her bottom lip as guilt played on her conscience at the reminder that Darius hadn't eaten lunch. "I'm sorry. I really didn't mean for this to last so long. I forget myself sometimes."

Darius didn't respond. Instead, he parallel parked the SUV and escorted Gabriella through the double doors of an exquisitely decorated restaurant. After being outside under Manhattan's bright streetlights, Gabriella's eyes took a moment to adjust to the semi-lit lighting of the entry.

Passing through the heavy wooden doors and into the ornate entranceway, Gabriella's steps faltered. Darius might have been properly dressed for such a formal restaurant, but judging by the patrons, she wasn't.

"I'll take your coat."

She aimed a sidelong glance at her bodyguard and seeing no amusement in his expression, turned to put her back to him. Remembering again what she wore underneath, her fingers hesitated in unbuttoning her coat.

"Thank you," Gabriella murmured. She turned politely as Darius assisted in taking off her coat. As his fingers touched her shoulders, she inhaled the scent of his cologne mingled with the heavy smell of bread.

Gabriella kept her chin up and her bearing proud. She'd learned from some of her classmates who had graduated and gone into runway modeling that it wasn't all about what you wore, but how you wore it. As she crossed the carpeted restaurant with Darius's hand on the small of her back, she caught the glances of a few female patrons who followed their progress. Several mistook her for a model and made note of her clothes so they could search for them tomorrow, while others kept an eye on the dangerously handsome man by her side.

As they were shown to an area in the back of the main dining room, her eyes took in the elaborate mosaics across the walls and ceiling, and ornate carpets and cushions draped across chairs and loungers. Rich-looking tapestries covered the windows. The place vibrated with color, from the intricately painted ceiling to the complex patterns on the sofas and pillows.

The waiter led them past other diners to a secluded low-sitting white linen-draped table, and Gabriella took her seat on a lowered divan. Before she could recover from the sensory overload, another waiter bearing a metal bowl and an etched metal ewer approached the table.

"Give him your hands."

Gabriella blinked a few times, then raised her gaze from the menu. "What?"

"Raise your hands over the basin," Darius ordered.

She held out her hands and the server winked before pouring warm water over her hands and then enveloping them in a soft hand towel.

She sat back and watched as the man repeated the ritual with her dinner companion. Picking up her menu, Gabriella pretended interest in its exotic selections. She'd already made up her mind to have Darius order dinner for both of them.

After a few minutes spent perusing the menu, Gabriella placed it on the table and leaned back on the divan. Her musically trained ears caught hold of the spiraling melodies of the mandolin, the tam-tam, and the sitar. She fought the urge to close her eyes and shut out everything except the subharmonics of the traditional Moroccan instruments.

"Ready to order?"

Gabriella shook her head to clear her thoughts and smiled. "If I could, I'd embarrass myself by ordering everything on the menu and then only eat a quarter of it."

"Like you did that first morning?" A slow smile crept over his face.

"Exactly. Would you mind ordering for both of us?"

"It'll be my pleasure."

After Darius placed their order he said, "Your father called while you were in the dressing room."

She regarded him in silence before reaching out to toy with the napkin. "What did he want?"

"He might be delayed. It seems your brother was involved in a skiing accident."

The expression on her face had not changed. He might have been reading the weather report. "It isn't serious." He paused and then added after scrutinizing her face, "You're not worried?"

She shrugged a shoulder. "I've never met my half-brother."

"How do you feel about that?"

"I don't feel anything. I accept it," she replied in a cold voice.

"Do you?"

Through the prism of the flickering candlelight she'd seen the warmth in the way his dark eyes looked at her. Her eyes settled on him in perplexed curiosity. She studied his face for a moment as though they had discovered something new and unfamiliar, then looked toward her empty plate.

Gathering her scattered thoughts, Gabriella reached out and picked up the pewter goblet filled with water. "How about we talk about happier things?"

"Such as?"

A smile tugged at her lips. "End of season sales? Maybe we could negotiate my next shopping expedition."

She caught a flicker pass over his expression and her smile turned into a wide grin. At that exact moment, in the absence of all his smooth confidence, she liked him. *Darius Yassoud, the fearless warrior*, she mused smugly. *Not by a long shot.*

They spent a few minutes discussing food, travel, and soccer until the first of several communally served courses arrived. They started with tomato-lentil soup and fresh buttered bread. Next came *bastilla*, a luscious chicken-nut-egg pie wrapped in *phyllo* and dusted with powdered sugar. The main entrée—chicken cooked whole and drenched in lemon and green olives, chickpeas and onions—followed. There was also couscous and salad.

After finishing the last bite of the decadent meal, Gabriella lifted her napkin and patted her mouth before sitting back from the table to relax into the softness of the seating. Just when she thought she would burst, dessert came. Gabriella groaned at the sight and picked up her glass of mint tea. "I can't eat anymore."

"But you must try this." Darius picked up a fork. "*Basbousa* is an Egyptian specialty and there is none better than what you have in front of you."

"And there's no room in my stomach as it is."

"Maybe if you stretch out."

Without warning, he took her legs and placed them in his lap. Gabriella barely managed to keep from tipping over. "Okay . . . okay. I'll try it," she laughed.

"Good. I used to fight for the last slice when my aunt made it."

"Darius?"

"Yes?"

She peeked out from under her eyelashes. "Maybe I can manage a bite."

"Just make sure that afterward you don't go getting any ideas that you can have mine." He raised an eyebrow and his eyes sparkled. Yet what really made her heart warm was the sight of the whipped cream on the corner of his mouth. She watched in fascination as he licked it off.

Unclenching her fingers, Gabriella picked up her fork and cut into the diamond shape. She lifted her hand to catch sugar syrup dripping from the fork onto the plate. The moment it hit her tongue she closed her eyes. The moist, fluffy, sweet, and buttery dessert tasted of a baker's care and heaven.

"And the verdict is?" His voice purred with smugness.

Her smile only increased. "You're right."

He started to reach across the table. "I'll finish that up for you."

"I don't think so." Gabriella playfully threatened to jab the back of his hand with her fork.

"A man's got to try."

"Try waving down the waiter and ordering yourself another dessert," she retorted.

Those deep-set dark eyes twinkled with amusement, and for a moment Gabriella went still as her gaze strayed over his jaw and settled on his firm lips. Once she'd seen him as a nuisance, and now she couldn't look at him without remembering the musky scent of his cologne, the heat of his fingers upon her skin, and the way his tongue danced with hers.

"Ahh," he laughed. "My father warned me about women who like their sweets."

"Really?" She leaned forward and rested her chin in the palm of her hands and deepened her smile. "And what exactly did he say?"

"That they can become a habit."

"Which? The dessert or the woman?"

The intensity of his gaze answered her question better than any spoken word. With great delicacy, Darius raised his fork and brought the last bite of *basbousa* to her lips. His eyes never strayed from hers as Gabriella opened her mouth slowly. Needing no further invitation, he slipped the fork between her lips and pulled away.

As they waited for the check, her eyelids grew heavy and the furniture seemed to invite her to recline yet further.

After returning to the apartment later that night, it seemed that neither of them wanted the evening to end. So standing in the corner of the living room window with the lights turned low and leaning back against Darius, Gabriella watched the twinkling lights of the East Side skyscrapers through the steadily falling snow.

She rested her ear against Darius's chest, and as he spoke, they traveled together to far distant countries and she saw old cultures through the eyes of a boy. In turn, she re-opened the doors of the Upper West Side townhouse and waded back into the warm crystal clear waters of her mother's home island. Time flowed and they continued to talk as the clock in the hallway chimed, the noise of the streets receded, and the city of Manhattan settled into a restless sleep.

Chapter
Seven

Gabriella sat back and threw her pencil on the desk. Only a week had passed since her arrival in New York and she'd already caught a case of cabin fever. On her left sat two newspapers. Next to them a phone book. She didn't want a job; she *needed* it—anything to keep her mind off the present situation. Just as she picked up the paper and flipped to the next page in the 'Help Wanted' section, there came a knock on her open door.

"What?" She swung her head around to see Darius leaning against the opposite wall looking quite sexy in a black sweat suit. A snide voice in her mind wondered if the man owned any piece of clothing that wasn't black.

She watched as his eyes momentarily left her face and trailed downward to her bare legs. "Overslept?" he smirked.

"I'm not going jogging today," she stated and looked back toward her desk. Gabriella didn't hear him enter the room; she felt him. The man moved like a ghost, she thought.

"Are you feeling under the weather?"

"I'm fine." She began to clear up the mess of papers on her desk.

"What's this?"

She shook her head, startled by the swiftness of his advance across the room. Darius reached past her to pick up the copy of the *New York Times*.

"The classified ads," she replied, pointing out the obvious.

"Help Wanted section," he commented. She could hear the amusement in his voice. "Looking for cleaning help?"

"No," she responded coolly. "That's what I've got you for." She watched as he raised a thick eyebrow. "Touché."

"I'm looking for a job."

"Oh, doing what?"

"I've always liked animals and I need to be able to support myself outside of the performance realm. I'll work for a veterinarian or at an animal shelter."

He shook his head. "Not happening."

"Look Darius, I need to earn money. And I won't live off of Sebastian. To be honest, I'd rather be on my way to independence before he returns."

"The answer is still no, Princess."

Gabriella threw a section of the newspaper in the waste bin. "Why not?"

"Can't compromise your safety."

"My safety," she emphasized. "How could it be compromised by working in an animal shelter?"

"The more places you're seen, the more forms you fill out, the greater the risk someone might be able to locate you."

Her eyes narrowed into slits as she struggled to keep Darius from seeing how much his hard tone upset her. For a moment her eyes drifted downward as Anton's image floated to the forefront of her mind. He had used a similar tone the morning after the murders. The coldness of his voice had confirmed the promise of murder in his eyes.

Running her fingers roughly through her hair, she pulled away from the memory and looked Darius in the eyes. "I will not be locked in a cage. Not for Vasilei and especially not for Sebastian."

"This isn't fun and games, Gabriella. Van Ryne is intent on keeping you safe."

"And apparently in danger of debilitating boredom." She gritted her teeth. Deciding to try a different course of diplomacy, Gabriella moved closer to the window. "Am I wrong to assume that as long as I use my new identity, there's a limited chance of Vasilei finding me?"

"If you're bored, why don't you just adopt a dog or a cat?" he suggested.

Gabriella's laughter caught him off-guard, but what surprised him even more was his response. He enjoyed the sound and the reaction it produced.

When her laughter faded, Darius watched as she reached out and touched the windowpane. "Even if he managed to track me to America, it would take months or years for him to know I was here in Manhattan. By then I'll be long gone."

"Van Ryne—" Darius started.

"You and I both know that Sebastian's fully occupied at his family's home," she smoothly interrupted. "Jensen needs Daddy as well as a legion of doctors."

"How about I get you some board games?"

Gabriella barely stopped herself from letting out a scream of frustration. Instead of giving in to the desire to throw a tantrum, she closed her eyes, counted to three, and then re-opened them. "You're supposed to be my *protector*, not a jail warden."

"Looks like what you need is a housekeeper," he commented, stepping away from her untidy desk.

"Hey . . ." Gabriella warned while picking up the clothes she'd dropped on the floor.

"Have you eaten breakfast?"

Gabriella's brow wrinkled. "I had a banana."

Darius scanned her rail-thin body and then turned around.

"What?" she asked trailing behind him.

"A banana is a snack, not a breakfast," he stated while scanning the contents of the refrigerator.

Gabriella crossed her arms and leaned back against the kitchen countertop. "Are you always this critical, or am I just lucky enough to be on the receiving end of your controlling nature?"

"Neither," he replied.

She watched as Darius proceeded to take out eggs, milk, and butter from the fridge.

"I don't make good omelets," she pointed out, remembering the breakfast at the diner.

She watched as his lips curled upward in a smile. "I wasn't going to ask you to."

She leaned her head to the side. "You're cooking breakfast?"

"That was my intention. Surprised?"

"That you know how to cook? Yes."

"A man without a wife must learn to feed himself or starve," he quoted.

She gave him the once-over. The man with his physically fit body didn't look like he'd missed many meals. "I'm not the best cook," she replied honestly. Actually, she couldn't bake, and the prospect of preparing a full meal consisting of ingredients other than pasta and sauce intimidated her.

"What? Something your elite education didn't teach?"

Gabriella slid a playful glance his way. "It was assumed that none of us would ever need to see the inside of a kitchen. We were trained to be leaders, diplomats, musicians, financial wizards, and politicians—not cooks."

"I see."

"Good." She smiled and then moved toward the sink to wash her hands. "Can I help?"

"Yeah. Help me find the cinnamon, vanilla, and some sugar."

"What?"

"We're going to make French toast," he said with a grin.

"I haven't met many men who cook," she commented offhandedly while moving to search through the kitchen cabinets.

"Something tells me that you haven't met too many men. A lot of us are self-sufficient."

Gabriella paused before rooting through the cupboard in

search of cinnamon. "You're the first I've met so far. I just hope you're not the last."

Damn she's beautiful, Darius mused. Foregoing his intention of getting fresh fruit from the refrigerator, he leaned against it. He watched while Gabriella stood up on her tiptoes to peer into the spice cabinet. Intelligent, musically gifted, warm, generous, and couldn't boil an egg or make couscous. She was all those things and more, yet he couldn't help but pay most of his attention to the lovely place where her thighs met the curve of her nicely proportioned rear.

He wanted her. Only her. And he had to keep his hands and his thoughts off her.

Shaking his head, he turned around and pulled some items out of the fridge. After washing them, he placed the honeydew and kiwi fruit on the countertop, then pulled out a cutting board and knife. Expertly handling the blade, he flipped a smile in Gabriella's direction. "Might want to take notes, Princess. Someday you may want to serve your husband breakfast in bed."

"I don't think so. The institution of marriage doesn't seem to be very popular in my family and who would want to marry—"

"Don't say it," Darius interjected as he sliced completely through the creamy green rind. "The circumstances involved with your birth have nothing to do with you."

"But the circumstances surrounding my engagement do. Why are we arguing, Darius? Why are we even talking about weddings? I don't want to marry."

"You might fall in love one day and change your mind," he prompted as he quartered and removed the seeds from the melon.

"So might you."

"No, I'm a soldier. We go away for months at a time; my branch has one of the highest divorce rates in the military."

"I'm sure there's a woman out there who would be willing to share you with your work."

"Think so?"

"Of course."

"Why don't you get the batter started by cracking a couple of eggs for me?"

She did as he asked and Darius noted every move she made, from simply cracking the eggs to using the wire whisk to whip all the ingredients together.

Later, after she'd placed the batter-dipped bread into the square griddle, Darius gave voice to the question that nagged him. "Would you?"

"Would I what?"

He looked up from the golden brown toast. "Consider marrying a soldier?"

She stilled and turned her body toward Darius. His question knocked her off balance. The idea of marriage period held little appeal after the debacle with Vasilei. Yet marriage to him? Tying her life to a soldier? Living with a man who would leave her alone just as her father left her mother? No, she couldn't do it. The wondering and waiting would kill her.

"Would you repeat your childhood on your own children?" Gabriella countered. "I'm sure you had a wonderful time growing up with your aunt and uncle, but wouldn't you have liked to have had more time with your parents?"

"Yeah, I would have. But that doesn't answer the question I asked you."

She sprinkled more cinnamon into the batter. "Honestly, no. I hated it when my father went away. My mother said to me, 'Your father is an important man; we can't have him all the time.' But I still hated his long absences, especially since my mother usually threw herself into long shifts at the hospital. She didn't need money, but she didn't want to spend her time pining for Sebastian."

Gabriella dipped a thick slice of French bread in the batter, allowed the excess to drip off, and then placed it alongside the others on the griddle. "One of the reasons I allowed myself to love Vasilei was that no matter what, he made time for me. In the hidden part of my heart, I dreamed of a house with a garden and stone walls colored green with ivy, and a husband who came home at six o'clock." She looked up at him and the resignation in her voice was profound. "More the fool was I."

Darius waited, but she said nothing more.

Neither did he. Each word from Gabriella's lips had pierced his flesh like a red hot bullet. Irrational anger shot through him, the same anger that responded to situations beyond his control. He couldn't deny what she said. The truth was that the family life wasn't meant for some soldiers. And he wasn't so sure it was for him. Pulling out two plates, he arranged the French toast and carried them into the dining room. The domesticity of the moment wasn't lost to him.

When the day came that he met the woman who would carry his heart, Sergeant Darius Yassoud, the man with most of the answers, would face a dilemma he wouldn't know how to solve.

After cleaning out the lint filter, Gabriella placed four quarters in the coin-operated Maytag dryer. She turned to stand at the opposite side of the folding table and pulled a still warm pair of jeans from the laundry cart. Looking over, she noticed how Darius smoothed out the wrinkles and folded the shirt with the precision of origami. "You're something of a Renaissance man aren't you?"

He looked up and she noticed that even under the laundry room's harsh fluorescent lights, his skin still carried a warm bronze tone.

"What makes you say that?"

"You fight wars, cook gourmet meals, and read philosophy. Plus," she pointed toward his stack of clothing, "you're good at this sort of thing."

"I was trained well."

Gabriella nodded. "Your mother must be proud."

"I'm sure she is, but I didn't learn to do laundry from my mother."

"Your aunt taught you?"

"No," he laughed. "The military taught me. The way of my uncle's household was such that I didn't have to help with these sorts of chores."

She eyed him curiously and repeated, "The way of the household?"

"My aunt and cousins took care of such things."

Her body shook with laughter at the wistful expression on Darius's face. "I imagine doing your own laundry came as a shock."

"That would be an understatement."

She followed Darius's gaze to the small pile of multicolored lingerie. His lips tilted up into a smile while a thick black eyebrow rose. Gabriella resisted the urge to grab the zebra striped bikini panties. There was no doubt in her mind that he was familiar with women's undergarments.

"I'm sure you appreciated your aunt's taking care of the household duties," she hinted, trying to turn the conversation back.

"Uh-huh." He blinked twice. "Yeah. I had three cousins in Detroit. Two girls and a boy. Nadia's the oldest and she's married and owns a Middle Eastern restaurant in Philadelphia. Kalila has a set of twins, a newborn and a husband who dotes on her every whim. And last but not least, Bashr, the youngest cousin, is the one who would have been here had I not volunteered to come in his place."

"Why couldn't he come?"

"My aunt has found him a wife and I'm sure his fiancée would object to him staying in such close proximity to an unmarried woman."

"But it's okay for you?"

He shrugged. "I'm the second son of open-minded parents, so life isn't so strict for me."

Gabriella smiled wistfully. "It must have been wonderful growing up with your cousins."

"Not really," he shrugged. "It was something short of a nightmare. Nadia and Kalila used to dress me up in their *habib* and parade me in front of everyone at family parties."

"*Habib*?" Gabriella repeated the foreign word.

"They're the long gowns and head coverings Moslem women wear in public. My cousins no longer wear them, but one Halloween they blackmailed Bashr and me into wearing them and going around a rich neighborhood to trick-or-treat."

"Oh." She put her hand over her mouth.

"Go ahead. Laugh." Darius glanced up from folding a shirt. The sound of her hastily silenced laughter warmed his heart. Everything Gabriella did in some way made him happy. Even the powder fresh scent of his clothes amused him after she insisted on pouring a liberal amount of fabric softener into his washing machine.

"I bet your aunt thought you were adorable."

"She was so ashamed, she didn't leave the house for a week. When my parents came to visit and my uncle showed them pictures, my mother laughed so hard she cried."

"Your family sounds so close-knit."

"My father and uncle are twins. Put them together in a room and only the difference in skin tone gives them away. The bonds of blood and family are close, although we live oceans apart. It wasn't the same for you, was it?"

"No," Gabriella mused, averting her eyes to watch as her clothes spun round and round in the dryer. "I lived two hours away from my father for five years and I only saw him four times. Each time he brought me an expensive gift, met my teachers, and took me to dinner. Then he disappeared again."

"That had to have been difficult."

She shrugged. "That's life. How about we talk about something more interesting?"

"Such as?"

Gabriella tossed a pair of socks into the laundry basket.

"You know all about my personal life. I think it's fair if I know something about yours."

"All right, ask. I'll tell you everything."

"That was easy." Her eyes narrowed. "Tell me about your girlfriend."

"Can't."

She pointed a finger at his chest. "See, you lied."

"I can't tell you about someone who doesn't exist. I'm a soldier, Princess, and that means I'm on a mission for most of my life."

"What about your future wife?" Something tightened in her chest. For some unknown reason, his response to her question mattered.

"I'm sure my aunt will find a suitable wife for me when the time comes in say . . . fifteen years."

"Fifteen years? You'll be old."

"And she'll be just out of college. Perfect, don't you think?"

"Perfectly hideous. You're not a man, you're a lecher." She threw his shirt at him and it hit him square in the face.

"Being a well traveled young woman, I wouldn't have thought you could be so culturally insensitive." The teasing smile on his face warmed her better than the Caribbean sun.

"What?"

"Under Islam, older men with younger wives are common."

"So now you're claiming your father's roots? I hope your family picks a woman who gives you gray hair and screeches you into deafness," she tossed over her shoulder while grabbing her still hot clothes from the dryer.

Darius dropped his boxer shorts down on the counter and grabbed Gabriella from behind, grasping her delicate wrists within one of his hands. "Easy, little one. I wasn't serious."

"Why don't I believe you?"

He turned her around. "Because you happen to be jealous." Her eyes flashed up to meet his. "*As-tu perdu la tête?*"

"No, I haven't lost my mind or my senses." He held tight as she tried to pull away.

"I am not—" she vehemently protested.

"Excuse me, is there a problem here?"

Darius let go of Gabriella's hands and placed his arm around her waist before turning her around. They both turned their heads toward the uniformed apartment security guard.

"Nope, Henry. My fiancée and I just decided to have a little *quality time* while finishing up the laundry."

"Oh, it's you, Mr. Yassoud. Sorry, didn't recognize you from the back and all."

He maneuvered Gabriella so that she stood beside him but was practically glued to his hip. He smiled down at her with his mouth, but his eyes held a clear warning.

"Well, I'm happy to see she's making a good recovery."

"Recovery?" Gabriella echoed.

Darius smoothly jumped in. "She's not back to her old self yet, but the bed rest has helped. I've got to thank you for keeping an eye out."

"No problem. I wish my wife were like her. Man, come rain, hail, sleet, or influenza, nothing keeps her in the bed. Not that I can blame her with those kids of ours."

"Well, give Mary my regards."

"Will do. And you two enjoy finishing up that laundry."

Darius braced himself for a storm and took two steps back from Gabriella. The clouds in her eyes were matched by the tight line of her femininely thin arched brows.

"Why did that man think that we were engaged?"

"Because I told him," he stated. "Part of our cover story."

"And my *illness*?"

"Explains why you can't be let out of the building and why I'm staying here with you."

"Darius, what exactly is wrong with me?"

"Post-traumatic stress disorder."

"Wh— what?" Her voice rose in disbelief.

"Your car accident caused a temporary loss of cognitive

skills due to blunt trauma to the brain. The medication you're taking can make you forgetful and impairs your judgment. If you left the building, you'd never be able to find your way back, so I bribed the security staff to make sure that you don't leave without me."

"You . . ."

He watched her chest heave and the way she opened then closed her mouth without a word coming out. In laughter, she was beautiful. In anger, damned if the fire in her eyes didn't make her all the more stunning. And while he should have been coming up with thoughts to placate the woman, all he could think about was sex. Long hours. Hell, he wanted weeks of just the two of them in a bed. He'd gone for days without food and he could do it again in a heartbeat if she was with him to feed the hunger he was feeling at that moment.

Gabriella threw her hands up and turned her back to him. Darius couldn't help but grin as he suppressed a chuckle. Looking down at the pair of boxers in front of him, he allowed himself a moment of pride. For the first time since they'd met, he'd left Gabriella Marie speechless.

Chapter Eight

"Who are you?"

Gabriella raised her face and looked toward the open doorway from her seat on the Persian rug. Soon after helping Darius clean up the dinner dishes, she'd changed into her pajamas, then retreated to the study with her flute. "What do you mean?"

"When you have that flute in your hands, it seems that all the confidence in the world dances on your fingertips, but outside of this room I see the shadows of fear in your eyes."

She placed the instrument in her lap and gave in to the urge to stretch her back. "You're reading too much into this."

"Am I?" he queried softly while taking another step into the room. "Tell me, how do you feel when you're playing?"

"It's strange, but I feel as though I'm the center of the universe. That the sound I make and the movements of my fingertips command the earth to move and the sun to spin."

"Exactly." Darius's eyes lit up when he looked down at her with a wide grin that showed perfectly placed teeth and made her heart catch. She liked his lips. Averting her glance with a brief stopover at the apex of his legs, her eyes returned to his face. Gabriella toyed with her flute. While half of her wanted to bury her face in her hands and confess everything to Darius, she pushed back the urge. "Why is it that you seem to have made it your mission to analyze as well as protect me?"

"It's all part of the bodyguard tenets. Didn't somebody tell you?"

"No," she replied dryly.

"Well, now you know."

"Now that you've proven your point, would you like to take a seat and stop hovering over me? I feel as though I might get a crick in my neck staring up at you."

"I was wondering how I'd forge through this wall of papers you've surrounded yourself with." Darius kneeled down, cleared himself a path, and sat beside her. Leaning forward, he deftly reached down and picked up a yellowed page, but they weren't the elegant type printed symbols he'd seen all his life. No, these notes were handwritten and didn't sit perfectly on each line; many of the notes were written with different color inks.

"He kept all of it," Gabriella murmured absently.

With one hand he placed a finger under her cheek and turned her face to gaze upon his own. "What do you mean?"

"My father—Sebastian. He kept all of them. From my first scale, to my first composition."

She reached past his lap and picked up a bound set of music. "I fudged this solo recital because I had the flu, and when I blew, even my flute sounded sick."

Her fingers touched another page. "We wrote this one for my mother's birthday. All of her friends came to the party and she cried when Father and I played a duet."

"Tell me more," Darius asked, moving closer to Gabriella. It was an instinctual thing; he put his arm around her, drawing her to him. And she rested there as if she belonged, as if she had been in his arms all along. "I'm not well versed in the art of music."

"Because you're a master of the art of war?" she teased.

"No, because I don't have an ear for tone. My parents liked it when I sang on our more adventurous trips into the

African bush. You see, my singing would scare away the small scavengers."

"I'm sure you're not that bad."

"Don't bet on it." He grinned, then gestured toward the papers. "This is another language to me."

Gabriella picked up a sheet. "I read the notes and hear the music in my head. My music teacher always stressed to me that music is attuned to math, but I always thought it to be closer to reading. Only there are no words, just sound. Sometimes during the orchestra's off-season, I would go weeks without touching my flute. The music in my mind sounded far better than my own playing." She paused and pointed to a bound set of music. "I played this piece at the national competition. I was so frightened. Even the Secretary of the United Nations came to hear us play."

"You miss it, don't you?" He watched her intent expression as she looked over the papers, her white teeth gnawing on her bottom lip, and he felt a sense of unexpected lust spring to life. He couldn't ignore the longing in her voice, the way her fingers trembled.

She sighed. "I miss many things, Darius. My mother, my friends, the comfort of having my own possessions, the security of my own apartment. What's one more?"

"You would let your pride keep you from playing?" Darius questioned softly. In the past, his intuition had never failed him, but while holding this vulnerable woman in his arms, he hesitated. Now would have been the perfect opportunity to take advantage and gather information regarding her powerful fiancé. "Lexer may have broken your heart but not your dreams."

"You don't understand. It's complicated." She turned, using her hair as a shield.

But he would not allow for barriers. Instead he pivoted to sit in front of her. "Help me to understand. You have a beautiful gift that should be shared with the world."

He took her hands within his and gently kissed her fingers.

"Your lips bring music, your fingers can mimic a bird, but now they are both silent."

"Darius." The huskiness of her voice drew him in and was all the invitation he needed. Momentarily throwing off the yolk of duty from his shoulders, he leaned forward and whatever she was about to say would forever remain a mystery as one leaned in toward the other and their lips met. The sweetness of the kiss caught in his throat and he wanted more. Slanting his mouth, his tongue touched hers and his fingers, like a man on a cliff, found a well-sought ledge in the softness of her hair.

Gabriella's hand lay flat against his chest, at first resting and then gently pushing him away. Darius moved his lips hungrily over the slope of her jaw to feast on her neck. The room, with its books, Persian rugs, and heavily curtained windows, swallowed the harshness of their breathing, ate the delicateness of her sighs. When he finally pulled back, his breath came hard and fast.

"Goodnight," she whispered and quickly fled the room with her flute.

Darius watched her departing back from his throne on the floor. He had not been trained as a bodyguard; he'd been trained as a soldier. But there were basic rules and he had broken one. Never get emotionally involved. Yet, it was too late and had been too late for a long time.

That same night, Darius turned and drew his gun and aimed within the blink of an eye. Just as quickly, he lowered the Glock's barrel toward the kitchen floor. His eyes went from her raised hands and shocked expression to the digital readout on the microwave oven: 2:36 A.M.

"Damn it, Gabriella. What the hell are you doing up so late? I almost shot you."

"For being up past my bedtime or for catching you with your hand in the cookie bag?"

"Both. What were you doing sneaking up on me?"

"Getting warm milk to help me fall asleep." She walked over to the refrigerator door and opened it. He had to admire her coolness as he clicked the safety back on the gun and tucked it safely behind his back. His heart hadn't started up again yet from the realization that he'd almost shot her.

She pulled out the carton of milk and he leaned back against the kitchen countertop, the bag of Mrs. Fields cookies still clutched in his hand.

"Aren't you cold?" He frowned. As she moved, her robe fell open a little exposing a black chemise and matching pants. Whoever had purchased her sleeping attire should have been shot. The lightweight cotton top and pants wouldn't last half a second outside the steam heated apartment.

"No, it's a little warm in here."

Darius couldn't agree with her more. Especially after he caught glimpses of her bare belly button as she stretched. Her smell wafted close to his nose, and it seemed so natural. At two o'clock in the morning, with her hair spread in disarray over her shoulders and bare feet, she was beautiful.

The troubles of the day seemed to vanish when they were in the same room. Darius clenched his teeth as her golden eyes went from the bag to his face as she came alongside him and opened the cabinet door. "So the warrior has a weakness after all."

"Fondness," he interjected, easily reaching over her to grab a mug and then placed it in her hands.

"For White Macadamia Chocolate Chunk Cookies."

"It's genetic."

A mischievous smile lit her face. "I can't wait to hear the explanation for that one."

"My uncle and my father are twins. One of the things they have in common is an uncontrollable love of sweets."

She gave him a skeptical glance. "Really, Darius, there's no need to lie. Just share the cookies. Would you like a cup of milk?"

"Thanks." He reached in and grabbed another cup. Darius took a seat and placed his elbows on the table as he watched her pour the milk and place the mugs in the microwave. His eyes trailed downward and landed on her feet. Somehow, the woman even made furry slippers look sexy.

Tired of tossing and turning on the most comfortable bed he'd slept on in years, Darius had gotten up and dressed only to discover that he had the distinct choice of going into Gabriella's bedroom and watching her sleep or slipping out into the dead cold of night to the twenty-four hour corner store and picking up a bag of cookies. Slumping in the kitchen chair, he rubbed his eyes with resignation. It had been a foolish hope to think cookies could satisfy the craving he'd developed for the woman crowding both his waking and sleeping thoughts.

"Here's your milk. Now hand over a cookie." Gabriella sat down on the other side of the table. Darius pushed the bag to a spot smack dab in the middle of the table.

Her lips curled upward into a satisfied smile after taking a bite. "I thought all soldiers had a weakness for blondes, beer, and being heroes."

"I'm a man, not an actor, Princess. On real missions, everyone doesn't make it back; I've seen my fair share of happy reunions and grieving widows."

Her brows drew a straight line as her smile disappeared. "Why is it that you don't talk about your work? This is the first time you've referred to a mission."

"Combat isn't a polite topic."

"Who said you had to be polite?" She tilted her head to the side and pointed a half-eaten cookie in his general direction. The sight of her bobbing ponytail brushing against her skin made his fingers itch to free her hair. "I thought we'd gotten past that stage when you ruined my morning jog."

Darius thought about his past assignments—both the covert operations and the undercover infiltrations where he'd had to change identities and nationalities. His mind automatically scanned through the night incursions in Jordan, the field missions in Iraq, and search and rescue in Afghanistan. Very few of his deployments had gone by the standard procedure or been a simple matter of reconnaissance. "What I do and who I am when I do it, is classified. But my not speaking about my life in the military isn't because of any rules. It's to protect—"

Darius blinked in surprise as she cut him off. "I'm so sick of hearing that word. Everyone wants to protect me from something. Vasilei from his enemies, my father from Vasilei, and now you."

"You didn't let me finish. I was going to say myself."

Gabriella's skeptical glance spoke louder than words. Darius looked down at the steam as it rose from the hot milk. "I've done things I don't want to remember, Princess. And the only way to live a semblance of a civilian life is to push back the memories and lock them away."

"So it's that famous American phrase. *Don't ask, don't tell*."

He picked up his mug and took a drink. "In a nutshell. Think you can deal with it?"

She seemed to ponder his words a little longer. "Something tells me that you aren't just any soldier."

Darius finished a cookie and took stock of his situation. No doubt about it, he was in trouble. Not the knee deep and sinking in quicksand but with the hope of finding an escape kind of mess. But more of the trouble in which he sent out a call for help and ran like hell. He met her light brown eyes over the rim of his cup and swallowed hard as the thought of leaving crossed his mind. Instead, he swallowed the lukewarm milk and reached for another cookie.

Chapter
Nine

She was right, he mused. Darius put his hands behind his head and stared upward toward the twilight of dawn coming through the curtains. Outside, the city that never slept shook its mantle of darkness to shift into high gear as people poured into the streets from the subway tunnels of Manhattan.

He'd spent another night restless and aware—aware of the woman located less than twenty feet from his current location. The milk and cookies had done their work all too well; so well, in fact, that he'd carried her to bed after she'd fallen asleep on the couch while watching late night television shows. But he'd stared at Gabriella long after pulling the down comforter over her shoulders. Her face was beautiful in stillness, yet more so when her eyes were open and smiling at him.

He couldn't keep her inside all day. It wasn't just maddening, it was unbearable. With New York City right outside the window, there were plenty of distractions. Needing to cool the attraction that had begun the night he'd first seen her and intensified every moment they spent in close quarters, Darius showered and dressed in record time.

It hadn't taken too much convincing on his part to get Gabriella to go out. On a weekday in the center of the financial world, they would play. It was like sneaking out of school and playing hooky. After bundling up in their hats, coats, gloves, and scarves, they walked hand-in-hand down the street, joining the river of commuters and passing cars and buses stuck in traffic. The scent of diesel lingered with tantalizing smells of street vendors with coffee and sweets. The smell of the subway tunnels was released through metal grates.

Car horns, police sirens, squealing brakes, and the sound of a thousand footsteps and voices.

They had oversized freshly baked bagels and coffee. Darius ate two: one with butter and jelly and the other with warm cream cheese and smoked salmon. Not only because of an empty stomach but also hunger for that moment. The husky sound of her voice as she laughed at a street mime's performance, the sight of her smiles, and peacefulness of the day.

"May I please have this skate?"

Gabriella turned from smiling at Darius's difficulty lacing up his boots to the man standing over her. She'd seen the older skate instructor with his red scarf and snowman toboggan when they'd arrived at the ice skating rink in the middle of Rockefeller Center. The man looked harmless, but she sent a questioning glace toward Darius.

"Go ahead," he urged. "I'm going to be a while."

"Are you sure?"

"Have fun and I'll keep score."

She took the man's hand and they went out onto the ice. At that time of day the rink was practically deserted. Gabriella smiled as the ice skating instructor pulled her out onto the smooth ice.

She could fly on the ice and she did so while being careful not to plow into a small gathering of teenagers. Joy poured through her heart, but it was tempered by a certain person's absence. She wanted him with her. Her bodyguard. Her Darius. Turning to her partner, she smiled and then made her way toward the object of her thoughts. He stood perfectly still on the outside of the ice circle.

"You take to the ice like a fish to water," he observed.

Gabriella carefully stepped off the slick surface and, after catching her breath, responded, "The lake near the Academy froze over during the winter. We would go out on a Saturday with food. After cutting the ice for most of the day, we'd start a fire and roast marshmallows."

"Don't worry about me, I'll be out soon."

"You can't fool me, Darius." Gabriella's lips trembled with the beginnings of a smile. "This might not be your first time on ice, but you haven't skated in a while."

His midnight brows rose. "Two decades to be exact. I went a few times after coming to stay with my aunt and uncle. I never imagined ice in such large quantities. And to skate on it?" he chuckled. "Suicide."

"You'll be fine," Gabriella encouraged. Sliding her arm under his, she guided him onto the ice. Positioning herself on the inside, she made sure to stay close to the side of the rink to give Darius the safety of grabbing onto the wall should he feel uneasy. "Now push out a little more with your right leg— now left—get into the rhythm—good job."

"You make one heck of a good teacher, Princess," Darius commented. "Maybe when you retire from traveling, you can pitch your tent next to an ice rink and give private lessons."

"Thanks, I think," she replied wryly. Then, to keep his mind off the increase in speed, she asked, "Do you really like skating or did you do it to humor your family?"

"The novelty wore off as the cold settled into my bones. I'm a child of the desert, not the Alps."

She slowed them down as they came near a group of junior high school students. As many dropped onto the ice in a storm of laughter, Gabriella maneuvered around the kids. "I've always wanted to explore Egypt."

"Maybe one day I can take you. You would love my family, and my grandmother would adore you."

Gabriella's smile dimmed at the reality that their time together would be over soon. "We'll see. So, I imagine you fell a lot when you first went ice skating."

"I've probably still got bruises," he joked.

"Well, I think you've done a good job," she remarked as they completed their first complete circle of the ice rink.

"Don't get too confident."

She stopped them both and turned toward Darius. Gabriella met his eyes, and their darkness sparkled with diamonds.

"I won't let you fall," she promised.

At that moment, the sun came out from behind the clouds and the breeze fluttered through the courtyard, catching in the flags. For an instant, wetness spiked her eyelashes and rainbows appeared. But the tears didn't form in her eyes because of the sun's brilliance, but for the beauty of the moment. Under the watchful eyes of the statue of the Prometheus, her skin tingled while her pulse sped and the wonders of the world shown in his eyes. She felt the weight of his hands at her waist and unmindful of the presence of others, leaned into him.

"And I won't let you down." He smiled at her until she could have melted the ice.

When the much anticipated kiss came, her vision and the sweetness of his lips mingled with the scent of chestnuts and all the fairytales, all the stories about princes and kisses, came true.

Later, after skating until their legs ached with exercise and cold, they strolled up the avenue toward Eighty-Sixth Street with the wind at their backs and the sun hidden behind tall buildings. She tugged on his hand when she wanted to stop and gaze at window displays of the world's haute couture, and he would release an overdramatic sigh. However, they soon found themselves in complete agreement when they turned down a side street and Darius led her to the small doorway of a restaurant named *Bella*. Even before stepping through the narrow entrance, she caught the scent of warm bread, olive oil, garlic, and herbs.

Gabriella allowed herself a feminine sense of satisfaction as Darius unwound the scarf around her neck and took her coat. It was a show of affection and possession, but she did not mind. Slipping her leather gloves into her purse, she moved back to his side, as the host, a small man with a cute little mustache, little creases around his eyes, and laugh lines, greeted them personally and led them past crowded tables to seat them at a nice secluded table in the back corner of the restaurant.

She let her lips curve into a smile as Darius held out her seat. "Thank you."

While the waiter poured the water and presented the menus, Gabriella looked around the restaurant. The decor was warm and inviting. Dark wood shone and the lighting made for a cozy and comfortable atmosphere. She could hear the barest jingle of pots and pans from the kitchen as Pavarotti sang out from invisible speakers.

She ordered the lasagna rolls and Darius requested the spinach fettuccine with chicken and sun-dried tomatoes.

Darius sat back in his chair. "I have to take a small trip tomorrow."

Gabriella nearly smiled at the thought of being on her own for the day, yet Darius's next sentence dashed her hopes.

"One of my colleagues will fill in for me while I'm gone."

"How nice," she said half-heartedly, her voice automatically softening to match the voice level of those around them. "But completely unnecessary. I'm sure I can keep out of trouble for the day."

"I made a promise, Gabriella, and I mean fulfill it."

She paused from stirring her tea and looked up at him. "Who is she?"

"What?"

"A man has certain needs." Her eyes narrowed.

"This is business."

Gabriella fell silent for a moment, remembering the main topic of their 2:00 A.M. conversation over cookies and milk: "don't ask, don't tell." "I shall try to be on my best behavior."

"One more thing."

"There's more?" She deliberately leaned her head to the side and smiled seductively at him.

"I need to clear the air."

"Go ahead." The upturn of her mouth flattened in response to the serious expression on his oh-so handsome face.

"I want you."

"To do what?" she teased, trying to deflect his true meaning.

"No games, Gabriella. Just you, me, and the truth."

"All right." She took a sip of her ice water and licked her lips. "You're attracted to me."

"I'd say this is a mutual attraction, wouldn't you?"

She met his eyes and shivered as her body clenched in response to the melodious tenor of his voice. A light fluttering started in her stomach; a sensual quiver ran along her nerve endings and made her feel feminine. She had not reacted this strongly to any man's nearness, not even to Vasilei. "I won't deny that I have certain feelings for you, but what are you getting at, Darius?"

"The problem is that I can't."

"Can't what?"

He drew a hand roughly over his hair. "Have these feelings. When this is over, I have to walk away. And until that time comes, I have to be objective in order to do my job."

She leaned forward and turned her hands over as though laying her cards out on the table. "We could just ignore it."

"It won't work," he replied bluntly.

"Then tell me what will?"

"That's the problem, Princess. I don't know." Where earlier today, a faint dimple had come unhidden during his smiles, now, Darius's mouth was set in a pencil straight line with no betrayal of expression on his face.

For several moments, silence reigned and during that pause, Gabriella glanced at the families and couples enjoying an early dinner. More than ever, she craved the normalcy of their lives. Releasing a pent up sigh, she averted her eyes, then glanced upward to lock with Darius's ebony pupils. She followed the flicker of candlelight to survey hollows of his cheek and realized how romantic their surroundings were. The words left her mouth before her brain could stop them. "As you just said, Sebastian will return to New York in less than a week. Then your duty is over and we will say our good-byes. So, why should we worry about the in-between? Contrary to your ego, Darius, you're not irresistible."

"You think so?" he replied.

"At least to me."

"You seem confident of that."

"I'm trying to be." Needing something to do with her hands, she reached for a piece of bread and placed butter on it. Hoping to stir the conversation into less emotionally charged waters and indulge her curiosity at the same time, she inquired, "So tell me, why did you join the military?"

"There was a need." Darius met her eyes and his voice lowered.

"Do you always do what is needed?"

"No, not always, but most of the time. I have to thank my parents for that."

"I thought you hadn't spent much time with them."

"True, but I learn best by example. They showed all of us that a part of being who you are is doing what is needed and my country had need of my skills."

"Maybe that's a part of your attraction to me?" she mused aloud, taking a small bite of French bread.

"Explain." The word dropped from his lips like a command from a four-star general.

Tilting her head to the side, hurt and anger fought a lightning quick battle, with cold anger finishing up first. "You feel the need to protect me," she said with a detached calm, then placed her hands down on the cotton tablecloth. "Maybe this is why when we get close—"

"What passes between us has nothing to do with my profession or my obligations," Darius interjected. His hands came down from their steeple position and covered hers.

"And it has nothing to do with my being on the rebound," she added, enjoying the look of surprise that flickered over Darius's expression.

"Touché." He removed his hands, then raised his glass of water in a mock toast.

The food arrived and a companionable silence fell over the table. Gabriella relished every bite of the lasagna rolls and savored the satiny finish of the cream sauce. In fact, the meal was so good that Gabriella put aside all the maxims drilled into her by the ladies at the Swiss Academy. That night, for the second time since she'd arrived in New York, she disregarded polite European table etiquette to enjoy twirling the pasta with her fork and lapping up the red cream sauce with bread.

Once the waiter cleared the table and brought the after-dinner beverages, she drank deeply from the tall cup of café mocha topped with whipped cream, the rich chocolate thick on her tongue. They shared a dessert and she wiped a spot of cream from Darius's lips as each battled the other for the frosting on a double layer carrot cake.

Much later, after they'd waved down a cab to transport them back to the apartment, Gabriella leaned on Darius's shoulder as he talked sports with the cab driver. She watched the lights go by and sighed replete within his arms.

He had walked her to her bedroom door and bid her good-night with a chaste kiss on her brow before the realization of what they'd done sunk in. She'd just been on a date with a noble man, a marvelous date that had lasted all day. And the best part of the day hadn't been the excitement of skating or the restaurant. No, in retrospect, the food could have been straight from a grocer's freezer. Rather, it was the naturalness of Darius holding her hand, the lingering smile on his lips, the sound of laughter in his voice, and the thought of a future without fear that warmed her soul and left her dreams wonderful.

* * *

He hadn't adjusted to being back in civilian life. At least that's what Darius told himself as he shut the bedroom door behind him. He'd just spent the day ice skating, after all. He let out a long sigh. Part of him wished he could eliminate the memories of the day, but his mind, much like a computer, collected information and once stored, no matter what happened in his life, some fragment of the complex emotions he'd experienced with Gabriella would forever remain.

Smothering a curse, he pulled off his turtleneck sweater and shucked his shoes. He removed his gun and took both the extra ammo clip and his cell phone out of his pockets, then laid all the items on the bed. He immediately crossed over to the center rug and kneeled down to the floor. Putting one hand behind his back and balancing on his toes, he went to work. During basic training, he'd been forced to do pushups in the summer mud with the additional weight of a thirty-pound rucksack strapped to his back.

Doing the exercise on the floor of a temperature controlled luxury apartment would be all too easy. He pressed his hand into the softness of the Persian rug, sank down, and pushed up in a controlled motion. Then his actions blurred as he increased his speed and like an engine, pumped furiously as his arm muscles bulged. Embracing the burn, he pushed harder, switched arms, and got back into the zone. His stainless steel military dog tags hung from his neck and glanced off the carpet. In the low lamplight, the metal disks caught the light and flashed into his eyes. Beads of sweat began to drip down his face as his body heated up and his chest glistened with sheen.

This leave of absence was the longest time he'd ever been apart from the team. He had an idea of where they were, but he wasn't there. The frustration of being on the sidelines poured out into his limbs and he kept going, ignoring the tell-tale signs of impending muscle failure. He'd pay for it in the morning, but right now he needed something to keep from punching the wall. His breath came fast and harsh in the silence of the room as his heart pounded and blood rushed through every vein in his body. The repetitive exercise didn't clear his mind of everything but instead followed the direction of one thought alone: *never give up.*

When he got to the point that he couldn't lift himself one more time, Darius lay flat on the rug with his arms still in position and his palms flat and ready to push off. Every time he went on a mission, he placed his dog tags in an envelope with a letter he'd written the day after he'd completed Delta training. As it stood, he'd never lost a member of his current combat team. They'd been shot, cut, bruised, and kicked to hell, but they'd come out of every situation stronger and alive.

His team, his family of twelve. He hadn't lost a member yet. Not because they were the military's elite with thousands of hours of training by the subject matter experts, physical conditioning, or access to custom-built advanced weaponry, but luck. Delta Omega Team was lucky. They'd taken on guerrillas, terrorists, hijackers, rescued kidnapped Americans, and operated covert missions in some of the most dangerous regions on earth.

When he focused again on the here and now, Darius sat up and leaned against the bed. He reached behind his neck and slid the tags over his head. While thoughts of Gabriella intruded upon his thoughts, he rubbed his fingers over the rough imprinted information on the rectangular tags.

"All that is left behind," he murmured to no one in particular. Every soldier knew the origins of the practice. During the Civil War, the bodies of the soldiers had become so disfigured and decomposed that they sometimes could not be identified. Most soldiers carried them into battle, but not Delta operators. If he were killed behind enemy lines, there was a good chance his remains wouldn't make it back home. And his legacy to his family, the last gift to his parents, would be his tags.

The cell phone rang and sparing a quick glance at the caller ID, he picked it up. Only two people had the number and it was the second person who called. "Yeah."

"Are you still coming?" O'Brien's gravelly deep voice asked.

"Unless you've gotten over your fear of planes and trains," Darius responded. "I've got a seat on a 12:30 P.M. nonstop into Reagan National."

"I'll meet you at the airport. Just want to warn you that we've got to come back to my office. I can't get the information out of the building so you have to come in."

When he finished talking to the FBI agent, Darius peeled out of his remaining clothing, went into the bathroom, and turned on the shower. Not waiting for the water to heat, he stepped in and closed the door. He ducked his head under for the simple pleasure of being washed clean; yet his enjoyment was short-lived.

Gabriella's image remained etched behind his eyelids and at that very moment, he knew, like he knew the exact time the sun would rise in the morning, that she lay with her arms curled around a pillow with her lips parted slightly and her dark hair fanned across her face. How did he know?

Darius dropped the soap and ducked his head under the water. Because he'd watched her. In the early hours of the morning, as the twilight snuck through the windows and warmed her cheek, he'd stood at the foot of her bed, in the very same place he'd watched her the first night he'd carried her into the apartment.

He'd enjoyed her company today. Too much. The allure of being an ordinary man and leaving the military behind sat too close. He'd spent so long being the best of the best, how could he give it up? The madness and beauty; the fear and triumph. Darius turned off the shower and leaned his head against the cool ceramic tile. Looking down, he watched the droplets of water fall from his body and disappear down the drain.

Chapter Ten

The next morning when the doorbell to the apartment finally rang, Darius stood from his relaxed position on the sofa and made sure he had easy access to the gun at his waist. Quickly crossing the living room and entering into the foyer, he came alongside the door and pressed his ear to the wall.

"It's me, Darius."

He relaxed at the sound of the familiar Texas accent and opened the door. "What took you so long? I saw you walk through the lobby over thirty minutes ago."

Darius reached out and gripped the hand of Reese Houston, known affectionately by the Delta team as 'All-Star'.

"Man," the Delta sniper flashed a wide grin, "you wouldn't believe who I met in the elevator."

"Does *she* have a name or did *he* have a jersey number?" Darius asked after closing and locking the door. All-Star was tall, dark, and built like an all-conference tackle. Smart and sports crazy, Reese had earned his nickname for the awesome number of awards he'd gathered on his high school and college football teams. With a high IQ and some of the best long-range marksmanship the military had ever seen, the Texas cowboy had risen to the top of the army's selection pool and caught the attention of the Special Forces recruiting team. He'd earned his hat as a Green Beret before being tapped for Delta Team 3.

"Would you believe I just met Lycia Andrews?"

"Who is she?"

"I keep telling you that you don't get out enough. The woman is one of the best actresses I've ever seen on screen and she can actually fight. I'm not talking that martial arts stuff either; her pop used to be a heavyweight boxer."

"What did she want with you?" Darius asked.

The Delta sniper took off his leather coat and shrugged. "What all women want from All-Star: a nice candlelit evening and a night trying different variations of the horizontal tango."

"In your dreams," Darius scoffed.

"Haven't had many of those lately." All-Star removed his leather gloves. "Those British SAS operatives don't mess around. I've had some serious sleep deprivation for the past five weeks."

"The girl?" Darius reminded him. Low profile normally meant no profile. The more people with whom they came into daily contact, the greater the chance that they could be recognized and thus jeopardize the safety of their charge.

"Chill, Dare. She just wanted to know if I could be her personal trainer. Nice set-up you've got here," All-Star commented after taking off and storing his aviator styled glasses.

The usage of his *nom de guerre* reminded him of all the missions they'd completed. Darius took up a position beside the piano and leaned against it while examining his Delta teammate. For the second time that morning, he reconsidered calling off his trip to D.C. After five weeks of rough training away from his team, All-Star's mission was of a shorter duration than previous missions but it was still an extended time to be without the company of women. Especially when the All-Star was still recovering from his ex-girlfriend's marriage to his current best friend.

Yet, there was no one else on the planet that he would trust more than a member of his Delta force. All-Star may have been raised in Texas, but the man could change in the blink of an eye. In the streets of Libya he could be African, in the mosques of Iran, a devout Moslem paying homage to Allah. Gathering intelligence was one of many roles he played as a Delta operative. "Yeah."

"Where's the video set?"

Darius pointed back toward the hallway. "The monitors are in an empty bedroom at the end of the hall. I'm hooked into cameras covering the lobby, car port, elevators, and this hallway."

"Looks like this is a pretty easy assignment."

"You think so, huh?" Darius's grin was every bit of forced. Being in close proximity to Gabriella was anything but easy. Even after coming to an agreement that giving in to their mutual attractions was not an option, it didn't lessen his frustration one iota. He may be a proper gentleman, one of the finest soldiers the U.S. military ever trained, but he was a human being—and a man with inherent needs—sexual needs.

"Darius, did the doorbell ring?" a soft, feminine voice called out from the hallway.

The two men turned to see Gabriella. Her entrance certainly made a strong first impression. From the flush of her skin, dilated eyes, the still damp hair spread over her shoulder and her bare feet, it was obvious that she'd just come from the shower. Darius inhaled and instantly regretted it as a floral scent—a woman's scent—drifted up his nostrils, shimmied down the back of his throat, and worked its way down to wake up his groin.

"Darius, aren't you going to introduce us?" Her voice was low and husky with a purr that was uniquely French.

Gabriella looked at him with her lips pursed in a sweet smile and one eyebrow raised. He knew exactly what she was doing. She wanted him to leave her alone and unprotected and he'd torpedoed the suggestion. This was payback pure and simple. And he was falling for it hook, line, and jealousy sinking into his gut.

Darius's eyes narrowed as he watched Reese's face go

slack, then his eyes widened. *Damn it*. If he didn't need the file on Lexer so badly, he would have called it off, right then and there. He'd seen All-Star look at women, and he'd stood back watching the way they reacted to the Delta operative, but he'd never seen his teammate react with dumb silence instead of instant charm.

"Gabriella Marie, this is Reese Houston. He'll be watching out for you until I get back."

"Nice to meet you, Ms. Marie," he drawled as he held her hand.

"You as well, Mr. Houston."

"You can call me All-Star." Reese grinned, taking her hand within his own. For a moment Darius thought the Delta officer would kiss instead of shake it. "Everybody does."

"I prefer the informal ways of American culture, so please call me Gabriella."

"I'd never go against a lady's wishes."

"Looks like we shall get along famously then," she announced. "Now, All-Star. Could I get you something to drink?"

"He's just fine." Darius gritted his teeth as Gabriella's smile widened.

All-Star moved to sink his six-feet, four-inch frame into the couch. "I could use something to take the chill out of my bones. Guess I didn't realize that New York would be so cold."

"Make yourself comfortable. I'll be right back with some tea," she smiled.

Darius wanted to grab her arm and drag Gabriella back to her bedroom and lock her in. Each move she made as she tilted her hair or stuck her hands in the robe's oversized pockets served to deepen the V of her robe and allowed him greater visual access to her creamy skin. His eyes were drawn to the sparkling diamond on the ring around her neck. The sight may have put a damper on his libido but it fired up his anger. "I'd like the same if it wouldn't be too much trouble."

She shot him a sideways glance before taking off toward the kitchen.

"She's the client?"

"She's the one you have to keep safe."

All-Star leaned in close and said in a low tone, "Partner, you had me thinking she was some old rich bird."

Darius suppressed the urge to throttle the younger man as he eyed Gabriella's enticing backside as she left the room. "Just remember the job. I'll be back sometime tonight."

"Don't rush on my part." Reese glanced back toward the kitchen doorway. "I'm just going to enjoy the sights."

The misgivings Darius had came back stronger than before. "This isn't a game," he snapped before standing up.

"No worries." The smile slipped from the other man's lips. "I'll protect her with my life."

"Have a nice trip in?" Darius questioned in an attempt to scale back the tension.

"Yeah, after making parachute jumps off the coast of Dover for the past month, the flight over the Virgin Atlantic was nice and smooth."

"You slept?"

"Like a baby."

"Good. Under no circumstances are you to let her out of your sight."

"Who's the hunter?" All-Star sat forward putting all kidding aside.

"Vasilei Lexer."

"The younger Lexer brother," All-Star whistled. "She's got to be the missing fiancée. She's a flutist, right? Think I saw her picture on some of the barrack walls. Those Brits might put on a good face, but get them back to their quarters and that whole perfect gentleman, suave, and charming James Bond 007 reputation is just a load of crap. Those are some kinky, perverted SOBs."

For a second, Darius's fingers clenched at the thought of anyone looking much less thinking about Gabriella with less than pure thoughts. Not that it mattered that his thoughts weren't entirely pure.

Gabriella took that moment to reenter the room bearing a serving tray. "Here's your tea, All-Star. I didn't know if you wanted cream and sugar so I brought both."

"Thanks, ma'am." He reached out and took the single cup off the serving tray. "I'm a simple boy, I just take it plain." His southern accent poured out with the thickness of old maple syrup.

Darius clenched his jaw and swallowed the urge to pull Gabriella away. "Shouldn't you be getting dressed?" he said gruffly, pretending not to notice the deliberate slight on her part. He'd asked for tea as well.

All-Star caught the furious glance directed his way and ignored it. Instead he leaned back and gave her a pointed grin. "Wouldn't want you catching a cold now, would we?"

Pushing back his irritation, Darius stood, grabbed his coat and gloves off the opposite chair, then headed for the door. "I'll call you when I get off the plane, and All-Star?"

"Sir?"

Darius's eyes narrowed at All-Star's cocky grin. "I left you some books on the desk in the library. You might want to brush up on your Farsi."

"Anything else?"

"Yeah." Darius took a step away from the door, glanced down the hallway to make sure that he wasn't observed, then took three long strides toward All-Star to get up close and personal in his teammate's face. He didn't want the other man to miss a word and so his voice was loud enough to echo. "Screw this up or touch her and I'll have you pulling scorpions from your boots on the Iranian border."

Delta Airlines flight 1753 touched down at Reagan National Airport exactly twenty minutes past one o'clock in the afternoon. The flight from New York to Washington, D.C. had left on time and arrived earlier than scheduled, but Darius still hated being on commercial airplanes. It wasn't the fear of flying; he just hated the lack of control. In the military, someone he knew and trusted operated the cockpit controls. If something were to go wrong, he could say a prayer, strap on a parachute, and jump.

"Damn." Darius let out a string of Arabic curses the moment he stepped foot onto the concourse and spotted his contact, Roger O'Brien, sandwiched between two other men dressed in dark gray suits and black patent shoes. *FBI*. He caught the apologetic look on Roger's face as the other man held out his hand.

"Sorry about this, Darius. They knocked on my front door at six o'clock this morning."

Darius nodded his head before turning his attention to the taller of the two agents who'd come to stand beside him. He believed Roger; the two had shared quarters at Quantico for six months. He'd spent hours drilling the older FBI agent on the vocabulary and pronunciation techniques he'd need to help with investigations involving recent émigrés from Middle Eastern countries.

"Sergeant Yassoud, my name is Paul Higgins and my partner here is Bill Turner. We need you to come with us."

The man was pushing six feet, thin and balding. From the way his eyes continued to survey the room, Darius could tell that the agent had been in the field for quite a while. His partner had the look of a new recruit. Nervous energy leaked off the man, and his attention never wavered from Darius.

"What's this about, Agent Higgins?" he asked, careful to keep his voice even and hands in clear view by his sides. He could take them both down and escape. But that was before September 11, 2001. Now the odds of his evading the National Guard and undercover agents placed in strategic locations throughout the terminal were low. Remembering his reasons for coming to D.C., Darius relaxed his stance. He'd come for information, not to start a battle.

"We have some people who need to talk with you, that's all." Higgins gave him a look that said he didn't want trouble. The fact that he stayed out of arm's reach and kept his tone friendly let Darius know that either this man had guessed or had been told that Darius was a member of an elite military squad.

"I've got a rather tight schedule." Darius didn't budge, even as their small group began to gain the attention of arriving passengers in the boarding area.

Agent Higgins actually cracked a smile. "Don't worry, we'll have you back in plenty of time to catch your return flight."

Shrugging his shoulders, Darius glanced over his shoulder at Roger before falling in line behind the agent. The procession through the terminal took only a few minutes and as he exited the airport, the sun broke through the clouds and Darius was escorted into one of two waiting black sedans while Roger was placed in another. As the car pulled off, he leaned forward and casually asked, "Are you going to tell me exactly who it is that I'm going to be meeting and why?"

"Sorry sir, I don't have access to that information. We were only told to pick up and deliver."

Flexing his fingers, Darius settled into the leather seat and directed his full attention to the passing highway signs as they drove farther and farther away from inner D.C. Soon they'd be out of the beltway all together. It was still too early for the congestion of afternoon traffic to slow them down, so twenty minutes later they pulled into a small nondescript office complex. Darius was politely ushered into an elevator and then into a conference room on the fifth floor.

"Can we get you something to drink or eat while you wait?"

"No." Darius surveyed the room. One exit point, no windows or outside phone lines. A wall screen, long wooden desk, and twelve leather chairs.

He walked toward the back of the room and took a seat; he'd only been waiting ten minutes before a group of men came through the door. Darius studied their faces carefully, memorizing each person's individual features so that if he had to identify or sketch them he'd have no trouble.

"Sorry to keep you waiting."

Darius didn't stand nor did he take his hand. "Where's Roger?" he asked in a cool voice.

"Mr. O'Brien will join us in a moment."

Darius glanced toward the deep voice belonging to the newest arrival. The tall, broad shouldered man with silver hair and piercing eyes wore a tailored Italian suit with loafers that probably cost a month of his take home pay. It took him a moment to access his memories and come up with a match. Only one man could take over a room in such a manner and that was Warren Peters. His expression settled into a mask. If the heir apparent of the FBI was behind this meeting, then things were going to be very interesting.

"All right, I suggest we get the introductions out of the way so we can get down to business. Sergeant, I'm Warren Peters, deputy assistant director of the FBI international criminal investigative division. These two gentlemen are Krouder and Taschinov. They are law enforcement counterparts from Russia."

He made sure to keep his face devoid of emotion. "Why am I here?"

"Because I don't like wild cards," Peters said matter-of-factly while staring intently at Darius. He gauged his reaction, then pointed a remote at the television screen.

The lights dimmed and a picture of a couple came on screen. His fingers tensed on the side of the chair. Gabriella sat in front of Vasilei Lexer on a tall white horse.

"I assume you recognize the woman in the picture?"

"Yes," Darius nodded.

"And the man?"

"Vasilei Lexer," he responded shortly.

The picture changed. "Do you know this man?"

Not by deed or look did Darius betray his recognition of Anton Lexer's photograph. The dictator's oldest son stood against the railing of a sleek Ferretti super yacht. "No."

"You're looking at Anton Lexer," Peters continued. "He's

brilliant, elusive, and a criminal mastermind who has managed to pull off some of the biggest private brokered arms deals in history. This one man is responsible for selling and transporting close to a quarter of the ex-Soviet Ukrainian military supplies to Africa and the Middle East."

Peters placed his fingers into a steeple position. "As we all know, after the fall of the Communist regime, the former Eastern bloc arsenals have come up for bid at fire sale prices. Lexer has used his connections with former military and political leaders in the region to set up one of the largest and most efficient arms smuggling operations in Eastern Europe and the Middle East."

Darius's eyes narrowed on Peters before he redirected his attention back to the screen.

"And he has made a fool of our government in the process." The heavily accented voice came from the dark-haired Russian seated closest to Darius.

Peters sighed. "Look, Yassoud. Russian Federal Security Service has asked us to lend them a hand on this one. As far as the FBI was concerned, this was just another case of corruption and gun running."

"What's changed?"

"The disappearance of these two men coupled with some highly classified intelligence from the CIA."

The picture changed and Peters continued. "Two members of the Russian security service were undercover working on the case. It seems that they were extremely close to getting the goods on a particularly large shipment of antiaircraft missiles when they failed to report in about three months ago."

Three months. The timing set off warning bells in his mind. That was around the time Gabriella went on the run. "What does all this have to do with me?" he demanded.

"Directly? Not a damn thing. The person we need is Vasilei Lexer's fiancée, Ms. Gabriella Marie. We've got nothing to link Anton with either the disappearance or the weapons. No photos, witnesses, evidence, nothing. Nobody talks within his organization, and those suspected of betrayal, disappear."

The Russian joined into the conversation. "We have spent months gathering information on the brothers. While the older one has ties with organized crime, the younger son is the head of the family's global empire, which is known to have provided money laundering and other services to corrupt Russian officials. They are well connected and protected."

"Ms. Marie is the only break they've had since they began watching him," Peters interrupted. "The German authorities want to shut down the arms smuggling operation, the Russians want revenge for the deaths of their agents, and my superiors want to make damn sure those antiaircraft missiles don't make their way into the hands of any terrorist groups or a rogue state."

Darius interrupted the man's monologue. "That's all well and good, but get to the point."

"We believe that Vasilei Lexer's fiancée went into hiding because she witnessed the murder of the agents. Our surveillance team observed her fleeing the Italian villa forty-eight hours before the agents failed to make their scheduled check-in. If that's the case and she saw the crime, then Anton Lexer can't afford to let her live."

"This isn't a Senate hearing. Just tell me what you want so I can get the hell out of here," Darius briskly ordered.

"I believe that you have access to Ms. Marie and we need her."

"You want to set her up as bait," Darius surmised.

"Yes, we want to lure him in and trap him or get Vasilei to turn on his brother. Either way, Anton goes down. In order to do that we need to have the girl unprotected, and you happen to be our quickest and easiest link. Anton has to have opportunity. All we need is to catch him in the act and we put him away."

Darius didn't move a muscle. "Why wouldn't he have someone else do it?"

"Anton Lexer's psychological profile won't let it go down any other way."

"Why not just bring the girl in and question her?" Darius worked hard to keep his growing anger off his face and out of his voice. His gut was churning too hard and too fast. "See what she knows about the disappearance and use that to lock Anton up."

"Too circumstantial," Peters shook his head. "They'll never issue a warrant, much less convict on just her testimony alone. Plus, the defense will say that she's prejudiced being that she was the fiancée of the younger brother."

"Even if you manage to get him on attempted murder, what's to say he won't beat that charge as well?" Darius asked.

"We don't need him to be charged, Sergeant," the other Russian agent interjected. "We have on good information that within the next two to four weeks, Anton will have finished brokering a deal to sell a missing shipment of Russian IGLAs to the Chechens."

Darius sat forward and put his hands on the table. "Now how does a person get their hands on that kind of hardware?" He knew the destructive capability of the IGLAs. The shoulder-fired surface-to-air missile could bring down a helicopter gunship or a low-flying combat plane.

"Stolen from our military base, of course," Taschwa responded.

"How about sold? Not much fun having your toys used against you, is it?" Darius pointed out, enjoying the way the man's face flushed with the innuendo.

Peters dropped his pen on the table. "That's beside the point. What we need to do is get to Lexer and we need to do it publicly. If we cut him off from all his outside sources, then they'll turn on one another. We'll have a small window of opportunity to find out where the arms are and seize them before they fall into the wrong hands."

Darius sat back as the lights rose and the screen blinked off. "My job is to protect Ms. Marie. This mission of yours will make her a target."

Peters tapped his fingers on the table. "She always has been. Interpol has had the Lexer brothers on their radar screen for the past three years. The disappearance of those agents is a serious matter. This wasn't an isolated investigation and it's become a major priority to shut them down."

Darius shrugged. "That's their problem. I've given my word to keep her out of harm's way."

"I'll make sure that nothing happens to the girl. My men will be watching at all times, and when Anton makes his move we'll catch him."

"Before or after he kills her?" he replied sarcastically. The whole situation left Darius with a bad taste in his mouth.

Peters blinked his eyes slowly, took off his glasses, then produced an ivory handkerchief and meticulously cleaned the microthin lenses. "Look, Yassoud, I'd hate for this to get to the point that I have to treat you like a hostile recruit, but my hands are tied and I need your cooperation whether you like it or not. Ms. Marie may have been an eyewitness to a crime, but we have neither the evidence nor the jurisdiction. We've also got a German court that likes its celebrities and its industrialists. But what Anton Lexer can't beat is an attempted murder charge of a U.S. citizen and the daughter of Sebastian van Ryne."

Darius's jaw clenched at the director's threat of forced cooperation.

"Let me put my cards on the table," the deputy assistant director began, after spreading his fingers like a card dealer at a high stakes poker game. "I may not be able to touch you directly, but if you choose not to cooperate, I'll be forced to make life extremely uncomfortable for your family. Now we'll leave you to rethink your decision. In the meantime, I'm sure you'd like to catch up with your old friend."

Darius stood as the small group filed out of the room. The door had barely swung closed when Roger came in.

"What the hell have you stepped into, Darius? I've had the organized crime unit crawling all over my office." Roger dropped a file on the conference table.

"How did they get word of my involvement, Roger?" Darius questioned in a cold voice.

"After I got your call, I went on line and tried to pull up anything I could on Lexer and the girl. I managed to print half the file before I was locked out."

"How did they know about me?" he repeated.

"I figure they tapped in on our phone call. They were knocking on the door even before I got out of the toilet this morning."

Darius ran his fingers roughly through his hair. He'd woken up with a bad feeling in his stomach and it seemed as though it was only going to get worse. "They're blackmailing me, Roger."

"What do they want?"

"The girl. Apparently, she's the missing piece. They can't get to Lexer without the girl, and they can't get to Gabriella without me."

"What are you going to do?"

Clenching his fingers, Darius took a deep breath. He needed time—time to figure a way out of the trap he'd stepped into. He couldn't allow his family to come to harm, but honor dictated that he keep his promise and protect Gabriella.

"I don't know yet," he said for the benefit of those listening.

"Well, you may want to take a look at these files before you make any decisions."

"What are they?"

"Peters asked me to give them to you. They're files relating all the intelligence information they've managed to get on Lexer's organization. I've never seen the like. Both brothers are connected to the highest sections of government in every Eastern European country. It was a mess to begin with, but then you add the girl and the stink her father can raise if he gets a whiff of this. Sebastian van Ryne won't stand by idle when all this starts to go down."

"Have they approached him?"

"No, they believe her father would most likely move the girl to another country. That's why they're trying to keep him out of the picture as long as possible."

"The son's skiing accident . . ."

"Set up."

"Damn," Darius cursed. "This makes little sense. Why don't they just pressure van Ryne into turning her over? Threaten to tell his wife?"

"The file indicates that the wife already knows about the girl."

Before he could say anything else, the door opened and Peters entered the room. "So have you come to a decision?"

Darius bent to pick up the files Roger had placed on the table. "Yes."

"Good, good," the director responded. "Now where is she?"

Darius gave the older man a smile that did nothing to warm the icy glint in his eyes. "Well, you see, that's something we're going to have to talk about. I don't think she'll cooperate."

"Show her these." The assistant director tossed a manila envelope on the table. "She'll help."

Four hours later, Darius gave in to the urge to rub his temples as the airplane accelerated down the runway. He'd seen the fear in Gabriella's eyes and he could bet that Anton was the cause. He couldn't ask her to pick up the phone and call

Vasilei. No, the only way to bring him down would be an up-close and personal encounter.

Bitter frustration welled up in his throat. If Peters was right, in less than three days Anton would be on a plane to New York. He didn't like the idea of civilians in combat, but if anything that the agents said was true, then the arms dealer needed to be eliminated. Opening his eyes and looking out the cloud-filled window, Darius unclenched his fingers from around the file folder and set it on his lap.

The Feds had set the plan in motion even before he'd boarded the plane. If Anton didn't know where Gabriella was now, he soon would after the German authorities tipped off an informer on Lexer's payroll. Sometime soon, Anton would learn about Gabriella's father. The enormity of the matter stunned him. To emotionally abandon one's child? The files explained so many things about her. It was no wonder she'd spent her life doing the things she did. Even her relationship with Vasilei made sense.

If it were up to the FBI, Gabriella's newly fought for peace would come crashing down around her. How would she feel about being the sacrificial lamb for anti-weapons proliferation? More importantly, how would she react to the sight of her ex-fiancé? Darius shifted uncomfortably in his business class seat as the reality of the situation settled in his gut. When it came down to it, he'd brought this down on both of them.

One thing he had on his side was knowledge. He thought about how he would misdirect the FBI. They'd have a lot of ground to cover, and finding Gabriella in New York would be akin to looking for a needle in a haystack. Darius only hoped that until he could come up with a solid plan and marshal the needed resources that he could keep it that way.

A knot of tension disappeared from his stomach as a steely resolve took its place. He would ask for her help and then he would do what he'd been asked. And that was to stay close and keep her safe.

Chapter
Eleven

Gabriella dressed with care for what she hoped would be her first time out on the town in months. As the cool silk slid over her skin and clung to her curves like a second skin, instead of feeling proudly rebellious, her fingers twitched with nervousness as she ran them through her thick hair. She'd spent most of her day out of the apartment enjoying the hustle and bustle of the city. All-Star had been great company as well, acting as more of a friend than a bodyguard.

He would have driven her around, but Gabriella preferred to take the subway. She knew that All-Star was rather annoyed at her choice of transportation, but she liked the roaring sound of the train's entrance and the groups of people from all different nationalities, ages and ethnicities. It was strange to think that she'd spent the first twelve years of her life in the city. Yet listening to the quick fluid voices as the express train sped downtown, she felt more like a tourist than a Manhattan native.

Earlier that day, Gabriella had exited the train at Fifth Avenue and Rockefeller Center. She breathed a sigh of relief after emerging from the subway. The stores and boutiques might have changed from when she was a girl, but the energy and vitality of the area remained the same. Tucking her scarf underneath her long wool coat, she picked a direction and set off. The sidewalks were filled, as shoppers and workers hurried in their thick winter coats and boots to find a place to grab lunch before returning to their desks to finish out their day.

Gabriella sighed before turning to examine her image in the full-length mirror. She looked the same yet different. The time spent on the run had made her even more slender, and the black silk cocktail dress only emphasized her narrow waist and full breasts while showing off her black sheer stocking-clad legs. She'd discovered the dress on the back walls of Fendi's boutique. The saleswoman had assured her that it had recently arrived from Milan. Of course, she'd purchased black leather slingbacks to match.

She pushed back her hair and moved to put on her only pair of silver earrings and stopped as the ring on her necklace slid over her throat and nestled in the valley of her breasts. Her heart froze when she looked into the mirror and caught sight of the diamond's intense glitter. Without conscious thought, her right hand moved to touch the engagement ring. She'd held her inner pain at bay so long, she'd almost forgotten about it. But now as she reached up to take off the necklace, the realization that she was free of Vasilei's control hit her square between the eyes.

A shiver crept down her spine, an obvious sign of the tenuousness of her bravado. It was her fault the two men had died, and it was her blindness that allowed Vasilei so much control of her emotions. Instead of giving her a sense of comfort, the ring felt like a tremendous weight that threatened to pull her down, or pull her back to the man who'd so utterly betrayed everything she thought they had both believed in. Her hand went to her throat and she touched the ring.

The battle between her mind and her heart had raged on for so long, a stalemate of sorts had occurred. One thing that Gabriella did know was that she was tired of living on the edge and she would take advantage of the moment to live a little before running again. She couldn't stay in New York forever, and there was no way she would allow Sebastian to control her life. Reaching behind her neck, she unclasped the platinum chain and took it off.

After placing the chain and ring inside her small jewelry box, she dotted the insides of her wrists with perfume. Gabriella opened the door and walked into the living room. That evening would be the only break she'd get for a while. It would soon be time to move. Although she trusted Darius to keep her safe, Gabriella still couldn't trust her father's motives.

Having spent most of her time in New York cooped up in the apartment or having a disapproving Darius looking over her shoulder, she was ready to let her hair down and have a little fun. She remembered the stern look on his face before he'd left that morning. The dark eyes seemed to pierce her soul and for a moment she'd imagined they'd softened with something akin to tenderness. She shook her head and stifled the urge to laugh.

No, the man was still arrogant, controlling, and conceited. The fact that he was so sure that she would obey his every order only served to make her even more determined to go out and have a good time. She slipped on her low-heeled shoes and glided gracefully out of the room.

"All-Star," she called out sweetly.

"In the kitchen, Ms. Marie."

She walked into the kitchen and leaned against the doorway. The angle gave her an unimpeded view of All-Star as he studied the contents of the refrigerator. Darius's substitute certainly knew how to make an impression. The formfitting black shirt and pants couldn't conceal the fact that there wasn't an ounce of fat anywhere on his body and his muscular arms and tight abs had a homegrown and not gym made look about them.

When she'd first seen him earlier that morning, the bald head, hazel eyes, twin dimples, and perfect teeth had given her impressions of a singer or rapper, but his crisp accent and constant alertness had her rethinking the idea. Reese. The name, along with the holstered gun at his side, conjured images of spies and secret agents in disguise. Only the slightly puckered scar on his chin marred the otherwise asymmetrical face and gave him a dangerous look.

"Didn't we agree that you're supposed to call me Gabriella?"

"Sure did. I forgot about that. What can I do for you?"

"How about we go out?" She watched as he turned from the refrigerator and looked at her. Gabriella suppressed a smile of feminine satisfaction at the way his mouth dropped slightly open as he gave her the once over. His gaze lingered on her legs before returning to her face.

"What?" His brows descended. All-Star was still getting over the sight of the woman standing less than five feet away from him. The Gabriella he'd spent half the day following from boutique to boutique had worn a ponytail and looked like his little sister. But the sophisticated lady standing in the kitchen was something else. He had to struggle to get his libido under control so he could think clearly.

"I want to go out to a *club*," she emphasized before picking up a red apple from the fruit basket and taking a small bite.

"Gabriella," All-Star cleared his throat. "I don't think that would be a good idea." In fact, he was quite certain it was a bad idea. This was his first trip back to New York in over four years and the thought of going out and having a good time was appealing, especially after having spent his past tour enduring the grueling and isolating training with the British Special Forces.

But, the possibility of getting busted by his senior commander put a damper on his enthusiasm. Darius had been the second-in-command of his Delta unit and neither time nor distance had lessened the feelings of loyalty he had toward the man who had not only saved his life but also prevented him from making fatal mistakes.

"Why?" Gabriella smiled innocently, oozing flirtation as she took a step closer.

All-Star cleared his throat a second time before answering. "Darius gave me explicit orders to keep you safe."

"Did he mention anything about not leaving the apartment?" she countered. They'd already gone out shopping.

"No."

Recognizing that she had an opening, Gabriella pressed the point. "It's Friday night, I'm going stir crazy in this apartment, and we're in New York City. What harm could come if we just go out for an hour or two?"

"You know, I've got a better idea. When my sister was grounded, she called up her best friend and invited her over to the house. They'd kick everybody out of the den, then set up some crazy hybrid of a beauty salon and nail parlor."

"All of my friends are across the Atlantic, All-Star," she pointed out. "You're practically the only person I've had contact with besides Darius."

"Whoa." All-Star shook his head. "Now that's got to be rough. The man's like a miser when it comes to talking. Especially about himself."

Her brows drew together in surprise at his last comment. Darius had been very free about himself. "Really? He's talked a lot about his family."

"Not to us. He knows the whole team's business. He actually helped me out." All-Star closed the refrigerator door and leaned against it.

"How?"

"It was his idea that I sign up for a special training session."

"Were your skills not up to par?"

"Nah, I'm perfect. I just needed to get out of going to my best friend's wedding."

She gave him a curious look. "Are you afraid of weddings?"

He placed the lunchmeat next to the loaf of bread on the counter. "In general, no. But it's complicated."

"How complicated?"

"My girl married my best friend."

"Oh." Gabriella lowered her gaze to the floor as her cheeks flushed with embarrassment and empathy. Love, it seemed, had not been generous with her and apparently not with All-Star either. Nevertheless, she held on to the promise that the emotion or the strength of the heart could overcome most odds.

"You know," All-Star said, picking up the cheese and meats, then placing them back in the refrigerator, "maybe I could use that drink right about now."

"A real dinner, drinks, and a few dances," she coaxed. "Some good food and music. That's all I want."

"It's not that safe."

"You're a big guy," she laughed softly. "I'm sure you're more than capable of taking good care of me."

"And what about the boss?" Reese's eyes narrowed.

Annoyance flickered through Gabriella's eyes. The thought of him just made her want to disobey more. "I'll handle Darius."

She watched as a grin spread over Reese's lips. "Well, can't hurt to get some air."

"All right then," she laughed excitedly before turning to leave the kitchen. "I hope you like to dance, because I'm more than ready to hit the floor."

The night stars were glittering brightly as they drove through Manhattan. A low-pressure front had pushed the clouds out over the Atlantic, leaving snow on the ground and a full moon in the sky.

After having a fantastic dinner at an upscale Latin restaurant in Chelsea, Gabriella wasn't surprised at All-Star's choice of nightclubs. He'd managed to secure a parking place within two blocks of their destination. With his arm secured around the small of her back, Gabriella wasn't bothered by the cold.

As All-Star escorted her toward the building, she examined

the structure and admired the architecture of the name, *Envy*. The club was more than living up to the promise of its name. Lincoln Town Cars and limousines stopped to drop their decked out passengers onto the purple carpeted entranceway while others shivered as they waited in a long line. Even standing outside, she could feel the beat and bass of music and hear the loud buzz of people inside.

He walked with complete confidence up to the front door and nodded to the crew of muscular black clad men standing there. Not only did they not hesitate to let them inside, but they were also shown to the VIP section.

Gabriella leaned on his arm and whispered, "How did you do that?"

All-Star's face broadened as his grin revealed ivory teeth; his right eyelid dropped slowly over his eye, then rose upward. "If I told you, I'd have to kill you."

Right then and there she did some eye movement of her own, but it wasn't to wink. Gabriella let out an exaggerated groan and rolled her eyes as they went up the carpeted stairs and waited behind three nicely dressed couples in line.

She eyed the waiter as they took their seats in a lounge outside of the dance floor. A series of tattoos ran up and down his massive arms. His large shaved head and diamond earring didn't seem to go with his soft Irish accent and green eyes.

"I'd like something special—a New York kind of drink," Gabriella shouted over the music.

He smiled, revealing a set of perfect teeth. "How about a Long Island Iced Tea?"

She nodded and sat back. Her companion ordered a gingerale.

"Having fun yet?" Reese inquired.

"Of course," she smiled and leaned over the iron railing that separated the lower dance floor. They had renovated the space so that instead of one floor there were two with a semi-circular staircase connecting the dance floor to the lounge upstairs.

The club was the size of a large musical practice room, but at that moment it was filled with people instead of instruments. Studio lights pulsed to the music and Gabriella had a clear view of the deejay booth from their table. Businessmen in tailored suits lined the bar while women in the latest fashions milled around the upper floor.

Gabriella turned to find that the waiter was back with the drinks. All-Star reached into his wallet to put cash on the table, but the waiter backed away as though he was afraid. "Boss said to tell you everything was on him tonight."

Her eyes narrowed at the interchange. "What was that all about?"

All-Star picked up his soda and raised it toward the upper cordoned level of the bar. "An acquaintance of mine owns the place."

"I should have known." Gabriella smiled, then picked up her drink. "Shall we have a toast?"

All-Star eased his lengthy body forward. "To?"

"Food, fun, and friendship," she said mischievously.

"I'll drink to that." All-Star clicked his glass with hers.

Gabriella took a long sip of her beverage and found the taste fruity and sweet as it slipped over her tongue, warming her throat on the way down.

"How's the drink?" he asked.

"Tastes good."

The loud music made it hard to carry on a conversation, so Gabriella sat back and sipped her drink while soaking up the atmosphere. She enjoyed the smooth beats and the energy, but most of all she savored the freedom.

All-Star watched Gabriella from the corner of his eye. He could tell the moment the alcohol hit her system as she began to sway with the music. He was just about to suggest they head out to the dance floor. The sooner she got the energy out of her system, the sooner they would be on the road back to the apartment. Each minute that ticked by, he grew more and more aware that Darius would be arriving back in the city.

Just as he opened his mouth to ask, his cellular phone vibrated in his pocket. Reese pulled it out and looked at the coded number flashing across the indigo lit panel and let loose a mild expletive. Too late. Darius was back. He gripped the phone and watched as another call came in with the identical phone number. He flipped it open, but the background noise prevented any possibility of a conversation.

"Go," Gabriella urged. "I'll be fine."

"Stay here until I get back," he ordered, standing up and moving quickly toward the back hallway for privacy.

"Sure," she called out to Reese's departing back.

She returned to sipping the drink, glad to have a moment alone. About three-fourths of the way through her second glass, she felt more mellow and relaxed. Just then the music slowed.

"Dance with me, *cara*?" A slightly accented Latin voice interrupted her solitude.

Startled, Gabriella turned toward the owner of the voice. With straight black hair beginning to lighten with silver, the handsome man raised her appreciation of Latin men. His chiseled face was smooth and colored by a natural tan. She guessed him to be in his mid-thirties. The blood of the Spanish conquistadors mingled with Aztec to give him sharp piercing green eyes. He reminded her of Darius, except this man's eyes were open and admiring instead of closed and cautious.

Gabriella finished her drink, and placed her hand in his as he assisted her from her chair. Almost furtively, she glanced back in the direction All-Star had gone. But she lifted her chin in defiance and followed the gentleman downstairs and onto the crowded dance floor.

He placed his hands on her hips, then leaned in close to her ear.

"My name's Javier."

"Lisa," she replied after a slight pause. The false name resonated in the back of her head and stirred up feelings of guilt.

"Lisa," he repeated in her ear. "What a beautiful name for a beautiful woman."

"Thank you," she replied gracefully, not falling under the spell of the charm that seemed to ooze from his pores. She wanted so badly to lose herself in the moment, but another's face swam before her eyes. *Darius*. Although he was miles away, the handsome bodyguard still had the power to affect her.

Gabriella had to admit Javier was smooth and a good dancer. But she felt his fingers begin to play in her hair and barely suppressed the urge to take a step away. Finally she pulled back, putting distance between her and her dance partner.

"So your date has left you all alone. I would not have taken him to be so foolish."

"What do you mean?" She frowned slightly at the familiar way the man referred to All-Star.

"The man I trained with knew how to protect what was his."

"I belong to no man," she shot back.

"Of course," he smoothly replied. A warm, sensual smile curved his lips and deepened the lines at the corners of his penetrating eyes. "Both beautiful and spirited. What a pity it's wasted on All-Star. He's a natural born playboy."

"And I suppose you're different?"

"Night and day, *bella*." Gabriella eyed his intense expression and checked the urge to pull even farther away. The look in his dark eyes had changed in an instant and hinted of a hidden warning. She blinked and it was gone. Javier's lips had curled into an edgy grin as he looked over her shoulder. Gabriella turned and followed his gaze.

Darius. The music changed and slowed as the semi-lit room resonated with the magnetic tone of the guitar and the heavy, sensual beat of drums. Her breath caught in her throat as her eyes locked onto a familiar figure; he stepped from the shadowed corner of the room. Dark piercing eyes framed by inky black lashes stared back at her.

None of the lighthearted banter or softness she'd witnessed the past few weeks showed in the man. Gabriella froze as he moved toward them. A stillness seemed to follow him as he maneuvered through the dancing couples. When the beat of the music gave way to the furious beating of her heart, she bit the inside of her lip.

Darius didn't look like her bodyguard; he looked like her keeper. She fought the urge to run, but the warning expression on his face coupled with the pleading look she caught from All-Star kept her feet still. When he was three feet from them, his gaze raked up and down her body before turning to the man at her side.

"Take your hands off her, Javier."

The menacing undertone of his voice broke the spell that Darius's abrupt entrance had wrought.

Gabriella's dance partner took a step in front of her, partially shielding her from Darius's view. "Well, well. Looks like the snowballs are dropping in hell. What are you doing here, Yassoud?"

Darius didn't turn his attention from Gabriella after speaking to the former Ranger. He'd come to the nightclub with the express purpose of finding Gabriella and yanking her out of the place, not getting into a brawl. But the second his eyes locked on her, twin emotions of relief and desire flared into being. Her naturally curly hair hung straight and smooth over her shoulders. "I believe you have something of mine and I'd like it back."

"You know nothing comes for free," the other man taunted. "And a woman of Lisa's beauty and taste is worth far more than you can afford on a military salary."

When Javier stepped back and placed his arm around her waist, Darius checked the urge to take his fist and plant it into the other man's face. Jealousy and envy ran rampant among all the ranks and services within the military. Only the best were invited to join the Special Forces and those that failed to gain entrance never forgot the bitter taste of defeat.

"I think letting you keep those nice teeth of yours is payment enough." The lack of emotion in Darius's voice made the threat all the more lethal.

"You think you can take me, D-Boy?" Javier responded. "Your team isn't here to back you up."

Darius noticed the rapt attention Gabriella was paying to their conversation and again fought the instinctive urge toward physical violence. "D-Boy" was just another of the Army's euphemisms for Delta. Rivalry between the armed forces was an everyday event, but to be effective, Delta force members had to remain a secret. And the last thing he wanted was for Gabriella to know. Someday after he resigned from his post, he'd tell her the complete truth about his role in the Special Operations branch, but not now.

"Think hard before you push this, Javier. I was alone when we last tangled." He looked pointedly at the man's right arm. "And your ego may have allowed you to forget the outcome, but I'm sure the scar on your arm is proof enough."

Several heartbeats passed before Javier took a step back and returned his attention to the woman at his side. "He's got me on that, *cara*." Instead of moving away from Gabriella, Javier stepped closer and moved her into a position that to other people would appear to be an intimate embrace. "Be careful you don't get burned."

Gabriella had but to tilt or sway and they would kiss. Her eyes flashed upward and locked with emerald green, before she pulled her head back. "We would both go down in flames," she promised.

Javier took her right hand within his own and she watched in bemusement as he gallantly kissed it. "Thank you for a wonderful dance. Should you need a better partner, I'll be waiting."

She gifted Javier with what she hoped was a flirtatious smile since she was more than aware that the Latin gentleman hadn't taken his eyes off Darius for a second. "Thank you for the advice."

An Important Message From The ARABESQUE Publisher

Dear Arabesque Reader,

I invite you to join the club! The Arabesque book club delivers four novels each month right to your front door! It's easy, and you will never miss a romance by one of our award-winning authors!

With upcoming novels featuring strong, sexy women, and African-American heroes that are charming, loving and true… you won't want to miss a single release. Our authors fill each page with exceptional dialogue, exciting plot twists, and enough sizzling romance to keep you riveted until the satisfying end! To receive novels by bestselling authors such as Gwynne Forster, Janice Sims, Angela Winters and others, I encourage you to join now!

Read about the men we love… in the pages of Arabesque!

Linda Gill
PUBLISHER, ARABESQUE ROMANCE NOVELS

P.S. Watch out for the next Summer Series "Ports Of Call" that will take you to the exotic locales of Venice, Fiji, the Caribbean and Ghana! You won't need a passport to travel, just collect all four novels to enjoy romance around the world! For more details, visit us at www.BET.com.

**SPECIAL OFFER!
4 BOOKS FREE!**

ARABESQUE

BET★ BOOKS

www.BET.com

A SPECIAL "THANK YOU" FROM ARABESQUE JUST FOR YOU!

Send this card back and you'll receive 4 FREE Arabesque Novels—a $25.96 value—absolutely FREE!

The introductory 4 Arabesque Romance books are yours FREE (plus $1.99 shipping & handling). If you wish to continue to receive 4 books every month, do nothing. Each month, we will send you 4 New Arabesque Romance Novels for your free examination. If you wish to keep them, pay just $18* (plus, $1.99 shipping & handling). If you decide not to continue, you owe nothing!

- Send no money now.
- Never an obligation.
- Books delivered to your door!

We hope that after receiving your FREE books you'll want to remain an Arabesque subscriber, but the choice is yours! So why not take advantage of this Arabesque offer, with no risk of any kind. You'll be glad you did!

In fact, we're so sure you will love your Arabesque novels, that we will send you an Arabesque Tote Bag FREE with your first paid shipment.

* PRICES SUBJECT TO CHANGE.

YOU'LL GET 4 SELECT ROMANCES PLUS THIS FABULOUS TOTE BAG!

ARABESQUE

Visit us at: www.BET.com

THE "THANK YOU" GIFT INCLUDES:

- 4 books absolutely FREE (plus $1.99 for shipping and handling).
- A FREE newsletter, *Arabesque Romance News*, filled with author interviews, book previews, special offers, and more!
- No risks or obligations. You're free to cancel whenever you wish with no questions asked.

FREE TOTE BAG CERTIFICATE

Yes! Please send me 4 FREE Arabesque novels (plus $1.99 for shipping & handling). I understand I am under no obligation to purchase any books, as explained on the back of this card. Send my free tote bag after my first regular paid shipment.

NAME _____

ADDRESS _____ APT. _____

CITY _____ STATE _____ ZIP _____

TELEPHONE ( ) _____

E-MAIL _____

SIGNATURE _____

Offer limited to one per household and not valid to current subscribers. All orders subject to approval. Terms, offer, & price subject to change. Tote bags available while supplies last.

Thank You!

AN045A

Accepting the four introductory books for FREE (plus $1.99 to offset the cost of shipping & handling) places you under no obligation to buy anything. You may keep the books and return the shipping statement marked "cancelled". If you do not cancel, about a month later we will send 4 additional Arabesque novels, and you will be billed the preferred subscriber's price of just $4.50 per title. That's $18.00* for all 4 books for a savings of almost 30% off the cover price (Plus $1.99 for shipping and handling). You may cancel at any time, but if you choose to continue, every month we'll send you 4 more books, which you may either purchase at the preferred discount price. . . or return to us and cancel your subscription.

* PRICES SUBJECT TO CHANGE

THE ARABESQUE ROMANCE BOOK CLUB
P.O. BOX 5214
CLIFTON NJ 07015-5214

THE ARABESQUE ROMANCE CLUB: HERE'S HOW IT WORKS

PLACE
STAMP
HERE

All-Star took that moment to slap Javier on the back. "Why don't we grab a drink and catch up?" Darius's replacement inclined his head toward the upper level bar.

Gabriella watched the two men walk away and a part of her wished she could go with them. Taking a deep breath, she pinned a smile on her face and turned to Darius. Whether it was fear or bravado, she didn't know.

Before she could think of something appropriately witty, she found herself being pulled until her body came into full contact with Darius's. "Come to drag the wayward home?" She tossed her hair over her shoulder and glowered at him. "Dare."

"You overheard." The skin around his eyelids tightened.

"As you meant for me to. You'll be pleased to know that All-Star hasn't laid a finger on me."

"Smile at me," he ordered. His mouth drew into a thin, uncrossable line when she didn't immediately comply. But the fingers clamped on her waist gave her no other option than to force a fake smile on her lips.

"Good, now put your arms around my neck."

Gabriella balked as the alcohol gave her delusions of disobedience.

"Now, Princess."

She did as told but turned her face away from him.

His breath whispered against the nape of her neck, tickling her skin and sending quivers of heat down her spine. "All-Star doesn't need to touch you, Gabriella. He is a man and all he has to do is look at you. Just like any other man in this establishment."

"Like you look at me, Darius? As though you want to touch me in places, intimate places?"

His grip tightened and Gabriella shuddered as he leaned down and the deep warmth of his breath trailed over her bare throat. His musky scent caught her nose, turning her nipples hard. "You may have been smart enough to give Javier the fake name, but that does nothing to mitigate the irresponsible and reckless decisions you've made tonight."

Gabriella raised her chin and said in a loud voice. "I take full responsibility for my actions."

"As do I. We will dance for one song. Only one, and then without drawing any more attention, we will leave."

"What if I don't want to leave?" Gabriella drew back as far as his hands would allow.

His fingertips trailed over the hollow of her throat and she was swept by a deep shiver. "And what if I want you to defy me, Princess? Because I'm itching to put you over my shoulder and carry you out with your legs under my arms."

"Didn't you mention something about not calling attention to ourselves?"

"I'll risk it," Darius bit out between gritted teeth.

When he'd called All-Star from a subway payphone and had been told that they were at a club, he'd let out a string of curses and contemplated tearing the man limb from limb. Now as he looked into a set of glowing amber eyes, his resolutions faltered. Darius's newly found knowledge of Gabriella's past weakened him. Just like that dress that clung to her body like an ATV on a tight turn. Unconsciously his hand loosened as his eyes kept getting dragged back to the smooth line of her bare neck and the raven colored wisps of hair at her nape.

As the tempo of the music rose and fell, she found his rhythm and matched it perfectly. "As I said, Princess. We're going to dance and then we're going to return to the apartment, and you and I will talk about the consequences of your actions."

Gabriella didn't stir from her comfortable position in Darius's arms. Maybe the alcohol had dulled her senses to the point that she no longer recognized danger, or maybe it was just that she didn't care. All that seemed to matter was the heat that seemed to wrap around her. It was like the cracking of ice warmed from the new heat of a spring sun. The strong muscled arms held her close. She was warm and lush, filled with seduction and anticipation. Her breasts tightened as they came into contact with his chest.

"Do you always have to be so rigid?" she questioned, looking into his eyes. "Have you never wanted to get away from your life? To lose yourself in the moment?" Her voice came out calm but inwardly her blood thumped in her temple.

Darius bent his head to hear her words and the sound of her husky voice coupled with the scent of her perfume sent a flood of arousal throughout his body. Instead of answering the question she posed, he moved his hands up the back of her dress and caught hold of her neck and kissed her. His lips were hard and hot as his tongue forced its way into her soft mouth. It was the sweetest taste he'd ever had, and like a man who had bitten the most forbidden fruit, he savored it for the moment and then let go. "Is this the answer you were looking for?"

"Yes." Her tongue dashed out to wet her lips. "I've tasted freedom tonight and I like it. I want more of it."

"Be careful," he warned. "Freedom left unchecked by caution can lead to ruin."

She pressed her body into his while her arms wrapped around his neck. "Then save me, Darius."

"How much have you had to drink?"

She met his gaze with a hint of a smile on her lips. "If I said nothing, would you believe me?"

"No, I can smell the alcohol on your breath. How much?"

"Not nearly enough," she whispered.

He watched as her thick eyelashes fanned upward revealing pupils darkened with desire. Once more, her tongue flicked out to lick her lips and Darius fought the urge to kiss her again. He should have been dragging her off the dance floor and shoving her into the back of the Land Rover without a backward glance, but all he wanted to do was move with her and stare down at her delicate mouth that reminded him of cherubs from nineteenth century paintings.

When she burrowed closer and wrapped her arms about him, Darius lowered his head and rested his chin atop her hair. No doubt about it. He was utterly compromised.

"Are you not speaking to me now?" Gabriella questioned. Her slurred words blended with the French accent. Darius hadn't said a word after dropping All-Star off at a hotel. She'd tried to defend the man as Darius cut into him the second they'd left the club, but All-Star had politely asked Gabriella to mind her own business. The silence in the car would have been unbearable if she hadn't felt so fluid and relaxed from the potent effects of hard alcohol in her bloodstream.

He looked at her for the first time since they'd walked out of the nightclub.

"You're inebriated, Gabriella."

"No, I'm not," she denied as the elevator stopped and the doors opened. She moved unsteadily into the hallway and with each step the walls seemed to move. While trying to get her keys, she dropped her purse. Gabriella bent to reach for it but Darius's hand moved faster.

"Let me."

"Thank you, but I can unlock the door just fine." She snatched the key dangling from his finger and unsteadily attempted to place it in the lock.

Darius growled with frustration. He was a Communications Sergeant within one of the most elite fighting troops on earth. He could build and utilize any kind of telecommunications equipment, from satellite systems to transistor radios, but he couldn't get through to one woman. Placing his hand over Gabriella's, he guided the key into the lock and turned. After letting them both into the apartment, he flicked on the hall light, then took off his jacket.

"Why don't you take a seat on the couch?" he called out while laying his jacket over the back of the living room chair.

I'll fix you a cup of coffee and once you sober up, maybe you can tell me why you disobeyed me?"

"Ohhh, so inviting," she sarcastically answered. "What more could I want than to listen to you lecture? I think I need another drink to fortify myself."

He gave her an impatient look and watched as she slipped her shoes off and walked over to the side tables to stumble into the sofa. Darius looked on as Gabriella closed her eyes and laid her head against the sofa's arm. Curling her legs up on the sofa, with her hair in disarray, she resembled a disobedient child. All the anger he felt melted away.

When he'd first spotted her on the dance floor at the nightclub, the way her body swayed to the music and her arms moved in dance, she'd looked like a seductive siren. There was no doubt he'd wanted her. Every man in the room would have given half his soul to possess her. Yet, he would also give his heart.

Shaking off the thoughts, Darius turned away, went into the kitchen, and prepared two cups of strong instant coffee. He returned to the living room a few moments later. "We need to talk."

"I don't want to talk. I want to do something else," she murmured. The husky tenderness of her voice made his body react strongly.

She ignored the coffee mug and moved closer to him. Almost in his lap, her breath was sweet in his ear.

"I'm so tired of being afraid, Darius. I want ice skating and the smell of chestnuts. I want the sweetness of your lips and the sunshine making rainbows between my eyelashes. Give me that again, Darius. Make the darkness go away."

Somehow, they leaned into one another and kissed, then gradually the kisses grew longer and deeper and their hands grew bolder, erasing any real or imagined boundary between them. She nipped his lip and their mingled breaths and the caress of her tongue mimicked the exploration of her fingers.

Gabriella's hand moved southward and settled on the hard evidence of his arousal.

All too soon, Darius pulled back. He took her hands gently within his own and turned to settle her into his lap as her body began to tremble. He drew in a deep breath to strengthen his weakened resolve. "What is the darkness you're afraid of, Gabriella?" he whispered in her ear. He couldn't help but feel the violent tremor that racked her body.

"Anton," she whispered.

"Tell me about Anton," he encouraged but she seemed not to hear him.

"He's a monster."

"Why did you call him that?"

"They were human beings." Gabriella went quiet for a moment and then continued, her voice low and confessional. "They were men in chains. He'd had two of them hung naked from chains. And he cut them. Cut them so much their skin turned red with blood. They couldn't scream because of the tape covering their mouths, and I thought I could hear them moan, but later it wasn't until after I ran back to the main house and locked myself in the bathroom that I knew the moans were mine. Oh, Darius, when I close my eyes some nights I see his smile. Anton was smiling as he cut them. And he didn't stop. He didn't stop even after seeing me in the window."

His heart stilled at her words, yet quick on the heels of his shock came anger. "Are you sure he saw you there, Gabriella?"

"Yes." She let out a sharp cry of laughter. "Oh, yes. He looked into my eyes when he slit the first man's throat. And the next morning he spoke to me of the pleasure he would take in my death."

Darius gently guided her face toward his own. He needed to know the answer to stop the churning in his gut. "Does Vasilei know about his brother's activities?"

Her golden eyes seemed to glow even more brightly. Her hiccups of laughter held a hint of hysteria. "Of course. He stood there watching." The dam holding back a month's worth of grief and horror burst and tears flowed unchecked. She buried her face in his neck and he held her tight as she whispered, "He stood there watching."

Chapter
Twelve

My aching head. Gabriella groaned before squeezing her eyes tight in the hope of blocking out the sudden burst of light streaming through the windows.

"Good morning."

The familiar musk of Darius's aftershave met her before his words penetrated the layers of fog surrounding her mind. She cracked her eyelids slightly and a blurry shadow slowly resolved itself into the familiar figure of her bodyguard. "Go away and let me die in peace," she croaked.

"I'm afraid I can't do that, Princess. What kind of bodyguard would I be if I didn't make an effort to save you? Now sit up and I'll leave you after you drink this."

"How about you leave me after drawing the curtains?" she asked hopefully. Some of her good humor resurfaced along with the memories of past hangovers. There had been a few times when she'd joined the jet-set circuit and danced the night away with bottles of the best French wines.

Instead of an answer, she felt his arm about her back and let him lift her upward as the pounding in her head rose to un-precedented levels. What had she drunk last night? In a flash, everything came back, including Javier's handsome face and her own reckless behavior. *Bodyguard.* She repeated the word in her mind. Not friend, not lover, but bodyguard. She'd tried to seduce him, only to succeed in crying all over his shirt. Gabriella turned in an attempt to bury her face in the pillow as shame burned her cheeks. But arms wrapped around her back and cool fingers cradled her neck. Something cold pressed against her lips, but Gabriella still refused to open her eyes. She wrinkled her nose at the smell and her stomach rolled.

"Is poison to be my punishment?"

"It may smell bad, but I promise it will make you feel better."

She could hear it in his voice. Gabriella opened one eye to confirm. Yes, the miserable wretch had an amused smile on his face. Swallowing the urge to vomit, she put her hands over his and tipped the contents of the glass toward her mouth. The taste was worse than the smell but she drank it all and when he removed his arms she sank gracefully back into the pillows and rolled onto her stomach. Only then did she notice the accelerated beat of her heart, the tingling warmth of her palms.

He does that to me. She squeezed her eyes tight as his fingers began to gently knead her shoulders.

"Get some rest. When you've showered and dressed, meet me in the study because we need to talk."

"About last night?"

"No."

"What else is there to talk about?"

"When you're ready, come into the study," he repeated.

Gabriella opened her eyes and studied his face. He gave no hint of what was going on but a trickle of discontent rose in the back of her mind. "All right."

"Sleep well, little one."

"Darius?"

He stilled and returned his unwavering attention to her face. "Yes?"

For a moment she couldn't speak as she was held spellbound by the glimpse of tenderness in his eyes. Gabriella smiled and burrowed under the duvet. It was a smile from her heart as she recalled the way he'd helped her last night, the tenderness of his touch as he removed her clothing and put her to bed. She re-

called every word she'd spoken of Anton and Vasilei and his as-
surance that none of what happened was her fault. "Thank you."

It was after three in the afternoon when Darius heard
Gabriella leave her bedroom. The sound of the door opening
seemed to echo through the apartment. He closed the folder
holding the photos and placed it in the center of the coffeetable.
She trusted him to keep her hidden and inadvertently he'd betrayed that trust. The FBI would know from his flight information that she was in New York.

"Darius, what's the matter?"

He stood and pushed the chair back. Walking around the
large rosewood executive desk, he came to a stop a few feet
from her. His gaze swept over her pale features and his gut
twisted. The last thing he wanted to do was upset her. But he had
no choice. His fingers curled into fists with the effort to keep
from brushing back the rebellious strands of her hair that had
left the confines of her ponytail. Darius made the mistake of inhaling deeply and his eyes locked on the bare lips he'd tasted the
night before as the scent of her perfume sent tremors through
his entire body. "Are you hungry? Do you want something to
eat?"

"No." She smiled. "I'm fine. Now will you just tell me?"

"We need to discuss Anton."

She recoiled as if he'd punched her in the stomach. "Why?"

"Because like it or not, he's coming here."

Darius watched for signs of fear and read them in her face.
First, her lips trembled, then the gold in her eyes shrunk as her
pupils dilated. The smile slipped from her face like butter in a
hot skillet. If possible, her creamy skin grew translucent and
turned the shade of alabaster.

He touched her shoulder and tried to guide her toward the
sofa but she pulled away. "Sit down before you fall down."

"Don't give me orders!" Gabriella yelled as her eyes skipped around the room like a trapped animal seeking escape. "Just tell me how he knows where I am."

"In less than forty-eight hours, government agents will tell well-placed informants in the lower ranks of Anton's organization information as to your whereabouts."

"Why would they do something like that?"

"The interests of international security."

"International security?" she echoed in disbelief. "How can this be?"

"Sit down, Gabriella." This time he didn't give her a choice; he just wrapped his arms around her and sat her on the couch. "Anton Lexer's a powerful and dangerous arms dealer who deals in the currency of death."

"Mine." Her usually sparkling eyes took on a haunted look. "He's come to kill me."

"No, I promise you that won't happen."

"You can't stop him. Vasilei had often boasted that he was the only person in the world who could challenge his brother in anything."

"Gabriella. No one." He took her shoulders and turned her toward him forcing eye contact. "No one," he emphasized, "wants you harmed. Anton is the head of a vast criminal arms dealing network that spans the globe and has caused the death of more innocents than all the diseases this world could produce. He trades arms for drugs, sells them for diamonds, and launders all the cash through Vasilei's corporations. They can't get him in the courts, they can't take him down legally, but that won't stop them from trying to shut him down. In less than three weeks, he's set to broker the sale of a large cache of anti-aircraft missiles. The Russians want those arms back and they have determined that you are Lexer's only vulnerability."

"I've got to go." Her eyes darted from him to the front door.

"No, you don't," he replied vehemently. She shook her head and did the opposite. He pulled her in closer even as she pushed to get away. Careful to keep his sensitive parts away from her kicking legs, he held tight as Gabriella's struggles ceased and her shuddered breathing calmed. Her voice lowered as her body shifted away from him.

"The trip you made . . ."

". . .was a ruse."

He ran his hand roughly over his head. "Initially I was to get more information on Vasilei Lexer. Intelligence agents picked me up at the airport, where I was to meet my contact. I was briefed and ordered by the deputy assistant director of the FBI to keep you safe but visible."

"You plan to make me the target of a killer." The bitterness in her tone filled the room and clawed at his heart.

Darius flinched. "I have no choice."

"Wrong answer."

Darius reached out to touch her and barely had enough time to block her fist. "Don't touch me!"

She stood up and he followed, heading off her attempt to leave the room.

"We need to settle this."

"We have. I'm leaving," she bit out. "Without you."

"Trust me to get you through this."

"Trust you? Oh, that's brilliant." She threw her hands up toward the ceiling. "You go behind my back to the government and set me up as bait for Anton and you still have the unmitigated nerve to ask me to trust you?"

"There was no choice."

Gabriella seemed to shrink inward, her gold eyes going distant. Where the hurt had ripped him with sharp claws, the sting of her withdrawal was worse. He wanted her hot with anger.

"You always have a choice. Just leave me alone, Darius." Tears did not fill her eyes but he could have drowned in the pool of hurt that he heard in her voice.

"Yes, and I made it." Darius grabbed her by her shoulders and she fought him tooth and nail, but he made no move as she beat at his chest. He just let her vent, even as part of him recoiled from the strength of her anger. This situation was of his own making. He'd gained her trust, snuck into her private life, and pulled her into a dangerous situation.

Even after Gabriella's repeated attempts to pull away, he knew she was listening; the amount that got through he wouldn't be able to tell but at least he could try. For the first time since he'd seen the look of betrayal in her eyes, he felt hope.

"Little one," he murmured softly, lovingly, even as guilt stabbed him hard. She had trusted him completely and in his quest to keep her from harm he may have diminished something precious, something that would take time for him to regain. "My duty has always been and will always be to protect you, no matter what. I would never leave you vulnerable to attack. By allowing the FBI to think that I would help them, it gives me time—time to figure a way out of this mess and to keep you safe."

She took a deep shuddered breath. "What is it exactly that they want me to do?"

"They need you as a decoy. The more energy and time Anton puts into finding you, the more time it gives them to locate the arms cache. They need you to be bait."

"And what about *you*?" she emphasized. "Do you need me to be bait?"

"I need to keep you safe."

"Liar." Her eyes held a diminished level of anger and the tightness in his chest eased somewhat. Anger was something he could use to keep her focused.

"I've never lied to you and I don't intend to start. My mission has never changed and that is to protect you. I had no knowledge of Anton's activities; only in my quest to keep you safe was I caught in this web. In the intelligence business, information is a double-edged sword. In trying to gather information on Vasilei, I used my nonmilitary sources and that got me pulled into the joint FBI/FSB operation."

"Secrets and lies, Darius. You can lie by omission. Just like my father, just like Vasilei. So tell me, what else have you kept from me?"

"I've been ordered to bring you out of hiding, but I won't."

He caught the slight quiver of her bottom lip. "Then there's no problem."

"Yes, there is, Princess. The clock is ticking and they will find you, Gabriella. It's only a matter of time until they do. The FBI has considerable resources and somehow they will get to you either by tracking or by force. They aren't above giving up your father to Anton."

"Whose side are you on, Darius?" she asked.

He brushed back her hair, then took her face within his hands in order to fully connect with her. "Yours. I'm asking you to help bring this man to justice. Assist the authorities in taking him down and you won't have to run and hide. You'll be able to play the flute in any venue to thousands or a small audience of one."

Her lip trembled and he used the pad of his thumb to caress it. "I can't," she whispered. "Please don't ask me."

"Gabriella." She took his hand within her own and then moved forward catching him off guard to place her lips against his own. Her kiss tasted of desperation and despair. Her tongue sought and gained entrance in his mouth as her fingers found purchase on the back of his neck and pulled him to her.

He would have given anything to have taken her there on the couch. He wanted to pull her against him and get lost in the need that had been growing ever since he'd laid eyes on her.

Darius didn't want to walk away from her any more than he could cut out his own heart, but he had to. He pressed his hands to the side of her cheeks and separated them. And it cost him because he had halfway fallen in love with her. The price of that emotion was paid by every muscle in his body tightening to a point that bordered on pain. "Listen to me."

"No."

He stared into her eyes darkened and unseeing with passion. As she tried to kiss him again, he grabbed her wrists and held them.

"Listen," he repeated. "You can't run and you can't hide from this."

She took his words like a physical blow and her face turned away even as her body bowed away from him. Darius pulled air into his lungs, then gently shook Gabriella to get her full attention. "Anton Lexer has profited off of the deaths of hundreds and will spill the blood of thousands of innocents, but you have the power to help stop him once and for all, Gabriella."

"They can just find another way to get to him."

Loosening his grip on her arms, he gentled his voice. "If you need to find something to give you strength, something to hold on to that eases your fears, then know that you are needed. This is about more than you. People's lives are at stake and the Gabriella who snuck hundred dollar bills to homeless men outside of Penn Station is not a selfish woman."

Darius stood up and pointed to the folder on the coffeetable. "When you're ready to do the right thing, open that folder. To do what's right, open it, and look at the suffering that Anton has caused."

It had to be the hardest thing that Darius ever had to do to leave her curled in a ball in the study. Before leaving the room he looked back for only a moment and saw her slender fingers reach for the folder. He closed his eyes and quietly shut the door behind him.

Darius left the room and went into the kitchen. He looked down at his watch, careful to keep his movements quiet so that he could hear the sound of Gabriella's footsteps. When he finally heard them, they didn't come in his direction but opposite.

"Damn it." He rushed toward the back hallway and reached the guest bathroom in time to see her bent over the toilet as her body was wracked with dry heaves. He'd seen the pictures. The wreckage of a small plane, little boys holding guns. Dead bodies in decay, maimed soldiers, but he was sure that it was the sight of children that sent her into such a state.

"I have tea prepared in the kitchen." He spoke calmly while

wetting a washcloth with cold water, then placing it on the back of her neck.

"He's a monster." Her voice trembled.

Darius remained silent as she pulled away and second by second seemed to recover herself.

"I'll make a bargain with you," she said after rinsing her mouth a second time. The taste of her fear and disgust still clung to the back of her throat. "If I am going to help you, then all I ask is that you give me one day to go wherever I want and do what I want."

"Gabriella—"

"I have no need to hide, right?" she cut him off. "The only way that Anton will stay focused is if he has a visible moving target. And if I'm to be the deer to his hunt then there's someone I need to see."

"Your father called while you were asleep. He's expecting to return in two days."

"Fine." Gabriella averted her eyes from Darius's. The dark orbs of his seemed to look past her skin and read her soul and she could not let him see her deceit. She wanted to see Nonna, her old nanny, before she ran. It would seem that she would see her father as well.

Katherine Lexer blinked her eyes to keep the tears from falling. That Vasilei had sought out her counsel in private was a moment she'd spent half her life hoping for. Yet, it was the cause of his sudden visit and mood of the conversation that upset her so. Her son was in pain.

Restless, she stood up from the settee and left the sitting room. Her satin slippered feet moved quietly over the thick carpet. Most early evenings she loved the silence of the house, but today it seemed that thoughts of her son—of both her sons— would allow her no comfort. Before she knew it, Katherine entered the music room. It was her favorite room in the large manor Dmitry had purchased after their exile from Slovenia.

Taking a seat at the piano, she ran her French-manicured fingertips along the keys and stared absentmindedly out of the lace-covered French windows leading to the garden. The world outside was unnaturally brightened by the moonlight reflecting off the snow.

Katherine had never seen Vasilei so happy as when Gabriella was with him. It was a joy to watch from the sidelines as her son wooed the beautiful American. The strength of his pursuit reminded her of the days when she and her husband had been first married, before his rise to power in the Communist party.

She'd despaired that Vasilei would always be alone or spend his life discarding one mistress after another. Yet, somehow the young woman had managed not only to capture her son's heart but Katherine's as well. For a brief moment, true happiness had returned to the Lexer family.

Anton would not have it so, a part of her whispered.

Her fingers stopped as the image of her oldest son rose in her mind. Katherine had miscarried three times before giving birth to Anton. Vasilei had been a surprise to them all and they had all loved him, Anton more so.

"You wished to see me, Mother?"

Startled, Katherine's finger pressed down and a discordant note rang through the room.

"Anton." She stood and waited as he walked over and kissed her cheek. "You look well."

Indeed, he looked almost happy, and although it made her heart glad, she had to wonder at the cause of this cheer.

"As do you." His manner had always been formal yet polite. Katherine had marveled at how such a young boy could be so well mannered and quiet. Anton never disobeyed and was seldom far from Vasilei as they'd grown up. The two had been inseparable and remarkably similar in physical characteristics. Both shared uncommon good looks, broad shoulders, and proud carriage.

"Shall we talk in the sitting room?" he asked.

"Of course. Would you like something to drink? Brandy?"

"No thank you, Mother." He smiled sweetly. "I have a business engagement later."

"Anton," she scolded, "you work too hard. It's hardly fitting for someone at your level to be conducting meetings at all hours of the night."

He shrugged. "I do what needs to be done. Now what is it you wanted to speak to me about?"

"Your brother."

"What has happened?"

Katherine drew back at the intensity of Anton's voice.

"Nothing," she said quickly and settled herself on the sofa. "I'm just worried."

"Your talk did not go well?"

She nodded. Even as children, Anton would know of Vasilei's location at all times. It was her husband's doing. It had come to a point when they were teenagers when Katherine suspected that Dmitry had trained their oldest son to be the protector of their youngest.

"Even though he did not once mention her name, I know he misses Gabriella terribly, Anton. Do you know why she disappeared?"

"You've heard the rumors."

She waved a dismissive hand. "Vasilei is too much like his father. If—and I mean if—he were to have an affair, it would be discreet and never with such a brainless woman."

"Does it matter why she left? She was not right for him."

"She made him happy."

"Is he happy now? She ran like a thief in the night, crushing my brother's heart." As he spoke, Anton's Russian accent thickened.

"She was in love with my son. Of that I am sure."

Anton shrugged. "What is done is done. Vas will learn to accept it."

Katherine shook her head. "But I won't. I want to talk to Gabriella."

She watched as he drew himself up. "You should stay out of this."

"When I am old and on my deathbed, then you can dictate to me. Until that time comes I expect to be treated with respect and obeyed without question. Bring her to me."

He sighed and ran his fingers through his silver tinted hair. Katherine's eyes fell upon his signet ring and her heart caught. Dmitry had been so proud the day he had given the rings to their sons.

"It's not that easy, Mother. Vas already has investigators searching for Gabriella."

"You don't approve?" she surmised. Decades of practice reading her husband's minute movements and expressions had taught her well. The way Anton's eyes narrowed as he crossed his legs sent warning bells off in her head.

"I want to find her as much as Vasilei, but I won't lie to you." He crossed his legs and leaned back. "She isn't worthy of him," he bit out. "That she is common is not the worst. She is a woman of great beauty, but she is a mongrel. Vas should choose amongst those of his class and breeding."

"Anton . . ." she sat back stunned at his vehemence. Katherine had only been aware of the tension between her sons when the topic of Vasilei's upcoming nuptials was discussed. Yet, the blazing dislike in his eyes bordered on irrational hatred.

"I mean no disrespect, Mother." He leaned forward and rubbed his hands roughly over his legs. "But what is it with this woman? Gabriella can bring ruin down on us, but Vas speaks of nothing else but her. We're on the line to deliver a shipment in less than two months, and I must use valuable resources to locate her."

Katherine sat still as her oldest son stood and began to pace. "She is a witch; maybe she has cast a spell over my brother. It would be better for everyone if he forgot about her."

"You know as well as I do that Vasilei won't let go so easily."

"This time he won't have a choice."

She stood and moved closer to him. "What have you done, Anton?"

The ringing of a cell phone interrupted the conversation.

She looked away, pretending not to strain for every word. "You are certain she is in New York?" he demanded to the person on the other end of the line.

Someone on the other end spoke. "Have the jet fueled and ready to take off. We leave tonight," Vasilei replied.

"Anton, what have you done?" she asked for a second time.

"I must go."

"Wait, we aren't finished."

He paid her no heed. "Take care, Mother."

Her son came over to the sofa, kissed her on the cheek, and left the room. Katherine stared at the empty chair, unable to shake the feeling of foreboding that ran down her spine. Anton would never harm Vasilei; the love he had for his younger brother was at times frightening in its intensity. Her husband had only encouraged the bond.

Katherine shivered as she made her way along the silent hallway toward the stairwell. The staff had long since retired for the evening. Stopping at the bottom stair, she placed her left hand on the cold banister. It had taken only one night to make her feel the sum of her age and the full sorrowed frustration of Dmitry's death.

Slowly taking the stairs one-by-one, Katherine wiped a furtive tear from her eyes. She'd tried so hard to provide the proper guidance for her children, but her sons were changing right before her eyes. In her heart of hearts, Katherine knew she would never sway Anton from the dark allure of power. But she wouldn't let that happen to her youngest son. If reuniting Vasilei with Gabriella would keep him from falling under Anton's influence, then she would make sure that in this chase, her youngest came in first.

Chapter
Thirteen

Gabriella pulled the brush through her hair, styled it into a bun, and then stared at herself in the mirror. She hadn't worn a bun since her mother died when she was thirteen years old. Her Aunt Colette had woken her in the pre-dawn hours to get her ready for the funeral. Her mother's family and the people on the island had remarked upon how beautiful Gabriella was. How like Josette.

She gave herself another critical going over, straightened her long skirt, secured the last button of her blouse, and then left the bathroom. She walked past the balcony windows and into the kitchen, paying no heed to the beginning of snow falling lightly outside. Instead, Gabriella measured out coffee, filled the machine with water, and stood there staring at the dark brown liquid dripping into the glass coffee pot.

Even the smell couldn't distract her from the thought that in less than an hour she would be seeing Nonna, the Dominican woman who was so much a part of her past and one of the closest links she had to her childhood except for Sebastian. She wondered what Nonna would think of her. She had written her ex-nanny every day when she had first arrived at boarding school, but her musical study and increasing schoolwork had slowed the regularity of her letters. Yet, without fail, every month a letter from New York would arrive and Nonna would tell her news of her family and the exciting life of Harlem.

After the coffee finished brewing, she pulled out a mug and poured herself a cup. She had just finished adding milk and sugar, when the creak of an opening door alerted her to Darius's impending presence. Holding her cup, Gabriella walked out of the kitchen and met him in the living room.

"You're still going?"

Gabriella nodded, then took a seat on the couch. She inclined her head toward the kitchen. "There's a fresh pot of coffee in the kitchen. Help yourself."

"We might want to get a move on before the snow gets any heavier."

She glanced out of the glass balcony doors. The rate of snowfall hadn't changed since she'd gotten dressed that morning. "I don't think a few more minutes will matter too much."

He shrugged. "It's your appointment."

She gave him a close look. It wasn't like him. Then again, after her aborted seduction, drunken confession, the revelation of Anton's arrival, and their subsequent fight, nothing was like him. Instead of smiles or gentle suggestions, Darius delivered instructions and warnings in a brusque and cold manner.

It seemed that during the night his companionable spirit had been stolen away. She shivered at the remembrance of waking up in the morning and wanting his closeness only to turn and find herself alone in the bed. The sense of purpose clung to him more openly, and she couldn't move without him being close.

"So where is it that you want me to take you?" he asked, leaning against the doorway.

"Harlem," she answered, not liking the way he regarded her. It wasn't as though he stared through her as Anton had done in the past. Darius's look was intense, as though he would strip her of all her thoughts and lay bare the secrets of her soul.

"Who or what's in Harlem?"

"Is that any of your business?" she snapped back, watching as he unbuttoned his leather coat and settled himself comfortably in the seat opposite the couch.

"If it affects your safety, yes."

"A friend of the family." She stood up and stepped past his legs and made her way back to the kitchen. Gabriella placed the cup in the sink and wiped her hands on the towel.

"There's no need to make this any harder than it already is, Gabriella." His voice came from the direction of the doorway.

"Tell me, Darius." She took a step forward with her chin raised. "How much harder can this be? I feel like a caged animal when what I truly am is bait."

She spun on the heels of her boots, left the kitchen, and walked toward the front door of the apartment. Gabriella grabbed her handbag and was reaching into the closet for her long coat when Darius's arm shot past her and grabbed it off the hanger.

"Let me." His voice was more of an order than an invitation.

She gave him a questioning glance, turned around, and let him help her into her coat, then waited for him to move away.

When he didn't move, she inhaled a sharp breath at the sensation of his fingers gliding over the nape of her neck. It seemed as though something warm and smooth lapped over her skin. She could smell the faint scent of sandalwood that clung to him as everything slowed.

Kiss him, an inner voice taunted her. *Kiss him and see if he loses his cool. Find out if you're the only one burning.*

Her head fell forward in a gesture that almost begged invitation to a kiss on her neck. And the warmth of his breath on the back of her neck sent shivers ricocheting throughout her entire body.

When he turned her around, she still didn't lift her face to his. Only the slight pressure of his finger on her chin forced her to look upward. Her tongue darted out over her parched lips and she watched in amazement as Darius's eyes darkened.

"You're staring," he told her.

"I'm trying not to." Although she said the words, she was no more able to look away than she was to stop herself from breathing.

"I want . . ."

"What?" The shallowness of her own voice surprised her.

"To kiss you until you moan."

Gabriella swallowed hard. "But?"

Darius reached out and ran his fingertips over her cheeks. "I've said this before. I'm your bodyguard, Gabriella. We can't get personally involved. Not now. Maybe not ever. Hell. I can't promise you anything because all I have I've always given to my country. My team."

"I haven't asked you for anything."

"That's the trouble. You don't have to."

She shook her head. "I don't understand."

"You don't have to ask for things I would give freely." He loomed over her and placed his hands on either side of her face.

Just looking up at him made the place in the center of her stomach warm as though she'd swallowed a glass of brandy. His face. God, there should be a law against the beauty of his features. The bronze of his skin against the white of his teeth, the midnight-black eyebrows. She would never forget his face. Unlike nightmares that haunted her dreams, this would be far worse. Gabriella stuck her hands in her pocket and turned away from Darius, but it would do no good. In the deepest space of her heart, he would always be there.

The trip to Harlem was accomplished in minutes. The northern Manhattan neighborhood lived up to its acclaimed past and vibrant present. Snow-covered cars lined the streets as groups of heavily bundled school kids trudged down the barely shoveled sidewalks. When Darius turned onto One Hundred Thirty-sixth Street, his eyes scanned to the right and left, glancing over the numbered homes as he looked for the address on the piece of paper Gabriella had given him. The well-kept townhouses along with the newer model luxury cars reassured him of the relative wealth of the neighborhood.

Seeing a lack of parking spaces, he circled around the block three times before finding a spot to parallel park the Land Rover. "You okay?"

"I'm just reliving some great memories." Gabriella turned toward him with a soft smile. "Sometimes when my mother picked up a late shift, Nonna would bring me home and I would stay the night."

"So your childhood wasn't all bad, was it?"

She dropped her gaze and then leaned her head back against the headrest. "I never said it was all bad."

"Really?"

"Yes," she gave him a sideways glance. "Now would you get that smug look off your face so we can go?"

"Yes, ma'am." Darius flicked off his seat belt, then leaned over and trailed his fingers over her cheek. Something in him calmed when he touched her. Even the casual touch.

She took his fingers within her own and sighed. "Thank you." Gabriella shook her head. "Am I ever going to be able to stop thanking you?"

"I hope not."

Darius looked up and down the tree-lined street after getting out of the truck and then escorted Gabriella to the house and up the stone steps to ring the doorbell of a large chestnut door.

"Welcome."

Politeness dictated that he allow Gabriella to enter the door first, but safety necessitated his inching forward and following behind the older woman who had greeted them. He caught Gabriella's look of irritation out of the corner of his eyes. He shrugged and resumed examining the layout of the home.

African-American art blended smoothly with its ancestral roots. The gleaming wood floors were covered partially with a plush handwoven rug. Paintings, which were softly backlit with track lighting, graced the cream-colored walls. The scent of home cooking blended with the faint musk of incense and jasmine.

The living room opened to a dining room that was more family oriented than formal. A table of deepest mahogany was graced with a bright arrangement of flowers. Twelve-foot ceilings allowed for both space and comfort.

"Let me take your coats."

"Thank you, Marcella." They both shed their coats and waited as the woman put them into a side closet.

"Now that we've got that out of the way, I think introductions are in order." Although the woman addressed the comment to Gabriella, Darius noted that she never took her eyes off him.

"I'm sorry. This is Darius Yassoud." She hesitated.

Darius took advantage of her brief silence to place his arm around her waist, draw her close, and place a kiss on Gabriella's cheek. "The man that wants to marry her if she'll have me."

The comment earned him a swift jab in the side. Yet, he lost neither his grip nor his smile. The idea had come upon him in an instant, and the words penetrated somewhere deep in his soul.

A large smile spread over Marcella's face. "Well, well. I would love to hear the story behind that announcement, but I'm sure Nonna wants to get the scoop first. She's been asking about you all morning."

Gabriella smiled at Nonna's daughter. "I appreciate you allowing us to drop by at such short notice."

"No problem at all. I just ask that you try not to wear Grandmamma out."

"Go ahead, Gabriella. I'll be right here," Darius urged.

"No." She took his hand. "I want you to meet her."

Surprise held him still for a moment, but he gave her hand a gentle squeeze and let her guide him toward the stairs leading to the second floor. Gabriella raised her hand and knocked on the door farthest from the stairwell.

"Come in," a voice called softly.

He let go of her hand and stood in the doorway, watching as she rushed across the room and into the arms of a small woman who sat enthroned in the king-sized bed among half a dozen pillows.

A TV remote control, paperback novels, an aged, tattered leather Bible, knitting needles, a ball of yarn, and a stack of magazines littered the woman's bed. This was but one of Gabriella's stipulations that he'd agreed to. In return for her cooperation, he'd agreed to allow her to visit this house and see her old nanny. The second, a trip to the Metropolitan Museum of Art, would be taking place the next day. Darius scanned the room and knew that this would be the easier of her two requests. The museum, with its crowds of tourists, would provide Anton and his people ample opportunities to come after Gabriella.

"Oh child, if you don't look the spitting image of your mother," the woman said before turning her bespeckled gaze toward Darius. "And who is this young gentleman? He sure doesn't look Eastern European."

He took five steps into the room and bowed his head respectfully. "Darius Yassoud at your service, ma'am."

"Well, don't just stand there." She waved a long fingered hand. "Have a seat."

Darius grinned, as his earlier assessment of the older woman rang true. A queen on her throne. He eased gently into an overstuffed recliner and kept his feet planted on the floor instead of taking advantage of the matching ottoman. Superbly comfortable, Darius relaxed and waited. He listened as Gabriella talked about boarding school, her friends, her trips, her music, and at the end, her life with Vasilei until she felt her voice would give out.

"You've made such a success. I used to worry that I'd made the wrong decision calling your father and telling him it'd be best to take you away from your mother's people."

"You called Sebastian?"

Darius drew to attention at the high pitch of Gabriella's voice.

"Yes, I did." Nonna nodded. "I stayed with you down on that island for two weeks and each day I felt I'd made the wrong decision. Your mother's people didn't let you run wild because you were grieving. They were ashamed that your mother never married your father."

"What?"

"Oh yes. Those Maries were something else, Baby. The only reason they wanted to take you was for the money, not any sense of family obligation."

Nonna coughed and Gabriella instantly reached for the carafe of water to pour her a glass.

"I've prayed about you so."

"I don't know what to say." Gabriella shook her head.

"Just tell me you're happy."

"Of course."

Darius smiled, then excused himself to go downstairs. Nonna's daughter looked up from writing at an antique secretary. "So, potential marriage candidate, would you like a cup of coffee?"

Darius smiled and glanced back toward the stairs. "I'll just have a glass of water if you don't mind."

"All right. Come on back. Watch your step though; I'm having a security system put in and the man just left for lunch."

"Trouble?"

"I've lived in the house half of my life and we've never had any problems." Then she caught herself. "That is, there haven't been any problems until the other day."

Darius focused all his attention on Marcella, but forced himself to ask casually, "What did they take?"

"Nothing."

"What?"

She smiled, pulled a glass out of the cabinet, then walked toward the refrigerator. "I know. We were in church that morning and came home to find the front door cracked open. The police thought it was crazy, too. Apparently the person entered through the second floor window."

"Do they have any clues?"

"Not a one. The police thought it might be some of the local youth playing a prank, but I know all the kids that live in the area. No matter, the thought of some stranger coming into our house and going through our private belongings is unsettling."

"Thanks." He smiled and took the glass from her outstretched hand. He took a sip and the ice-cold water poured down his throat and over the rock that had formed in his stomach at the mention of the break-in. Following behind Marcella as they made their way back to the front of the house, Darius shook his head and looked toward the curtained window. Time, it seemed, may have already run out.

Chapter
Fourteen

The Upper West Side of Manhattan was every beautiful image she remembered and more. Flush with a large Spanish lunch, hot tea, and butter cookies, Gabriella turned toward Darius. "Some Saturday mornings when Sebastian left for Europe, my mother and I would wander around from room to room at the Metropolitan Museum of Art looking at various paintings, sculptures, and artifacts and wondering about the people who made them. What were their lives like? What would they think if they knew that their mummified bodies or personal possessions were on display?"

Darius turned and looked at her with a thoughtful expression on his handsome face. "I never thought about that."

She shrugged, turned up the collar of her long winter coat, and put on her gloves. "It's not a comfortable idea. I even shy away from the thought of someone centuries from now digging up my coffin and putting me on exhibit for all to see."

They turned the corner on Eighty-second Street between Park and Madison Avenue. The street was lined with small trees and beautifully restored townhouses that served as homes or offices. As luck seemed to constantly smile upon him, Darius found a parking spot. Then he held out a hand to Gabriella as he helped her from the Land Rover. His hands were as strong and long fingered as any surgeon's. Yet she could also imagine them wrapped around a gun.

He turned toward her with a grin. "You'd make a nice looking mummy."

Gabriella laughed as she walked over to him, then paused, staring at his outstretched hand.

"Princess, just for today, why don't we just block out the world and imagine that we are all alone without a care," he said.

She looked into his face and didn't need to see the eyes behind the sunglasses to know that he was sincere. He wanted them to be a normal couple on a date and Gabriella couldn't help but want the same thing. Taking a step forward onto the sidewalk, she placed her hand in his. As they walked toward the museum, she began to explain her fascination with Egyptian art and excitement at seeing the new exhibit.

"So you wanted to be Indiana Jones as well as a concert flutist?" he asked smiling.

"Not necessarily." She shook her head. "I wanted no part of the danger stuff. I imagined that I would be digging through caves, exploring the pyramids, and combing excavation sites for shards of pottery or pieces of jewelry."

"What would you have found?"

"I think my obsession would have been to find the burial site of Nefertiti. There's so much mystery surrounding her life; no one knows where she came from or who she was. She just appeared out of the shadows and went on to become one of the most famous and beloved of all the ancient Egyptian queens. I was able to see the bust of her on display in the Egyptian Museum in Berlin. The person who created it has to be one of the most skilled artists of all time."

"You are a wonder. I had no idea that you were such a historian," he commented.

"Thanks," Gabriella replied, embarrassed and warmed by his praise.

They approached the steps of the museum and joined the tour group heading for the entrance. It seemed people had barely begun to trickle into the Met when they arrived. Being one of the most popular tourist destinations in New York City, the place would be packed by noon. Darius motioned for her to wait on the side of the entrance gate while he bought the tickets. The line moved swiftly and within moments he returned to her side holding the entrance pins.

Holding up a bright green metal pin, he asked, "May I?"

"Please."

Darius slowly lowered his hands to a stop over Gabriella's heart and gently slipped the pin on her shirt. After he placed his pin on, they entered into the first hall and walked toward the entrance.

She had only taken a few steps before muted silence and Egyptian artifacts surrounded her. To the right were displays filled with colorful jewelry, pots, ornaments, and miniature statuettes. All the pictures she had seen in books were brought to life before her eyes.

The atmosphere of the room was soft and warm. Tall ceilings and subdued lighting served to accentuate the ancient pieces on display. It would be easy to imagine being transported back to the days when Egypt was the center of the world. Caught up in the moment, Gabriella forgot that she wasn't alone. She turned to see Darius staring at a royal Egyptian necklace.

"It's beautiful, isn't it?" she said quietly.

He nodded. "I was just reading the translation of the hieroglyphics in the pendant. 'The god of the rising sun grants life and domination over all that the sun encircles for eternity to King Senwosret II.' My grandfather told me once that the ancestors believed that jewelry worn by ancient Egyptian women was more than cosmetic or status related. Egyptians felt that the precious stones and metals that comprised the jewelry were symbolic."

"In what way?" Gabriella asked.

"I read that the ancient Egyptian women believed that their jewelry gave them supernatural powers. They would use those powers to support the King, and he in turn would benefit from the power in the jewelry worn by the females in his family. That's why the hieroglyphs note the name of the king and not the princess who wore it."

"Figures," she commented dryly.

Quietly chuckling, Darius placed his arm around her waist and they slowly moved through the exhibits with the growing crowd of tourists. The third room they entered was the largest of the areas that they'd previously visited. The room was filled with light and open space. Large Egyptian statuettes and columns hung on all of the walls. Toward the back of the room, she saw the object that had first drawn her to the study of Egyptian history. Letting go of his hand, she ignored the coffin that Darius was intent on studying.

There, off to the side but bathed in a soft spotlight, lay a sphinx. Walking around the statue, she felt a childlike excitement and fought the urge to run her hands along its side. Glancing up, she saw a museum guard. As though he could read her mind, he smiled at her wonder before turning his head to survey the room.

The sphinx looked as though it was carved from some smooth blue stone. With the body of a lion and head of a king, it lay in a crouched position. The statue was in excellent condition. The rear of the lion smoothly transformed into human hands, arms, and a youthful face. The statuette was remarkably preserved.

She was so intent in studying the human head, which was covered by a royal headdress with the image of a cobra in its middle, Gabriella started at the touch on her shoulder.

"You okay? I called your name but you didn't answer," Darius said. "Want to tell me about him?" He gestured toward the artifact.

"It was a while ago so I might not have all the facts straight. Because lions were the strongest and most feared animals in prehistoric times, they were linked with the Egyptian kings. The sphinx was considered to be a powerful guardian against evil. With the body of a lion and the head of the king, it was symbolic of royal power. The Egyptians viewed the standing sphinx as that of a conqueror and the crouching sphinx as a guardian of holy places. It's stunning."

"I couldn't agree with you more."

Gabriella turned and found Darius's eyes intent upon her face instead of the statue and quickly looked away as her heartbeat sped up. Turning away from the sphinx, she continued walking toward the doorway to the next room.

Time seemed to hold no meaning as they went from piece to piece exploring the rooms filled with artifacts. Taking a break, Darius and Gabriella sat on a small stone bench and observed the people who passed by. They both smiled at a group of parents and their children and watched as the mothers tried to keep their kids from touching the museum pieces while the fathers paged through the guidebooks trying to find the nearest bathroom or exit.

Gabriella cut her eyes sideways at Darius. Even in such a safe setting with tourists and kids of all ages milling around, he moved warily with an animal alert motion. It seemed that his attention never stayed in one place. Here they were, surrounded by some of the most fascinating objects in history, yet he scanned the area for danger. He didn't have his gun in a side holster, but if she lifted the back of his leather jacket, she'd see the dull black handle of one.

Two days ago, she'd learned Anton was getting closer to killing her. Today, she'd learned that her nanny was the one who'd asked Sebastian to ship her off to boarding school. With all those thoughts whirling like a storm in her mind and practicing the flute not being the least bit helpful, she'd asked Darius to bring her here.

Gabriella sighed and turned her attention back toward the viewing screen that advertised the museum's admission prices and special exhibition time schedules.

Nothing would ruin this day, she vowed, pulling herself out of her gloomy thoughts. Something that she had thought lost after leaving Vasilei had returned: hope. Maybe her life would return to some sense of normality; maybe she could come to forgive her father; maybe she could make peace with the past and have a happy future.

All those thoughts and more she put to the back of her mind, letting the ambiance and the wonder of the moment along with the excited voices of the school kids sweep over her. After collecting tickets for the butterfly exhibition, she smiled and impulsively reached out and took Darius's hand. The look of surprise on his face was well worth the risk.

"Darius." She pulled him closer to the edge of the hall. Gabriella had gotten caught up in the school children's excitement at seeing the ancient artifacts, famous paintings, sculptures, and other exhibits, but it was here that she stood transfixed. The exquisite reproduction of a rainforest, with the myriads of butterflies flitting about the curved roof, took her breath away.

She unconsciously took a step toward Darius, seeking somehow to share her wonder with him. They'd waited in the queue for less than ten minutes and all the while she'd gazed through the transparent wall to see the inside of the nestled structure. It was a world within a room and it was beautiful.

"Little warm in here, don't you think?" Darius commented after they stepped through the arched entranceway.

Gabriella turned her attention from watching a small butterfly glide over her head. The smell of blossoming flowers mingled with the thick warm smell of verdant earth. Her lips curled into a soft smile. "No, it reminds me of home."

"This reminds you of New York?" he asked incredulously.

She shook her head and drew him aside to let a couple pass. "My mother was born in Curaçao, raised in St. Martin, and then moved to New York to be with my father. Each summer we'd go to the island and spend time with her family."

"Is it this . . . green?" His eyes stopped their scanning and centered on her face.

She laughed softly. "No, this is a simulation of a rain-forest. There's a lot of vegetation but nothing like this."

They resumed their walk along the narrow serpentine path. Tropical plants of various shapes and sizes surrounded them as did the silent fluttering of butterflies either in the air or dancing among the orchids and ferns. *So fragile*, Gabriella reflected, watching as a small tiger-striped butterfly landed on a leaf by her hand.

"So I guess you know a lot about butterflies?"

"Not really." She gave him a quizzical look. "I just paid attention during biology class. Some things about butterflies might surprise you."

"Such as?" he encouraged.

"They communicate by smell."

"Ah."

Gabriella watched Darius raise an eyebrow. "Their antennae are very sensitive to certain odors," she continued.

"So they can smell us?"

"Most likely, but they're not interested in us."

"Why is that?"

"The male butterfly produces pheromones to seduce the females. He uses his eyes to locate her and then woos her with scent."

He moved closer and tugged a stray lock of Gabriella's hair. "So if he has the right cologne, he can have his own harem?"

"Something like that. In some cases, they perform an intricate courtship flight."

"What else?"

"See the color of the wings?" She pointed toward a group of Monarch butterflies. "They're actually covered with tiny colored scales, much like a snake."

"That one, too?"

"No, that one's different." She eyed a winged creature the size of her two fists together. "That's a moth."

"How'd you know?"

She chuckled before pointing to a picture of the giant moth in her brochure.

Darius shrugged. "Still looks like a butterfly to me."

"Being in your line of work, I would have thought you'd know that looks can be deceiving."

"Sometimes I forget. Yet it seems that fate has a habit of sending me a reminder."

Half an hour later, as they prepared to leave the building, Gabriella reached the second floor level and turned back to look at Darius only to see that both of them were surrounded by a group of high school students as they entered into the alcove separating two of the exhibition halls.

"Darius." She waved and tried to move toward him but was pushed back. Just then she noticed a young Latino woman nearby who was also trying to move away from the stairs leading down into the lover level of the museum.

Gabriella felt a touch on her sleeve and instinctively pulled away. Her hand flew to her mouth as the woman she'd been standing next to let out a shrill scream. All she could do was watch in horror as the woman tumbled down the stone stairwell. For a second, silence reigned and then pandemonium broke out amongst the students.

Gabriella stood stupefied, barely cognizant of the conversations swirling around her.

"Did you see that?"

"Man, I saw her fall."

"You? I saw it all. The dude with the cap pushed her, man."

"Yeah, man. She tried to grab that other chick's jacket and then she went flying down the stairs. It was just like in the movies."

"Gabriella!"

She looked over to see Darius at her side. "We've got to get out of here."

"The woman—" she muttered, but couldn't finish as he grabbed her hand and pulled her away from the increasing crowd of people.

"She'll be fine." With fast and efficient movements, they weaved through the crowd of onlookers toward the exit.

"I shouldn't have jerked away," Gabriella finally managed to get out once they reached the museum's entrance rotunda. It was all she could do to keep up with his fast-paced strides.

"It would only have brought both of you down."

She lengthened her stride as Darius led them out of the building and down the sidewalk toward the car. Gabriella's breath came in puffs and the sound of motorists driving up and down Central Park West cut off any hopes of conversation.

However, Gabriella wouldn't give up on the idea that she could have somehow prevented the woman's fall. "Still—"

Darius increased his pace while pulling her into a crowd of people. "Look, stop second guessing yourself. It was an accident."

Much later that night, after returning to the apartment and making some phone calls, Darius leaned back against the headboard of the bed and sighed. The possibility that today's incident had been an accident had all but dropped to zero. Anton's agents had followed them to the museum. Yet, he'd made damned sure they didn't follow them back to the apartment. The knock on the door startled Darius from his reading. "Come in."

"Hi."

He put the notebook computer on his lap aside, then moved to stand up.

"No, don't get up." Gabriella motioned but Darius instantly disobeyed. The sight of her eyes locked on his bare chest lit a match to his sexual desires. Falling back on the excuse of propriety and not the temptation of allowing her looks to lead his thoughts along with his body in a more physical direction, he reached over and put on his shirt.

"What can I do for you?"

"This is the first time I've been in your bedroom."

Nervous, he concluded. Gabriella was definitely nervous. There was nothing remarkable in his room except the large iron-framed bed and the heavy wood furniture. "It's a little late for a tour, don't you think? Or is it a midnight snack you're after?"

"Would you make me one if I asked?"

"Maybe."

The smile disappeared from her lips and he wished he had answered the question in a different way. Even in the low glow of the light, he could see her face, the delicate mixture of Caribbean and Dutch.

"I can't sleep."

"Nightmares?"

She nodded.

"Want me to read you a bedtime story?" he asked. All kidding aside, he'd do it; he'd tell her a story from his childhood. Hell, he'd tell her anything to erase the shadows under her eyes and the pinched expression on her lovely face.

Her lips thinned as she walked over to the bed; he barely managed to dodge the flying pillow. "Hey!"

"I'm trying to be serious here."

"As was I." He rose from the bed, stood, and walked toward her. "Tell me what's on your mind."

"Today at the museum. That woman's fall wasn't an accident, Darius. I think that she was pushed."

"Gabriella," he interjected, seeing the paleness of her tightly clenched hands.

"Don't lie to me or sugarcoat the truth. I need to know if Anton's in New York."

"Not yet. But I got confirmation that a few more of his men arrived last night."

She sucked in a deep shuddering breath. "Oh, God."

This time, not even duty would stop him from taking her into his arms. Each shudder that racked her body slit a line in his heart. "Shh, I'll protect you."

"But who will protect you? Who will protect the people who get in Anton's way?"

"Let's not borrow trouble, Princess."

"Like the woman in the museum?" A tremor wracked her body. "Part of me just wants this over with."

"It will be. Anton'll make a mistake and the authorities will be there to put him away, permanently." That was if Darius didn't do it first. "Come on. Let's get you back to bed."

"Can I sleep here with you?" She looked up at him with wide trusting eyes.

"I don't think that'd be a good idea."

"I trust you."

The problem was that he didn't trust himself. Especially given the fact that he still held her in his arms and couldn't seem to let go. The herbal scent of her hair was damned intoxicating.

"Your bed is just as large as mine," she observed. "You can stay on one side and I'll stay on the other."

"Look—"

She cut him off. "Are you trying to tell me that such a deadly soldier is afraid of a half hysterical woman?"

Darius sighed and pulled away with a smile on his face. Standing there with her hands on her hips, Gabriella impressed the hell out of him. Damned if she didn't know to go for the pride and the jugular. "Well, you put it that way."

He didn't get a chance to say more before she walked around the bed and lay down in the warm spot he'd just vacated. She then reached over to turn off the table lamp. "Good night," she murmured. He heard the sound of genuine smugness in her voice.

Darius ran a hand over his hair and shook his head. *Good night*, he repeated the word in his head. If his pride hadn't been on the line, he would have gladly grabbed a blanket from the closet and bunked on the sofa. "Gabriella, there's one thing you need to do before going to sleep."

"What is it?"

"Lift your head up, Princess."

She turned to look over her shoulder aiming a puzzled glance his way. "Why?"

"My gun's under your pillow," he stated wearily, pulling back the heavy covers and sliding into the bed. Careful to keep his distance, he propped his head on his elbow, then grinned down at her. "And I don't want you shooting me while I sleep."

By all the gods. Darius smothered a curse. He opened his eyes in the pre-dawn darkness and then slammed them shut as Gabriella's movement brought her tantalizing rear end into closer contact with his groin. All night long, he'd tried to avoid touching her. Yet, the queen-size bed and king-size pillowed wall he'd erected between them two hours earlier were pathetic defenses against the woman who'd invaded his room and taken over his bed. It'd been a while since he'd been in bed with a woman. It'd been a long while since he'd touched another human being as he did now and it felt real good.

Seasoned soldiers like himself had the ability to fall asleep immediately. Like food and water, sleep was a commodity you took whenever you could get it. There was a truth to being a warrior, one his survival of Hell Week had proven. Pain made a soldier stronger. It was the fire by which all Delta soldiers were forged.

Whether it was sleep deprivation, twitching muscles on the verge of collapse, the burn of oxygenless lungs, the extreme weather, the Ranger training, Airborne, or Special Forces selection—by sheer willpower alone a warrior harnessed all the aches, all the pain and exhaustion and transformed it into power, vigor, and the determination to win. But as Darius lay there struggling to keep from wrapping his arms around her frame and burying his face in the hollow of Gabriella's neck, he couldn't summon up the will to wish he were anyplace on earth other than where he was at that moment.

"Darius," she murmured as he began to ease himself out of the bed.

He froze like a deer in the headlights. "Don't move . . ." his voice trailed off.

"You can hold me if you like."

"I want to do a lot more than hold you, Princess." His voice slid down an octave.

"And if I wanted it as well?"

"We can't." Some of his internal struggles were reflected in the strain of his tone. Against his request, she shifted against him. Feeling her intention to turn, Darius's hands flashed out and grasped her hips and held her still. "There are consequences for everything we do in life, Gabriella. And a man can only carry so much guilt."

"I'm not a virgin." The irritation of her voice cut through the darkness and brought a small smile to his face.

"That doesn't matter."

"I don't want a wedding or happily ever after, Darius. I don't need false promises and whispered declarations, just uncomplicated sex."

He shook his head. "Sorry, but that's the one thing I can't give. I'm about as complex a man as you'll ever run into."

She sighed and placed her hand atop his and pulled his arm around her like a blanket. "But you're a man and I'm a woman."

"You do have a wonderful grasp on the obvious," Darius bit out harshly as she placed his hand under her pajama shirt. The contact with her flesh raced from his fingertips throughout his body. "Your father trusted me."

"With my life, not my chastity."

"Same thing," he answered resolutely. "Where the body goes, the mind follows. You're not naïve enough to think that we can make love and walk away."

"I think I can."

"Well, I can't," Darius asserted as he began to relax. The more they talked the easier it became for Darius to lie still, using his brain to think instead of his lower body to feel. "Let this go, Gabriella. It'll be easier."

"Nothing in my life is easy right now."

"It can be if you let it."

"You mean let Anton try to kill me or let you get hurt while keeping me safe? How about letting my father break my heart?"

The confused hurt in her voice caught in his chest. He'd heard it before in his mother's voice. The morning he left for West Point was one of the greatest and saddest moments of his life. And now he lay here, able to do nothing except hold her. God, how he hated not being able to wipe away her fear.

Choices. He made choices in an instant and lived with them for a lifetime. It was an integral part of his life as a soldier and as a man. He'd chosen his path long ago. But now as he lay with the pad of his thumb absently stroking the warm velvety skin of Gabriella's stomach, the consequences of his actions sat heavy on his shoulders. Darius lowered his chin into the curve of her neck and burrowed his left arm underneath Gabriella to pull her fully into his embrace. The intimate contact of her rear end against his groin sent a groan of pain through his body.

"Just close your eyes for me," he instructed softly. "Close your eyes and relax for me, little one. I promise that nothing . . . no one will harm you."

In the long minutes between his last words and the instant Gabriella succumbed to the temptation of sleep, he gently touched her hair. God, how easy it would be to make love to her. But the possible consequences . . .

"Ah, hell," Darius swore under his breath and then pulled her all the more tightly against him. He closed his eyes as little by little the tension drained out of her spine and her legs crept toward his. Holding her like the most precious thing in the world, he sighed into her hair. Bone deep weariness crept into his body and as the sun came up, he fell into sleep, and fell unwittingly deeper in love.

Chapter
Fifteen

The next morning, Gabriella hit her stride and turned a corner in Central Park. The crystal cold air of winter cut her lungs and the breeze made her eyes water, but she kept jogging. The passing of the wind and the white of the snow freed her of the dark cloud of terror.

Yet, it was still impossible to forget the fact that sooner than she'd like a decision would have to be made. Sebastian wouldn't be away forever and when he returned there would be questions she'd have to answer, conversations that had been years in the making.

It had seemed like such a good idea at the time—running away from Vasilei. *Maybe I inherited the habit from my father,* Gabriella thought bitterly.

As soon as she'd gotten on the first train out of Italy, she'd been assailed with doubts—doubts about herself, doubts about the man she had sworn she would love for the rest of her life. And now she contemplated leaving again. Disappearing into the vastness of America.

"Wait up."

Gabriella turned her head to see Darius stop to tie his shoe laces. Ignoring his request, she turned back around and headed down the path toward the apartment building. If she needed another reason to leave, then Darius was it. Something had grown between them. Some emotional connection had crept uninvited over her walls and stolen into the protected recesses of her heart.

Gabriella drew a shallow breath and kicking in a burst of speed, ran faster. She would be at the edge of the park in a few minutes. It was crazy that she should be attracted to another man, trust another man. Betrayal had become par for the course for her. She should pack a bag and leave, she decided, slowing down as she came to the marked crosswalk.

With the walk signal in her favor, she set off. The screech of tires was her only warning. All of a sudden everything seemed to slow as her perception of time transformed seconds to minutes. Gabriella turned her head in time to see a big black SUV barreling around the corner. She threw herself forward toward the snow piles but was still grazed on her side and shoulder.

"Damn it, you should have waited for me."

Gabriella felt herself being lifted up and shook her head as Darius's concerned face came into focus.

"Are you all right?"

"I'm fine," she lied. "What happened?"

"You almost got killed," he bit out as they started walking toward the apartment.

"Did you see the driver?"

"No."

"He probably didn't see me."

"I doubt it. He might not have seen you when he turned the corner, but he couldn't have missed the sound of you hitting his car. The bastard didn't care."

She took in a shallow breath, trying to calm the unaccustomed panic that shot through her veins. "I'm just glad I got out of the way."

"Me too. If you hadn't jumped . . ." He stopped.

By the time they reached the lobby of her apartment building, the shock had worn off.

"Maybe we should take you to the hospital."

"No," she almost shouted. Gabriella hated hospitals. Ever

since she'd watched her mother die, she'd never stepped foot in one.

"Gabriella."

She shivered, not from the thought of walking through the hospital doors or the memories of the doctors and nurses crowding into the private room and pushing her aside; no, it was from the way Darius said her name in the small space of the elevator.

The elevator doors opened at her floor and Gabriella began to feel the pain on the right side of her body, which had made contact with the speeding car.

Darius unlocked the apartment door for her and she walked past him. The door closed and she didn't turn around. Taking a deep breath, she took off her gloves and started to unbutton her jacket when Darius stepped up beside her.

"Let me help."

She gratefully let him pull off the jacket.

"Take a seat; I want to look at that arm."

"It's okay." She pulled away and winced.

"I'm not leaving you alone until I see your arm, little one."

"If I died in an accident would you be blamed?" she asked, needing some distraction from the throbbing ache of her bruised shoulder.

"No one dies on my watch, Gabriella. Now raise your arms so I can take off your sweatshirt."

As soon as he had a clear sight of the bruise, all the anger mixed with fear Darius had felt when he'd witnessed the accident rose again. Careful to roll up the sleeve of her T-shirt, he let out a short whistle as self-reproach sucker punched him in the stomach.

"That bad?" she asked.

"It's not pretty."

Her smooth almond-colored skin already displayed a myriad of blue, red, and purple shades.

He looked up from her shoulder to her face, noticing for the first time the way she held her body stiff and her eyes away from him. She had more courage than some of the recruits he'd help train in boot camp. The woman was a surprise. Just when he thought he knew everything about her, some new facet showed itself and made him desire her even more.

"I'm going to get you an icepack and some ointment. Just try to relax and I'll be right back." Darius lowered his voice as he moved to stand. Before preparing the pack, he returned with two tablets and a glass of water.

"What are those?" Gabriella's eyes rose from his hand to his face.

"Aspirin. They'll help you with the pain and swelling," he lied smoothly. No hint of distrust showed in her eyes. She put the painkillers into her mouth and then chased them with a drink of water. Darius suppressed a smile at the grimace on her face. He well recalled the alkaline taste of the medicine.

Careful not to move her arm, she stared at his back until he left the room. Leaning back onto the sofa, Gabriella closed her eyes and tried to ignore the throbbing pain in her side. Time was running out. Sometime that day, her father would return, and at any moment either Vasilei or Anton would come for her. The sudden coldness on her arm brought her upright.

"Better?" Darius's voice intruded upon her thoughts. She opened her eyes to stare into his concerned face. He held the icepack gingerly against her skin.

Placing her hand over his atop the pack, she said, "Much. Thank you."

"Anything else I can do?"

Slowly, Gabriella returned her eyes to his face and gazed deeply into his eyes. She was tempted to be poetic and say she could get lost in their mysterious depths. Yet, the feeling of safety, trust, and—dare she even think it—love peeled away all of her misgivings and made her vulnerable. "Yes, hold me please."

"I don't want to hurt your arm."

Without giving Darius a chance to move away, Gabriella relaxed into his chest, let out a pent up breath, then inhaled slowly. Gradually the pain seemed to be receding and in its place, a lassitude followed. "I know you'd never hurt me," she said sleepily.

The warmth of his body, security of his scent, and rhythmic stroking of his fingers over the nape of her neck sent Gabriella into a blissful sleep.

Two days after the accident, Gabriella looked away from the car window and down at her nails. They were a perfect pearly oval against the backdrop of her burgundy dress. This evening she had been invited—no, summoned—to have dinner with her father. An invitation could be declined, but a request delivered via a stern-faced bodyguard could not.

Darius wasn't dressed so casually tonight. The sweats had been replaced by an Italian dark gray suit; but instead of a shirt and tie, he wore a black turtleneck, which set off his rich bronze skin well. *Too well*, Gabriella observed.

Darius hadn't said a word since they'd left the apartment. He'd offered her support and was very careful not to touch her arm, but the man seated beside her in the driver's seat acted like a stranger. Everything about him, from the way his fingers held tightly to the leather-encased steering wheel to the way his eyes scanned the traffic, alert to the lightning quick lane changes of the other cars, was all business. Nothing of the kindness or the kiss they'd shared earlier that afternoon showed on his face.

Gabriella swallowed a sigh as with each block they came closer and closer to Sebastian's penthouse. She knew the address by heart, not because she had ever visited the building, but because it was the return address for all the cards, checks and other correspondence she'd received from him.

She'd never wanted to see the place, but here she was being driven to see the man who'd killed her mother, by the bodyguard he'd hired to protect her from the man who'd been her fiancé. Her heart lurched as her mind went into overdrive.

What was she doing?

As a teenager, she hadn't been able to comprehend—much

less accept—that Sebastian had led another life with a wife and a son she would never meet. Yet, the past aside, she loved Sebastian, the man who was a kind father figure who moved in and out of her life. She loved him because her mother had died with his name on her lips. His picture laid underneath her left hand as Gabriella held the other. She loved him because he'd been her giant as a child.

"I'll be waiting downstairs. When you're ready to go, just buzz the front desk," Darius commented.

His calm voice filled the silence of the SUV. Gabriella tried to relax and couldn't.

"What if we kept driving?" she asked, turning toward him. "I've never been to New Jersey."

"He loves you."

"Sebastian abandoned me."

"We all make mistakes, harm the people we love and ourselves. For those of us who are lucky enough, somewhere down the line we wake up and try to make amends." He glanced at her profile and saw her frown even in the shadowed interior of the jeep.

"I don't want to see him."

"We all have to do things that we don't want to do, Princess."

Gabriella turned off the stereo. "Darius, why do you defend him?"

"The better question is why you don't."

Her finger curled into fists. "He killed my mother."

"Her hospital records indicate that she died of natural causes," he stated.

The air in Gabriella's lungs left in a whoosh as a wave of old and bitter anger almost overwhelmed her. "If you define a broken heart as natural, then yes."

"Princess, what has he done to you?"

"He sent me away from my family and left me to rot in an academy like I was spoiled meat. I had a home, friends, memories and he took that away."

"He placed you in an academy with the best instructors, who

helped you secure a place at Sorbonne University, right? You were able to pursue your dream of playing the flute and you were very well taken care of."

"Stop it!"

"Truth time, Princess." Darius slammed on the brakes, pulled over to the right side of the road, and put on his hazard lights. When he turned toward her, Gabriella fought the urge to stick her fingers in her ears.

He continued. "Your father made mistakes, but you can't blame him for every wrong in your life without giving him some credit for the right. You are a beautiful, accomplished flutist with a bright future. Let that be enough."

"You make it sound so easy. Am I supposed to snap my fingers and forget what he's done?"

"No, I want you to forgive." He reached out and placed a finger underneath her chin, forcing her to meet his gaze. "Forgiving and forgetting are two different things."

"It would be too hard."

"Hard, but not impossible."

She shook her head slightly and then took his hand within her own. "Are you a bodyguard or a psychiatrist?"

"Neither." His voice softened. "I hope to be the friend you need."

"Why?" Gabriella asked a moment later as Darius resumed their drive toward Sebastian's penthouse.

"Why what?"

"Why are you being so nice to me? Is it because of guilt?"

"No, little one." She watched as his lips curled upward into a full grin. "It's because I'm afraid you'll beat me up if I'm not."

She sighed and turned to read the passing street signs. "Funny, I guess you get to add comedian to your résumé."

"Loosen up, Princess. It's dinner, not a hanging."

"I'm not tense," Gabriella denied.

"Then what are you?"

"Tired." Her answer was muffled.

"Then you should have taken a nap as I advised you to this afternoon."

"I've slept more in the past week than I have in months. I've had more than enough beauty rest."

"You sure?" Darius smiled. "You're not looking too hot as far as I can see."

Her vanity stung, Gabriella glared at him. "Was that crack supposed to be funny?"

Darius laughed and the deep husky sound filled the car. "No, just wanted to rile you up a bit. You look so upset, I'm debating whether or not to pull over and get you a stiff drink."

Gabriella played with the seatbelt for a moment. "You told me before that you're in the military."

"Yes," Darius confirmed.

"I understand if you don't want to talk about it. But . . ." she stopped, wondering if she really wanted the answer to the question she'd been about to ask.

"Go on," Darius encouraged.

"Have you ever killed someone?"

He paused, considering how to answer her question as well as giving thought to the reasons behind her interest in his background. "I've seen a lot of time behind enemy lines, and I've had to do a great many things to secure the success of my mission." It was as close to an admission as she was going to get. "Why do you ask?"

"I was just curious, that's all."

Darius shot her a look from the corner of his eyes. He was going to question her further but instead slowed to look for a parking place near the luxury condominium on Park Avenue where van Ryne took up residence when he was in New York.

"You can just let me out at the front," Gabriella instructed as he slowed.

"Don't touch that door handle," Darius cut in. He turned the car into the underground parking garage in the building and found an empty space on the first level. He took off his seatbelt and twisted in his seat. "Where you go, I go, Gabriella."

"I'll be fine," she asserted.

Darius reached for his door and opened it. "You disobeyed me the other morning and almost got killed."

He came around to the passenger side of the SUV, opened her door, was careful to avoid her injured arm, and provided support as she climbed out.

They walked to the elevator and took it to the lobby. Neither spoke as the concierge led them to the private elevator. Gabriella watched as the older gentleman inserted a key and pressed the button.

"I'll be right here," Darius reassured her.

Gabriella allowed herself a tight smile before the elevator doors closed and whisked her upward to the penthouse. Time had not worked to lessen her anger but the cold had. The icy prison called boarding school had chilled her emotions, turning teenage rage into an adult coldness fueled by generic greeting cards with money, sporadic visits, and few phone calls. Year after year, she'd hoped he'd retrieve her, call her, share with her something of the love her mother had known. Her father was a man she barely knew.

She was brought out of her reverie by the elevator's sudden stop. The doors opened into the entrance hall of the penthouse. Gabriella stepped into a grand high-ceiling entrance alcove. The architecture of the apartments may have been modern, but Sebastian's taste could be seen in the interior design of the antique furnishings.

She walked straight ahead to the balcony doors, passing alongside a large Viennese sofa flanked by two Russian chairs. The sound of her shoes over the mahogany floors echoed in the empty space. It was there, standing by one of the penthouse apartment's wraparound windows gazing out over Central Park toward the beckoning lights on Manhattan's West Side, that she felt afraid.

The day she'd arrived in New York, she had been unsure as to whether or not she'd recognize him if they had met.

You have your father's heart. Her mother's loving adoration drifted through her mind as she walked toward the dining room after having taken ten minutes to find one of the bathrooms to wash her hands.

After wandering through the penthouse studying porcelain vases, inhaling the sweet scent of freshly cut flowers, and cataloguing the French antique furniture, Gabriella looked impatiently at the closed door to her father's study. Absentmindedly, she toyed with one of the exquisitely crafted glass Harlequins on display. The figurine's lips smiled as its eyes cried black tears on a white mask; it was the epitome of mockery.

Gabriella approached the entrance to the dining room. A painting on the wall of the enclave caught her attention. She stepped closer and stared at the lady dressed in her wedding gown. The woman would have been stunningly beautiful with her chestnut hair and timeless features, but there was no realness, no warmth to her bearing. Most glaring seemed to be an absence of happiness and affection.

At the sound of footsteps, Gabriella straightened her shoulders but did not turn.

"Dinner will be served in about ten minutes. Would you like a glass of wine?" Sebastian asked, having come upon his daughter.

"Who is she?"

A stab of remorse touched him. "My mother," he stated simply. "The painting was given to my father two days after their wedding."

"She doesn't look happy."

Sebastian came to stand beside Gabriella. "She wasn't, neither of them were. Mother wasn't given a choice in the matter and my father was too busy building a political empire to care. As long as she performed the duties of a wife, then he was content."

"Is your marriage like your parents'?"

She caught his nod from the corner of her eye. "It was arranged by our fathers. But my choosing to live up to the expectations of my family has been one of the biggest regrets of my life."

"Why do you say regret? Why not mistake?"

"If I hadn't married Sylvia, I'd never have met Josette."

At the mention of his beloved's name, Sebastian watched helplessly as his daughter took a step back. He looked into a face of indifference where only moments before there had been sympathy.

"Dinner is served, Monsieur van Ryne." The French accented voice interrupted the silence.

"Thank you, Jean-Paul." He turned back to his daughter. "Hungry?"

"Yes, of course."

She followed him into the separate dining room that contained a long, black polished table resplendent with flowers, candles, and cut glass. Elegant serving dishes sat alongside two place settings of platinum embellished china, translucent crystal goblets, and elegant silverware.

They took their seats at the table and started the meal. Sebastian waited until after the first entrée was removed before breaking the silence that had fallen between them.

"I apologize for having to leave so abruptly after your arrival."

"Your son needed you. How is Jensen by the way?" The inscrutable look on her face mimicked the tone of her voice. It was a knife to his heart to see her look at him in that manner, but he couldn't blame her for it. In her eyes, he was the worst of men.

"It was only a minor accident." Her father took a sip of wine. "He has recovered."

"There was no need for you to come back so soon."

He placed the glass down gently on the table. "My daughter needs me; that is reason enough."

"I don't need you." For the first time since he'd looked upon Gabriella at the airport, he saw some emotion flicker in her eyes. Even anger was a welcome change from cold indifference.

He sighed and put down his fork and knife. They sat three

feet away from one another at the dish-laden dining room table. It may have been an ocean as far as Sebastian was concerned. He closed his eyes briefly as grieved memories washed over him. Having wanted for so long to see Gabriella, to hold her close and beg her forgiveness, he didn't know how to begin.

Sebastian settled his gaze onto the face so similar to Josette's that he flinched as the old grief became new and the image of the woman whom he had married in his soul stared back at him. When she lowered her face and tucked her hair behind her ear, he blinked. Sebastian knew the gesture very well. He watched her closely and saw that her movements were graceful and fluid. But then he saw the coldness in his daughter's eyes, which he himself had put there.

"You're right," he acknowledged. She'd have done well on her own if it hadn't been for Lexer. "You don't need me, but I need you."

The admission had come from a place deep down in his soul. "I need you to give me another chance, Rella."

Sebastian didn't know if it was his honest admission or the use of the childhood name, but something had shaken her as she quickly lowered her head, again.

"To what?" Gabriella asked carefully, modulating her voice to sound as cool and unemotional as she could even as her fingers clenched her napkin underneath the table. "To give you another opportunity to break my heart?"

Years of yearning and anger came pouring out from the dark place within her. The useless tears and dashed hopes overflowed into her mouth, mixed with the waiting bitterness that spilled off her tongue. "My mother died loving you, wanting you, thinking of you. She placed her child into your keeping and you took me from my aunt's house and left me to strangers."

"You were so distraught with grief. At the time, I thought I was doing what was best for you. It was a mistake."

"A mistake?" She shook her head violently and struggled for some shred of control. "No, you were doing what was best for you. I would have had some semblance of a family, but you had to take that away. I was miserable. And you," she spat the word, "you had another family to concern yourself with. A wife and son. I have an older brother who knows nothing of me. If this is a sudden attack of conscience, then I want nothing to do with it. Find some other way to relieve your guilt," she ordered coldly and picked up her utensils.

Leaning close over the table, Sebastian did not just want to reach across the space separating them. He wanted to reach across the years of brittle silence and pull her to him. To let her know that he loved her, he was proud of her, and he'd cried over her pictures as he read Josette's letters over and over to the point where the ink bled easily on his fingertips.

He fought the urge to back away and allow her space. The truth was that he'd taken the easy way out the first time and had regretted it ever since. Now he would finish what he started and air the truth no matter how painful it was.

Sebastian took a deep breath and then spread his hands out on the table. "Jensen is not my son."

Her fork clattered upon the plate.

"I have loved no woman other than your mother. Jensen is the product of one of Sylvia's lovers. We had an agreement of sorts; I could live my life with Josette, and the price was not exposing the truth of his birth."

"I—" Gabriella started and stopped, then blindly reached for her water glass to wet her dry throat.

Sebastian held up his hand signaling for silence. "I wish to God I could go back in time. There are so many things I'd do differently, so many things I'd say. But I can't change the past. The only thing I can do is make up for it."

Gabriella shook her head.

"I spoke with my attorney the day after your arrival in New York. Tomorrow, you'll be recognized as my daughter in all ways. You will have a new name—a name you should have had at your birth. You will be a van Ryne. I have also designated you as the primary beneficiary of my estate upon my death. In the meantime, I've transferred a quarter of my wealth into the

Swiss bank account I had set up the day you were born. By the end of the month, you'll be in possession of a sizable fortune."

"No." Gabriella barely kept from dropping the wine goblet in her hand. "I don't want anything from you."

"You don't have a say in the matter."

"Stop it." Her voice rose with an edge of hysteria.

Sebastian picked up his napkin and calmly wiped his lips. "I can't."

"Don't give me that," she bit out. "You started it; you can undo it. I don't want your money."

"I don't want you to hate me," he said softly.

"If you want me to forgive you, stop this." Gabriella was grasping at straws as the world turned on its axis. Jensen wasn't her father's son; Sebastian was legally and publicly recognizing her birth; and now. . . .

"Rella, I've purchased an estate on the outskirts of Montreal. The main house has a music room. I've even set up an audition for you to play for the symphony. The master flutist has agreed to be your mentor. Darius has been given orders to take you to Canada tomorrow. In two days, it'll be announced that I'm stepping down as CEO. I want to start a new life; I want a fresh start and time—time to get to know the woman that my daughter has become. And I want you to get to know me as well."

She looked into his face and all of a sudden the pain in her shoulder grew stronger. She'd dreamed of this moment for so long and it was happening. The words, the gestures. Her heart thudded in her chest and she wasn't sure she could stand.

"I . . ." She didn't know what to say. Time seemed to be slipping through her fingers. The feeling that all too soon Anton or Vasilei would find her. Sebastian's act of generosity would forever put her in the spotlight; there wouldn't be any dark avenues for her to slip down, no possibility of remaining anonymous. The world never forgot its heiresses.

"You have some time. Not a lot. The FBI paid me a visit this morning, and once the papers are released to the public, Lexer will know you're my daughter and be able to find you through me. I would spare you any further pain."

"The FBI was here?" Her voice shook.

He gestured to her wineglass. "Drink it."

She hesitated and then brought the glass to her lips and drank it all. Sebastian picked up the bottle and refilled her glass. "Two agents came to my office this morning. They wanted to know about why you left him. It seems that you're wanted as a potential witness in the disappearance of two government agents." He watched her even more closely.

Gabriella pressed her lips together as her mind raced. She had to get out of the city and fast. The noose seemed to be tightening around her neck.

"Did you tell them anything?"

"No. I told them I haven't seen you in years."

"Did they believe you?"

"I think not." He shook his head. "I wouldn't be surprised if they came back tomorrow. Rella, would it not be best to talk to them? It might be just the thing to keep him away from you."

Gabriella remained silent.

"They said they could help. If what the FBI suspects is true, then Lexer had a hand in the murder of two agents."

"Don't say anymore." She stood up and backed away from the table.

"What happened? Did he threaten you?"

"No, Vasilei didn't threaten me."

"Then why are you so terrified?"

"Anton." She spoke his name quietly as if he were one of the make-believe demons mother spoke of as a child.

"What about him? Tell me, Gabriella." Sebastian came around to her side of the dining room table.

"I saw what Anton did with the knife. There was so much blood." She spoke his name in a hushed whisper as though saying his name aloud would bring evil down upon them.

Sebastian pulled her shaking body into his arms. "Everything's going to be okay. I won't let anything bad happen to you ever again," he vowed.

For a moment, she allowed herself to slip back to the time when as a child she believed in her father, and at his word all things were made possible. But, Gabriella put her hands up and disentangled herself from her father. He'd said those exact words when she'd fallen off her new bicycle.

"No. Just leave me alone." She turned around and unsteadily made her way to the entrance alcove of the penthouse.

"Rella!" She heard her father's raised voice but ignored it. Instead, she hit the button on the elevator and thankfully the doors slid open. Confusion dogged her every step. She couldn't think, didn't know how to feel. Once she entered the lobby, Gabriella ran to Darius and took his hand, pulling him toward the elevator to the parking lot.

"What happened?" he asked.

"We need to go." Tears gathered in her eyes, but she refused to say anything until they were both in the car.

Darius keyed the ignition and put on his seat belt. "Where to?"

She wanted to say anywhere and nowhere. The urge to run seemed to beat through her body but the want of peace was stronger. The image of her mother bowed in church flashed through her mind. It was the only place she knew she could go and hope to find some direction.

"Confession." She squeezed herself into a little ball after putting on her seat belt. "Take me to the Catholic Church near the apartment."

Darius took another look at Gabriella and didn't ask any further questions. Instead, he started the car, exited the parking garage, and headed north.

Chapter
Sixteen

Darius brought the Land Rover to a halt outside the small Catholic church and sat quietly as Gabriella fled the car. From the looks of it, dinner with her father had not gone well. A churning started in the pit of his stomach.

He didn't like keeping silent when at that exact moment the Lexer corporate jet carrying Vasilei Lexer would be landing at New York's John F. Kennedy airport. Anton had entered the country a mere twenty-four hours before. Darius had men watching the arms smugglers' every move yet still he'd slipped up and Gabriella had almost died.

Sitting back in his seat, he fought the urge to get out of the car and follow her into the church. Only his respect for Gabriella's privacy kept him there. Sighing, he stared at the doors as he waited. This was the calm before the storm. Anton was running out of time and sooner than later, he would make his move.

Gabriella stepped into the church and took a deep breath of the cool air. She wanted more than anything to drop to her knees and weep, but instead she turned toward the candle-lit vestibule. The wooden floor creaked as she walked slowly past the back pew and came to a stop in front of the raised table of candles. A statue of the Virgin Mary seemed to cast a loving glance her way, but Gabriella couldn't look at it. Instead, with shaky fingers, she picked up a match.

She remembered the times she'd been alone in the small chapel near the boarding school—the times she'd knelt down and lit a candle in memory of her mother.

And now she did the same thing in lighting the votive candle. But it wasn't enough. She needed to talk to someone, to get guidance, or receive some semblance of relief from the guilt lodged in her throat. She had watched two men die and had done nothing. Now more than ever she needed to confess her sins and receive a penance and absolution.

She stepped into the confessional, closed the wooden door, and took her seat. "Bless me Father, for I have sinned. It's been five months since my last confession," Gabriella recited.

"Speak to me, my daughter." His voice was thick and raspy through the partition.

She drew a shaky breath.

"What is it, my daughter?"

"I witnessed the murder of two people." She wrestled with the words. "And I did nothing."

There was a long pause and she heard the sound of fabric rustling. "Go on, my daughter."

"Oh Father, how could I have known?" The memories poured from her lips. "I ran into the men while they were leaving my apartment. They explained themselves by claiming to be building repairmen, saying that a woman downstairs reported a leak in her bathroom ceiling."

Gabriella thought nothing of it until she saw them again a month later getting into a van with Anton at the Lexer estate. When she'd mentioned the coincidence to Vasilei, he'd shrugged and took her mind off everything by proposing a getaway to his Italian villa. She didn't see anything amiss when he wouldn't let her go home and sent someone for her clothes.

She finished telling her story and took a deep breath. Oddly, the scent of smoke filled her nose. She sniffed again and the distinctive smell of sweet tobacco grew stronger. Her heart started to race and adrenaline sharpened her senses.

Anton smoked only the best Spanish cheroots.

"Father, do you smell smoke?"

A chill crept over her, making her body go rigid and tense. Every second seemed to stretch out like minutes and the grain of the wood in the partition screen seemed vibrant and distinct.

"Father?" Gabriella whispered again. Hearing no response, she opened the door and approached the other side of the confessional.

She tried to swallow but her throat didn't seem to work as a foreboding chill swept through her body. "Father, are you all right?"

Her hand moved out to slowly open the door. Peering through the darkness of the vestibule, the sight that greeted her eyes would forever haunt her nightmares. Gabriella's entire body shrunk away as her hand rose to cover her mouth, barely managing to hold in the scream stuck tight in the back of her throat. Her heart beat quickly and violently against her ribs. The priest was leaned against the outer edge of the confessional. A line of red circled his throat and blood dripped down onto the Bible still gripped in his fingers.

"Oh God!" Gabriella began to shudder violently and back away. "Help!" She let out a wild scream and looked around the church for someone—anyone. Every pew stood empty, the aisles clear. Scrambling up from the floor, she ran to the front doors of the church and tried to push one open but nothing happened. She took a deep breath and coughed from the heavy smell of smoke. She tried the door again and then kicked at it with her heels but it didn't move. Nothing she could do would budge the solid wood doors that had kept the sacred church safe for centuries only to burn now in a murderous blaze.

Gabriella looked over toward the alcove in time to see the heavy velvet wall-carpeting burst into flames. The unholy light reflected off the stained glass windows, making the angels of heaven who had been so comforting mere moments ago into specters of menace. More like an animal than a rational human, her eyes scanned the nave for another way out. The rapidly advancing fire cut off any chance at escaping through a back exit. The windows along the side walls were too far up to reach even if she managed to break them.

"Gabriella!" a voice called from behind the entrance doors.

"Darius!" She sobbed with relief to hear his voice, then began to cough as the acrid sting of smoke bit into her lungs. "Darius, it's Anton . . . Anton."

"I know. Listen to me, Gabriella. Stay close to the floor and find something to cover your mouth and nose. Move away from the door and wait for me."

"Wait?" Her mind seized upon that one word. *Wait.* The fire was spreading faster, the roar of the flames became louder, and she slunk low, struggling to breathe through the wool of her coat. Unbidden, her eyes strayed back toward the confessional and a shudder wracked her body. Just then, the double doors of the church burst open and Gabriella fell back against the stonewall. Her eyes caught on the familiar sight of the black SUV as the passenger door flew open. "Get in."

Gabriella struggled upward on shaky legs and lunged into the car.

"Fasten your seat belt." Darius put the vehicle in reverse and backed up hard, barely managing to keep from hitting a bystander. He bit out a curse as his peripheral vision caught the sight of Gabriella lurching sideways. He reached over and grabbed the seat belt clasp from her trembling fingers and pushed it into the slot. He'd been shot at and she'd almost been burned to death. Mentally, he went through all the obscenities in all the languages he knew, yet none of them equated to the churning fear and rage coiled in his stomach.

The only thing that worked was a vow. Not a promise; a vow. Anton Lexer would die by his hand.

"We need to ditch the car tags; then we're getting out of the city. We were followed. We've *been* followed most likely for the past few days."

"Where were you?" she whispered. The abandoned and hurt tone of her voice cut through his bravado. She'd needed him, really needed him, and in the end he'd been there, but he should have been there sooner.

"Anton wasn't alone. He followed you into the church while two others came after me." Darius slowed as they passed through Harlem. It had only been ten minutes after Gabriella had left the car that he'd felt the prickle of unease in his gut. Careful to make sure that the car's dome light was turned off, he'd eased out of the vehicle with his sidearm drawn only to hear the first gun shot. Taking out the shooters hadn't been a problem, but the acrid scent of smoke had stopped his heart. Looking upward toward the stained glass windows, he'd seen the flickers not caused by candlelight but by fire.

Darius continued driving until he came to a neighborhood that met his requirements. The old brownstones hidden under layers of graffiti had seen better days. The cars that lined this street didn't need alarms; they had been stolen too many times and returned.

"Don't move from the car." Pulling into an available space on a street lit from above by only one unbroken light, he cut the engine and got out. Darius used his Swiss Army knife to unscrew the New York City license plate and replaced it with the Connecticut plate from a nearby older model jeep.

Once he'd finished covering their tracks, he crossed the two-level George Washington Bridge and drove northwest into New Jersey. After slowing down to grab a ticket for the turnpike, he set the cruise control at the speed limit and began scanning for signs of their being followed.

After refueling the car, Darius waited until he'd reached a less populated county before stopping at a family run motel. He'd deliberately chosen a small establishment and paid cash in order to make the record of their stay inaccessible to anyone tracking them by computer. Just to make sure, Darius registered them as Mr. and Mrs. Jerrod Brown of Norwalk, Connecticut.

Chapter Seventeen

"Why?" Gabriella questioned aloud through clenched teeth. The bathroom's cloudy mirror didn't respond, but then again it didn't need to. The obvious answer was Anton. She shuddered as though someone had laid flowers on her own grave. In her mind's eye, she could see him smiling as his long fingers held the knife.

She jumped at the knock on the door. "Are you all right?"

Just the sound of Darius's voice was enough to calm the furious beating of her heart. She didn't want him to see her like this. Didn't want the fear that curled on her stomach to spread out and touch everything and everyone around her. The two-foot distance between Gabriella and the door seemed more like a chasm. "I'm fine."

"Are you coming out?"

No, a childish part of her wanted to answer. *I'm going to stay in here and hide.* Hide from the monster that wanted her dead. Hide from the seductive pull that appeared every time she got close to Darius.

"Of course." She reached out and opened the door. Wrapped in nothing but a towel, she stepped out into the cool air of the suite.

"I'm going to grab a quick shower," Darius said gruffly as he stared out, then let the curtain fall back into place. He turned from the window and tried to keep his eyes anywhere but on Gabriella, anywhere but on her loose and damp hair or the luminescent glow of her skin. A seductive siren and a terrified woman stood next to the television and he wanted her. "There's food on top of the fridge. Help yourself. Just stay away from the windows and the doors."

"You think he can find us here?"

"Not this soon. I just don't want to take any chances."

He watched her nod and turn away to walk toward the small eating alcove. He'd been worried about leaving her alone while she was in the shower, but the small diner adjacent to the hotel had been quick to deliver the meals to his door. Picking up his duffle bag, Darius entered the bathroom and shut the door. But even that couldn't shut out the image of Gabriella. Her scent filled the small space. The smell of shampoo and soap served to arouse him more.

Darius turned on the shower faucet before placing his gun by the sink, pulling off his clothes, and dropping them to the floor. God, it had been a narrow escape. He felt cold thinking about how close he'd come to losing her. That moment when he'd seen the flames and heard her shout his name had crystallized the feelings he'd sought so very long to deny.

Darius Yassoud never left a man to die. He'd begun the mission to protect Gabriella. Now he'd discovered that he'd saved her life but had lost his heart. He was in love with a woman who for all intents and purposes was emotionally tangled with someone else.

Vasilei. His jaw clenched as the hot water ran over his skin, making his thoughts all the more unbearable. Darius reached out and turned the water to cold. As the icy spray beat down on him, he wondered how long it would take for the FBI to get the warrant. He needed this to be over.

Twenty minutes later, after having showered and dressed, Darius opened the door and found his gaze captured by a pair of golden eyes. "Gabriella?" He said her name softly, unsure as to why she was standing where he'd left her before going to take a shower. The only difference was that the lights were lower.

Darius checked to ensure that the safety of his gun was on before placing it on the bedside table. Then he moved back toward her. "Talk to me, Gabriella."

Gabriella. She stood still and turned her face toward the sound. Like the estranged daughter wandering in some foreign land, the deep melody of her name from his mouth felt like home. Not the physical trappings of her summer vacations, but something more. It rolled off his tongue like the foaming waters of her mother's birthplace while his voice chased away all her fears and brought the heat of the desert to the frost on her soul.

She needed warmth to beat back the chill that was within. She needed Darius to make love to her, hold her, and give hope that the nightmare her life had descended into had an ending.

The shield of numbness she'd wrapped herself in had begun to fall apart and she had to struggle to draw a breath. Her heart had begun to beat furiously in her chest, but it wasn't from fear. No, the pounding in her ears wasn't a response to Darius's nearness, but the split second decision she'd made, by the call of the home she could have in his arms.

Never taking her eyes off him, Gabriella crossed the space between them and stood so close that she could hear the raggedness of his breath and feel the heat of his breath on her bare skin. Gabriella tipped her head up and locked eyes with his. Something flickered in their dark depths, something that had her holding her breath. She reached to touch his cheek, but he moved back and gently caught her hand in his. The strength of those long fingers coupled with the silence of the hotel room lent an intimacy to the moment, an awareness of the closeness of their bodies. "I've tried so hard to tell myself that I wanted to be alone when all I've really thought about was being with you," she whispered.

"You're in shock, Gabriella. You don't know what you're doing."

He was right; she had never seduced a man. She'd always been seduced: by music, by the obsession of a powerful man. Somehow she'd thought it would be a simple thing, a look, a touch, a soft prelude that led to a grand finale. She took a step toward him and brought up her other hand to frame his face. Her finger slid over the slight roughness of his chin as her eyes enjoyed the rakish look brought about by the hint of a goatee.

"Yes, I do," she replied. Darius's muscles clenched as her tongue slipped over her lips. "I'm going to seduce you."

When she took his hands within her own, Darius sucked in his breath as her slender fingers began to knead the callous in the web of his thumb. All Delta assault team members had that same telltale callous on their firing hand. She brought his hand to her mouth and the air left his lungs as she placed a moist kiss in the center of his palm.

"You go wherever you're needed, but what about your needs, Darius?" Gabriella's voice hummed with anticipation.

Of all the things he'd expected her to ask, that was not one of them. Between the time she ran from Sebastian's penthouse and the moment he'd pulled her from the burning church, the world had stopped making sense. He had stopped making sense, but being this close to Gabriella felt too good to be ignored. There was no denying the desire that curled between them, and as he looked into her eyes, Darius could do nothing but yield to her, yield to the primitive attraction that had begun to bind them together from the first night he'd held her in his arms and carried her into the apartment.

He shook his head and closed his eyes, searching for one last shred of self control but couldn't find it. *Need*. The word permeated every muscle in his body. And the answer to her question came in the form of a rough growl from his throat. "Gabriella." At that moment, honor, promises, and duty were mere words and the power of her allure reduced them to

ashes. He needed her like he needed air. Darius Yassoud drew
a deep breath of her perfumed scent and surrendered.

Her arms curled around his neck and the towel dropped to
the carpet. Darius felt her body pressed against his, her lips
pressed against his own. The air smelled of soap and flowers;
her mouth tasted of sweet wine and a thousand honeyed
dreams. He wanted to savor the taste of her, the scent of her,
to take his time and love her gently.

Her fingers tightened on the nape of his neck and pulled
his mouth down to hers. With exquisite sensual provocation,
she traced the outline of his top lip before she turned her attention to the bottom. Darius held himself still until she
nipped with enough pressure to blur the line between pleasure
and pain. A shudder wracked his body and he pulled her
closer. Gabriella chose that moment to slip her tongue between his lips, taking full possession of his mouth.

There was an urgency to her kiss that he responded to.

Darius drew in a ragged breath and pulled back so that his
lips were merely inches from hers.

"I don't want you to regret this." His eyes bore into hers,
searching for the slightest hint of indecision.

"Tomorrow is never promised, Darius. And of all my possible regrets, making love with you will never be one of them."

From the first moment Gabriella had woken in his arms,
she'd made her choice to throw off the chains of possession
for the freedom of tender desire. Yes, she would be tied to
Darius in all ways, but it would be her fingers weaving the
thread, her hands working the loom.

When the back of her legs came into contact with the bed,
she stopped and her slender deft fingers made short work of
his shirt as his mouth moved over hers. He moved to unbutton his pants.

"No," she said. "Let me."

It took everything he had to hold himself motionless as
she unbuttoned and unzipped his pants. His gaze focused
downward at the creamy mounds of her breasts and his

throat went try. Gabriella released a shallow moan and he kissed the corners of her mouth and trailed his lips down her cheek to her neck.

Gabriella needed the solidness of the bed behind her to keep from falling. His hands were hot over her bare skin as his erection pressed up against her. Boldly she ran her fingers down his arms, over his chest. The muscle under his skin was unyielding and yet soft. Her eyes widened as she noticed the lines left by a knife fight in Algeria.

She ran her fingers over them, caressing them. "You poor man."

"They don't hurt." Darius's heart melted at the tender expression on her face as she ran her fingertips over the scars. They were old wounds from missions he'd rather have forgotten and in the past they had given him nothing but pain. Yet now—in that moment—as he watched Gabriella lean close and place a soft kiss on each one, his stomach muscles clenched and a wave of desire rolled over his body.

He moved away from her, turned back the covers, and watched as she slid between the sheets. For one brief moment, her body lay nude in the lamplight and all he could think to describe the vision was *jamiil*. Yet, even the Arabic word for beautiful could not encompass the feeling. Darius quickly removed his dog tags and shed his remaining clothes before getting into bed beside her. His mouth sought hers as his fingers roamed over her body. The need to touch her overshadowed everything in his life. The want to hold and love her became his reason for existence. Once he was fully undressed, the contact of her flesh against his took his breath away.

Gabriella moaned into his mouth as his hand cupped her breast, only to catch her breath as Darius lowered his mouth to her skin. The trembling harshness of her own breathing had given way to something low and aching. Overlapping emotions of pleasure and need ran over her body and filled her She sank into the pleasure brought on by the moist softness of his tongue on her nipples, the delicate scratch of his teeth over her sensitive skin. The more he touched her, tasted her, ran his hands over her, the more sharp notes of heat drove her to the brink. All thoughts unraveled as his fingers slowly caressed her inner thighs, finding her center.

His touch sent her spinning out of control as she writhed with need. She could feel everything—the cool sheets underneath her back, the trail of his kisses on her skin, the growing wetness between her legs—but Gabriella was blind to everything but the pleasure.

She opened her eyes. With her fingers cradled at the back of his neck, she dragged his mouth back to hers. His skin was hot underneath her hands; the hair on his chest cushioned her breasts. She had been a sleeping beauty waiting for her prince to come and wake her from sleep. Now with the hard heat of his body and the aching emptiness that screamed to be filled, she locked her legs around Darius and rolled so that she lay on top of him.

Her hair fell, making a screen for hiding their faces from the outside. She looked down into his beautiful face and lowered her lips to join his. She wanted to kiss but also needed to silence the words she saw pouring out his eyes. In one silken movement, she slid down bringing him inside her. The fullness of his presence rocked through her, causing her to arch her back and close her eyes to the sensation.

Nothing mattered. Darius looked up and lost himself inside her warmth, her tightness. Buried to the hilt, gut-wrenching pleasure spiked through his body. Nothing mattered outside the sight of her luscious breasts, her sighs, and the feel of her nails on his chest, the moans coming from the delicate quivering of her throat.

His brain, like the computers he knew so well, shut down completely. Darius took his hands from her hips and pulled her down for a kiss. He'd dreamed of her soft thighs against his own, her hair gliding over his skin. Of their own accord, his hips moved upward to meet her downward thrusts.

"Not yet," she moaned. Gabriella pulled back from his mouth and held herself still with her bottom resting on his bare thighs. Even as her mind struggled to comprehend the splendor of the joining, she didn't want it to end. She closed her eyes with her hand pressed against his chest, savoring the fullness brought by their joining. He was so deep a part of her, she didn't want to cross over to fall into the abyss.

But Darius gave her no options when his hands took control of her hips and he rose up and wrapped his arms around her, retreating and thrusting into her. She muffled the sound of her cries on his shoulder, sobbing half with relief and half with exultation.

"Can't . . ." he gasped as the beginning of climax roared through his body. He turned them both over, taking most of his weight on his forearms, and attempted to withdraw. But Gabriella wrapped her legs around him and squeezed, pushing him deeper. And as sand in the wind, Darius's thoughts and plans to pull away before spilling his seed were swept away as she moaned into his mouth and soft muscles clenched around him.

"Open your eyes, Gabriella," he spoke gently, low in her ear.

The darkness of her eyelids gave way to the shadowed countenance of Darius's face. "Look at me, Princess."

She raised her eyes and in awe she met him on their mutual climb as they reached the high point of the melody. His lips found hers. Her tongue met his and she clung to him, her fingers clutching his shoulders as he reached down into the center of her soul. When friction gave way to completion, her eyelids fluttered downward and she pressed her fingers into his back. Gabriella moaned the extent of her pleasure against his neck. In one remarkable instant, they shattered together and ecstasy laid waste to every emotion.

Dazed with repletion and bone melting satisfaction, she let him cradle her into the curve of his body and pull the covers over them both. Her heart slowed its breakneck pace as she

closed her eyes and moved toward the ever-beckoning call
of sleep.

"*Ana behibek,*" he whispered against her skin. With a sigh
of complete masculine satisfaction, he slid an arm under her,
then rolled over carrying her with him.

She did not understand what he murmured into her ear. His
words were neither French nor English, but as sleep claimed
her she knew in her heart of hearts that it was not enough.
With his body a perfect fit to hers, his breath was a synco-
pated whisper against her neck. She had not believed that
pain could come with too much tenderness. That one night
would never be enough.

After sitting on the edge of the bed, content with watching
the rise and fall of Gabriella's chest and remembering the im-
print of her skin against his body, Darius was reluctant to in-
terrupt her slumber.

He'd lost count of the number of times he'd watched her
while she'd slept, but this morning was different. He'd awoken
in the wee hours and turned his head. She'd lain so close.
Touching—not touching. Sleeping and waking. He'd watched
her as he did then and something warm filled him, rose through
his veins into his bones, filled his heart, and sat underneath his
skin. It was only now that he could identify it as love.

He hadn't thought it possible but last night had bound him
to her even more tightly. Gently he shook her and when she
opened her eyes and looked at him with trust and tenderness,
his stomach clenched. Darius bent closer and gently nuzzled
the softness of her cheek, inhaling the scent of her skin. She
yawned then wiped the sleep from her eyes after pulling the
covers closer. "Good morning."

Darius reached out, pulled her against him and savored the
smell of her skin, the warm solidity of her body, the sound
of their two hearts beating. Only her presence seemed to as-
sure him that the nightmare he'd had last night was only an

unconscious mechanism for dealing with his unacknowledged fears. Unasked for, the FBI profiler's comments echoed in his head.

"Anton Lexer is not a sociopath nor is he a psychopath and that makes him even more dangerous."

"Explain," Darius demanded.

"Extreme psychopaths kill without regret and with pleasure. Rumor has it that Anton enjoys torture and has perfected his methods under the tutelage of his father. You see, a person who cannot identify with human beings can therefore hurt them or even kill them casually. Each person who has ever been a serious threat to the Lexer family has disappeared."

He drew back and placed a tender kiss on her brow. "If we didn't have to go soon, I wouldn't let you leave the bed."

"I understand." She lowered her head and turned in an attempt to hide a disappointed expression behind her hair.

Darius reached out, placed his fingers underneath Gabriella's chin, and forced her to meet his eyes. "What we shared last night was a beginning we will both see to a very satisfying end."

She shook her head. "It won't work, Darius." The pain in her voice hit him hard. "He tried to kill me, and he won't stop until he does. I won't have you hurt because of me."

"I won't let anything bad happen to you, Gabriella," he said softly.

"I never thought . . ." She started and stopped. "He killed a priest and burned down a church."

"Who?" Darius asked, even though he had a damn good idea who was behind the attack.

"Anton. I smelled the sweet scent of the Spanish cigarettes he smoked." A tremor shook her slender frame. "They both must want me dead."

"Shh," he pulled her shivering body closer.

"I could have prevented this," she murmured.

His jaw tightened. Her voice was stronger now but the direction of her thoughts concerned him. Guilt was a powerful emotion and he'd seen first hand the damage it could do when left unchecked. "That's not a train of thought you need to follow too far. You can't blame yourself for the actions of others."

"This isn't something I can turn off and on at will, Darius." She pulled back from the circle of his arms. "I thought for years that my father didn't love me because of something I had done. During all the months of running from Vasilei, I was in denial."

He took her hands within his own. Gabriella's French accent appeared only when she was upset. And now her words rushed out in a fluid manner only the French could produce. "You can't know that for sure."

She shook her head violently. "I have to go, and this time I'll go *alone*."

"Do you really think that's the solution to everything? Being alone? Well it won't work this time because they're not going to leave you alone."

"They won't find me this time." Her eyes narrowed and she began to back away, but his hands snaked out. He wouldn't let her run from the truth.

"Did you think that I wasn't thorough? That your father hadn't made adequate preparations to keep you hidden? I didn't fail you Gabriella, this country did. The authorities want Anton Lexer badly and they're willing to sacrifice anyone to get him."

"I know."

"Then you need to hear it again. Princess, they will never stop. And all the players in this game have the money and resources to hunt for you from now until eternity. And let's not forget that Anton didn't find you; he was led to you."

"Will you take me to Canada as Sebastian ordered?"

"Your father is afraid just as I am, but he's a businessman, not a soldier. Computer databases are national and information only goes international if there's trouble or criminal activity involved. Although taking you to Canada would make your identity harder to track, it would only be a matter of hours before they found you again. Besides, once the authorities and Anton figure out that you didn't perish in that fire, they'll have him under intense surveillance."

Her eyes widened. "He's in danger."

"All-Star's guarding him as we speak, and he's been under the watch of the federal agents since he returned to New York."

"Why didn't you tell me?" Disentangling herself from his arms, Gabriella moved across the firm hotel mattress, dragging the sheet with her. He had touched every inch of her flesh the night before, but now she needed a shield. Something as insubstantial as the generic white sheet helped keep her emotions in check, helped keep her from curling into a ball and crying, crying until she slept; and in that darkness of sleep the memory of the past twenty-four hours would leave her.

Everything she touched turned to ash. Everyone she trusted turned away. Happiness was meant for other people. Even now she felt the effort to survive too much. Who would mourn her passing?

Only the sight of her clothing scattered on the floor stopped the train of her thoughts as she tried to keep her eyes from the bed and her mind from the potential consequences of their lovemaking.

"Gabriella." Darius's voice brought her attention back to the present, as the sound of her name sent a tremor of desire over her skin and warmth between her thighs. "I failed to protect you last night."

"How could you have known that Anton would be so evil as to kill a priest or burn down a church?" She pretended ignorance of his true meaning.

He moved closer to Gabriella, placing his hand on her bare shoulder, the only inch of her skin she had not covered. He turned her around. "That wasn't what I meant and you know it."

She held her tongue and looked everywhere but his face,

but he read her mind anyway. "We didn't use protection last night," he stated as though he'd just announced the weather forecast.

Her mouth went dry at the implication, but Gabriella didn't allow her alarm to show. "I didn't want to be protected. I wanted to be . . . ," she shook her head and took a breath. Darius fought the urge to pull Gabriella into his arms as her lip trembled and he watched her small teeth bite into her lower lip. "No matter, I'm safe."

"You can't be one hundred percent sure of that."

Gabriella averted her eyes. When she'd set out to seduce him, nothing else had mattered—not the past, the future, or the present. Now there was the possibility she would have to pay for that moment of selfishness. Yet, she couldn't muster any sense of self-recrimination. She had never known completeness like the moment he'd brought her to climax or like the happiness of falling asleep in his arms.

Wrapped in the warmth of him, loving him, being with him, burning with him. Last night, she had the crazy notion that the attraction would dissipate but she'd been wrong. It had only grown stronger. Now in the daylight everything had changed, only she knew that beneath her anger the love she bore for the man standing close had not. "I can never be sure of anything. You've seen to that," she shot back wanting to wound him. "But *if* I'm pregnant, I will handle it. I seduced you and I take full responsibility. *If* there's a child, you need not worry."

With the lightning speed of a scorpion, Darius's fingers found the curve at the base of her throat and he applied a slight pressure—not enough to hurt but just enough to impress upon her the seriousness of the situation. His child would be raised within his family and in his life.

She might be angry and hurt, but it would pass. He would ensure that it would pass. Last night had been a mere signature on an unspoken contract. What he felt for her was not a mere passing heat of the moment or thrill of attraction. Over the course of hours, days, and weeks he'd spent in her company he had come to love her. "Let there be no mistake here. Should you be carrying my child, Gabriella, we will marry."

"It was only once and it's not my time of the month. The chances are . . ."

Darius bent down and rubbed his cheek against hers. "*Insha'allah*, it is as God wills it. Children are precious in my family and among my people. If you are carrying our child, *we* will raise him or her together."

He took her hands within his own and the bed sheet pooled unbidden to the carpet. "You cannot deny that we are tied together, Gabriella. Can you look me in the eyes and tell me that last night did not matter? That the thought that you and I might have conceived a child does not make your heart catch with wonder or fill with joy?"

"I cannot," she whispered.

He inhaled the perfume of her scent and was grateful that he'd woken to check the perimeter of the hotel in the twilight hours and used the payphone to make two very important phone calls. The loosened fabric of his slacks helped to disguise evidence of his deepening awareness of her nude form. The remote chance of becoming a father, the image of her stomach thickened with his child, and a babe at her breasts excited him more than anything he'd ever known. The only thing that could come close was to have Gabriella as his wife. "Everything will be all right," he promised and drew her back into his arms.

"I can't breathe, Darius. I can't breathe past this thing in my throat." She raised her eyes to meet his. "This fear. How can I believe this will end well when there is all this death that seems to follow in my wake? I can't run, and I can't face Vasilei."

"Is it because . . . you still love him?" The question burned in his chest but he had to know. Maybe out of some unconscious defensive safety measure he'd declared his love for her in Arabic. And only when he was sure of his place in her heart would he be able to repeat it in English.

"No." She shook her head, then met his burning gaze. "What I felt for Vasilei wasn't a true love and what I feel for him now isn't true hate. I don't want to hate. I have known too much of it in my feelings for Sebastian. I don't think I'm that strong, Darius."

"There is nothing that you need to do. We have forty-eight hours, maybe more, until they figure out you didn't die in the fire."

"Where will we go?"

"To the only place that can give you what you need." He paused and laid his cheek against her temple. "We go to family."

Chapter Eighteen

They spent over half an hour wiping the room of finger-prints and getting prepared to depart. Leaving the hotel was easy, but the rest would not be. Darius ditched the Land Rover on the outskirts of Newark in a neighborhood that guaranteed that it would be stripped to the bare minimum and sold within hours of their departure. He had taken the extra precaution of removing the license plate and burying it in the bottom of a convenience store dumpster.

They purchased a change of clothing at a small shop next to the bus stop. Not only did he not like his pants, because they stayed at his waist only because of an oversized belt, but he disliked Gabriella's having to purchase a tight sweater. The only thing that worked in their favor was having to wear bulky parkas to keep warm. Another advantage was that his gun was easily concealed in his pocket.

After forcing her to eat, he made them disappear into the vastness of the public transportation system, switching from bus to train for the journey into Philadelphia.

"Is that a good idea? Hiding at your cousin's?" Gabriella asked as they exited the bus at the corner. It went against everything for her to ask for help and the thought of involving other people unnerved her.

He leaned over and kissed her on her brow. "You need to rest and feel safe. Don't worry."

Dawn had begun to wake the city of Philadelphia by the time Darius brought them to the quiet Bucks County suburb. The abrupt phone call he'd made to Nadia last night still weighed in his mind. He wondered what his family would think of his arriving unexpectedly with an unmarried female in his company.

Umar, Nadia's husband, was a moderate Moslem. The son of a wealthy Kuwaiti family had met his cousin while attending the Wharton Business School. Although he was concerned about the family's reaction, Gabriella's unnatural silence worried him more.

After turning down the block and slipping through the side of a neighbor's yard, he unlatched the unlocked fence and held her hand as he made to go up the stairs to the screened in back porch. Yet, Gabriella, who had willingly followed his lead, stopped on the first stair.

"They don't bite," he whispered.

A wan smile lit Gabriella's face but didn't reach her eyes. The golden orbs that had burned him with passion the night before were banked with sadness.

She ran her fingers through her hair and then rubbed her tight jeans. "I'm not exactly dressed for meeting your family." Her voice trailed off as she looked toward the simple oak door. Gabriella had been in the homes of European aristocracy but the thought of meeting Darius's cousin when in such emotional and physical disarray made her very uncomfortable.

"You could meet them wearing nothing but a sack and they would still welcome you. One word of warning. My cousin's husband is a little old-fashioned. Do not be upset if he does not shake your hand. Now let's get you inside before you catch a cold." He took her hand in his and before they reached the front stairs the door was thrown open.

"*Asalamtatum.*" The woman Gabriella assumed was his cousin embraced Darius and before she could move back, the same arms squeezed her tight. "Welcome."

The woman with her dark brown eyes and lightly bronzed olive skin had taken one look at Gabriella and as soon as the introductions had been made she was being swept up a flight of wooden stairs and into a beautifully decorated bedroom. She moved with the grace of a dancer and the confidence of a queen, Gabriella thought. *If only I could be so confident.*

"You must be so worn out from your journey." Nadia examined the woman her cousin had brought to their home. The woman's face, bare of any cosmetics, was lovely, as were her golden eyes. She let out a whisper of a sigh, feeling a slight prickle of envy. Gabriella did not need kohl to make them more beautiful.

Gabriella. Nadia shook her head. *French*, she concluded. Her name along with the slight lilt of her voice brought Nadia to that conclusion. She'd seen the way Darius had stared as she'd led the young woman from the room.

How the mighty have fallen. She shook her head, again remembering her cousin's youthful boasts. Darius had vowed that he would never allow a woman to rule him as her mother ruled her father. She had a strong feeling that one soft word from Gabriella's lips would send him running.

But her thoughts took on a touch of concern as she noticed the tension in the woman's posture and the yawn she was struggling to hide.

Expressing her annoyance, Nadia moved her chin back slightly and made a clicking sound with her tongue. "That cousin of mine. He has spent too much time surrounded by men." She glanced over her shoulder to make sure Gabriella walked behind her. "You would think he was raised without consideration. I would introduce my husband but he won't be home until much later. Come, I will draw you a bath and then after a nap you'll feel more refreshed."

Bemused, Gabriella followed the briskly moving woman down the hall and into the bathroom. "No, it's not like that," she protested in Darius's defense.

"Oh, and what is it then?" Nadia stopped and raised a naturally perfect eyebrow.

Gabriella blushed. "It's been a stressful week for me. I haven't slept much."

Nadia pulled a plush towel from the closet and laid it on the bathroom shelf. "All the more reason for you to relax," she stated firmly, reaching over the large marble tub to turn on the faucet. Truth be known she was filled with questions she wanted to ask but held her tongue. Tonight after the kids were asleep and she was alone with her cousin, the mystery would be solved.

"Please, you don't have to do this. I'm fine."

"You're tired," she corrected, pouring a capful of her favorite bathing oil into the warm water. It was her way to take charge. The demands of running a household and a restaurant would have taxed most women, but for Nadia it was her only way of life. After testing the water, she stood and smiled. "A nightgown and robe are over there on the hamper. Take your time."

Gabriella breathed in the lush steam-filled air and nodded her head. It would do her no good to lie. Although she'd touched the clouds of heaven in Darius's arms the night before, she had not slept well afterward, and although her body demanded rest, she didn't relish the thought of sleep. "Thank you."

"Be at peace," Nadia said solemnly. "You're with family."

Gabriella nodded as the door closed leaving her alone. The nice sized bathroom was beautifully decorated in a mixture of colonial American and Middle Eastern. Bronze sconces combined with sunlight filtered through a frosted windowpane to fill the room with a soft light, while the china white marble bathtub stood adjacent to a stand-alone shower. A mosaic of tiles painted the floor and an antique pewter sink and iron cabinet stood to the side.

Gabriella stripped off her clothing and placed it nicely folded on top of the wicker hamper. Stepping into the water, she sat down, rested her head back, and then sank down low, so low that her chin touched the surface. Within minutes, the combined strength of the warm water, the silence, and the steamy scent of jasmine forced her muscles to relax. A murmur of contentment escaped her lips before she closed her eyes.

It seemed that her world had been turned around again. Her fiancé was trying to kill her, her father wanted a place in her life, and Darius . . . Her thoughts stilled as the mere thought of his name conjured the image of his face. He was a light in the darkness, a constant star she had come to depend on for more than guidance; he was hope. She couldn't believe that it had only been weeks since they'd first met. It felt as though she'd lived another person's life in the space of a few weeks.

With his latest revelation, she did not know how to identify the feelings she had toward him. Yet, one clear note blazed through the confusion of her mind.

"Love," she whispered as a wave of steam lazily rent the air. She had lost her fragile sense of what love was a long time ago. It would be so much simpler if she could just say that she'd taken a lover. But this was so much more with consequences she couldn't fathom. And while her mind struggled to reach a solid conclusion, her body was still imprinted with the magic of his touch.

After bouncing his message off over two dozen satellites, Darius sat back in the leather chair of his cousin's over-the-garage office and sighed. If the world was going to end the next day and only one person could stop it, he would bet on Sergeant Clay Gordan, known to the Delta Omega team simply as "Sergeant."

In military circles, respect was earned by action, not by the number of medals or names on one's insignia worn on the right sleeve. The desert, where split seconds could be the difference between life and death, was a world where people measured revenge not in the space of a man's lifetime but in thousands of years. Darius had been in the military long enough to know that men with the patience, understanding, and intelligence of his senior officer were rare. He understood the intricacies, rivalries, and history of the Middle East region on a par with premier scholars of the world.

"Is everything okay, Darius?"

He focused his eyes on the doorway and forced a smile to his lips at the sight of Nadia. "It will be."

"May I come in?"

"Yeah, I'm finished." He turned around and powered down the laptop computer.

"How's Gabriella?"

Nadia's smile relaxed the tension in his shoulders he hadn't known was there. "She's fast asleep in the guest room."

A moment of silence followed until his cousin closed the door. "Father called and asked about you yesterday."

"How's he doing? When I was home he surprised me with the announcement that he planned on retiring."

"He's still going through with it." Nadia sighed loudly and then dropped into a chair. "Mother thinks that he will drive her crazy at home now. She plans to get him a hobby. Maybe golf."

"She's been begging him for years to retire and now she's having second thoughts?" Darius shrugged his shoulders and shook his head in bemusement.

"And third and fourth," Nadia continued. "But they both are concerned about you."

"I'm fine."

"Can I tell them that I've talked to you?"

"No." Darius placed his hands at his sides and was careful not to tense up. "They may be listening to your phone calls."

"Who are they?"

"I can't get into this now."

"Whatever you are in revolves around Gabriella, doesn't it?"

"Nadia," he warned. "This does not concern you."

Her heavy black brows slashed downward and Darius cursed inwardly. "Because I'm a woman? Do you know how much I despise that phrase? How many times I had to swallow my hurt and anger when my husband's family came to visit and questioned my presence in the restaurant I helped build, Darius?" Her foot snuck out and kicked him gently on the shin. "I had thought that growing up in this country you would not have caught the disease that men have in Egypt, but I see that I was wrong. You are just like Grandfather."

Darius's jaw tightened as he felt the urge to grip the armrests of his chair. Their paternal grandfather, while a good man, nevertheless believed in the old ways. And in the old ways, a woman's place remained in the home and nowhere else. "You know that's not true."

"Do I? You call me in the middle of the night asking for help and bring an unmarried woman into my home, and I'm expected to obey and not ask questions?"

"Your husband understands."

"Umar is not your blood; I am. He also respects my decisions and my mind. He has left this in my hands." She exploded up from her chair amid the rustling of her robe. "I think I will go talk to my new guest. Women often are smart about these things."

"Nadia, wait." Darius stood up. "The FBI has your house under surveillance."

"Why?" She'd stopped but her back was still to him.

"They want to bring down a powerful man and plan to use an innocent to do it."

"Gabriella?"

"Yes. I need to keep her safe and hidden until some solution can be found."

"You'll hide her here?" His cousin turned around to face him.

"No." He rubbed his brow. "It would be too dangerous. I've

made arrangements for us to leave tomorrow evening. All I need is for you to give us a lift to the restaurant."

"She is beautiful."

Darius blinked twice at the abrupt change in topic, but he made no attempt to deny her observation. "Yes, she is."

"Will you marry her?" Nadia's chestnut eyes narrowed on his face and Darius couldn't help but grimace at the look that was identical to his aunt's when she delved into his personal life.

"Nadia." He let out a loud sigh. "Now is not the time."

"The heart knows no schedule. And it is past time that you settle down and . . ."

To forestall the imminent lecture, Darius took two steps forward and enveloped his older cousin in a warm hug. "I always said I would keep my head if I fell in love. Then Gabriella entered my life and made a liar out of me. Don't worry, *bint khal*. When all of this has passed and I have received blessings from your father, Gabriella's father, and mine, I will give you a bride whose hands you may paint with the brownest of henna, and cheeks you can kiss."

"Promise on Mother's rice pudding?" Nadia drew back and arched her brow in a gesture exactly like her father's.

Darius laughed deep in his chest, remembering the fights they'd had over the last spoonful of Aunt Inas's signature dessert. "I promise. Now why don't we go and see to it that those little nieces and nephews don't wake up my future bride."

Long after they had eaten and Gabriella had returned to bed, Darius sat in the dark of his cousin's house watching the outside through a tiny opening in the curtains. Sure enough, an ordinary car sat across the street with two plainclothes men inside. He would not be moving anytime soon, but the speed of their reaction made him well aware that the Lexer brothers could not be far behind. He had to get Gabriella to a safe place, but the question was where and when.

*   *   *

Much later, hearing a half-scream from the bed, Darius moved from the chair he'd placed near the window to sit beside Gabriella. He'd spent the last few hours observing the FBI agents watching the house. Darius sat quietly holding her shivering body.

The delayed shock of the other night's activities had just set in. He'd seen it many times before when the adrenaline ran out, the danger passed, and the reality that one might not have made it out alive set in. He cradled her close and inhaled. The scent of soap and jasmine rose from her skin. The nightgown his cousin had given her to wear was a thin protection from his eyes.

"He wants me dead," she whispered through the roughness of her throat.

He looked down at her closed eyes in time to see a tear run fast down her cheek. "How could I have been so wrong?" she moaned.

"Shh . . ." Darius held her tight and spared one last glance toward the window. He knew she was thinking of Anton.

He must be getting desperate, Darius reasoned. To kill a priest and set fire to a Catholic Cathedral was an indication of someone who was running out of options and a person who had no limits to the evil he could commit. While Darius cursed the man, he also cursed himself. It was partially his fault.

Protecting Gabriella but also keeping the complete truth from her was like a double-edged sword, and the man who had no fear was afraid. She was an innocent and her generosity of spirit moved him as little had since he'd joined the military.

"You once asked if I wanted you to tell me a bedtime story," she murmured against his neck.

He nodded, recalling the night she'd taken over his bed. "Can I have one now, please?"

"What would you like to hear?"

"Anything. I just want to think of something—anything besides the priest's face or the flames." A shiver swept through her body.

Darius eased back against the headboard and cradled her in his arms. "We were driving through the Hamada el Homra on one of my first missions. Believe me, Princess, it's the loneliest stretch of road on earth. About ten thousand square miles of nothing but red ground and white sky. It had a reputation of dreadfulness in the region, but coming after the black basalt boulders of the Kharug, it was a smooth drive.

"The reason the place was avoided was because it is an empty wasteland without a single piece of vegetation for hundreds of miles.

But it was lovely, with its sand a pearly gray and red stones about the size of your hand set vertically on edge. When the sun was low in the horizon, each slope was a picture of beauty. The light poured down in different colors as we drove, from coral pink to dark crimson. However inhospitable, the desert was a wonder to look upon." His voice faded to a whisper at the evenness of her breathing. Darius looked at her half closed eyes. "Just like you."

He tucked the quilt around her shoulders and sent her to sleep with his memories of Sudan. Dressed in a Moslem robe, he'd watched the sun set while standing atop a bridge spanning the joining of the Blue and White Niles—a place referred to in Arabic poetry as the longest kiss in history. He left the room and went downstairs. It would be a long night.

Before the sun had risen to peek over the East Coast, Darius had woken from his doze on the downstairs sofa and crept up to Gabriella's room. With the grayish light of sunrise creeping into the room, he bent down to brush his lips across her unlined brow.

Her golden eyes opened and his heart caught with happiness. "Good morning," she whispered.

"I didn't want to have you wake up without this." He moved closer and kissed her deeply. "Although my cousin and her family are more Americanized than their parents, I don't want you made to feel uncomfortable by having a male in your bedroom." He grinned before taking a seat on the bed.

Darius watched as Gabriella journeyed from sleep to full wakefulness. "Did you get any sleep last night?" she asked.

"Of course."

Her light eyes narrowed on his face and he knew that his words belied his appearance. Darius had been to the bathroom for only moment and had neglected to shave. The stubble on his chin would soon grow into a beard unless he took a razor to it soon.

"How much?"

"Four hours," he lied without skipping a beat.

"Is that enough?"

"Plenty. Now how did you sleep, Princess? Was the bed not too hard or too soft?" He reached out and brushed a lock of her hair behind her ear and she caught his hand within her own.

"Too empty," she replied.

Darius exhaled and a smile pulled the corner of his lips upward. "Well if it makes you feel any better, the couch downstairs is too short and too narrow."

After few minutes of hastily suppressed laughter, Darius moved to the head of the bed and placed his arms around Gabriella's shoulder.

"Darius?" she whispered.

"Hmm?" he replied while absentmindedly stroking her shoulder. The calm he felt with Gabriella laying against his chest was unlike anything he'd ever experienced.

"I dreamed last night."

"Were they good dreams?"

"I saw white sand and blue rivers, mountains so beautiful they brought tears to my eyes."

"That wasn't a dream, Princess. It's a place. And one day we'll travel there."

"And I'll get to ride on a camel?"

"You can ride on a camel," he laughed. "I'll be in an air-conditioned jeep."

"It sounds so simple."

Gabriella moved her head away from his chest and Darius placed his fingers underneath her chin, forcing her to meet his eyes. "It will be."

"But he won't give up, will he?"

Darius chewed on her question before answering. Whether the *he* Gabriella referred to was Anton or Vasilei, it didn't matter. Neither of the Lexer brothers would give up.

"I used to think that I didn't have anything in common with Vasilei Lexer except that I love you."

She looked at him curiously. "But I was wrong, Princess. We do share something and that is determination. I never quit and what we shared the other night was a beginning we will both see to an end."

She blinked and he followed her gaze toward the window. One weak beam of sunlight had penetrated the thick velvet curtains. "Will my presence here put your family in danger?"

"I'm the bodyguard and the soldier, remember? Just keep away from the windows and we'll be fine. We'll be leaving here soon."

A minute passed and she buried her face in his chest, and then murmured, "I want to be strong like you, yet I just wish I could hide under the bed like a child. Even if I could go for five minutes without thinking of Anton, so many other things have changed overnight. My father has publicly named me his heir. Jensen isn't even Sebastian's son."

"You don't have to take it all in at once, Princess," he reassured. "Just know that everything is going to be okay."

"*Tu ne comprends pas*, Darius," she murmured in French. "I've built a large part of my life on hating Sebastian—on believing that he never loved my mother or me. Now it's all crashing down. I don't know what to think or how to feel."

He kissed her softly on her brow before urging her to lie

back down. She was wrong; he knew exactly how it felt to have his world turned on its axis. He'd experienced it the moment his mind accepted what his heart had known all along—he'd fallen in love.

Darius pushed her hair away from her cheek. "Every boy has a first love. I spent a summer working at a refugee camp in southern Nigeria. I became friends with the daughter of our translator. Imari was delicate, yet strong, beautiful, and a fighter. Just like you."

Her curious eyes rested on his face. "What happened to her? Did she marry another man and break your heart?"

"No, I returned there some years ago to find out that she had given herself to God and became a nun."

"Why are you telling me this story, Darius?"

He rubbed the back of his hand over her slender throat. "Because I've discovered something, Princess. I need you, like air, like blood and the thought of how close I came to losing you will haunt me for the rest of my life."

"Darius . . ."

"I don't make promises lightly, but this I swear to you. When this is all over, we will rebuild, together. You and me. Always and forever," he whispered against her soft lips, then drew back to look her in the eyes. "I love you and I promise that when this is over, we will have love aplenty, and I will give you joys outnumbered. We will share perfect moments, and children to turn our hair grey, and family to keep us rich."

"I love you," she stated. Her golden eyes shimmered with tears and he wanted to lie down and make love to her more than anything in the world.

"Shh," he whispered. "*Ne pleure pas.* Don't cry," he implored. With the pad of his thumb, he brushed away a teardrop. "Don't argue with fate, little one; just try to get some more rest. In a few hours, my nieces will be beating down your door."

* * *

An hour after Darius left her, Gabriella found her way downstairs and, following the sounds of laughter, walked into a room unlike any she had ever seen. The euphoria of knowing that Darius loved her still flowed through her limbs. The warm sensation staved off the morning chill and the harsh reality that government agents were watching the house.

Deep wide sofas wrapped around the room, thick carpeted floors and an eclectic mixture of metal art adorned the walls, and a gilded iron chandelier hung from the ceiling. She saw the small things she hadn't seen the night before—the pictures on the wall, toys peeking out from under furniture, and small shoes set in a neat row near the front door. The silence of the large home was broken by the sound of voices. The air was pungent with the delicious smell of cooking food, and her stomach reminded her it had been far too long since she'd eaten something solid.

She paused at the side of the doorway and watched Darius sitting cross-legged in the corner laughing at the antics of two toddlers playing on the floor. Something bloomed in the region of her heart, something she hadn't felt since the night she'd witnessed the murders: hope. The children's laughter bubbled through the room and erased all the dark thoughts that had been looming over her. It was impossible to resist the sheer enjoyment of the moment.

He looked up and his lips formed a wicked grin. "Sleeping Beauty has woken."

"What time is it?"

"Lunch time. Nadia's just finished putting together a virtual feast." Darius rose from the couch, quick and agile as a cat, and came over to take her hands. He placed a chaste kiss on her brow and led her farther into the room. "I'd like you to meet the youngest members of the household."

Sometime later, they sat in a sunroom at the back of the house. Although snow still blanketed the lawn, Gabriella was warm and toasty. Music played through the room and a supper of cheeses, roast beef, salad, and yogurt was spread out over a low bamboo table. But that wasn't all. Nadia's trips to the kitchen brought rice with vegetables and lamb, an assortment of dishes with beans and vegetables, including eggplant, zucchini, cauliflower, spinach, onions, parsley, and chickpeas.

After eating, Gabriella didn't know what to do. Taking her cue from Darius's cousin, she picked up plates and helped Nadia clear the table. Standing next to the sink, she began to rinse the dishes and place them into the dishwasher.

"You really don't have to do that."

"It's the least I can do." Gabriella looked over as the other woman wiped down the kitchen counter. "You've opened your house to a stranger."

"The woman who holds my cousin's heart could never be a stranger, Gabriella."

She lowered her gaze and smothered a blush. "He must have told you why we're here."

"He mentioned it, yes, but it really doesn't matter."

"Doesn't matter?" Her hands stilled in the dishwater. "I could have gotten him killed."

Nadia placed a comforting hand on her shoulder. "And if he'd been injured or had died trying to save you, then I could be no more proud. The men of our family are warriors, descended from a long line of extraordinary heroes and leaders. They fight, Gabriella. My father's battles are in business, my uncle's in saving the world. But one thing they have in common is the lengths they will go through to keep loved ones safe."

"I would do the same for him," she vowed.

Nadia flashed her a wide smile and something unfurled in the region of Gabriella's heart. "I know . . . As I would for my husband and kids. Poor Darius."

Baffled, Gabriella took the small spoon from Nadia's fingers as the other woman erupted into giggles.

"Sorry." Nadia placed her hands over her stomach. "It's just that in high school he vowed that he would go back to Egypt and marry a meek village wife. And to see how far the mighty has fallen has done me a world of good."

Later on that afternoon as Darius ensconced himself in front of the computer, Gabriella picked up the copy of the *Philadelphia Inquirer*. The tea kettle began to boil as she read: *Last night, St. Paul's Cathedral, one of America's oldest Catholic churches, suffered heavy smoke and fire damage. One priest was found dead and three fire fighters were injured. According to fire officials, the blaze is being investigated as arson.*

Fear seized her heart and she quickly excused herself and fled upstairs.

Chapter
Nineteen

Darius and Gabriella left the next evening amidst crying from the children and subdued glances from Nadia and her husband. They'd both huddled down in the backseat of his cousin's minivan; then at the restaurant they slipped out of the car and into an old pickup truck parked down a side alley.

They were traveling again. Only this time as she tried to bury herself deeper under the blanket Nadia had given her, there was neither the luxury of the Land Rover nor the smooth ride of the train. She could feel every pothole and rough spot on the highway as they traveled into the night. The pickup truck's engine roared and the radio had probably ceased to function a long time ago.

It wasn't until they reached the outskirts of Philadelphia that Darius stopped checking the rearview mirror every few minutes to see if they were being followed. She noticed he kept within the speed limit, used his signals, and did nothing to arouse suspicion. He only pulled over for gas and then he made Gabriella crouch down to the floorboard.

She didn't even know where they were going, but it didn't matter as long as they went away—away from Anton and Vasilei and away from her father. Darius didn't know how lucky he was. He had a family that adored and would do anything for him.

Turning from the window, she looked at Darius as he drove

and felt another pang of regret in her heart. He was the first man who had been true, who had neither played her falsely nor gone back on his word. He would risk his career and put his family in danger for her.

She turned back to the window and strained her eyes to catch hurried glimpses of the large billboards. Only when the two-lane freeway gave way to four lanes and the traffic became heavier did her eyes narrow. Highway signs became more prevalent and she wished she'd studied geography harder because she could not recognize any of the names.

After a couple of hours, he exited the highway and the truck slowed. All the twists and turns and the lines of shops gave way to rows of houses. She peered out as he pulled into a driveway and stepped out of the truck. Gabriella didn't watch as he went around the side, looked at the stone grey house, and then turned to look down the block.

The houses with their uniform vinyl siding lined up alongside one another stretched into what looked to her eyes to be a never ending row. She sighed and the smoky wisps of her breath reflected in the shadows cast by the streetlight. It was a fitting place for him to bring her. In the midst of this uniformity, this suburban jungle, there was little chance anyone could find her. As Darius raised the garage door, the knot in Gabriella's stomach eased. He would keep his promise to keep her safe; now all she had to do was convince him to keep her hidden.

After surveying the house, Darius stepped into the garage and closed the utility door behind him. Upon arriving at the house, the first thing he'd done was start a fire in the living room's gas fireplace, then went on a room-to-room search with few results.

Now, he scrutinized the garage until his eyes fell on a slight uneven edge higher up in the wall. Hidden in plain sight, the indicator of a false panel couldn't be discovered unless someone had been trained to look. He pressed in delicately, then slid the panel back.

Darius's lips curled upward and he let out an impressed whistle at the sight. Virgil Baxter, weapons master and sergeant in the United States Special Forces, was always well equipped whether in civilian life or during military action. Slipping his own military issue 9-millimeter pistol out of his back pocket, Darius ejected his clip and proceeded to re-load the half-empty cartridge.

Cocking the barrel to load one into the chamber, he placed the weapon on safety and repositioned it in the small of his back. Carefully closing the hidden compartment, he surveyed the otherwise empty garage. His teammate had purchased the house to be close to his ex-wife and young daughter. The tragedy of it was that the current situation in the Middle East kept his teammate on Army transport or on duty down at Fort Bragg. Everything in the house, from the light bulbs to the coordinated furniture, was brand new. Virgil had wanted the place as a home, not a hideout.

Darius's mouth compressed in a thin line as he opened and stepped through the garage door and into the connected laundry room. He could see the faint glow from the kitchen and inhaled. The scent of cooking took him completely by surprise.

"Hey," Gabriella stuck her head in, "I hope you're hungry."

"Smells good. What do we have here?"

"I grabbed something to make soup with from your pantry." Something in his expression made her step closer to him. "This is your place, isn't it?" she questioned.

"No, it's a friend's place."

"Oh no." Her brows drew together with guilt.

"Don't worry, he knows we're here."

"Will he be coming home tonight?"

Darius clucked and put his arm around her slender waist. "Not unless he can fly faster than the speed of light. Sling should be on duty in Afghanistan."

"Sling?"

"His *nom de guerre*. The real name of this place's owner is Virgil Baxter."

"Darius." She turned in his arms and her gentle eyes gazed at him with such openness and love that for a moment something tightened in his throat to the point he couldn't breathe. Many women had looked at him, enlisted and professional. The risk of being with a Delta, the thrill of sleeping with a Special Forces Agent. Yet, none had looked at him as Gabriella did.

"Why did All-Star and Javier call you Dare?"

"Easier to remember than Darius." He grinned, leading the two of them over to the stove. Something in him didn't want to tell her what he'd done to earn the nickname. It was that same part of him that wanted to keep his profession separate from the love he had for her. He didn't want the ugliness and death that he'd seen on the battlefield to touch her, nor for her to ever associate the hands that held her gently with hands that could kill.

Even so, the knowledge and the skills the military had spent hundreds of thousands of dollars honing would get her out of the situation with Anton Lexer. "Just in case you're curious, they also called me 'The Best.' Just like the meal I'm looking forward to sharing with you."

He looked down into her upturned face and then kissed her on the brow with the hope that he could put off for a little longer her crash course into his world. He turned to look at the clock on the microwave. In less than ten hours, three of his teammates would arrive to assist him in taking down Lexer. He intended to make use of every minute. "I thought you told me you didn't know how to cook," he commented.

He caught her narrow gaze and returned it. She shrugged a slender shoulder. "The box came with explicit instructions and complete ingredients."

He took his hands and her arms and put them over her

shoulder. He struggled to keep the grin off his lips as they intertwined around his neck. "I adore you, Princess."

"Even though I can't cook and your family probably thinks I'm trouble?"

In response, his fingers trailed down the smooth softness of her throat to trace the silver chain to the amulet, which rested comfortably in the upper hollows of her breast. "Did Nadia tell you about this necklace?"

"No." Gabriella's breath trembled at the rising heat within. She looked down at the silver filigree in the shape of a hand. In the middle lay an open blue eye. "Your cousin told me not to take it off until the danger passed."

"In Arabic it is called a *hamasa*, meaning "hand of Fatima", who was the daughter of Mohammed. It is a symbol for protection; the blue eye wards off evil spirits. Our grandmother gave this to her mother before she left Egypt to join my uncle in Detroit."

"I should give it back."

"She put this around your neck to show that my family welcomes you, little one. Nadia is one who would forever collect sisters. She says brothers are too much trouble."

Gabriella quickly lowered her face to hide the glistening of moisture. A sister.

"Come on." He tilted her chin upward and grinned again. "It's not like I'm not broken up with grief at the thought of having you as a sister."

She playfully smacked his hand. "I'd have run away from home."

Laughing, Darius let her go and opened a couple of the cabinet doors until he came to the pantry. Pulling out a bag of cornmeal and flour, he proceeded to find a bowl and spoon.

"I can't have you running outside, so how about I whip up some cornbread to go with this? You can watch and learn."

"Would you like an apron?"

"No," he said soberly. "Just you."

One eye closed in a wink as a smile broke like sunrise on

her face. "I'll set the table, then I'll be back to keep you from burning down the house."

After they took their seats at the small round table in the breakfast nook, Gabriella asked. "So where exactly are we?"

"New Jersey."

He watched as she almost lost her grip on the spoon. "Why? I thought we were trying to get away from Anton. Why are we closer?"

"By now the FBI and Anton realize that you didn't die in that church fire, Gabriella. Both of them will expect us to be traveling as far and as fast as we can away from New York. Our best chance of staying hidden is to stay close and stay down."

"Is that all?"

"No, my teammates are traveling over land to meet here. Once they arrive we're going to come up with a plan to get rid of Anton Lexer once and for all."

She placed her spoon gently on the table and reached across taking his hand within hers. For the first time she noticed the rough callous on his fingertips and the pad of his palm. "What are you planning?"

"All that you need to know is that we will protect you."

The hard inflection of his voice and the coldness of his face stuck in her stomach like a rock and threatened to send up the portion of the meal she'd just eaten. Gabriella pulled back so abruptly she almost tipped over her chair in her eagerness to stand. "You want to protect me? Fine, but I will not allow you or anyone else to kill for me! There is already too much blood on my hands."

"Stop this, Gabriella."

"No. You stop it. There's nothing to keep us from disappearing. Darius, we can just run away."

"What about Sebastian, Gabriella? Would you leave him as well?"

Emotion welled in her throat at the thought of leaving her father so soon after she'd reconnected with him, but she forced it away and gave a small shrug. "Until recently, we hadn't seen each other in years; will a few more be so much?"

At her nonchalant shrug, he pressed on. "Yes, every moment in life is precious and family more precious than all else. You've already let Vasilei and Anton Lexer take your innocence. Are you going to let them take away the opportunity to get to know your father too?"

"If it means keeping you safe, yes."

"I'm not at risk here."

"There is another option." She paused for several moments. "I can end this by going back to Vasilei."

Rage poured over every muscle in his body and he pulled her to him roughly. "Damn it woman, I love you and I would have you in chains before I'll let you go back to him."

"Will you?" She lifted her hands from his and then placed them around his. Her eyes flashed. "Will you kill him?"

"He is a threat to you, Princess. And I won't let anyone hurt you."

Her eyes narrowed as her hands pressed against his chest. "Does that include you?"

"Yes."

"Leave him alone, Darius."

"Listen to yourself, Gabriella. It almost sounds like you're protecting him."

She blinked twice, then shook her head. "Maybe I am a little. You don't understand the kind of childhood he had, Darius. His own father made him watch as he ordered his soldiers to torture prisoners to death. I can't help but feel sorry for Vasilei."

"We are all responsible for our actions, Princess. Vasilei must be held accountable for his."

"Let someone else do it. Not you. Run away with me." She pushed her hands under his sweater and rubbed her palms against his chest. She moved in close, trailed her lips over his

jaw, and whispered low in his ears. "You and I. We can fin
a small place far from here. Maybe Mexico or California?
can find a job at a beach bar or a coffee shop. You can join th
police force and visit me every day. I promise to give you fre
doughnuts."

"You tempt me. God knows you do."

"Prove it," Gabriella breathed as her nipples tightened in re
sponse to the heat of desire in his eyes. "If you love me . . ."

"Hush, little one. I won't let you become a fugitive," h
murmured as she clung to him. Swearing under his breath, h
pushed her back, back until she bumped against the wall op
posite the fireplace.

If you love me . . .

Darius buried outside thoughts deep in the back of hi
mind and let his heart's eye open fully to look upon he
face—the curves and hollows, the sweep of her eyelashes
the rise of her brow—and a wave of inarticulate hunge
swept over him. With her head tilted back, Gabriella's eye
were half-lidded as she looked up at him with those se
ductive, beautiful eyes. At the sound of her soft whimper
her lashes rose and their eyes locked. He could see her los
ing it a little as the shimmer of golden orbs caught in th
light of the fireplace, and before he knew what he was doin
he was sinking his hands in her dark hair, entwining hi
fingers in the thick, heavy waves, and kissing her hard
bruising her with his mouth.

He was a warrior and his was that of certainties. There wa
no if, only love. He felt a shock go through his body as thei
lips touched, surging through his chest and stomach and int
his groin, which was now hard and throbbing with an un
voiced need. The feel of her pelvis pressed against the tigh
line of his jeans brought home the fact that he needed her
wanted her. And even though they were in danger and some
where dimly he remembered this, for one brief moment i
time it didn't matter—none of it mattered.

"Now? Here?" she whispered against his mouth.

"Yes, now . . ." He pulled her shirt over her head and tossed it to the floor; all the while his lips never left her skin.

This was not a scared girl, but a passionate woman. Her fingers slipped under his sweater and scratched a hard, wicked line over the skin of his shoulders and chest before pulling the garment over his head. Not a kitten but a tiger met him, her sharp teeth biting his lips, sucking hungrily at his tongue as his fingers slipped down her back, over her hips and thighs, and then he had her in his hands and was lifting her and moving between her long, luscious legs.

Their movements were frenzied, the fumbling, breathless gestures of lovers too long apart. His fingers clamped onto the zipper to her pants, jerking it down so hard that he nearly ripped it. Then he came back closer and ground his erection against the hot place between her legs, those same limbs wrapping themselves around his waist and holding him there, tightly, as she flung back her head and moaned.

Black bra, black panties teased him, and he pushed the lace of her bra down and the soft cotton of her panties down so that she could kick them off. Then and only then did he pay proper homage to her breasts. He flicked his tongue across one pebble-hard nipple, then moved to the other.

"Darius . . ." Her lips parted with passion as she watched the hard line of his face at her breast, sucking her nipple hard, his black hair brushing against her sensitive skin. He touched her heat and found it moist. Darius slipped a finger inside and her muscles clenched around him.

He kissed her again, and she reached down, unbuckling his belt, unfastening his jeans, her fingers taking him into her hands and squeezing oh-so-gently and roughly all at the same time.

And when she had positioned him close to her entrance, he paused and a growl of frustration ripped from her throat. Yet at that moment reason took hold. At the last second, with every piece of his soul howling to possess what was his, he held back.

"Your friends," she gasped.

"Won't be here for hours."

"Why have you stopped?"

"I need protection, Princess."

"Do you . . ."

"In my wallet."

She raised a brow. "And I thought you were just buying me a chocolate bar."

"You got something you needed and I did the same."

Her hand reached around and dug into his back pocket. "I still have needs."

Seconds later, the sensation of her fingers on his shaft almost made him lose it right then and there. The moment she had him fully protected, Darius took her hand within his own and pushed them back against the wall.

There were no words, only breathing as he watched her golden eyes darken as he entered her slowly, inch by inch until he was completely sheaved within the heat of her thighs. And the sight of her heavily lidded gaze coupled with a low moan almost drove him insane. Nothing on earth could have enflamed him more. With that, he plunged into her slick, tight heat, and she cried out, wrapping her legs around his waist as her head flung back.

A tongue of flame followed his tongue on her neck as he nipped at her skin, as the trembling harsh sound of her own breathing filled her ears. He pressed against her whole body, throwing himself into her with his mouth, his limbs, his flesh and bone. In awe she met him—welcomed him—and even though Gabriella felt he could go no deeper, he filled her as everything dropped away and pleasure poured down.

"Love you . . ." he whispered, his breath soft in her ear. He slowed down then, cradling her gently. As he began to move against her again, his hands clenched convulsively around her waist.

She cried out and his eyes flew open in alarm. But she just clenched about him, as her harsh breathing matched his and sweat gleamed on her skin. He groaned watching her, feeling her. Then too soon, he jerked and came, spilling himself, his heart, his very soul into her. Her arms locked around his shoulders, her breath catching, and he felt the ripples of her own release in tandem with his own.

"And I you." Gabriella's voice broke at the hard streak of excruciating pleasure that shot through her womb. "Always." She buried her face in his shoulder and struggled to breath, struggled to hold on to the feel of his heartbeat against hers, the scent of his skin, the love of him.

Much later, after they'd gathered their clothes and settled into one of the guestrooms, Gabriella wondered what the future would hold for both of them. Her breathing eased as Darius settled into the bed behind her and pulled her back into his chest. As the line between being awake and asleep began to blur, she imagined a man whom she wanted as a husband. A man who had a passion for his career, loved his wife and family, doted on his children, was willing to give what he valued most, and did whatever was necessary to keep the family going. She imagined a man like the one who held her.

Even before she opened her eyes the next morning, Gabriella knew that Darius had gone. It was more than the coldness but the utter silence. His breathing had become to her the most beautiful sound in the world to fall asleep to and the most welcome upon waking. Gabriella sat up, careful to keep herself covered, and cocked her head to the side as she heard voices.

Men's voices trickled underneath the door and she remembered Darius mentioning the arrival of his teammates. Nude, she rose from the bed and went into the adjoining bathroom. After a shower, she would greet them—these men Darius spoke so fondly of that it bordered on love. These men whom he trusted with his life and with hers.

Chapter
Twenty

"Good morning, Miss," the men said in chorus upon Gabriella's entrance into the dining room. Darius suppressed a wince at the rough sound of chairs as they all stood up. He also rose from his chair to stand by her side. Introductions were necessary but he didn't want to do it. Not because he disliked Gabriella having contact with his military life, but because of the looks his two unmarried teammates gave her. Looks he could only respond to by glaring, but knew it couldn't be helped. With her hair still damp from a shower and the well-loved flush on her cheeks, they couldn't help but stare.

Hell, *he* was having a hard time.

"Gabriella. Meet Eric Lambert, Thomas Hart, and my command officer, Clay Gordan."

She moved forward with an attempt to shake their hands, but Darius forestalled the motion by taking her hands within his. Gabriella narrowed her eyes while his expression remained unmoved except for a slight twitch of his full lips. Tiny darts of arousal pricked her skin at the memory of how his lips felt on the intimate places of her body the night before. Gabriella lowered her face to hide the rush of blood to her cheeks.

"You still look half asleep, Princess. I was just headed to the kitchen to bring out a fresh pot of coffee."

"Really?" Gabriella caught his glance toward the kitchen and then surveyed the faces of the men. It didn't take a nuclear scientist to figure out that for the moment they wanted her out of the room. "Of course, I could use one myself," she replied.

"It's pretty strong, Miss." The heavy southern drawl pulled her attention away from Darius.

"It's Thomas, right?" The sun had tanned his complexion darker than hers and his eyes were so brown they appeared to be black, under thick lashes and heavy brows.

"Yes."

"Where are you from?"

"Born and raised just outside of Roanoke, Virginia."

"Thomas." She moved toward the table and addressed the brown-haired man with sideburns who had been straddling the dining room chair. None of the men looked like any soldiers she'd ever seen. For a moment she entertained the notion that the men weren't what they claimed to be but then dismissed the thought at the sight of their weapons, the pile of equipment, and black nylon duffle bags sitting in the living room. "Is that your cup?"

"Yes, it is."

"Would you like a refill?"

"That'd be nice."

"You just take a seat and get back to work. I'll be right back."

After the swinging door to the kitchen closed behind her, all of his teammates' attention turned to Darius as they sat down. His commanding officer spoke first. There was an undeniable sense of authority about Clay, and his word was always the final one, no matter the circumstance or the situation. "Dare?"

"Yeah?"

"Does she have a sister?"

"Not that I know of."

"Cousins?" Thomas spoke up.

Darius shook his head and stifled the urge to laugh at the frustrated expression on his teammate's round face. "Nope."

"Then you are a damn lucky man."

"I know." He looked thoughtfully toward the kitchen, then turned his attention back to the men at the table. "Don't know if I said this before, but thanks for coming up."

"Glad to get off the base," Eric responded. "My wife is at her mother's and they cancelled the training exercise because of hail and snow. So you had ten guys, fully armed, fully operational, and ready for war. The last thing they wanted was to be sitting in the squad with their thumbs up their rear end."

"Yeah, I was glad to get out too."

"Here you go," Gabriella announced while portraying the epitome of a perfect hostess even though two laptop computers, blueprints, and three weapons set the table instead of dishware.

Gabriella brought the coffee carafe, sugar, cream and empty mugs out to the dining room on a serving tray. If she hadn't been in the kitchen the night before, she would have sworn the coffee had been brewed and left to age for weeks.

She sat down in the only unoccupied chair and helped herself to a cup of coffee. She added at least three full scoops of powdered cream but to minimal effect. It was only after she'd stirred and lifted the cup to her lips that she noticed that she'd become the center of attention. Raising her cup, she took a sip and sheer willpower made her swallow. One breath later, acid began to rip away the lining of her stomach.

"Is everything okay? I made that batch myself."

She aimed a weak smile in the direction of the older man—Clay, Gabriella remembered. She could see Darius tense out of the corner of her eyes. "It's just fine."

"Good," he nodded. "So where were we?"

Gabriella sat back relieved even as her stomach protested. Without even realizing it, she wanted their respect. She looked over the four large men. Even seated they dominated the room. Eric's unlined mahogany complexion belied his deep voice and streaks of white peppering his hair. She had the impression that he would never be caught unaware because his eyes never stopped shifting. He'd been the first to see her as she'd tried to slip down the stairs without being noticed.

Yet, she would have known that the man named Clay was their leader even without Darius's introduction. Long dark silver streaked hair hung down his back. His skin bore the tan of a man who spent a great deal of time in the sun, while pronounced cheekbones and a sharp chin hinted at his Native American origins. He would be the first person everyone would turn to in a meeting even if he had not been seated at the front of the table. It was the way he pinned a person with his hazel eyes, as though he could look into your head and within seconds read the book of your life and pass judgment.

Eric answered. "All-Star just checked in. Lexer's men have the penthouse under observation but no attempts have been made against Mr. van Ryne."

Clay flipped a folder closed. "Anton Lexer is a distrustful S.O.B. The arms deal won't go through without him and according to my sources the Russians need at least one more week to pinpoint the location of the arms. He tapped the table before continuing, "Eric, how feasible would it be to grab Anton and keep him under wraps for a week?"

"Odds aren't good. He travels with his own personal guard and likes to keep to public places. We couldn't get him without putting bystanders in harm's way. The younger brother would be a better target."

"The Feds want him bad, but they want to do it by the book. The Lexer family has powerful friends in both the United Nations and down on Pennsylvania Avenue."

"There is another way," Gabriella spoke up. "I wasn't the only one to witness Anton's killing."

"No, Gabriella." Darius's hand clamped down on her arm.

"Let her speak," Clay ordered.

"Vasilei was there." More than aware of Darius's fierce glare, she continued. "Maybe I can convince him to—"

Eric finished her sentence. "To turn on his own brother."

"It's a chance—"

"That I'm not willing to let you take," Darius interjected. "Anton Lexer has tried to kill you not once but three times and we don't know if your ex-fiancé is in on it as well."

"That's a risk I am willing to take," Gabriella stubbornly replied.

"Forget it."

"Enough." Clay's softly worded command had the impact of a gunshot in the room. "I believe that Ms. Marie has given us the key to solving this problem."

"Commander," Darius started. This had gotten too far out of his control. He had never once doubted Clay. On his order he would run into a burning building if the man assured him he'd come out alive, but Gabriella wasn't trained.

"Darius, get your contact at the FBI on the line."

"What's the plan, boss?" Thomas ventured.

Gabriella swung her gaze toward Clay and his hazel eyes kept her pinned to the chair. Hidden underneath the table, her fingers clenched on the rough cotton of her jeans.

"Gentlemen." Sergeant Gordon stroked his chin. "We are going to give the Lexer brothers exactly what they want."

Darius stood up from the table and rubbed his hands over his eyes. They were all tired of looking at computer screens and blueprints. After gaining access to some of the government's classified information databases, they had analyzed every possible piece of information relating to the Lexer brothers. They even knew what shoe size Anton wore, his preferred cologne, the supplier of his Spanish cigarettes, and his exact location.

He gave Clay a silent look before heading upstairs to see Gabriella. Three days had passed since his teammates' arrival at the house, and in less then twenty-four hours, Darius and Gabriella would leave for a cabin in the Poconos in Pennsylvania.

He quietly knocked on the door of the guest room before entering. His eyes quickly adjusted to the darkness, and as he stepped into the room, emotion crowded into his heart. Just looking at her silhouette next to the window did it to him. Her scent did it to him. Somehow the air that perfumed around her made Darius Yassoud, Delta operator, one of the military's elite, weak in the knees.

"How goes the planning?" she asked, moving away from the window toward him. In the glow of the bedroom's single lamp, the slight sway of her hips through the shadows of the room sent heat pouring down to his sex. Ignoring his body's natural response, he unclenched his jaw. "I don't like it. So many things can go wrong."

She raised her hand and placed it gently on his cheek. He covered it with his own and turned his face to place a kiss on the palm of her hand. "This makes my idea of running away sound appealing, huh?"

"Yes, little one, it does." He smiled for the first time in two days. And it felt good—damn good—just like having her close.

"Don't you trust Clay's plan?"

"I trust the men downstairs with my life." The operation which had been set in motion forty-eight hours before couldn't be stopped, but that didn't mean he liked giving her up.

"But not mine. Or is it that you don't trust me?" Her chin came up and he locked eyes with hers.

"This has nothing to do with trusting you. I don't trust the bastard who wants you dead or the man who wants you back." He tightened his grip on her hands. "You are my heart, Princess. If something should go wrong . . ."

Silence descended between them and Gabriella took a step away. Darius resisted the urge to reach out and pull her back

"Trust in me this time, Darius, because you can't have it both ways. You can't expect my trust without giving it. You told me I was needed and I am. You helped me conquer my fears; now you have to let me do what I have to do."

"If something should go wrong . . ."

"It won't," she insisted. "I'll have all of you there to protect me."

He looked away from her. Darius had more than one reason for coming up to check on her.

"There's something else, isn't there? Something you're not telling me."

He hesitated. "It's your father. He's been kidnapped."

She paled and he reached out to catch her before she stumbled. "What? When . . . and how?"

Darius lowered her down to the bed. "They ambushed his car while he was on his way to a meeting with his lawyer. All-Star took a bullet in the side."

"Is he all right?"

"Luckily he was wearing his vest."

"And my father?"

Darius paused. "Anton has people watching our old apartment and your father's penthouse. My guess is they expect to trade him for you."

"Oh, God. This keeps getting worse."

"Shh, we haven't got it confirmed, but there is the possibility that Vasilei's people have your father. If that's the case, chances are that he won't be harmed." Darius sat her on the bed.

"We will do everything in our power to make sure he's found," he vowed.

She gave him a weak smile. "I know."

"Gabriella, this isn't the time or the place, but in less than twenty-four hours, everything's going to spin out of control."

"What is it?"

He went onto his knees and cradled her face in his hands. He'd imagined this moment a thousand times and during each he'd been sure his heart would thud with fear. But as he looked into her eyes, a sense of rightness descended upon him and a peace like standing in the eye of a sandstorm filled his heart. "You make me laugh and mesmerize me with your smile and the way your mouth pouts when you play the flute. You challenge me, reach inside me as no one has ever done and remind me of all the wonderful things in life. You make me remember why I became a soldier. I'm supposed to protect my country and I honored that duty to the best of my abilities. But as much as I love my work, I love you more."

Darius looked deep into her eyes, down to her heart, and the love he saw got him through what had to be the scariest moment of his life. "Marry me, little one."

One tear then two crept from the corners of her eyes and Darius caught them with his fingertip.

"Darius—"

A knock came at the door, cutting off her response. He swore under his breath and an unintentional growl escaped his throat. "Yeah?" he called out over his shoulder.

"We need you downstairs."

He turned his head toward Gabriella in time to see another tear glide down her cheek. "Go," she said.

"We're not finished here."

Her lips trembled when she smiled. "I know."

He kissed her gently, then rose from his knees. Not by word or deed did Darius show how much her silence hurt. "Try and get some rest."

She nodded. "I love you."

Darius toyed with a lock of her hair and taking a deep breath turned toward the closed door. It wasn't until he gently shut the door behind him that doubt began to kick him in the stomach. For a man who'd beat death and incredible odds, the thought of failure was as abhorrent to him as death. Why hadn't Gabriella answered his question? Interruption aside, the fact was that she loved him. Part of him ached with every step he took away from the bedroom and toward the dining room, which had been designated the temporary planning area.

Suddenly sick to his stomach, Darius felt as though he would vomit. His heart seemed to have jumped into his throat and the taste of something long buried rose in his mouth. It was the rush he always felt when embarking upon a mission. Taking a deep cleansing breath, he descended to the first floor and eyed the collection of weapons, vests, and combat equipment the team had brought in from the van. His fingers flexed. The sooner this ended the better. *The Lexer brothers are going down*, he vowed, and he'd be there to do it.

Chapter
Twenty-One

Darius shifted the firewood in his left arm to the side before turning the bolt on the cabin door. Even in the dim interior of the one bedroom mountain cabin, Gabriella's silhouette wasn't hard to notice. He crossed the room and placed the logs atop the pile.

"Is it cold outside?" she asked.

"Not yet, but the weather report mentioned a possible snowfall tonight." He looked into her upturned face as she gestured for him to sit beside her on the floor. "You should warm yourself by the fire."

He nodded and took a step back. "I just need to wash up. I'll be back in a minute."

"Okay."

Darius shrugged off his coat, then went into the bathroom and closed the door. Damn, he could still taste her scent on his tongue and just seeing her made him forget everything. For a moment resentment flared in a corner of his mind because she had such control over his emotions. He turned on the cold water and washed his hands before dashing it on his face.

Possessed of some semblance of control, he joined her on the rug in front of the fireplace. She had just begun to brush her hair.

"Let me." He gestured toward the brush in her hand. She

handed it to him without the slightest hesitation. Darius positioned himself behind her and slowly, gently began to comb the tangles from her slightly damp hair. Time passed measured by his stokes.

Gabriella was the first to break the silence. "Not that I don't like this new and tender side of you, Darius, but I'm curious as to why all of a sudden you want to brush my hair."

He inhaled the floral scent of her shampoo and closed his eyes as his body tightened with a flood of arousal. "Because it gives me pleasure to do so, little one."

"Oh." She paused. "Darius?"

He paused in mid-brush.

"You're very good at it."

He grinned and when he got to the point where her locks were tangle free and wavy, he put the brush aside and lifted the hair from her neck. He'd dreamed of kissing her, touching her, making love almost every moment of the past few days, but he hadn't. The presence of his teammates and the importance of their upcoming mission had commanded his full attention.

Lowering his head, Darius tenderly paid homage to the crest of her neck. Gabriella let her head fall back as his lips trailed over her. His fingers crept down her back, hooking into the bottom of the long flannel shirt and moving upward.

"Don't," he whispered huskily into her ear as her hands moved with the intent to help him. In under forty-eight hours, he would send the woman he loved into the arms of another man. The thought had eaten at him from the moment they'd put the plan to bring Anton down into motion.

Gabriella was his. His heart, his soul, his mate. And he would mark her as his in every way. After he'd pulled the shirt over her head and tossed it to the side, he devoured the sight of her naked skin in the flickering firelight.

"Lay down on your stomach for me, little one."

He caught the questioning look in her eyes, but kept his own expression blank. An unknown knot of tension unraveled

as she did as he asked. Tonight, his sole purpose was to learn
every inch of her body, to touch her as completely as she had
him.

Darius stood and removed his own clothing, then kneeled
next to Gabriella. She'd turned her head to the side and cradled it in her arms. The appreciative hunger in her eyes filled
him with masculine pride.

Careful to keep from touching her with any part of his
body except for his hands, Darius concentrated on helping
Gabriella relax. He started at her shoulders and kneaded the
warm skin, careful not to push too deep. At the sound of her
first soft moan, his lips curved into a grin. The heat from the
fire along with the arousal brought by touching her introduced a sheen of perspiration to Darius's brow. But he ignored everything but her. He made sure his hands slowly and
tenderly touched her body. Then he ran his fingertips gently,
so gently they barely touched her, along the curve of her
spine. She wiggled slightly, but he'd accomplished his objective of keeping her from succumbing to the relaxation of
sleep.

"Turn over." The tone of his voice was halfway between a
groan and a whisper. Darius's mental discipline aside, his
body's physical response to Gabriella's nearness could not be
disguised. Her eyelids rose slowly and met his gaze as she
turned over. His teeth clenched hard at the sight of her cocoa-
tinted breasts. He closed his eyes and released a ragged sigh.

"Do you know what you're doing to me, Darius?" The
throaty purr of her voice cut a little more at his self-control.

"No, little one. I only know what you're doing to me right
now."

Her eyes lowered and then swept upward. "I see." She
arched a lovely eyebrow. "I didn't know you liked self-
torture."

"I am practicing the art of self-control."

"You don't have to."

Her arms reached up to pull him down and he caught and

held her slender wrists in one hand. "Not yet. Tell me how you feel."

"I'm burning, Darius," she whispered.

"Just a little longer, sweetheart."

He ran his fingertips all over the front of her body barely touching the skin. For how long he didn't know. Long enough to need to put another log on the fire and to work his way from the tips of her ears on down. He circled her breasts with the palms of his hands and fingertips, moving to run over the soft curve of her stomach, then down her legs to work his way upward via the trail of her inner thighs. He wanted to drive her crazy and as she writhed and moaned underneath his fingertips, he was succeeding.

"Please, Darius, I can't take much more of this," Gabriella panted. She bit her lips and her fingers compulsively clenched on the rug. She freed her hands and reached to pull him to her.

"Not yet, little one."

And when she thought that the pleasure couldn't become more intense, he laid alongside her while turning her onto her side. Darius moved his hand and gently cupped her breast, then he slowly guided the nipple into his mouth. Gabriella sucked in her breath. His other hand tightened on her rear, squeezing the round flesh, and pulling tight against his body. The hair on his chest felt wonderfully soft against her sensitive skin. Darius sucked her nipple gently, his eyes still holding hers. He gripped it lightly between his teeth, teasing the tip with a series of butterfly-light flutters of his tongue.

"No more," she moaned. She cradled his face within her hands and pressed a hard, demanding kiss against his lips. Darius closed his eyes; both of his hands buried in the softness of her hair as he returned her kiss, their mouths parting, tongues hungrily tasting each other.

Gabriella gently moved her hips against his, rubbing against his erection. "I want you inside me, Darius," she whispered, breathing the words into their kiss. "Now."

Impatient, she placed her hands against his chest and pushed him flat on his back.

"Protection, little one."

It wasn't the sound of his voice that penetrated the haze of passion clouding her thoughts, but the arm locked like a steel band around her waist. Gabriella took a deep breath and took the foil lined packet which had suddenly materialized within his hand.

Very carefully, she rolled down the condom, and then returned her gaze to Darius's face as he lay below her. His dark eyes were alight, reflecting the fire's flame.

As she moved to bring him inside, the hands at her waist prevented their joining. Gabriella let out a growl of frustration and her eyes flashed upward to collide with his.

"Slow." His dark eyes locked with hers and she obeyed his command. Her cool, electrified fingers took his sex into her hands and squeezed it. She was guiding him between her legs, and he forced himself to slow down with one hand on hers as he pulled her down and buried his face in her neck. He smelled her sweet scent and his tongue left hot trails up her neck's graceful line as he managed to whisper in her ear, his voice coming out like a strangled growl.

"*Mon Dieu* . . ." Gabriella let her forehead fall against his shoulder, her eyes still closed as her chest rose and fell in hard little breaths. Darius's lips were close to her ear, his breathing harsh and raspy . . . and she moaned again as he ground his hips against hers, the feel of his erection delicious inside her. They remained that way for a moment, neither of them really moving, joined together as she sat straddling his lap. Holding his head in her hands, her slender fingers sinking into his hair, she kissed him again, catching his bottom lip between her teeth and sucking it as she slowly began to move against him.

Gabriella's hands slid over the lean muscles of his shoulders, his skin cool beneath her fingers, every thrust from his hips making her moan softly. She sagged down against his chest and gently cupped his face between her hands;

his mouth opened underneath hers and her tongue entered his mouth to explore him thoroughly as she continued to move up and down, pleasured by the languid, smooth rhythm of flesh against flesh.

As Darius grasped her hips and increased the pace, she moaned and closed her eyes.

So close.

And when her climax came, she trembled violently, crying out with an almost painful ecstasy. Darius's eyes had closed, the cords of his neck standing out visibly as he groaned through clenched teeth at the ceiling. Then seconds later his arms wrapped around her as he hid his face against her shoulder. A long, trembling groan escaped his lips.

"My God . . ." was all he had strength to say.

Silence crept back into the room, and a strong winter wind rattled the window, the only sounds in the cabin besides the soft, slowing pants of their breath and the crackle of the fire. Gabriella lifted a hand and gently touched the nape of Darius's neck, stroking it with her fingers so he shivered again beneath her touch.

"I love you, Dare," she whispered softly.

"Always, little one."

She felt him turn his head slightly, and he kissed the skin just above her collarbone. And as she fell into a contented sleep, she felt him lift her and place her into the bed, and then lying in a semi-fetal position, he put his arm around her, protecting Gabriella from her own demons. And warding off the thoughts of her leaving him.

Hours later, while curled underneath a wool blanket, Darius stared into the darkness of night, aware that the woman by his side was no longer asleep. "Second thoughts?" he asked after flipping on the small bedside lamp.

"And third and fourth."

He pulled her into an embrace and buried his face in her hair. "I'm proud of you."

"Don't be."

"I'm proud of you, little one," he repeated raising her chin to force eye contact. Darius felt the cold lump of fear in his chest give way to the flicker of heat in those golden orbs. Safe in the mountains, they could have remained hidden for months, instead of days.

"Tell me that when Anton doesn't loom over us like a dark cloud."

Darius laid his head back onto the threadbare pillow and pulled Gabriella closer into his chest. Sighing, he looked toward the ceiling as shadows of the wooden beams danced in contrast with the flickering light from the fire in the hearth. "He's only a man, Gabriella. Men can be killed."

"You speak of it so nonchalantly. Is that because you've taken lives on the battlefield?" she murmured.

His eyes turned downward to the crown of her head as it nestled against his chest. Lazily moving his hand, Darius stroked the silken softness of her hair. "No. I can say it because I have been trained to view the enemy as mortal and not some immortal demon that can't be vanquished."

"I'm still afraid of him. Anton doesn't lose."

"Ahh, Princess. Let's not spend our time together discussing Anton Lexer when I'd rather know more about you."

She shifted on the bed and her skin rubbed against his, causing Darius to lose his concentration for a moment. Gabriella yawned before asking. "What is it you'd like to know?"

"What's your favorite color?"

"The orange pink of sunset over the ocean. What's yours . . . And don't say black."

"How about green?"

"Just green?"

He shook his head slightly as his lips curled upward into a

full smile. "The dark moss green of military fatigues coming over the horizon to shore up your position."

"That sounds romantic."

He tickled her on the nape of her neck. "Don't knock it until you try it."

"All right.

After a moment of companionable silence peppered by the crackling of the dying fire, Gabriella asked, "Darius, are you asleep?"

"No, sweetheart. What's wrong?"

"After this is all over, what happens?"

He tensed slightly because in his mind he could hear her entire question. After this ended, what would happen to them? He drew in a deep breath before answering. "I've hurt, lied, stolen, killed, maimed, and terrorized for my country, little one. I've done things that stain my soul, but being with you, loving you has lessened that darkness."

"That sounds suspiciously like a good-bye."

"Your father won't back off when this is all over."

Love, honor, and integrity. The words seemed to beat in his chest. Darius had already said too much in regard to his life in the military. And to keep Gabriella, he would have to leave her. The call of duty was strong, but the love he felt for her surpassed all emotions he'd ever experienced. Yet, he couldn't blindly walk away from his teammates or his old life without first going back to tie up some loose ends. And he couldn't risk it all without the reassurance that Gabriella could love all of him, the Delta operative and the man.

"What does my father have to do with us?" she asked.

"Answer me this question: will you be open to giving him a second chance?"

"If I do, will you tell me why this is so important to you?"

"Yes."

"I think I can forgive him."

"Men like your father and I need second, third and fourth chances."

"You are nothing like my father, Darius."

"Wrong, Princess. We both are selfish and want your heart."

"You don't have to want for something you already have."

"God, you don't know how I need to hear that." He closed his eyes and pulled her toward him. Hours would shrink to minutes, then disappear into seconds. If Clay's plan went as scheduled, it would all be over soon; and even if it wasn't, he'd make sure that one way or another the Lexer brothers would never hurt Gabriella again.

When the time came in the pre-dawn hour, they didn't even get to say good-bye. One moment she sat on the old metal link bed and the next, she heard the sounds of glass shattering and the feel of a familiar hand reaching over and pushing her to the floor. Then came a smell so strong that her eyes watered and her throat began to burn, but none of that mattered more than the sounds of the door ripping open, the heavy footsteps, and the yelling.

"FBI. Nobody move."

She managed to crack her eyes open slightly and looked through the blurriness to find Darius. Instead, they picked out four letters: S.W.A.T. Her world narrowed as they pushed him down. Gabriella bit her tongue to keep from crying out when she saw him prostrate on the floor with men standing over him with weapons pointing down toward his back.

She must have moaned or said something when he raised his head and she met his eyes—hard, cold, predatory, and reptilian eyes that made her curl into herself and shiver. They were the eyes of her kidnapper, not those of the man she had come to love.

"Gabriella van Ryne?"

Stunned, she opened her mouth and then coughed at the sting in her lungs. Playing the role of victim had been easier than she'd imagined. The next thing she knew, strong arms curled around her and the impact of a shoulder in her stomach knocked the wind from her lungs as she was being hauled out of the cabin. Gabriella kept her head down and shut her eyes against the brightness of the sun.

Her eyes began to tear again even as a wet cloth was thrust into her hands and she wiped it on her face. Much to her relief, the stinging eased but her eyes continued to water from the chemicals in the gas.

"Take her to the chopper," she overheard, as unfamiliar hands lifted her again and carried her across crunching ground. Then she heard the slow beating of helicopter wings. Gabriella turned her head and stared back at the chaos of the cabin as the agent carried her away.

The moment she caught sight of Darius being led out of the cabin, a metallic taste of blood filled her mouth. She had bitten her lip. Her eyes met his over this distance and the lump in her throat threatened to choke her as the agents lifted her into the helicopter. Through the open door Gabriella watched helplessly as they led him into a waiting black Suburban with his hands cuffed behind him.

Minutes later, as the helicopter door slammed shut, someone crossed a seat harness over her chest, and the ground fell away. Gabriella took her eyes from the window and looked at the men who sat congratulating themselves; she huddled more deeply in the stiff seat. She didn't have to fake the twin tears sliding down her cheek. Next the hard part would come. The questions, the reporters, her having to lie.

Heiress rescued. Hostage ordeal ended.

At the tap on her shoulder, she turned from staring blindly out into the brightly lit sky as they headed north toward New York.

"Ms. Van Ryne." The lead FBI agent spoke loudly to be heard over the engine noise. "Everything's going to be all right. We're taking you home."

She looked at the men dressed in body armor who sat opposite her, each holding a wicked gun in his lap. Any one of them could be Anton's puppet. Gabriella swallowed hard against the acid bile rising in the back of her throat and forced what she wanted to be a grateful smile on her face.

"Thank you," she mouthed, then turned her face back toward the window. In truth, none of this was over; it had just begun.

Vasilei's personal guards, not the man himself, greeted Gabriella after leaving the FBI building. They ringed her like a Roman phalanx and walked her through the mob of reporters, television cameras and flashing light bulbs into a long Mercedes with tinted windows. She didn't have to pretend exhaustion; she felt it deep down in her bones.

They had questioned her for over an hour. About Europe, about Vasilei, the man who kidnapped her, her father. Her father. When the FBI informed her that he'd disappeared, she'd done as Darius instructed and fainted. After coming to, they'd taken her to another room where Gabriella had allowed herself to be subjected to a rape kit. She grimaced at the humiliation of the act, but she knew that Vasilei would undoubtedly receive a copy of the report.

She had asked no questions. His guards had never spoken to her. Under orders, she presumed, from their master. Only his assistant ever spoke. *Sergey.* The man gave her chills, and as though she conjured him up from thin air, it was his face that greeted her in the entranceway of the hotel's penthouse suite.

"Where is he, Sergey?"

"Vasilei will arrive soon. In the meantime, he left explicit instructions for your care. A bath has been prepared. See to it that you are dressed and ready by eight o'clock."

She took a step back. "Ready for what?"

"You'll find out."

She lifted her chin and managed to speak without her voice shaking. "And if I refuse?"

Sergey moved, faster than she'd seen anyone move except for Darius. Before she could inhale, his fingers locked on her cheek. The shock of his touch immobilized her. Pain shot up her jaw.

"Take your hands off me," she squeezed out through gritted teeth.

"I always thought you to be a clever girl, Gabriella." His voice lowered with hostility. "Don't make me regret that impression."

Sergey moved away and she allowed the slight pressure of his hand on her arm to guide her into an adjacent room. Shaken, Gabriella stood still and when the bedroom door closed, she didn't have to turn around and try the knob, instantly knowing Sergey had locked it.

Pull yourself together, she commanded herself. Drawing air into her lungs, Gabriella examined the suite's master bedroom. Her eyes marked the placed that Darius and his team had planted the surveillance equipment. Careful to keep her expression blank, Gabriella slipped off her shoes and entered into the steam filled bathroom.

A glimmer of a smile crossed her lips as she undressed. This would be the only location within Vasilei's penthouse suite without video surveillance. Yet, Darius had assured her that no matter her location, they would record every sound she made or word she spoke.

Gabriella approached the large Jacuzzi tub and inhaled. The rich floral scent of the bubble-filled bathwater tickled her nose. An even sense of foreboding, which had sat in her stomach since the night before, eased at the thought of taking a bath. She removed her two-day old clothing, stepped into the whirlpool bathtub, and sat down.

Crossing her arms over her breasts, she laid back and closed her eyes. Even in the heat, as the waves of hot water lapped against her skin, Gabriella shivered with the coldness of dread.

She stayed immersed for close to an hour. When the water

began to cool, she stepped out of the tub onto the fluffy mat beside it. Gabriella took one of the large towels and dried off before putting on the hotel robe that hung alongside an array of lotions and oils.

Wrapping the belt around her stomach, Gabriella exited the bathroom and stopped. Someone had been in the room. Whereas before only one of the lamps had been lit, now all the lights were on. Like a spotlight, her eyes were drawn to the bed and what lay atop the covers. The back of her hand moved to cover her mouth and stop the moan of horror from leaving her lips.

Across the bed lay a long ivory silk dress with a delicate lace bodice, an opulent string of pearls and teardrop earrings along with a diamond bracelet sat atop a sapphire blue velvet bag. The engagement ring she'd left on the dresser at the apartment sparkled darkly next to the long draping left sleeve. Alongside it sat her flute nestled inside its black velvet case. A shudder wracked her body, as she understood the implication of Sergey's earlier words. This was not just any dress. This was to be her wedding dress.

Twenty years was a long time to practice—a long time to learn an instrument, to spend countless hours with metal warmed by fingertips and hot breath. Playing the flute had been Gabriella's only love, her only passion. Yet it had only taken a brief glance, the erotic shiver of cold jewels on her slender wrist, and the sound of his deep voiced challenge in her ear to know that Vasilei would come to her soon. The hunt was over.

Gabriella turned and walked back into the elegant hotel suite from the balcony. At least in this meeting, he would come to her. It was a desperate gamble. He'd tried to have her killed twice, but the betrayal that sat heavily in the pit of her stomach paled in comparison to the anger. That he would kidnap and threaten her father was inexcusable.

Unknowingly, her hand crept up to the pendant around her neck. Darius. They had made love as though there would be no tomorrow. Together, they had soared to heights even her flute could not take her. It had been a wild storm tendered with a gentle rain. She'd needed him and the burning passion and warm intimacy as much as she'd needed the sweet oblivion that followed when the journey to ecstasy arrived.

Gabriella went into the bedroom and sat gingerly on the side of the king-size bed. Her flute lay at the center of a luxuriously made bed of silk and satin. Vasilei would sleep on nothing less than the thread of royalty. She picked up the musical instrument and held it close to her breast. The waiting would drive her crazy. Running and hiding had turned time into a cheetah; now minutes felt like hours and the chime of the clock became the speed of a tortoise moving across a riding field.

The image of Vasilei that had formed when she'd looked at him with a lover's eyes had long since faded. If she searched hard enough in the alleyways of her mind, she could still see him as he had been then—an Adonis with a deep penetrating stare, strong arms, and a sensual smile.

Because of him, she could no longer trust herself. Everything about him had been a lie. She could still see the priest's face. She, who had once used her flute to relieve Vasilei from his childhood nightmares, now had her own.

"Not anymore," she whispered.

A few seconds later, the click of a door unlocking penetrated the silence of the room. Gabriella slowly stood and turned toward the opening door. She looked up into a pair of winter green eyes and the flute in her hand dropped to the bed.

Chapter
Twenty-Two

"Vasilei. . ." Gabriella started.

He raised a finger and held it to his lips. It only took that small gesture to freeze the words on her lips. She stood still as a statue with her head slightly bowed and followed the progression of his feet as they made a circle around her.

Nervously, she wet her lips and began again. "My father—"

"Will witness our vows," he interrupted.

"How did you find me?"

"I searched for you on two continents, but it was my mother who informed me of your location."

Certain her expression would give away her surprise, Gabriella kept her gaze directed toward the floor. She hadn't communicated with Vasilei's mother.

"You should have let me go, Vasilei," Gabriella stated simply.

He came to a stop directly behind her and she could feel the heat of his closeness. She barely managed to suppress a slight jump when he reached up, removed her hair clip, and gently ran his fingers through the tresses. "I'm pleased that you have not cut your hair."

"Where is my father?" Gabriella began to turn around but the pressure of his hand in her hair held her still.

"Peace, Gabriella," he growled. The edge of menace in

his voice sent a shudder down her spine. "Do not mistake m
happiness at your safe return with forgiveness."

Dead silence. He pulled down the collar of her robe, the
she felt the silky tendrils of his hair against her ski
Gabriella's heart thumped against her chest as he lowered hi
face into the nape of her neck. The coolness of his indraw
breath brought goose bumps to her skin.

Aware that the situation could escalate to a point wher
Darius would intervene, Gabriella forced her shoulders t
relax and then reached back to take Vasilei's free hand withi
her own. "You have one of those migraine headaches you a
ways get when you work too hard," she scolded gently.

"I missed you," he admitted. Gabriella caught the edge c
weariness in his voice.

"Will you let me take the pain away?" she pleaded softly

The only sign of agreement was the loosening of his hand
in her hair. Taking it as a cue, Gabriella gently led him deepe
into the bedroom. She sat patiently while Vasilei removed hi
shoes and sat down on the floor, then settled himself betwee
her legs.

Please let his work, she prayed. It had been a ritual betwee
them. Whenever he came home in one of his dark moods, sh
would comfort him, just as his mother did when he was
child. "Let me take the pain away," she cajoled softly.

When he obeyed her request and stretched out his lon
legs, Gabriella gently ran her fingers through his hair, the
placed her fingertips along his scalp. She kept her attentio
focused on her ex-fiancé all while extremely conscious c
Darius watching and listening to their every word.

Only a few moments passed before she observed the low
ering of Vasilei's shoulders and the briefest whisper of h
sigh. Her heartbeat slowed and she aimed a glance at th
video transmitter hidden within the large screen televisio
This Vasilei—the cold and ruthless man replaced by the vu
nerable boy—she knew how to handle.

After a moment, she began to hum. An old lullaby, an in

provised classic. Slow and melodic she sang a sampling of songs designed to relax but not to put him to sleep. In order for their plan to work, she would have to regain some of Vasilei's trust before Anton's arrival.

When the last note faded, she stilled her fingers and withdrew them from his hair. "Vasilei, we need to talk." Her voice came out strong, even as her heartbeat accelerated.

"First, put it back on." His voice was husky.

"What?"

Vasilei didn't speak. Didn't need to. His head turned and she followed his pointed look toward the object lying on the silk purse.

"I can't put it on."

"Place the ring on your finger. Back where it belongs."

She shook her head and removed her hands from his shoulders. "No, I'm not sure that I can ever marry you. Not only have you deceived me, Vasilei. But you can't be the man I fell in love with."

"I have only told you the truth."

"Liar," Gabriella snapped with a hint of anger sharpening her voice. "You deceived me from the moment we met. You swore to me the night you proposed that with me by your side you wouldn't become your father's son. Yet, you did nothing as Anton tortured those two men to death."

"He is my brother." Vasilei abruptly stood from the floor and loomed over her. Gabriella lifted her chin and unafraid met this stare.

"And I am the woman you claimed to love," she countered as she rose from the bed. "You told me your father was a monster; you didn't tell me your brother was too."

"Quiet, Gabriella."

"Does the truth stab you in the heart, Vasilei? Or does it twist like a snake in your stomach?" she wondered aloud.

Instead of responding, he turned away and walked to the door. With his hand on the doorknob and his back toward her, he ordered, "Get dressed, put my ring on your finger, and join me in the living room. Our guests will be here soon."

"No." Gabriella balled her fingers into fists while hoping the fear that churned in her stomach did not appear on her face.

"You love me."

Her lips tightened and she said nothing.

"Do not deny it. You ran away to protect me."

She narrowed her eyes. "I ran because I feared for my life."

"I would never hurt you," he claimed. Gabriella made note of the fact that he had neither moved from his position by the door nor had he turned to look at her.

"But Anton would see me dead."

"He would never harm you."

Finally, Gabriella got a response as he turned back toward her. She took two steps forward, then raised her right hand and slowly held out three fingers. "He tried to kill me not once, not twice, but three times. The first time, one of his men tried to push me down a flight of stairs. The second time, was almost run down on the street. The last time, Anton killed a priest and burned down a church. He would have my death look like an accident."

"You cannot know it was my brother."

"I'm not a fool and the scent of his Spanish cheroots are unmistakable, Vasilei. We both know that he will stop at nothing to protect his family."

"Then after tonight you shall have nothing to worry about."

Gabriella crossed the room and stood less than a foot from Vasilei. This time there would be genuine pleading in her voice. As she looked into his eyes and witnessed a flicker of doubt, hope bloomed in her chest. Maybe she could save him. "Listen to me. You are a good and decent man. Anton will pull you down and destroy your soul, just as your father tried to do."

"What would you have me do? Turn on my brother?"

"Yes," she hissed. "Stop him before he destroys what goodness you have left."

"Maybe you're right. Maybe my brother's organization has corrupted me, but all I have done has been for you." He reached out and stroked the back of his hand over her cheek.

Gabriella's heart stopped at the implication of his statement. "What did you do, Vasilei?" she asked slowly.

His gaze shifted then returned to her face. "Someone had to be punished for your disappearance."

"Markus?" she whispered as her knees began to wobble with the implication of his words.

He ran his fingers through his hair before answering. "Is dead by my order. He paid a heavy price for your actions. Now you go freshen up. The priest will arrive with your father and you must look like the blushing bride."

Gabriella stood perfectly still. "I won't marry you."

"I didn't give you a choice. You and I are promised, Gabriella, and I will bind you to me in all ways legal and otherwise."

"My father?" she prompted as he turned away from her.

"Is safe as long as you cooperate."

"Leave my father alone!" Gabriella ordered through clenched teeth.

"Don't anger me, Gabriella. Put on the dress and the ring by the time I return."

"Or?" she challenged.

Vasilei turned quickly with his hand on the doorknob. Her eyes locked with his and a shudder wracked her body. "You will find out how much I am my father's son. Believe me when I say that for every hour you delay, I will order my men to relieve him of a finger."

After Vasilei left, Gabriella untied the robe's belt and let it fall to the floor. With trembling hands, she picked up the wedding dress, pulled it over her head. It fell below her ankles and took a few moments for her to adjust the bodice. Once it lay over her skin, she ran the palms of her hands over the fabric as a lump of anger curled tight in the pit of her stomach. As with everything that Vasilei touched, the dress was a perfect fit. Gathering every shred of her anger, she turned and walked across the bathroom's marble floor and opened the door.

Just as Gabriella exited the bathroom wearing the wedding dress, the door to the bedroom opened. She froze; even her heart went still as fear grabbed hold of her lungs and cut off the instinct to breathe as the suit-clad man stepped through the doorway.

Gabriella's first thought was of Darius. Would he wait or ruin their chance to put Anton away?

"Anton." She spoke with a calmness she in no way felt as terror's bony fingers gripped her throat.

"You were expecting my brother?" He grinned—an evil, cruel grin. "My apologies, but he'll be a little late."

She kept her arms to her sides and moved away from the bathroom doorway. "What do you want?"

Instead of answering, he laughed. "Your blood on my hands, sweet Gabriella. I want to exorcise your name from Vas's mind as I watch you die."

"Why?" She locked her eyes with his and saw something that chilled her to the very core. Insane hate stared back at her.

"Why?" he barked. "Before you, we were a team, he and I. He was safe."

Let Darius be listening, she prayed, trying to keep her gaze from straying towards the television. Gabriella didn't know how much longer she could keep up the act of being brave. "Safe from whom, Anton? Safe from everyone's influence but your own?"

"You know nothing of our bond."

"I know that you are sick, twisted, and willing to do whatever it takes to make Vasilei into a man as evil as you."

He seemed to shake himself. At that moment, Gabriella

caught sight of the knife tucked at his waist. "Where is my father?"

"Quite safe." He took another step forward. "You have been such a worthy opponent. It's almost a shame this has to end."

Gabriella froze as he walked around her and paused. His fingers reached out and touched the silk of her dress. She forced herself not to pull back as he ran a hand over her hair, then trickled a finger over her breasts. It took all she had not to slap him. She needed his confession and the location of her father.

"I've left a package with someone to be mailed out in the event of my death," she said, her voice a low monotone. Gabriella continued as the hand caressing her throat stopped. "In it I accuse you of torturing two men to death, setting fire to a church, and killing a priest."

"Bravo." He clapped his hands. "That's a very damning list, isn't it? But nothing you say will matter. You'll be dead and there is no evidence." ·

"Oh, but there is. The tape of you threatening to rape and kill me if I went to the authorities with what I saw the night before I fled will hammer a nail in your coffin." Gabriella bluffed in the hope of keeping Anton off guard.

If she had not seen him move so deliberately in the past, Gabriella would not have tensed in preparation of the back-handed blow that rocked her back on her heels and sent her neck snapping to the side. She bent and barely kept from falling onto the bed.

"*Bliatz*," he cursed, spittle flinging from his lips. "Look what you made me do. You would ruin my brother, our business, my family. You have cost me millions in delays."

Gabriella tasted the blood inside her mouth, then she ran her tongue back and forth over the cut inside her lip and tried to figure out what to do next.

Nothing had changed the goal. They still needed a taped confession and time was running out. She didn't trust Dar-

ius's patience and she knew beyond a shadow of a doubt that
All-Star's finger was curled tight around the rifle as his eye
peered at Anton through the crosshairs of a sniper's scope.

"Is that what you're planning, Anton? Beating your
brother's kidnapped bride on her wedding night?"

"Kidnapped," he laughed again. "You probably followed
the poor fool with your legs open and mouth full of lies.
Maybe he decided to cut you loose so you decided to have a
little revenge, eh?"

"You tortured two innocent men to death, then threatened
to kill me. I only ran to my father because I feared for my
life."

"Innocent? How blasphemous that word sounds coming
from your lips. Those men betrayed me; they got exactly what
they deserved. Just as you will."

"What are you planning?"

"What I should have done the day my brother brought you
into our lives. I'll kill you."

"Vasilei will hate you."

"Love and hate are but two sides of the same coin. He's my
brother and one day he'll come to understand that I only did
what had to be done." He watched her closely; she showed no
signs of fear. Anton killed for the pleasure of it; he loved the
power of fear. She could see his enjoyment at hurting her in
the wet gleam of his eyes. Yet at the moment when terror
threatened to overtake her common sense, Darius's words
came back to her.

You do what you have to do because you are needed.
Gabriella didn't know if it was because of love or the deple-
tion of emotion, but the constant fear she'd lived with since
that fateful night had disappeared.

"Are you disappointed?" she asked scornfully. "I'm not
afraid of you, Anton. You only like to hurt people who can't
fight back, like those men you tortured to death in the
boathouse.

"That's right," she taunted. "You're a coward. A little boy who kills priests and sets fire to a church."

He raised his hand to hit her again but some inner force stopped him. Instead, he reached under the right side of his jacket and drew out a wicked looking knife. Gabriella flinched at the sight of the light glancing off the blade. The man had tried to kill her three times and it appeared that this fourth time she might not be so lucky.

"We've got movement in the lobby."

Darius looked over at a member of the FBI's team. The man lowered his radio and cursed. "Someone's requested access to the floor. Apparently, it's a priest."

"Detain him," he replied coolly. Hell, it would be the waiting that did him in. Every instinct in his body told him to take hold of his gun and go downstairs and get Anton before he got near Gabriella. And with it all came the memory of her face as the FBI took her away from the cabin. Just the thought was like a knife to his guts. If this didn't work out right, he could lose her—lose the woman he loved, who might at that moment be carrying his child. His heart squeezed at the thought of having a son or daughter. Few of his missions failed, but there was always the possibility, and if he hated anything more at that moment, it was the chance that she could be hurt. And so he looked toward the ceiling and took a deep cleansing breath to push back his emotions.

"What the hell do you want me to do? The man's a servant of God."

Darius swore under his breath as all the reasons for not getting the government agency involved came back to him. He pressed the button on the transmitter. "Tell him the truth or tie him up. Do what you have to do but don't let him up," he ordered.

"Easy, Dare."

He turned his neck slowly as his jaw clenched and un-

clenched. First, he'd had to endure watching Vasilei touc
Gabriella. Now, the presence of both Lexer brothers with
close proximity to Gabriella had stretched his military ir
stilled patience to the breaking point. "I don't like this, Cla
We've got too many variables in the equation and Gabriell
is down there unprotected."

"Sit down and put that headset back on; Anton's in the bed
room with Gabriella."

. . . a shame this has to end. Darius caught the end of th
sentence when he put on the headset. With every word out (
Anton's mouth, Darius grew still. He didn't so much a
breathe because anything, no matter how slight a movemer
would set him off. And he so badly wanted to kill the bastar
The warrior in him reacted as trained, with calm and me
thodical violence. The man whose woman was threatened d
manded action.

Darius looked over at his commanding officer and withou
regard to the chain of command issued an order into his hea
set. "All-Star, if you have a clear shot, take it."

"Negative."

"Damn it."

"Cut the hallway lights and take out the guards because I'
going in." Darius ripped off his headphones and before any
one could stop him headed for the door with his weapo
drawn.

After barreling up a flight of stairs, a modicum of cautic
stopped him by the side of the elevator. With the gun hel
tightly in his right hand, he sent a silent signal to Eric with h
left. He needed to level the playing field fast and there w;
only one way to do it.

Less than five minutes later, Darius stood in the living are
of the suite with the nozzle of his gun firmly planted
Vasilei's temple.

Darius watched helplessly as Anton exited the bedroo

holding Gabriella against him. Anton had a gun to her head and a knife to her throat. He moved both of them away from the windows toward the inside of the penthouse. The possibility of All-Star taking a shot decreased to zero.

Anton taunted Darius. "The bodyguard comes to the rescue. Have you sampled her charms? Has she bewitched you as she did my brother and my mother? Would you die for her?" he whispered close to her ear. Evil crawled across her skin like maggots over flesh.

His fist tightened in her hair making her wince in pain. "If you harm one hair on my brother's head, you will die like this bitch, only more slowly."

"Anton." Vasilei's voice was amazingly strong, given the pressure Darius placed against his windpipe. "Do not harm Gabriella. She and I will marry and nothing she has seen can hurt us."

"Never," Anton spat. "You want this mongrel in our family? Our father would scream, Vasilei. No, I will kill her first and this obsession of yours will disappear. I promise. And we will be great. Just like before."

The knife cut deeper into her throat and Gabriella suppressed a scream as tears filled her eyes. Through the haze, she kept her eyes locked on Darius.

"Did I hurt you?" he sneered. "How does it feel to know that your death will mean nothing?"

"Anton, brother. Let her go. She and I will marry and there's no need to fear."

"She is a witch, Vasilei," he shouted as spittle flew through the air. "She has poisoned you and Mother against me. For that alone she has to die."

"They will arrest you."

"And I'll make a deal. This is America. Freedom can be bought, and I'm a very wealthy man." Smug confidence practically rolled off Anton in waves.

A shudder wracked through her body at his words. He would kill her and go free.

"For every mark you put on her skin, I will make an ide
tical one on your brother, Lexer. And I swear that if you har
her, neither of you will live to take another breath."

Every word seemed to embolden Anton. "Brave word
Sergeant."

"True. If I don't kill you then one of my men will. End th
and let her go before little Vasilei here loses the ability
speak, indefinitely."

"I have another idea. You will order your men to pull bac
Then I'll take Gabriella as my hostage. Once I have reache
a safe place, we will trade. This bitch for my brother."

Golden eyes locked with obsidian and in the space of tin
as brief as the flutter of a hummingbird's wings, she watche
as Darius's eyes flicked to her left then back. It took her a m
ment to comprehend the message and she blinked slowly.

Praying that she was doing the right thing, Gabriel
summed up her strength and threw herself to the side just
a loud pop sounded. Then the world went silent. The bur
ing sensation on her arm had no meaning as the carpet cam
up to meet her and shock slammed into her mind.

She watched in detached numbness as something red an
wet spread over the ivory dress. In what seemed like slow m
tion, the knife dropped from Anton's hand and he fell bac
ward.

She blinked once and Darius was on the carpet beside he

"Talk to me, Gabriella," Darius ordered. He couldn't thin
couldn't feel, as his body shook with self-directed rage. He
shot her. The woman he loved. And as he gathered her gent
in his arms, he shouted. "I need a medic!

"Everything's going to be fine, little one."

Her ears continued to ring as the hotel suite filled with pe
ple. She didn't recognize any of the men coming through t
door wearing bulletproof vests and holding weapons. Wh
the agent in the helicopter had said those exact same word
she hadn't believed him. This time Darius had made t

promise and his calm reassurance meant everything in the world. "I know."

"I need a medic," he ordered to a man who leaned over Anton's body.

He cradled her arm gently. Gabriella fought back a hiss as he pulled back the silken material from the wound.

"Sorry."

"It's okay," she managed a wan smile. "My father?"

"We found him."

"Is he . . ." her voice weakened.

"Alive and unharmed."

"Thank you," she replied before closing her eyes.

Darius looked at the woman he loved. The golden eyes he loved seemed to swallow her face. If he'd lost her . . .

The medics descended on Gabriella and moved her into the bedroom. Having been informed by the FBI that her father would be waiting at the hospital, he remained in the room. She would be well taken care of, but he still fought the urge to go with her. At that moment, his teammates were on their way to the airport to catch a plane back to Fort Bragg. The same flight he needed to catch.

Darius blended with the crowd of FBI agents until he could disappear into the stairwell. A determined expression set on his face. With Anton's death and Vasilei's arrest, he had fulfilled his uncle's obligation. Yet, one question remained unanswered. Could he choose between his Delta team and his heart?

"Time to wake up, lazy bones."

Gabriella opened her eyes and blinked twice.

"Darius, how did you get in here?" she managed to say with her voice thick with sleep. Staring into the eyes that had haunted her dreams, both waking and sleeping, the world and the night faded away around them.

"Roped down from the roof, Princess. I know that in the

classic fairytale the Princess let down her hair and the Princ
climbed up. But you were asleep and it's faster rappellin
down than climbing up."

Gabriella rose from the bed and stood with her arn
wrapped around herself. "You left me," she accused.

A long, clever hand reached out and tugged her hand awa
from her arm, guiding it to his shoulder as he steppe
smoothly against her. Her lips parted, releasing a sudden gas
as she felt his free arm slide easily around her back, fittir
her against him as if she belonged there in his arms. "I knov
There were some things I had to take care of and people
needed to see."

"Will you disappear again?"

"Only if you ask me to." He grinned, then his expressio
became more solemn. "I've said good-bye to the military li
now. What you see is what you get and I have the papers t
prove it. Starting sometime in the next couple of months, I'
just be Darius Yassoud, a plain ole intelligence officer wit
the National Security Agency. There'll be a few trips and a l
of time in a classroom for delving into paperwork."

"You gave it up for me?"

"No, I left for *us*. I can't stay in that world knowing that
have you here. You are my heart and I can't cut you out ar
give my all to the success of a mission."

"I wish I could believe you. But you can't disappear for
month and then climb through my window and expect me
welcome you with open arms."

Darius brushed her hair back from her cheek. Closing h
eyes, he ran his nose along her cheek all the while breathir
in her scent and marking her as his own, relived all the m
ments he held her close. "If I were to follow my father's way
then I am in gross error of Egyptian customs."

He turned toward Gabriella and her heart stopped at th
look shining bright in his eyes.

"If this were Egypt, Princess, my parents would visit yo
father's house to receive his agreement to our marriage." H

took her hands within his own. "And they would bring you two things: *Mahr*, money to help buy furnishings for our house, and *Shabka*, a valuable jewelry gift that gives substance to their son's love. Right now, I have neither of those things to give you. I only have my heart."

Startled, they both turned toward the door as it flew open.

"Gabriella!" Her father stood in the doorway. "I thought I heard you cry out."

The light flashed on and Gabriella winced at the brightness.

"What the hell are you doing in my daughter's room, Yassoud?"

Darius moved to stand alongside her. "Sir, I plan to marry your daughter."

Gabriella could never say that she had not seen her father speechless after that moment. For she saw his mouth move but nothing came out, as his eyes went from hers to Darius and back again.

"Is this what you want, Gabriella?"

She smiled and Darius captured the moment in his heart's eye, for it was beautiful. "More than anything in the world, Daddy."

Epilogue

"Okay girls, don't forget to work on your compositions. I shall expect to hear them next week. And Shanna?"

"Yes, ma'am?"

"Congratulations on making the national youth orchestra." Gabriella's lips relaxed into a smile. She looked at her pupils with pride, but it took her a moment to notice that their eyes were focused not on her but over her shoulder. It was then that she felt a familiar prickle on the back of her neck and the scent of the man she loved.

"He's standing behind me, isn't he?"

Her four private flute students engaged in synchronous nodding. Gabriella refused to turn around and instead laid her baton on the edge of the music stand. "Okay, this lesson is over. I'll see you next Saturday."

They filed out together and it wasn't until the door to the music room closed that she leaned back and strong arms embraced her from behind.

"You're home early," she commented.

"I took an earlier flight."

"Who picked you up at the airport?"

"Jensen."

Gabriella turned in his arms and lifted her face toward her husband. Memories poured over her at the sight of his dark eyes. Unlike the Egyptian brides of old, she'd ridden in a black limousine—not a camel—from the wedding reception to her new home. Her father had given her away, but it was her brother Jensen who'd decorated and welcomed them into their new home.

Everything was as romantic and wonderful as if she had been an Egyptian princess. Darius's mother and aunt made all the arrangements. And the day before the wedding, she had a *henna night* where all the women gathered in the home her father gave them for a wedding present. The older colonial was outside of Washington, D.C. surrounded by tall trees and had five bedrooms and a landscaped garden. It served as a perfect place for Darius and her.

They danced and sang, then used henna to tattoo intricate designs on Gabriella's hands and feet. Their wedding was billed as the romance of the year and swamped by the press. But it all came down to the moment her father walked her down the aisle. Her lips curved upward with the happy memories.

Darius kissed her on her brow, then her nose, and finally her lips. Desire swirled through her body and Gabriella marveled at how much she missed him when he went away.

"I brought something back for you," he whispered in her ear.

"Really? Where did you put it?"

"In the bedroom."

Gabriella's lips turned upward as she quickly slipped out of his arms, then dashed out of the room like a naughty child.

"Minx." The sound of his laughter followed her over the hardwood floors and up the stairs toward the master bedroom.

Much later, after the sun had begun to sink over the horizon, Gabriella rolled over to wrap her arms around her husband's warm back. She slipped her arm underneath his waist and then intertwined her legs with his.

"Husband," she smiled and closed her eyes again, falling into the sound of his heartbeat in her ear. The diamond pendant necklace he'd given her lay warm against her chest.

"Little one, we've got dinner reservations in less than an hour."

"I know," Gabriella hummed, then snuggled closer.

"That means we have to get up."

"I know that too," she smartly replied.

He laughed, then turned over and she found herself pulled against his chest. His hardness tucked between her thighs. "That means we can't start something neither of us can afford to finish."

"We don't have to go. I have all the ingredients we need to make French toast."

He fanned his fingers over the slight swell of her stomach and she looked into his excited eyes. The memory of the night she'd told Darius that she was pregnant brought tears to her eyes.

"Princess, are you feeling the same thing I'm feeling?" her husband asked.

Gabriella nodded as emotion welled up in her throat. Just as Darius's grandmother had predicted, their first child was scheduled to make his or her appearance in exactly one year after their honeymoon in Egypt. "Yes."

"It's the baby?"

He buried his face against her neck and Gabriella breathed heavily as she felt the wetness upon her skin. Her heart swelled until she feared it might burst.

"God, how I love you," he whispered.

Gabriella ran her fingertips over his shoulders and cradled his head in her hands. Gently, she drew his face back to rain kisses over his cheeks. "And don't you ever forget it."

He leaned forward and whispered against her lips as his fingers toyed with the diamond. "Always and forever."

Dear Readers

Once again your letters of encouragement have inspired me to write another book. Women love heroes, and I loved writing Darius and Gabriella's story. These two characters popped into my head at the weirdest time: while I was waiting to get my oil changed. It's taken months of writing and weeks of editing, but I'd do it all over again. I hope you enjoyed this story and that all of you have a Darius in your life or will very soon. While I'm waiting for my own hero, I'll be writing my book, a romantic adventure that will keep you guessing and smiling.

Happy Reading,

Angela
angela@angelaweaver.com
http://www.angelaweaver.com

ABOUT THE AUTHOR

Southern girl by way of Tennessee, Angela Weaver resides in Atlanta, Georgia where she gets most of her inspiration. An avid reader and occasional romantic optimist, she began writing her first novel on a dare and hasn't stopped since.

She is the author of three Arabesque books and is currently at work on her next novel.

COMING IN JUNE 2005 FROM
ARABESQUE ROMANCES

___**LOOKING FOR LOVE IN ALL THE WRONG PLACES**
    by Deidre Savoy $6.99US/$9.99CA
                                    1-58314-625-3

After a series of setbacks, Liza Morrow suddenly finds herself jobless, homeless, and fiancé-free. To top it off, the one man she doesn't want to see—freelance photographer and notorious playboy Jim Fitzgerald—is the only one who can introduce her to the man she believes is her biological father. But fate frowns on Liza once again when she discovers her father isn't quite the devoted paternal figure and that a dangerous man from his past is intent on seeking revenge through her. Can Jim keep her safe long enough to convince her that his love is the real thing?

___**WINDSWEPT LOVE** $6.99US/$9.99CA
    by Courtni Wright   1-58314-557-5

Joanne Crawford and Mike Shepherd met at the Naval Academy. Now their military assignments will take them far away from each other and the separation will put their newfound love to the test. Standing on the steps of the Naval Academy chapel, they vow to return and marry. Mike is assigned to a submarine and is constantly at sea, while Joanne is stationed in Hawaii. Can these two windswept lovers find a way to make their relationship and their military careers flourish?

___**BLIND OBSESSION** $5.99US/$7.99CA
    by Angela Weaver   1-58314-561-3

Gabriella Marie had the perfect life when she was in Europe and engaged to the man of her dreams. That world came tumbling down when she witnessed her fiancé commit a brutal murder, putting her life in jeopardy. Now she has no choice but to return to New York—to the father she despises and into the unwilling custody of Darius Yassoud. The mysterious Special Forces soldier may be her only chance to bring her pursuer to justice, but he's proving to be a temptation more dangerous than she could have ever imagined . . .

___**TOTAL BLISS** $5.99US/$7.99CA
    by Sean Young   1-58314-577-X

Alexis Shire is so busy trying to reach her professional goals that she has no time for a social life—until she meets entrepreneur Jaeden Jefferson. Busy working on his first million, Jaeden only has casual flings, not relationships. All that changes when his cousin introduces him to Alexis. The couple falls in love quickly and Jaeden pops the big question. But as they prepare for the most important day of their lives, the stress of planning a wedding starts to take its toll. With a never-ending stream of dilemmas standing in the way of their happiness, will they ever make it down the aisle?

Available Wherever Books Are Sold!

Visit our website at **www.BET.com**.